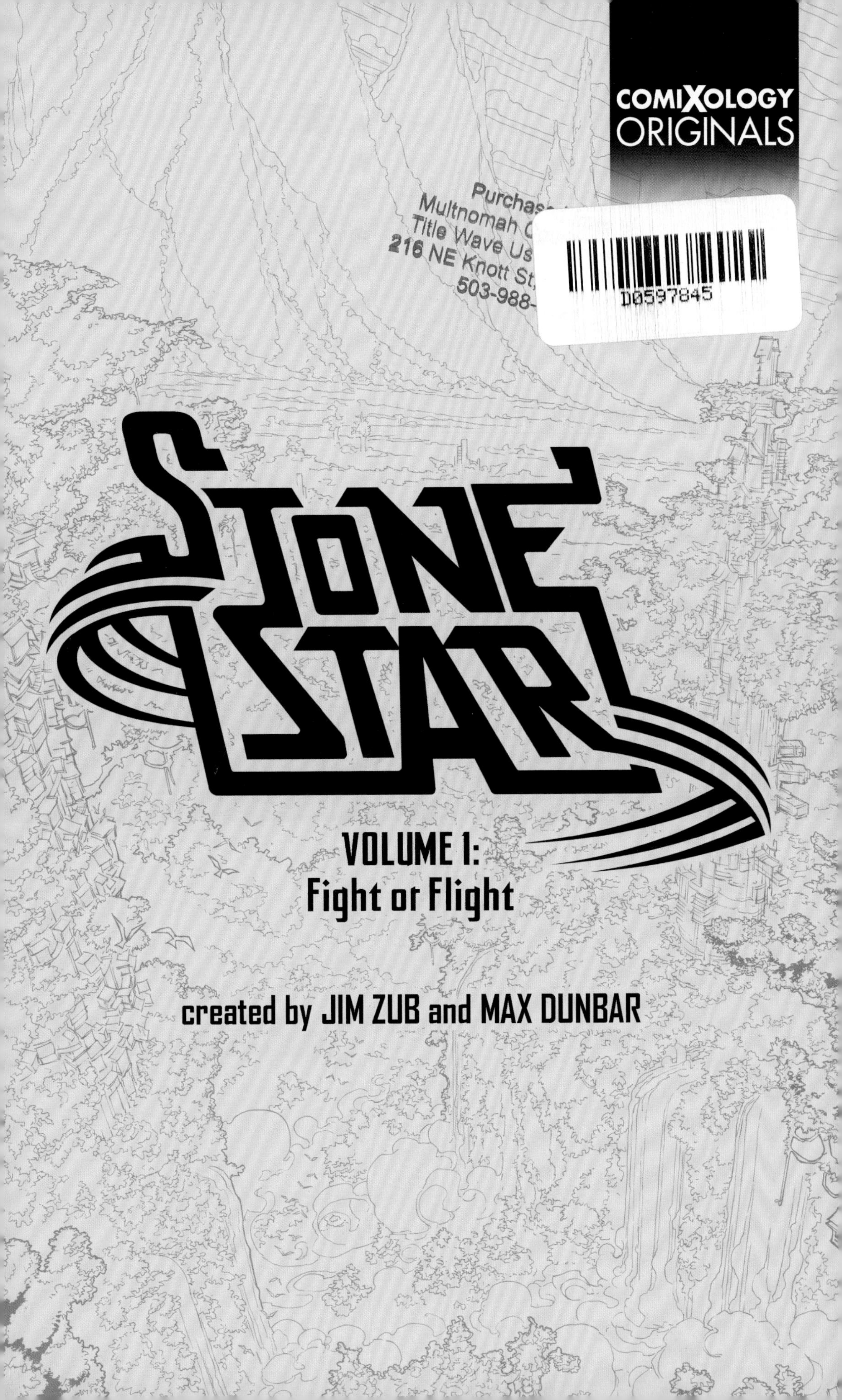

STONE STAR

VOLUME 1: Fight or Flight

created by JIM ZUB and MAX DUNBAR

This book is dedicated to Doreen King.
Mom, thank you for your endless support.

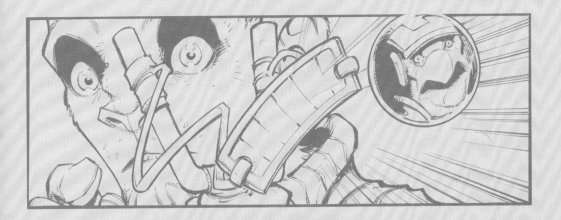

story • JIM ZUB
line art • MAX DUNBAR
colors • ESPEN GRUNDETJERN
letters • MARSHALL DILLON
logo design • TIM DANIEL
created by • JIM ZUB and MAX DUNBAR

Special Thanks
David Steinberger • Chip Mosher • Ivan Salazar • David Hyde • Pamela Horvath
Ludwig Olimba • Dane Cypel • Jose Sagastume

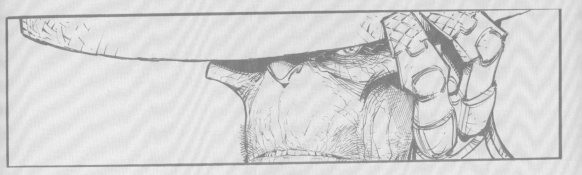

DARK HORSE TEAM

President and Publisher • MIKE RICHARDSON
Editor • DANIEL CHABON
Assistant Editors • CHUCK HOWITT and KONNER KNUDSEN
Designer • SKYLER WEISSENFLUH
Digital Art Technician • JASON RICKERD

Neil Hankerson Executive Vice President • Tom Weddle Chief Financial Officer • Randy Stradley Vice President of Publishing • Nick McWhorter Chief Business Development Officer • Dale LaFountain Chief Information Officer • Matt Parkinson Vice President of Marketing • Vanessa Todd-Holmes Vice President of Production and Scheduling • Mark Bernardi Vice President of Book Trade and Digital Sales • Ken Lizzi General Counsel • Dave Marshall Editor in Chief • Davey Estrada Editorial Director • Chris Warner Senior Books Editor • Cary Grazzini Director of Specialty Projects • Lia Ribacchi Art Director • Matt Dryer Director of Digital Art and Prepress Michael Gombos Senior Director of Licensed Publications • Kari Yadro Director of Custom Programs • Kari Torson Director of International Licensing • Sean Brice Director of Trade Sales

Published by Dark Horse Books
A division of Dark Horse Comics LLC
10956 SE Main Street
Milwaukie, OR 97222

First edition: July 2021
Trade paperback ISBN: 978-1-50672-458-4

10 9 8 7 6 5 4 3 2 1
Printed in China

Comic Shop Locator Service: comicshoplocator.com

Stone Star Volume 1: Fight or Flight

This volume collects *Stone Star* #1–#5.

Library of Congress Cataloging-in-Publication Data

Names: Zub, Jim, author. | Dunbar, Max, artist. | Grundetjern, Espen,
    colourist. | Dillon, Marshall, letterer.
Title: Fight or flight / story, Jim Zub ; line art, Max Dunbar ; colors,
    Espen Grundetjern ; letters, Marshall Dillon.
Description: First edition. | Milwaukie, OR : Dark Horse Books, 2021. |
    Series: Stone Star ; volume 1 | "This volume collects Stone Star #1–#5."
    | Audience: Ages 12+ | Audience: Grades 7-9 | Summary: "The nomadic
    space station called Stone Star brings gladiatorial entertainment to
    ports across the galaxy. Inside this gargantuan vessel of tournaments
    and temptations, foragers and fighters struggle to survive"-- Provided
    by publisher.
Identifiers: LCCN 2020058205 | ISBN 9781506724584 (trade paperback)
Subjects: LCSH: Graphic novels. | CYAC: Graphic novels. | Science fiction.
Classification: LCC PZ7.7.Z83 F54 2021 | DDC 741.5/973--dc23
LC record available at https://lccn.loc.gov/2020058205

Chapter 1: Pipe and Pits

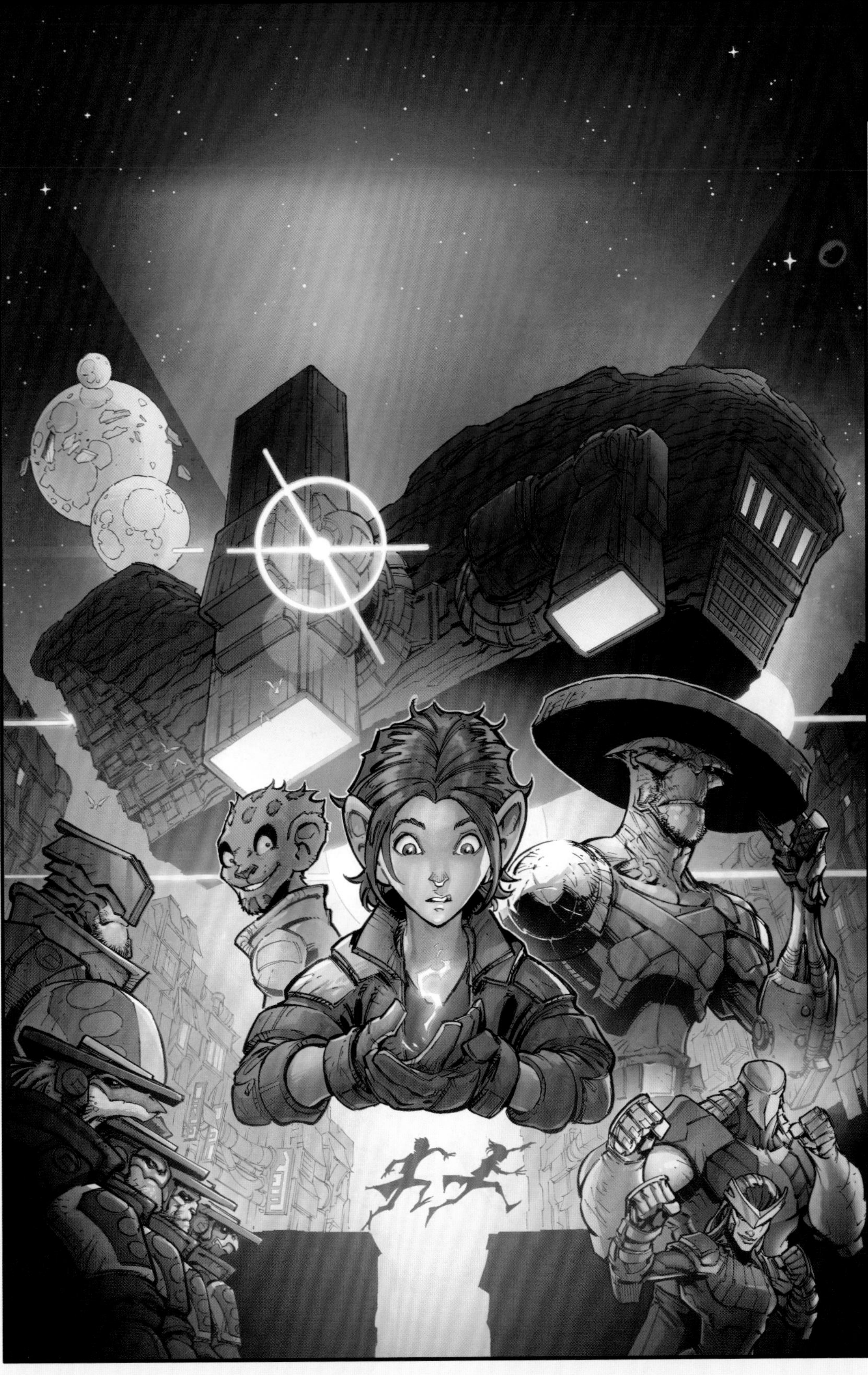

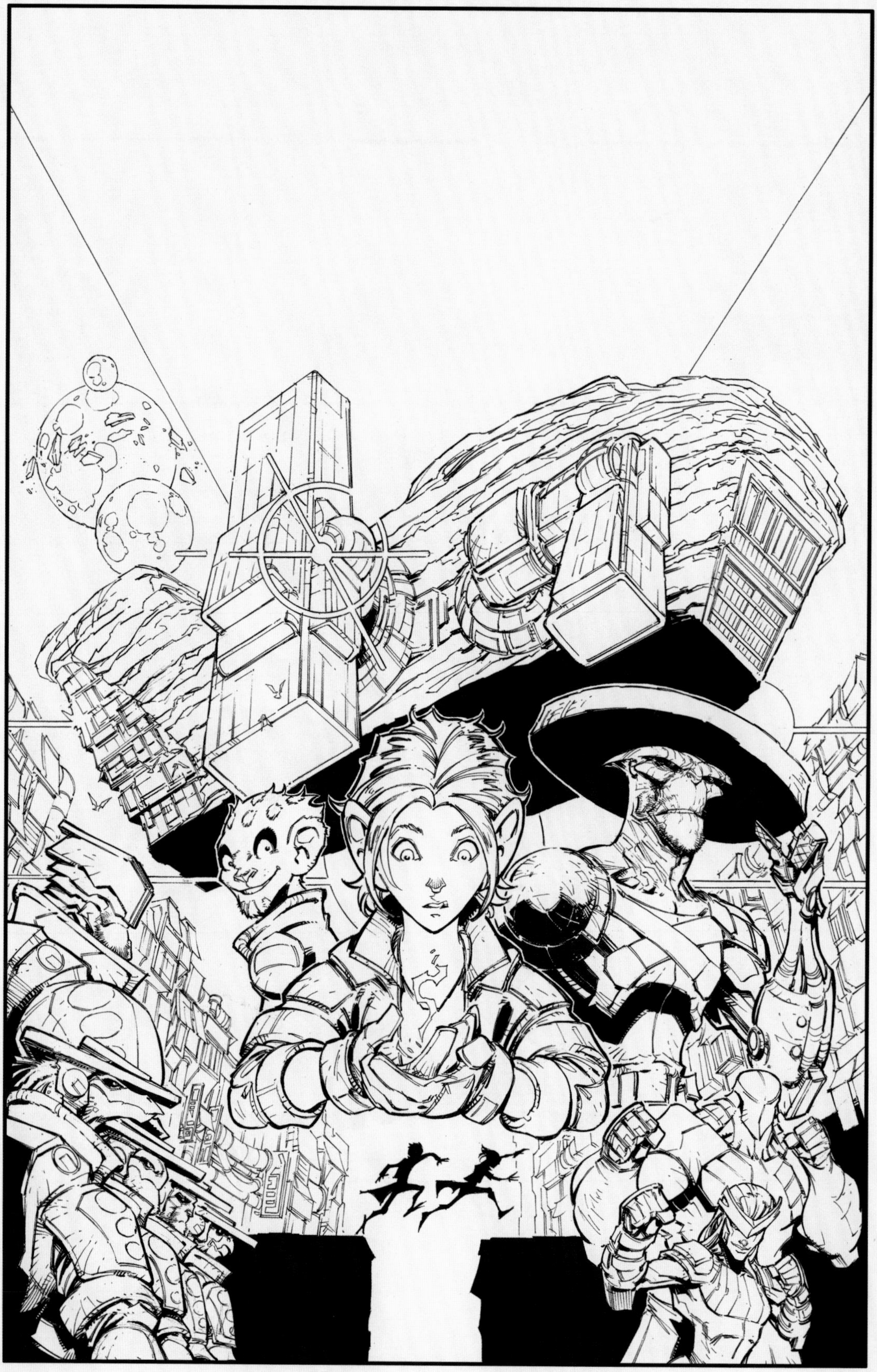

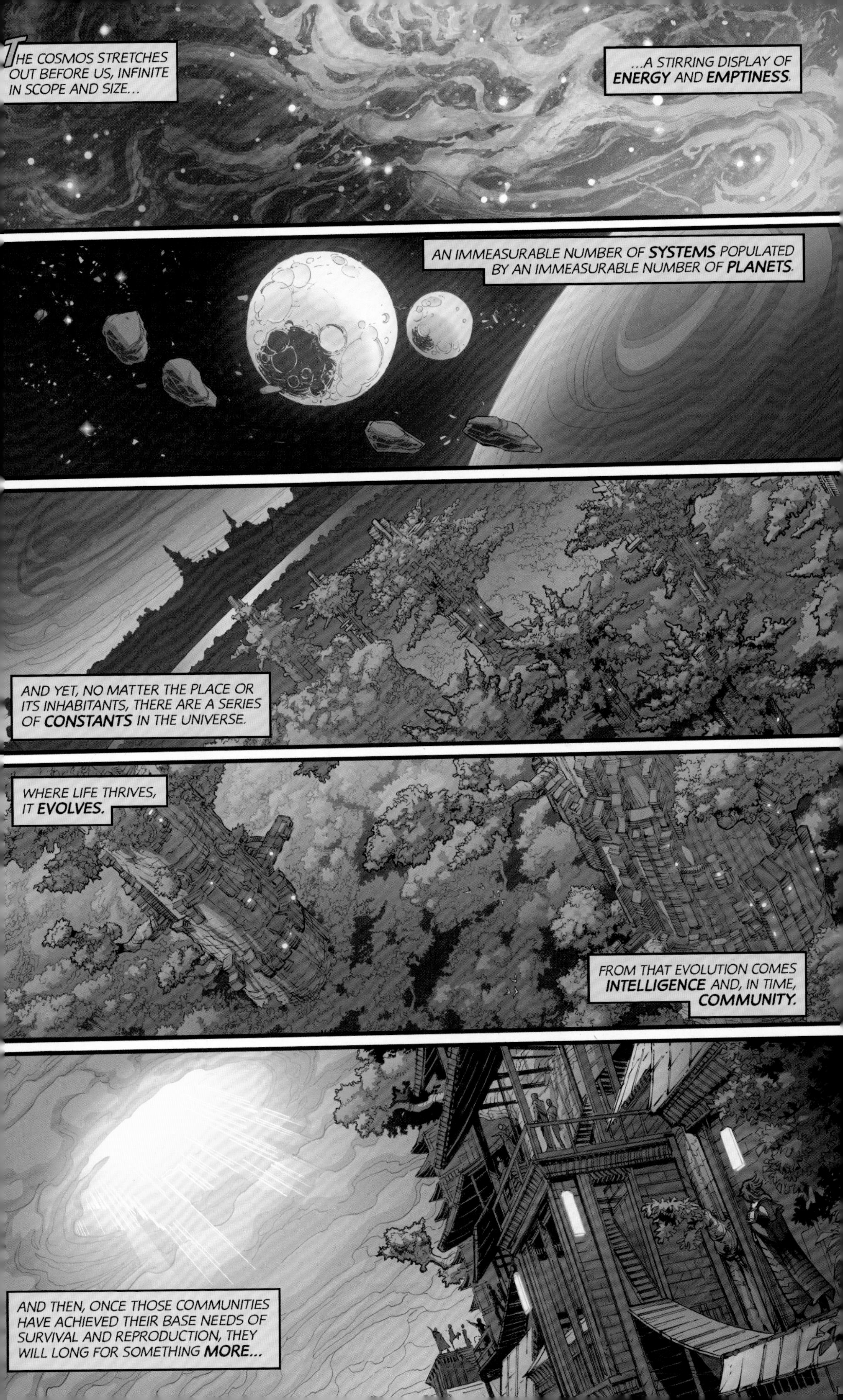
THE COSMOS STRETCHES OUT BEFORE US, INFINITE IN SCOPE AND SIZE...
...A STIRRING DISPLAY OF ENERGY AND EMPTINESS.
AN IMMEASURABLE NUMBER OF SYSTEMS POPULATED BY AN IMMEASURABLE NUMBER OF PLANETS.
AND YET, NO MATTER THE PLACE OR ITS INHABITANTS, THERE ARE A SERIES OF CONSTANTS IN THE UNIVERSE.
WHERE LIFE THRIVES, IT EVOLVES.
FROM THAT EVOLUTION COMES INTELLIGENCE AND, IN TIME, COMMUNITY.
AND THEN, ONCE THOSE COMMUNITIES HAVE ACHIEVED THEIR BASE NEEDS OF SURVIVAL AND REPRODUCTION, THEY WILL LONG FOR SOMETHING MORE...

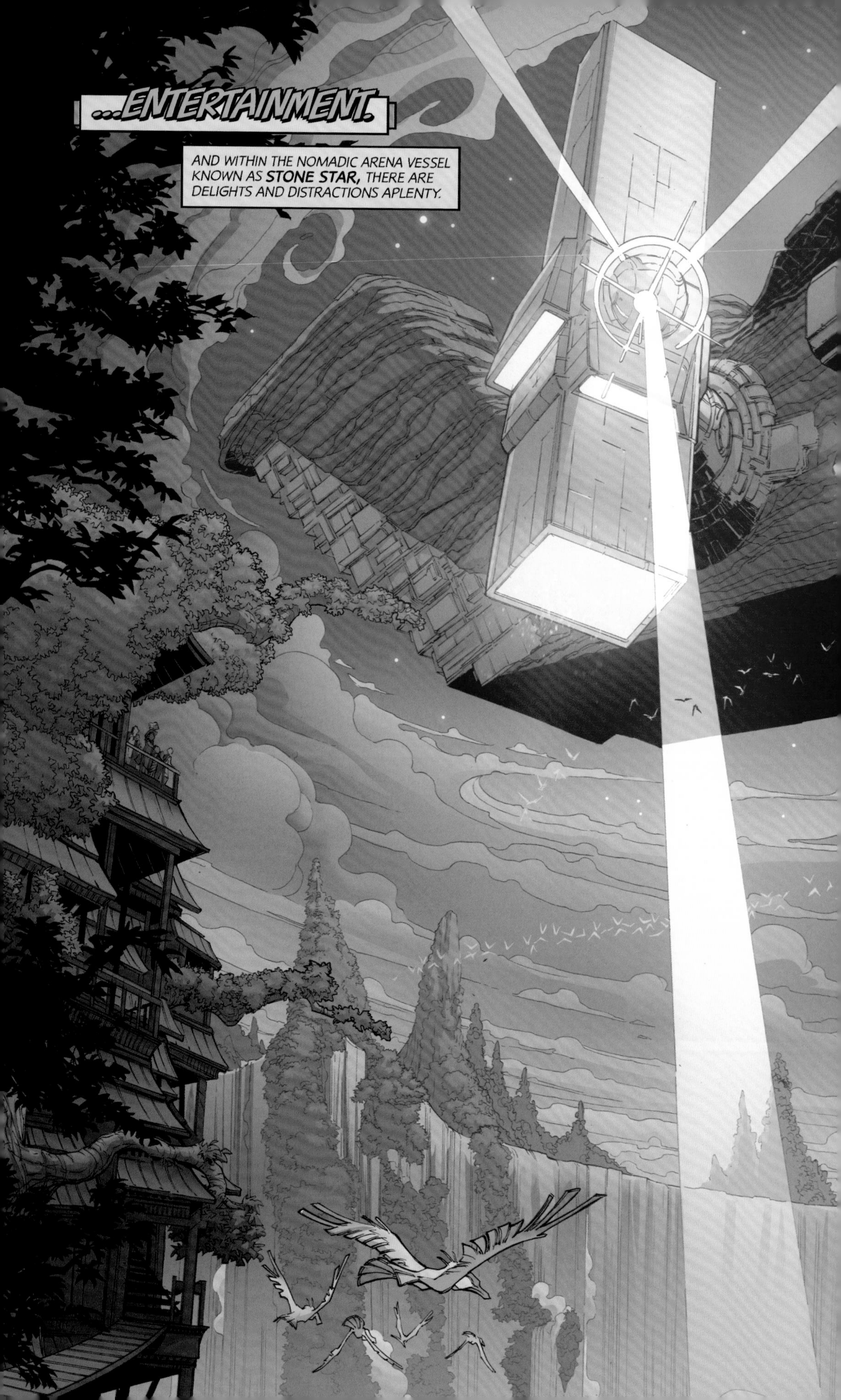
...ENTERTAINMENT.
AND WITHIN THE NOMADIC ARENA VESSEL KNOWN AS STONE STAR, THERE ARE DELIGHTS AND DISTRACTIONS APLENTY.

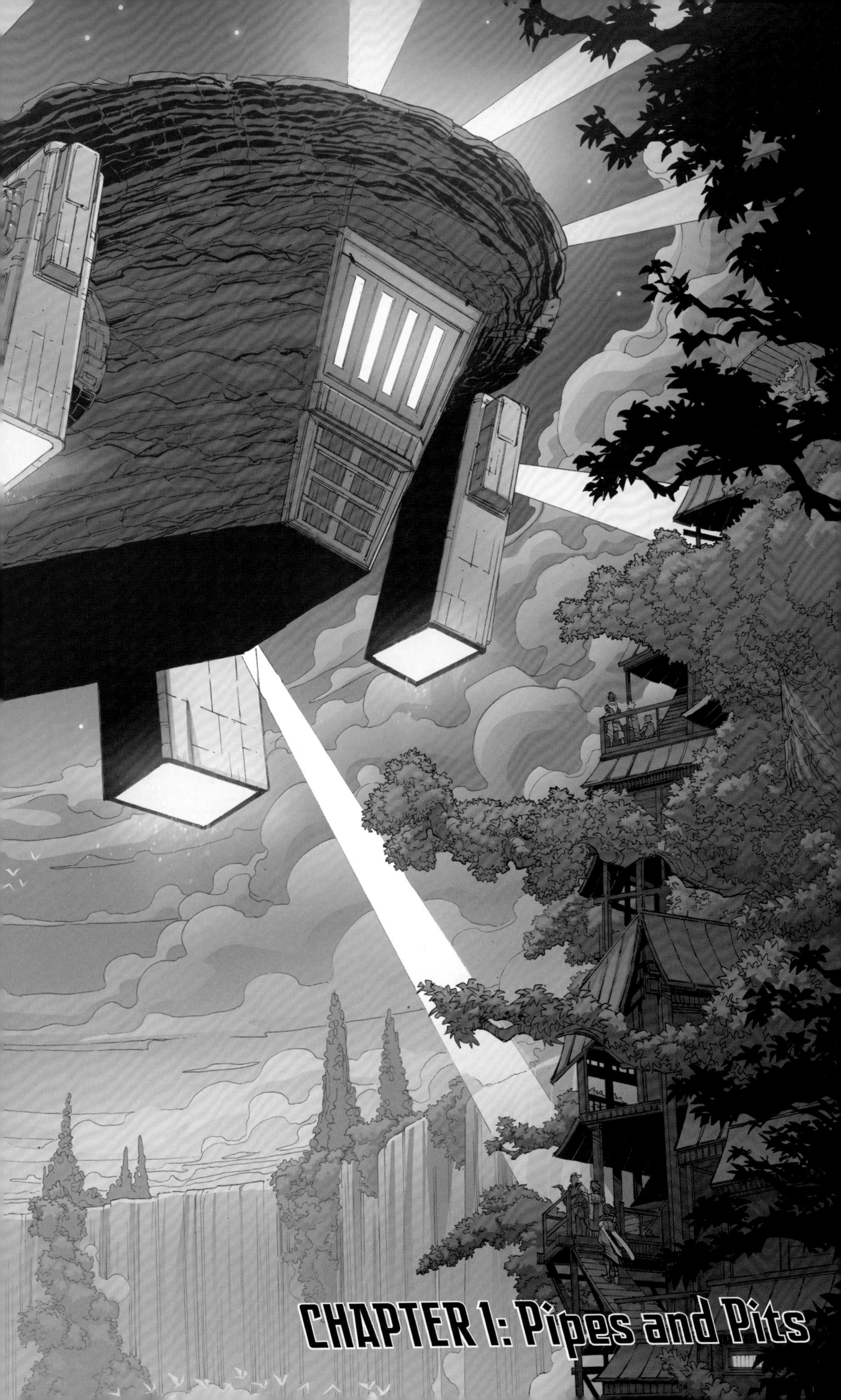

CHAPTER 1: Pipes and Pits

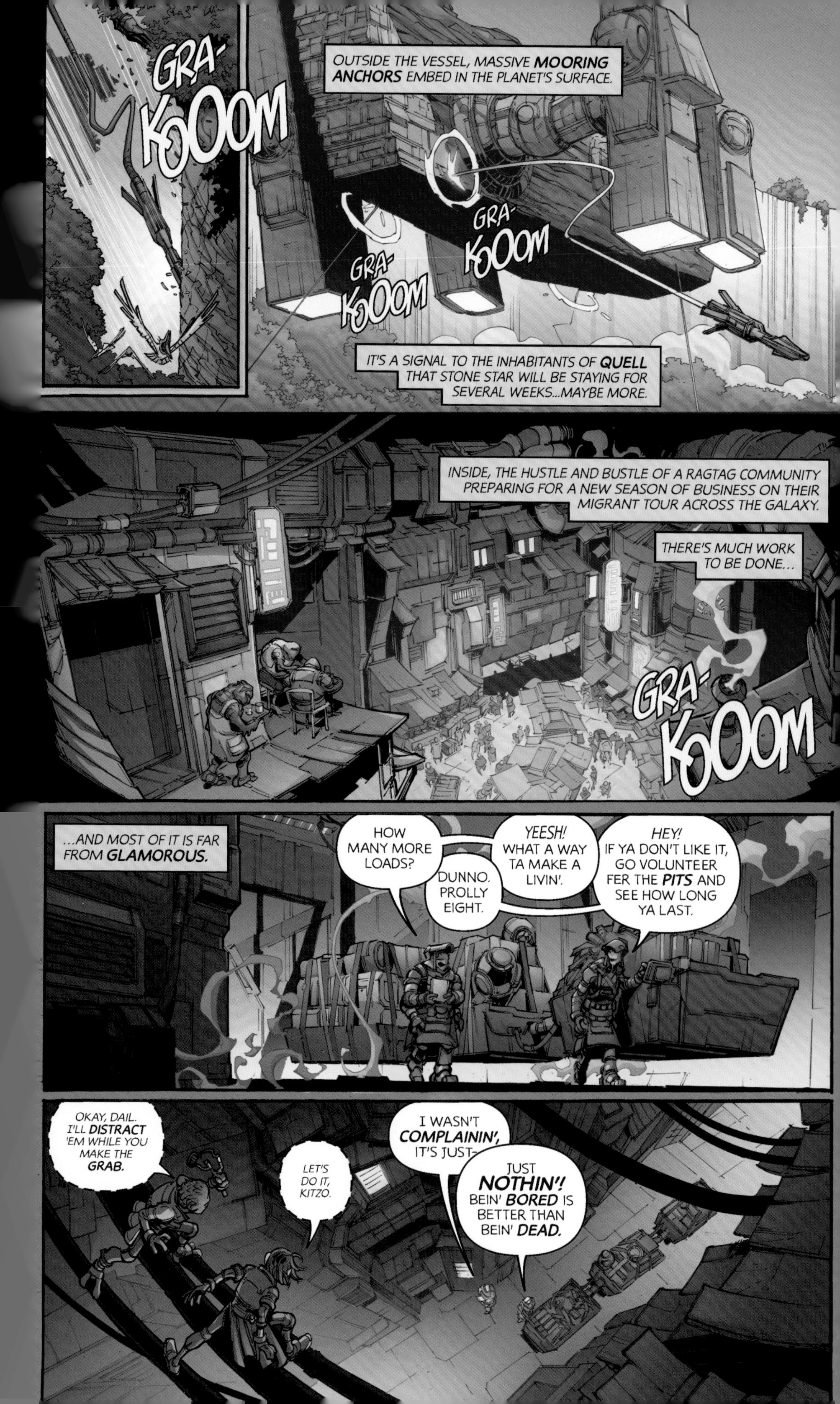
GRA-KOOOM
OUTSIDE THE VESSEL, MASSIVE **MOORING ANCHORS** EMBED IN THE PLANET'S SURFACE.
GRA-KOOOM
GRA-KOOOM
IT'S A SIGNAL TO THE INHABITANTS OF **QUELL** THAT STONE STAR WILL BE STAYING FOR SEVERAL WEEKS...MAYBE MORE.
INSIDE, THE HUSTLE AND BUSTLE OF A RAGTAG COMMUNITY PREPARING FOR A NEW SEASON OF BUSINESS ON THEIR MIGRANT TOUR ACROSS THE GALAXY.
THERE'S MUCH WORK TO BE DONE...
GRA-KOOOM
...AND MOST OF IT IS FAR FROM **GLAMOROUS.**
HOW MANY MORE LOADS?
DUNNO. PROLLY EIGHT.
YEESH! WHAT A WAY TA MAKE A LIVIN'.
HEY! IF YA DON'T LIKE IT, GO VOLUNTEER FER THE ***PITS*** AND SEE HOW LONG YA LAST.
*OKAY, DAIL. I'LL **DISTRACT** 'EM WHILE YOU MAKE THE **GRAB.***
LET'S DO IT, KITZO.
I WASN'T ***COMPLAININ',*** IT'S JUST--
JUST ***NOTHIN'!*** BEIN' ***BORED*** IS BETTER THAN BEIN' ***DEAD.***

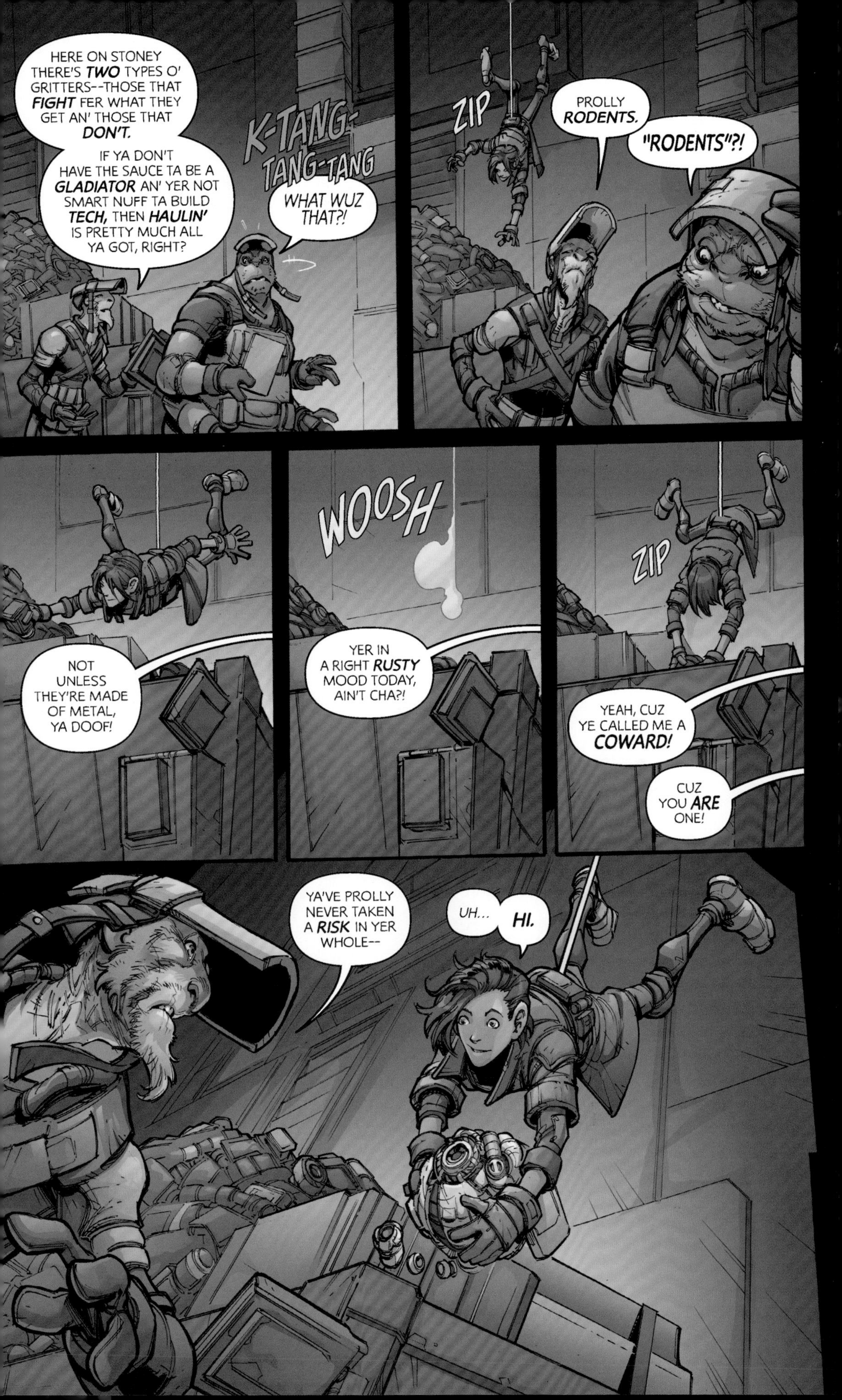
HERE ON STONEY THERE'S TWO TYPES O' GRITTERS--THOSE THAT FIGHT FER WHAT THEY GET AN' THOSE THAT DON'T.
IF YA DON'T HAVE THE SAUCE TA BE A GLADIATOR AN' YER NOT SMART NUFF TA BUILD TECH, THEN HAULIN' IS PRETTY MUCH ALL YA GOT, RIGHT?
K-TANG-TANG-TANG
WHAT WUZ THAT?!
ZIP
PROLLY RODENTS.
"RODENTS"?!
NOT UNLESS THEY'RE MADE OF METAL, YA DOOF!
WOOSH
YER IN A RIGHT RUSTY MOOD TODAY, AIN'T CHA?!
ZIP
YEAH, CUZ YE CALLED ME A COWARD!
CUZ YOU ARE ONE!
YA'VE PROLLY NEVER TAKEN A RISK IN YER WHOLE--
UH...
HI.

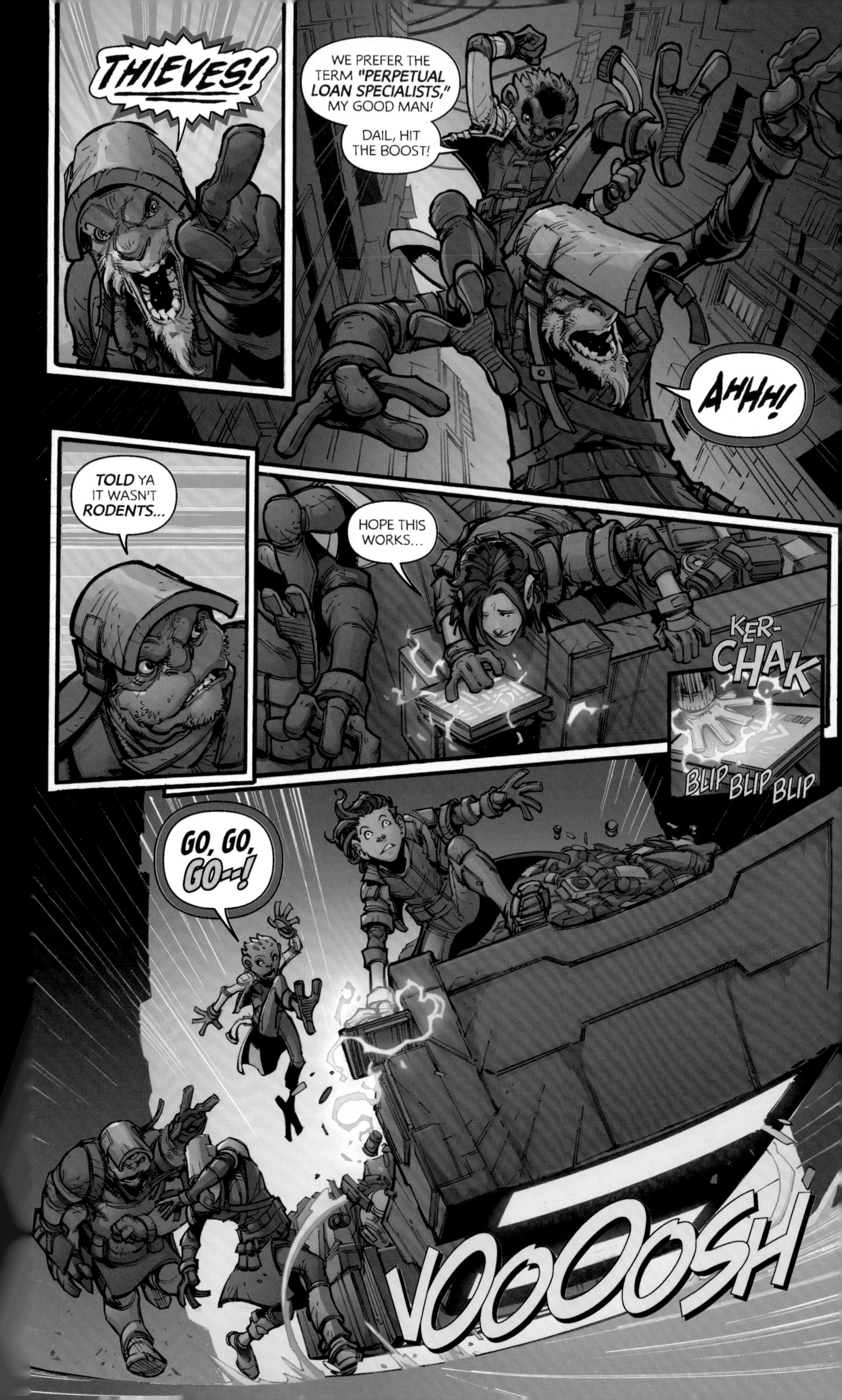
THIEVES!
WE PREFER THE TERM "PERPETUAL LOAN SPECIALISTS," MY GOOD MAN!
DAIL, HIT THE BOOST!
AHHH!
TOLD YA IT WASN'T RODENTS...
HOPE THIS WORKS...
KER-CHAK
BLIP BLIP BLIP
GO, GO, GO--!
VOOOOOSH

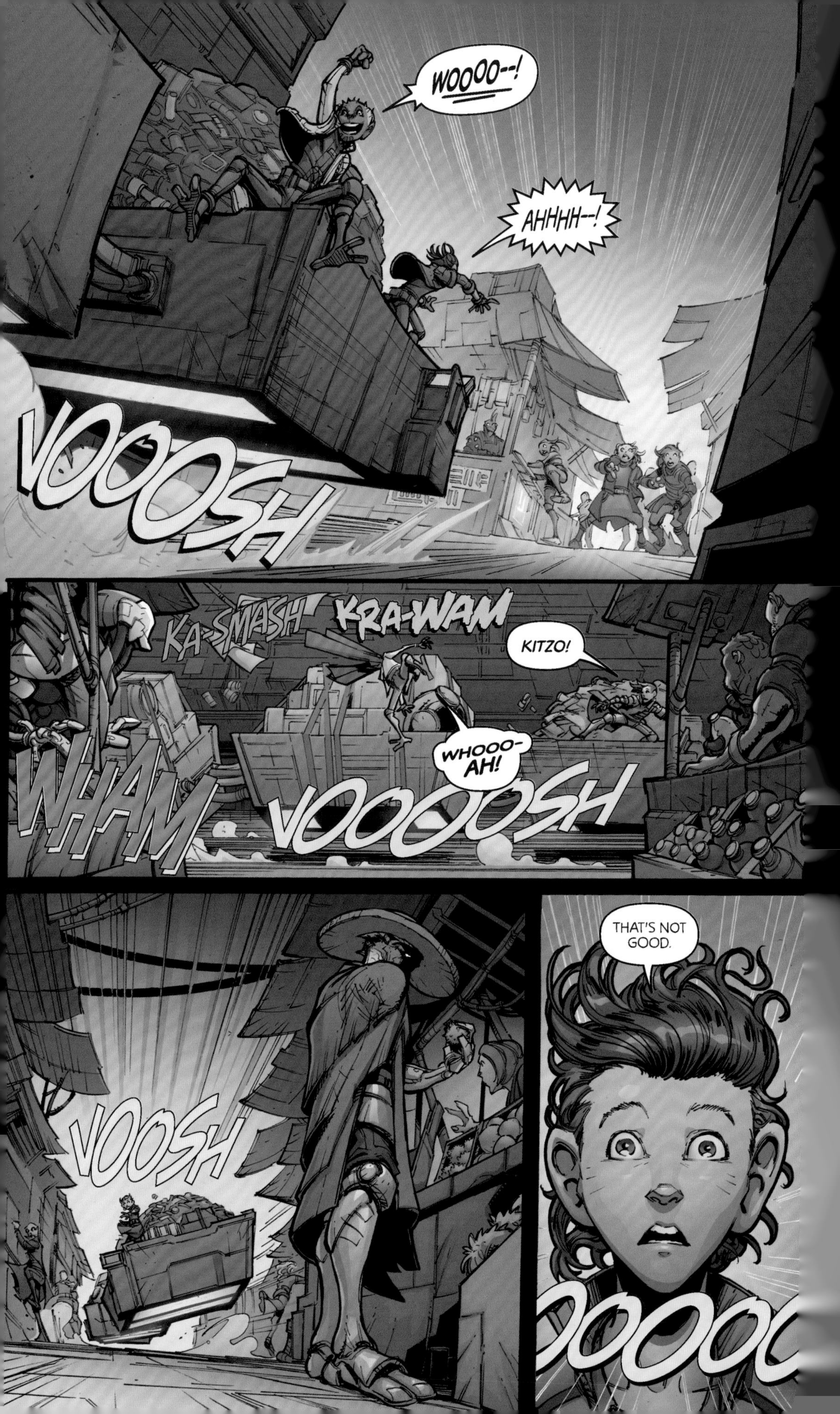
WOOOO--!
AHHHH--!
VOOOSH
KA-SMASH
KRA-WAM
KITZO!
WHOOO-AH!
WHAM
VOOOOSH
VOOSH
THAT'S NOT GOOD.
OOOOOO

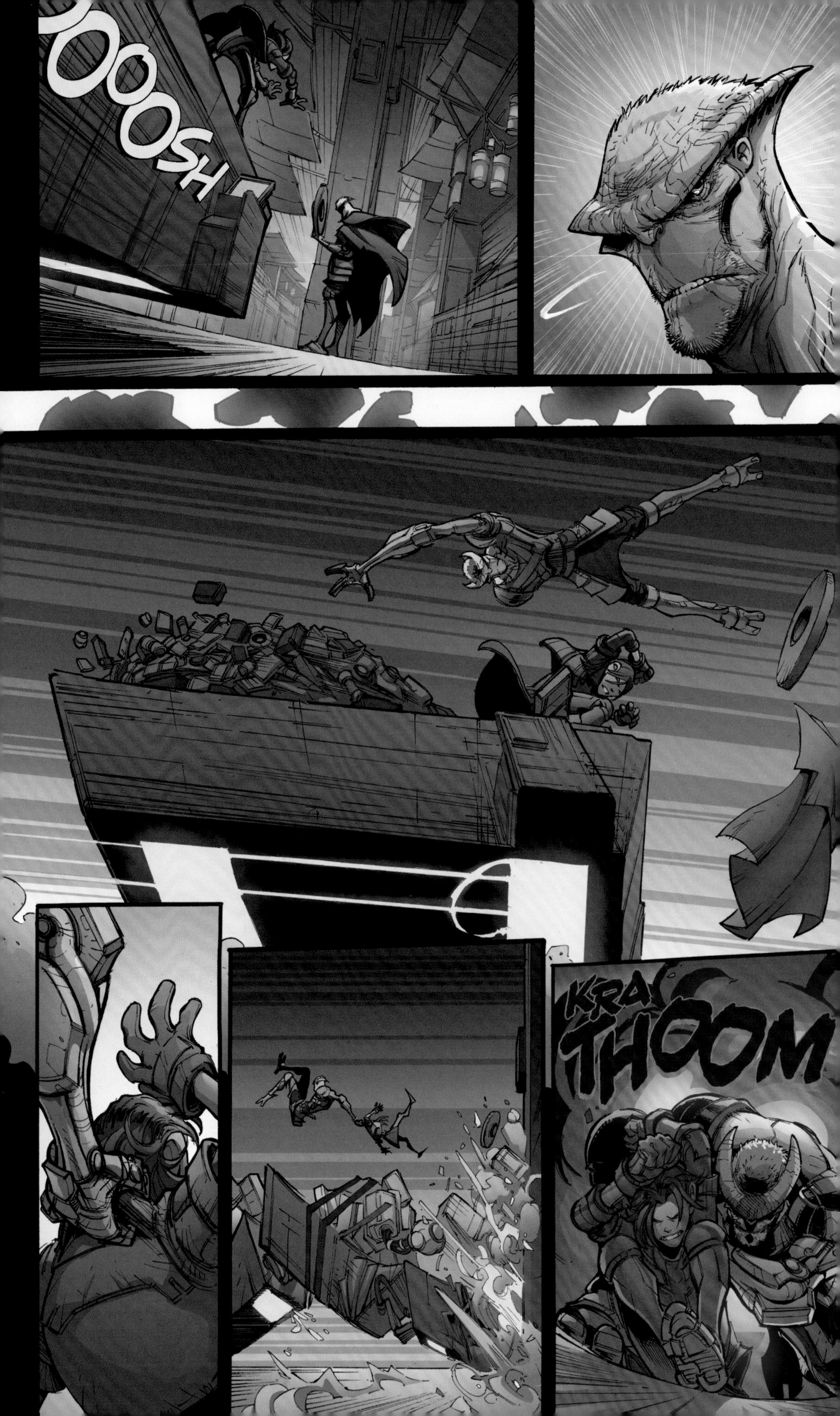
OOOOSH
KRA
THOOM

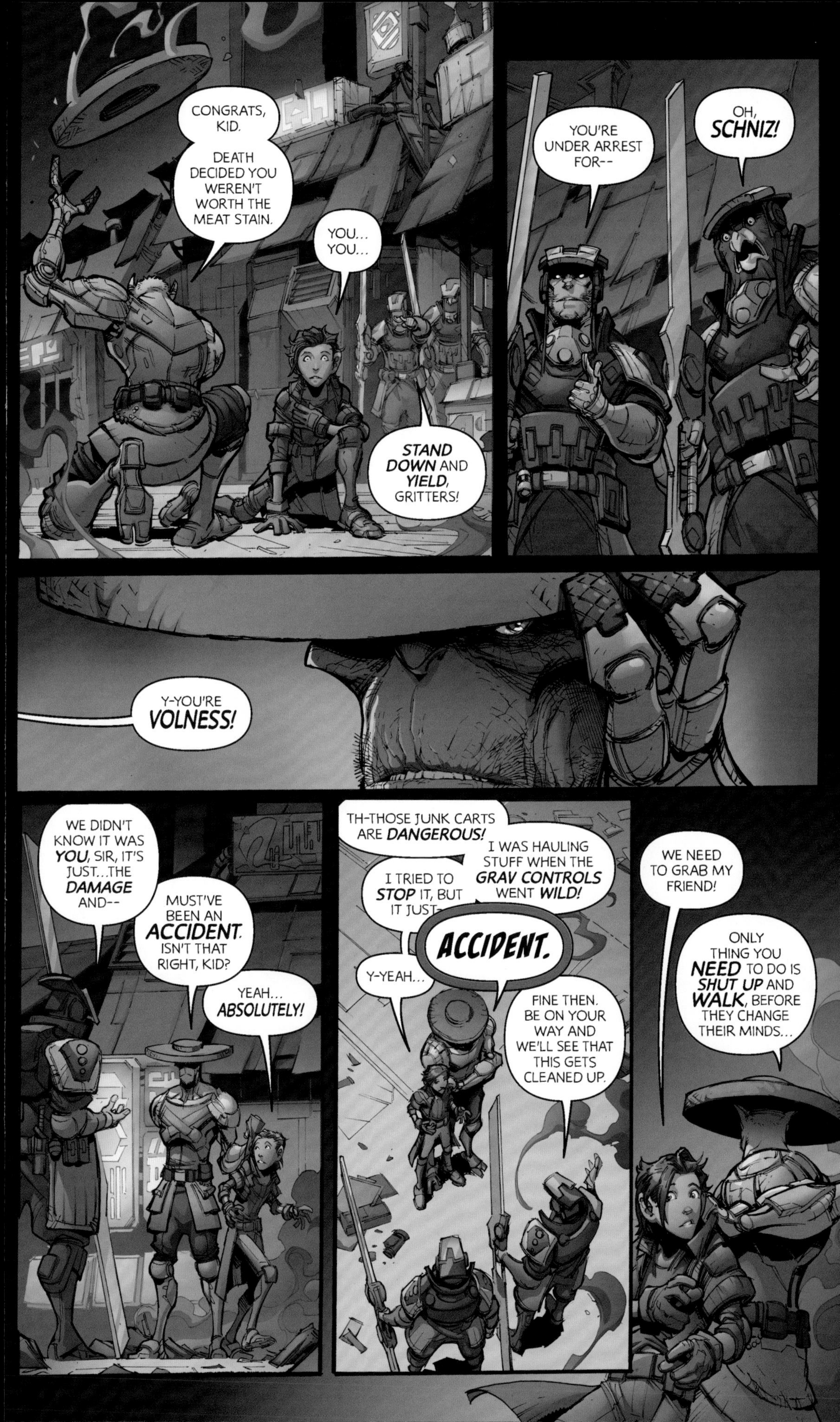
CONGRATS, KID.
DEATH DECIDED YOU WEREN'T WORTH THE MEAT STAIN.
YOU... YOU...
STAND DOWN AND YIELD, GRITTERS!
YOU'RE UNDER ARREST FOR--
OH, SCHNIZ!
Y-YOU'RE VOLNESS!
WE DIDN'T KNOW IT WAS YOU, SIR, IT'S JUST...THE DAMAGE AND--
MUST'VE BEEN AN ACCIDENT. ISN'T THAT RIGHT, KID?
YEAH... ABSOLUTELY!
TH-THOSE JUNK CARTS ARE DANGEROUS!
I WAS HAULING STUFF WHEN THE GRAV CONTROLS WENT WILD!
I TRIED TO STOP IT, BUT IT JUST--
ACCIDENT.
Y-YEAH...
FINE THEN. BE ON YOUR WAY AND WE'LL SEE THAT THIS GETS CLEANED UP.
WE NEED TO GRAB MY FRIEND!
ONLY THING YOU NEED TO DO IS SHUT UP AND WALK, BEFORE THEY CHANGE THEIR MINDS...

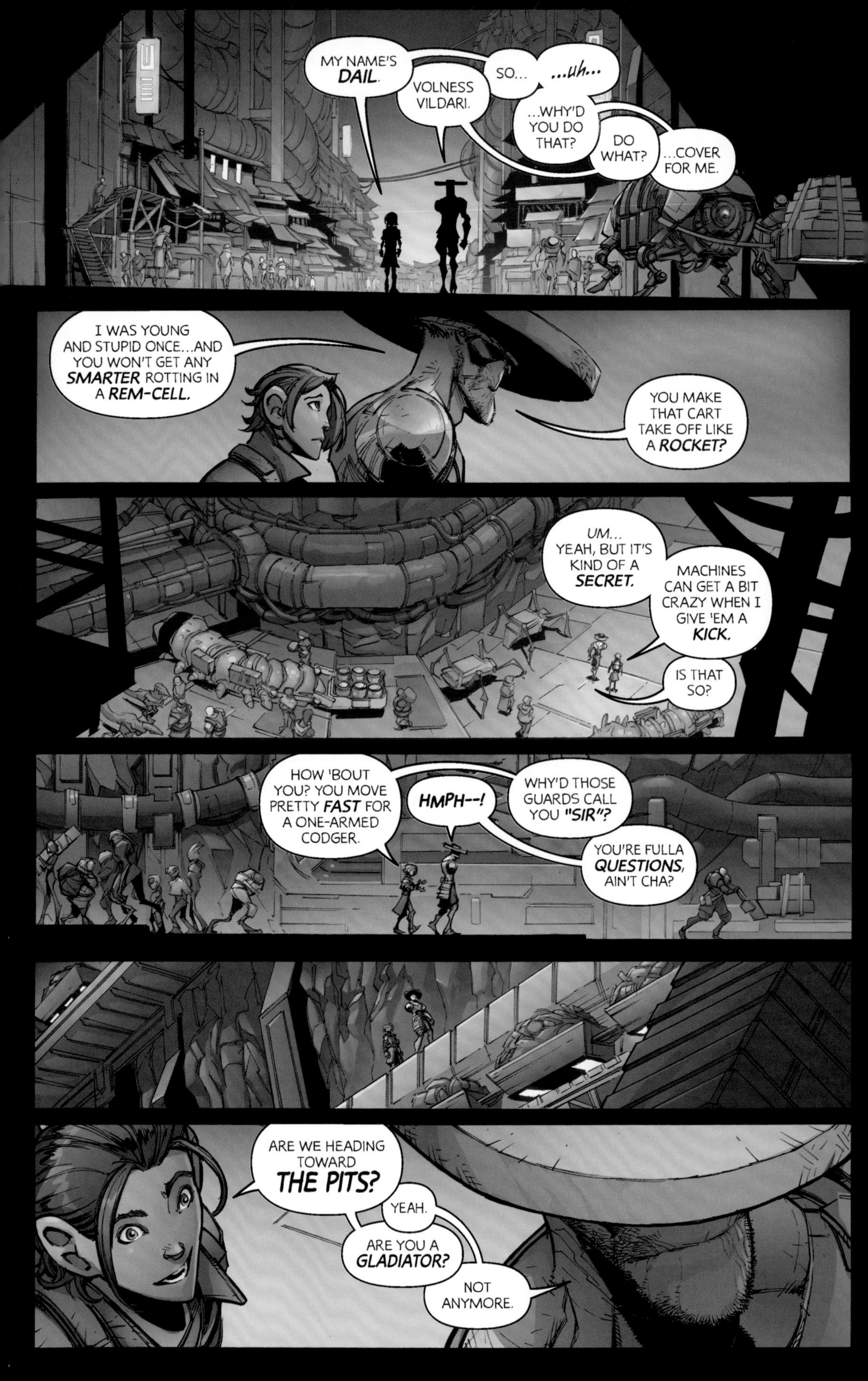
MY NAME'S DAIL.
VOLNESS VILDARI.
SO...
...uh...
...WHY'D YOU DO THAT?
DO WHAT?
...COVER FOR ME.
I WAS YOUNG AND STUPID ONCE...AND YOU WON'T GET ANY SMARTER ROTTING IN A REM-CELL.
YOU MAKE THAT CART TAKE OFF LIKE A ROCKET?
UM... YEAH, BUT IT'S KIND OF A SECRET.
MACHINES CAN GET A BIT CRAZY WHEN I GIVE 'EM A KICK.
IS THAT SO?
HOW 'BOUT YOU? YOU MOVE PRETTY FAST FOR A ONE-ARMED CODGER.
HMPH--!
WHY'D THOSE GUARDS CALL YOU "SIR"?
YOU'RE FULLA QUESTIONS, AIN'T CHA?
ARE WE HEADING TOWARD THE PITS?
YEAH.
ARE YOU A GLADIATOR?
NOT ANYMORE.

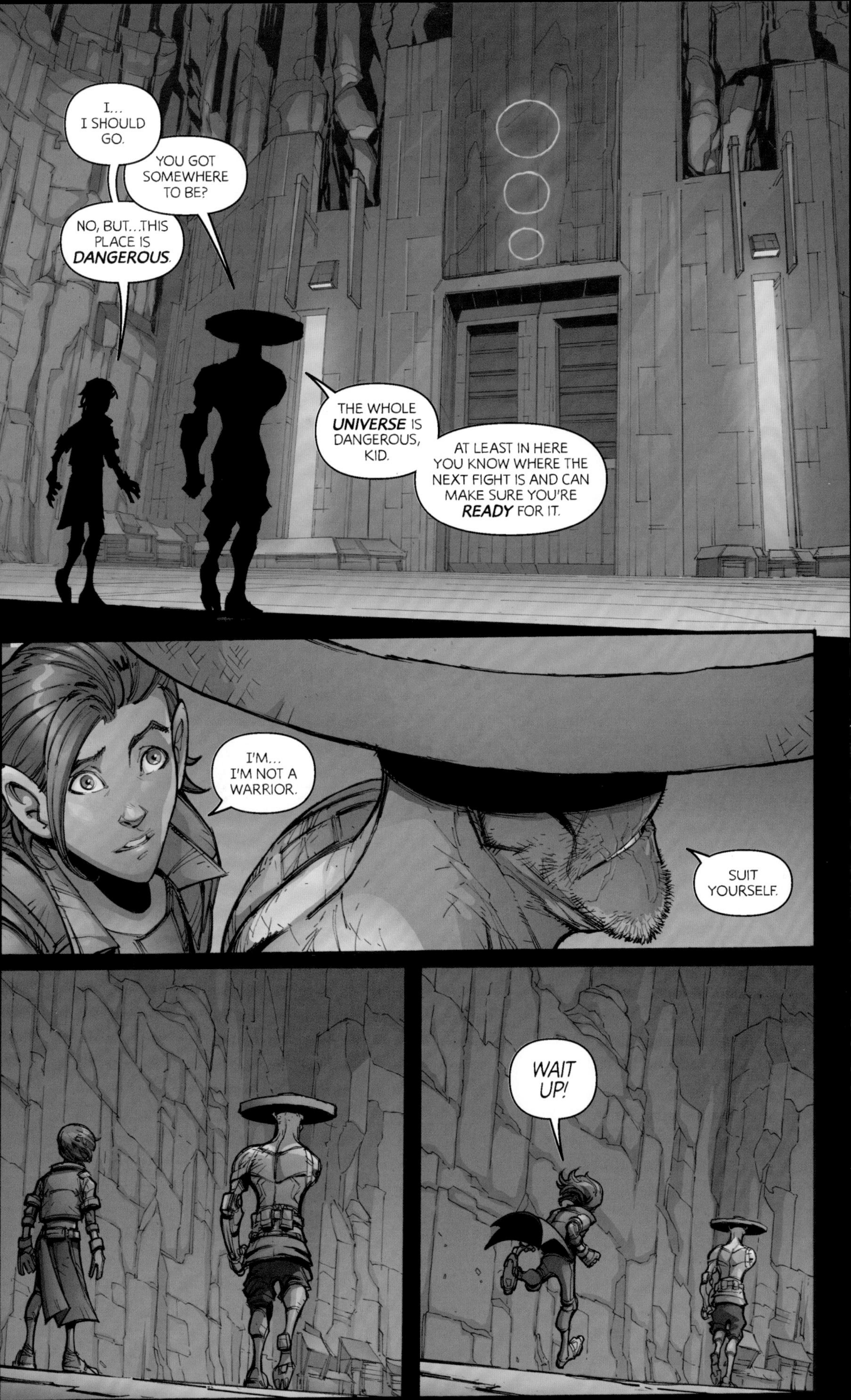
I... I SHOULD GO.
YOU GOT SOMEWHERE TO BE?
NO, BUT...THIS PLACE IS DANGEROUS.
THE WHOLE UNIVERSE IS DANGEROUS, KID.
AT LEAST IN HERE YOU KNOW WHERE THE NEXT FIGHT IS AND CAN MAKE SURE YOU'RE READY FOR IT.
I'M... I'M NOT A WARRIOR.
SUIT YOURSELF.
WAIT UP!

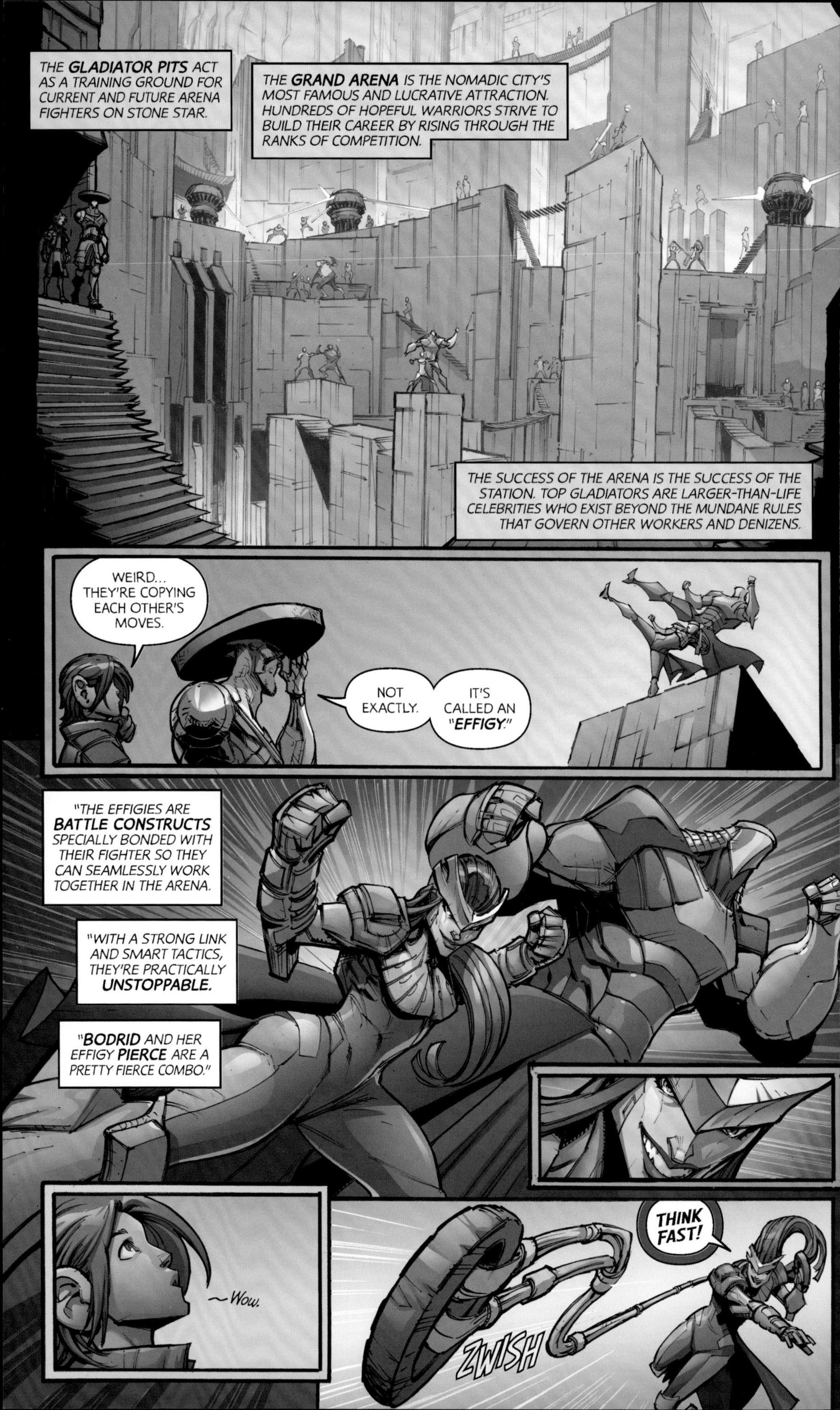

THE **GLADIATOR PITS** ACT AS A TRAINING GROUND FOR CURRENT AND FUTURE ARENA FIGHTERS ON STONE STAR.
THE **GRAND ARENA** IS THE NOMADIC CITY'S MOST FAMOUS AND LUCRATIVE ATTRACTION. HUNDREDS OF HOPEFUL WARRIORS STRIVE TO BUILD THEIR CAREER BY RISING THROUGH THE RANKS OF COMPETITION.
THE SUCCESS OF THE ARENA IS THE SUCCESS OF THE STATION. TOP GLADIATORS ARE LARGER-THAN-LIFE CELEBRITIES WHO EXIST BEYOND THE MUNDANE RULES THAT GOVERN OTHER WORKERS AND DENIZENS.
WEIRD... THEY'RE COPYING EACH OTHER'S MOVES.
NOT EXACTLY.
IT'S CALLED AN "**EFFIGY**."
"THE EFFIGIES ARE **BATTLE CONSTRUCTS** SPECIALLY BONDED WITH THEIR FIGHTER SO THEY CAN SEAMLESSLY WORK TOGETHER IN THE ARENA.
"WITH A STRONG LINK AND SMART TACTICS, THEY'RE PRACTICALLY **UNSTOPPABLE.**
"**BODRID** AND HER EFFIGY **PIERCE** ARE A PRETTY FIERCE COMBO."
~Wow.
THINK FAST!
ZWISH

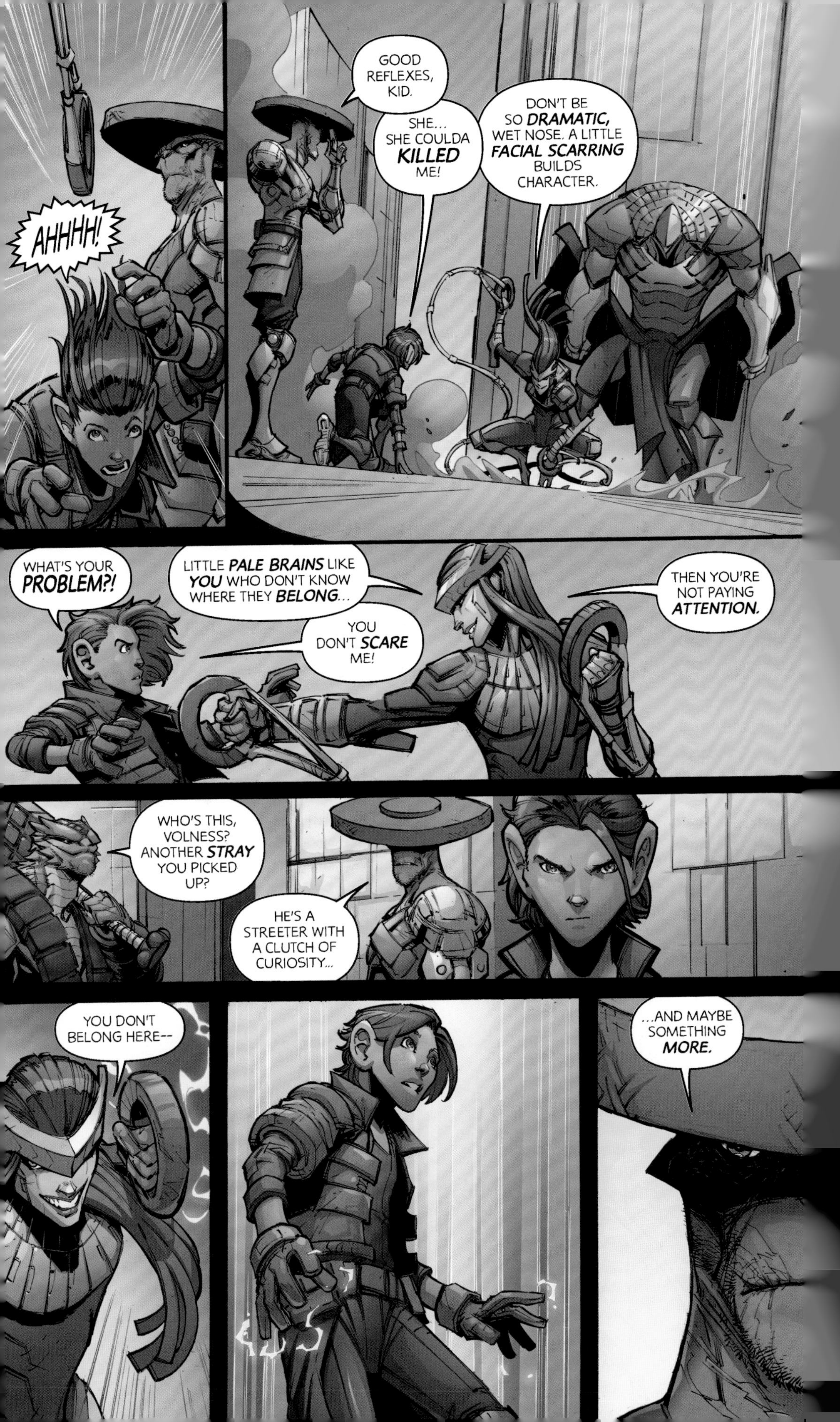
AHHHH!
GOOD REFLEXES, KID.
SHE... SHE COULDA KILLED ME!
DON'T BE SO DRAMATIC, WET NOSE. A LITTLE FACIAL SCARRING BUILDS CHARACTER.
WHAT'S YOUR PROBLEM?!
LITTLE PALE BRAINS LIKE YOU WHO DON'T KNOW WHERE THEY BELONG...
YOU DON'T SCARE ME!
THEN YOU'RE NOT PAYING ATTENTION.
WHO'S THIS, VOLNESS? ANOTHER STRAY YOU PICKED UP?
HE'S A STREETER WITH A CLUTCH OF CURIOSITY...
YOU DON'T BELONG HERE--
...AND MAYBE SOMETHING MORE.

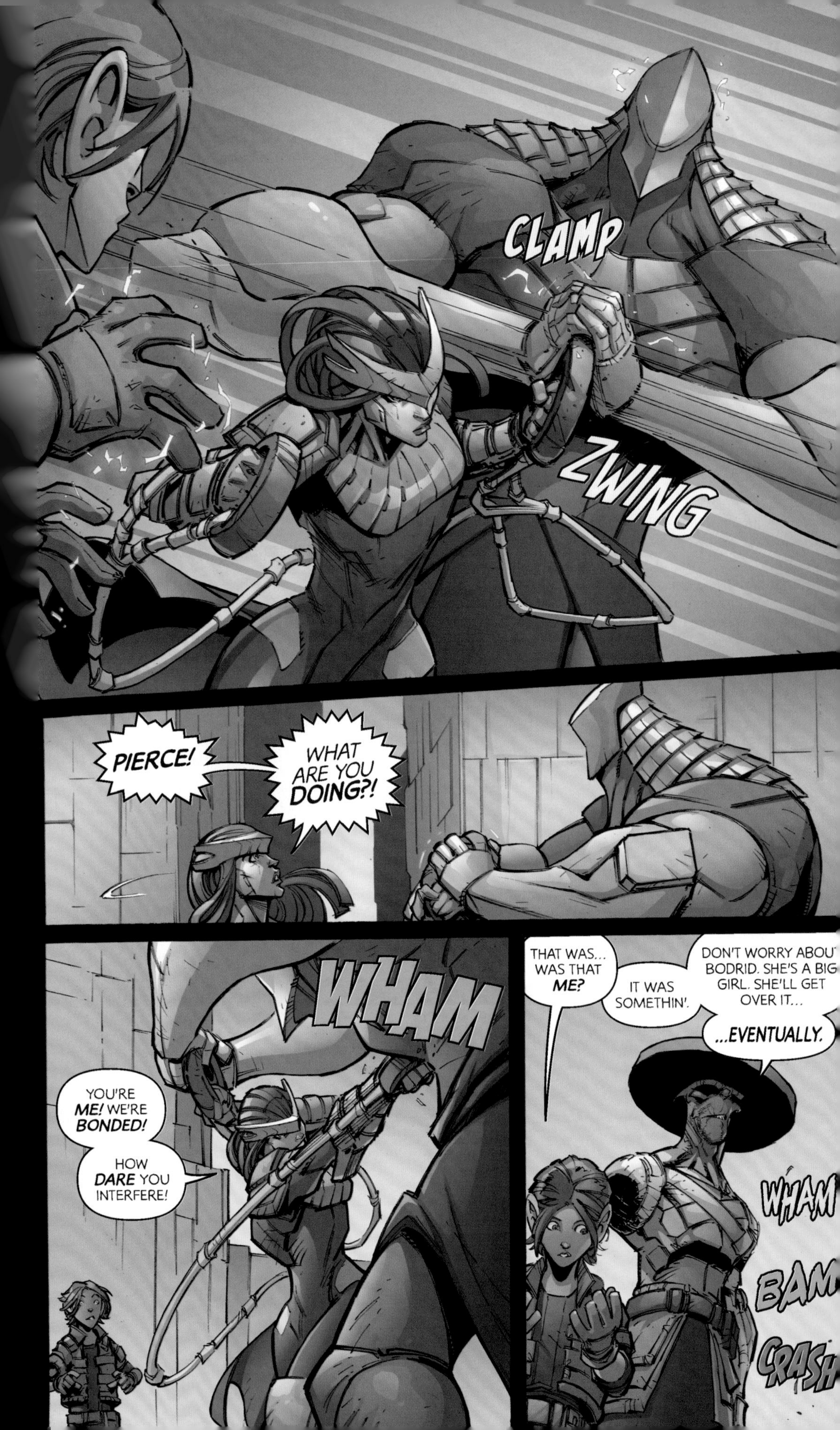
CLAMP
ZWING
PIERCE!
WHAT ARE YOU DOING?!
WHAM
YOU'RE ME! WE'RE BONDED!
HOW DARE YOU INTERFERE!
THAT WAS... WAS THAT ME?
IT WAS SOMETHIN'.
DON'T WORRY ABOUT BODRID. SHE'S A BIG GIRL. SHE'LL GET OVER IT...
...EVENTUALLY.
WHAM
BAM
CRASH

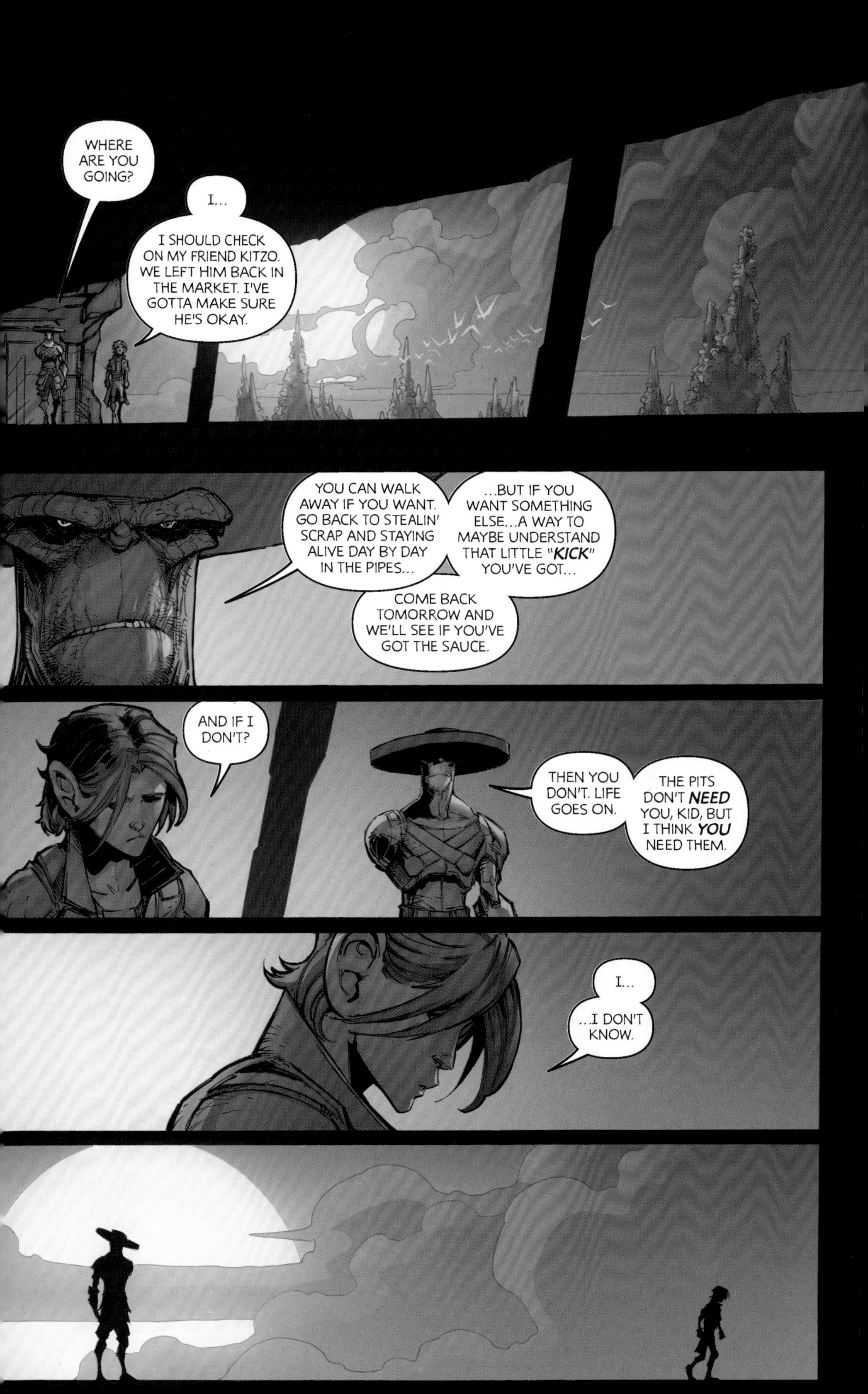
WHERE ARE YOU GOING?
I...
I SHOULD CHECK ON MY FRIEND KITZO. WE LEFT HIM BACK IN THE MARKET. I'VE GOTTA MAKE SURE HE'S OKAY.
YOU CAN WALK AWAY IF YOU WANT. GO BACK TO STEALIN' SCRAP AND STAYING ALIVE DAY BY DAY IN THE PIPES...
...BUT IF YOU WANT SOMETHING ELSE...A WAY TO MAYBE UNDERSTAND THAT LITTLE "KICK" YOU'VE GOT...
COME BACK TOMORROW AND WE'LL SEE IF YOU'VE GOT THE SAUCE.
AND IF I DON'T?
THEN YOU DON'T. LIFE GOES ON.
THE PITS DON'T NEED YOU, KID, BUT I THINK YOU NEED THEM.
I...
...I DON'T KNOW.

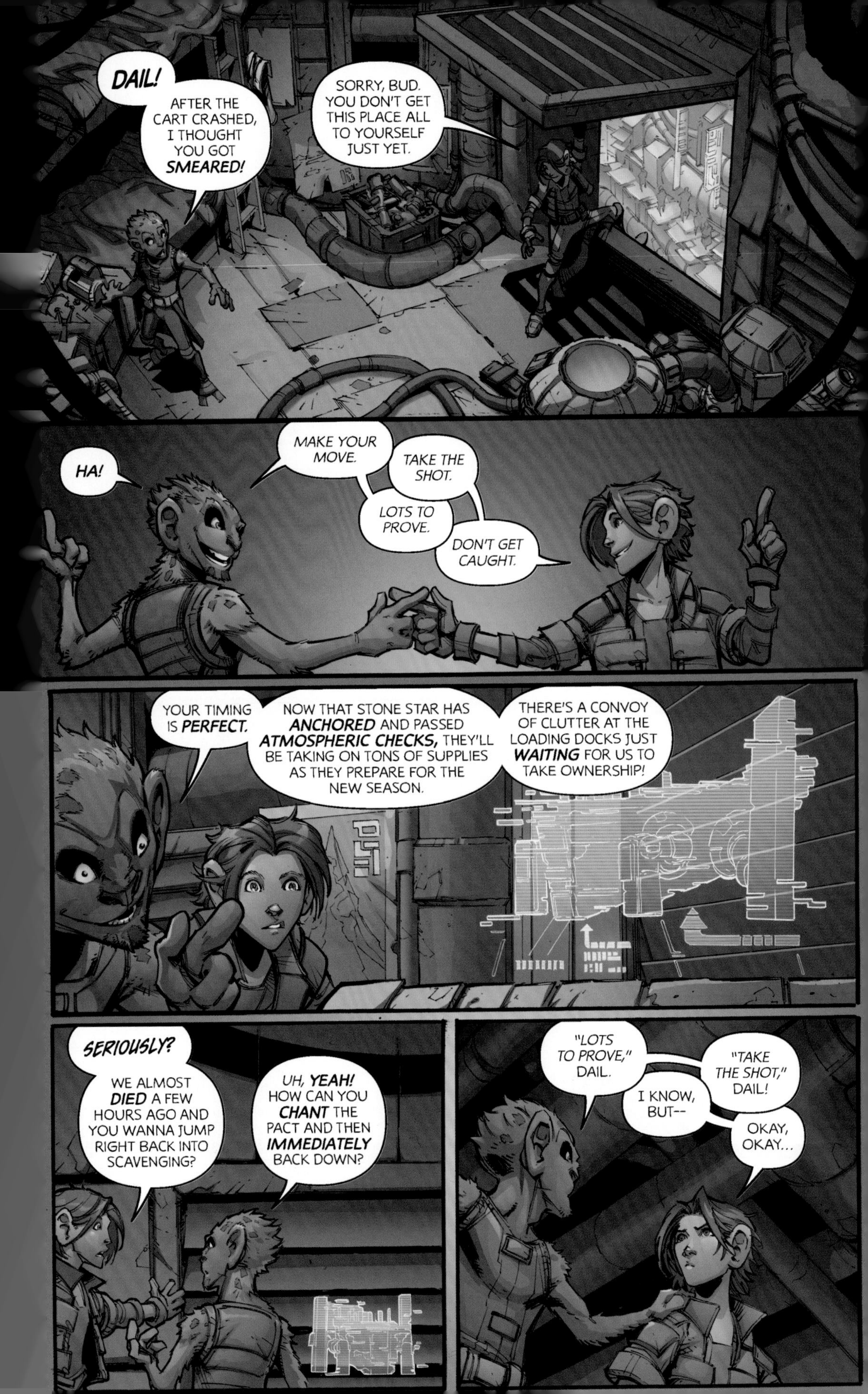
DAIL!
AFTER THE CART CRASHED, I THOUGHT YOU GOT SMEARED!
SORRY, BUD. YOU DON'T GET THIS PLACE ALL TO YOURSELF JUST YET.
HA!
MAKE YOUR MOVE.
TAKE THE SHOT.
LOTS TO PROVE.
DON'T GET CAUGHT.
YOUR TIMING IS PERFECT.
NOW THAT STONE STAR HAS ANCHORED AND PASSED ATMOSPHERIC CHECKS, THEY'LL BE TAKING ON TONS OF SUPPLIES AS THEY PREPARE FOR THE NEW SEASON.
THERE'S A CONVOY OF CLUTTER AT THE LOADING DOCKS JUST WAITING FOR US TO TAKE OWNERSHIP!
SERIOUSLY?
WE ALMOST DIED A FEW HOURS AGO AND YOU WANNA JUMP RIGHT BACK INTO SCAVENGING?
UH, YEAH! HOW CAN YOU CHANT THE PACT AND THEN IMMEDIATELY BACK DOWN?
"LOTS TO PROVE," DAIL.
"TAKE THE SHOT," DAIL!
I KNOW, BUT--
OKAY, OKAY...

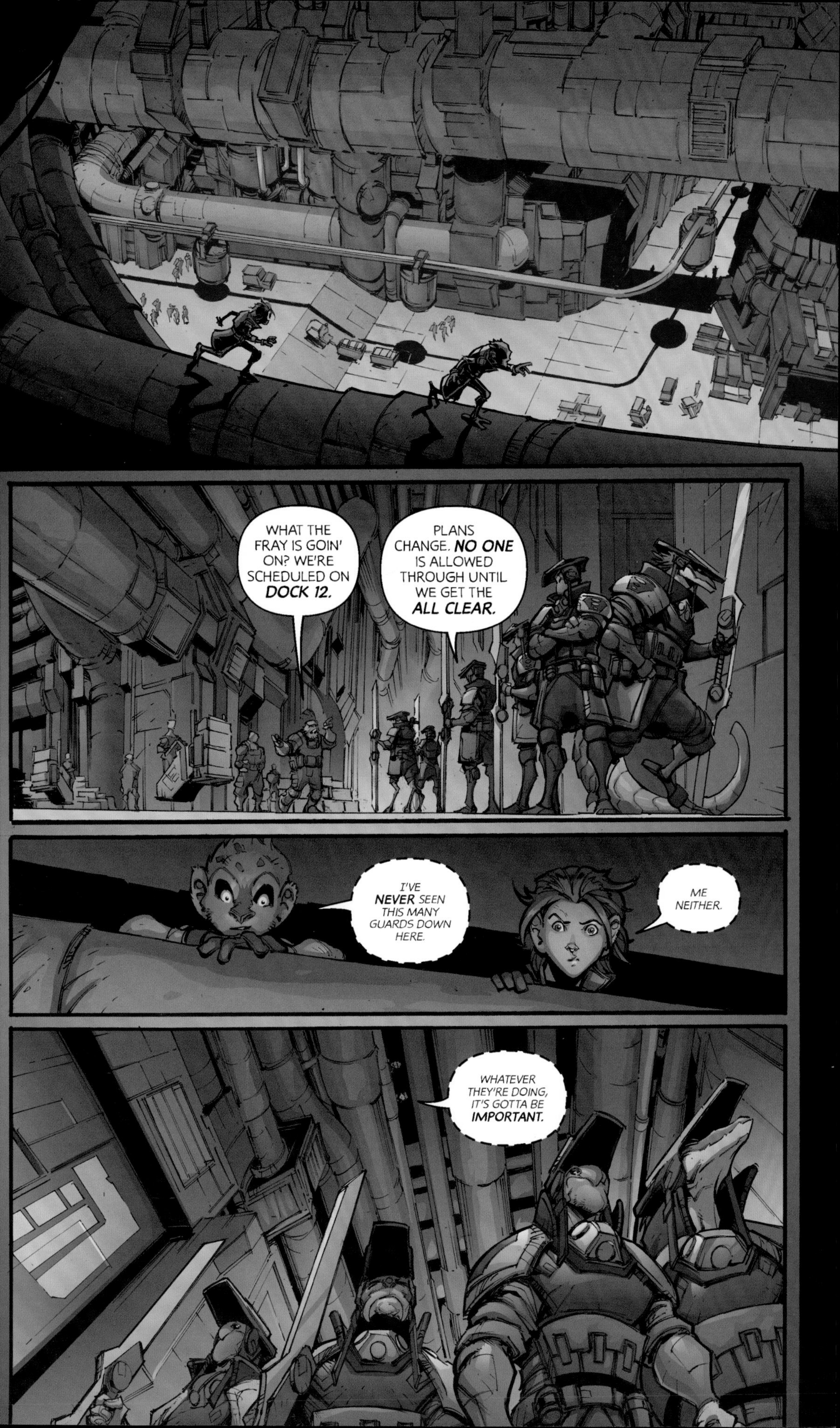
WHAT THE FRAY IS GOIN' ON? WE'RE SCHEDULED ON **DOCK 12.**
PLANS CHANGE. **NO ONE** IS ALLOWED THROUGH UNTIL WE GET THE **ALL CLEAR.**
*I'VE **NEVER** SEEN THIS MANY GUARDS DOWN HERE.*
ME NEITHER.
*WHATEVER THEY'RE DOING, IT'S GOTTA BE **IMPORTANT.***

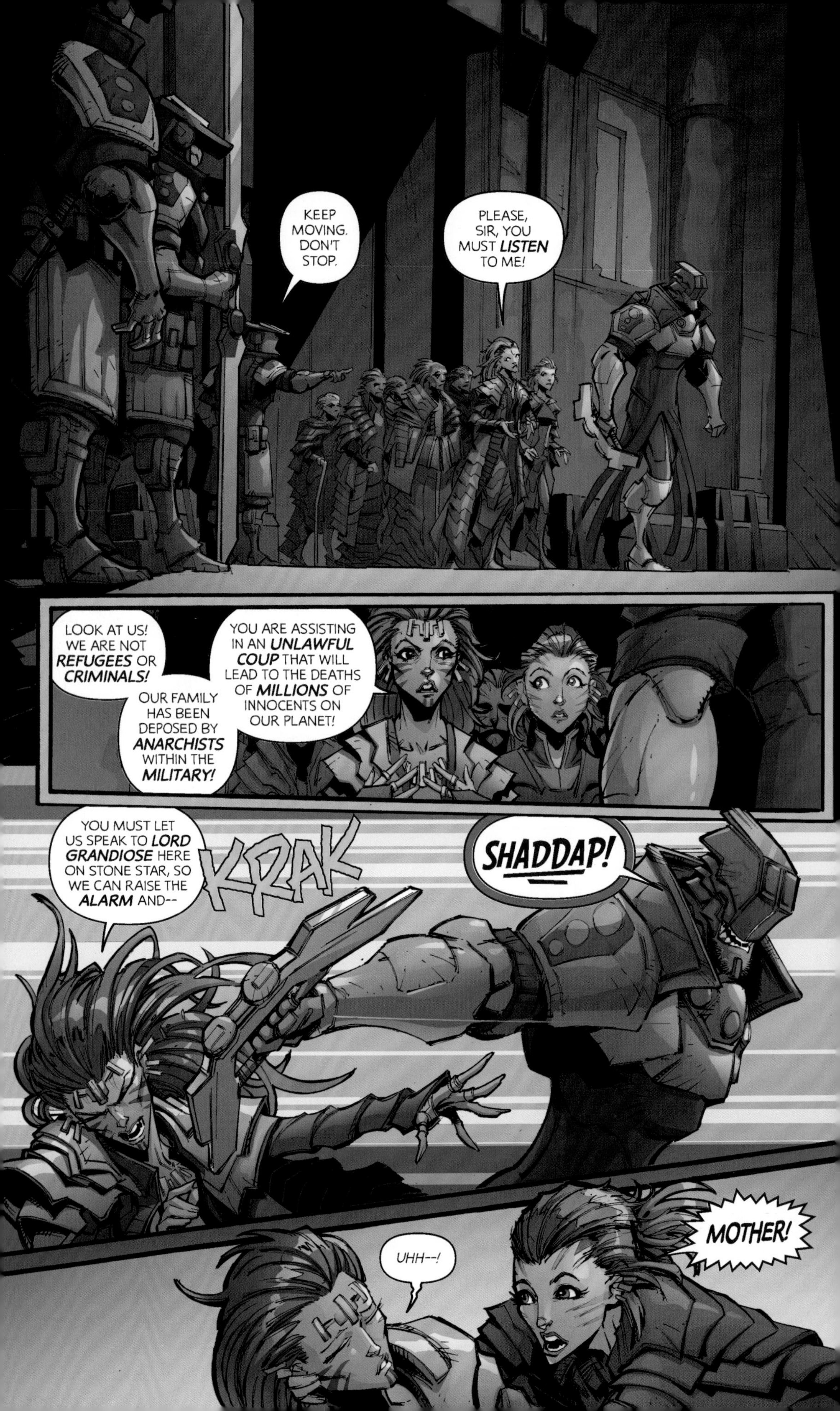

KEEP MOVING. DON'T STOP.
PLEASE, SIR, YOU MUST LISTEN TO ME!
LOOK AT US! WE ARE NOT REFUGEES OR CRIMINALS!
OUR FAMILY HAS BEEN DEPOSED BY ANARCHISTS WITHIN THE MILITARY!
YOU ARE ASSISTING IN AN UNLAWFUL COUP THAT WILL LEAD TO THE DEATHS OF MILLIONS OF INNOCENTS ON OUR PLANET!
YOU MUST LET US SPEAK TO LORD GRANDIOSE HERE ON STONE STAR, SO WE CAN RAISE THE ALARM AND--
KRAK
SHADDAP!
UHH--!
MOTHER!

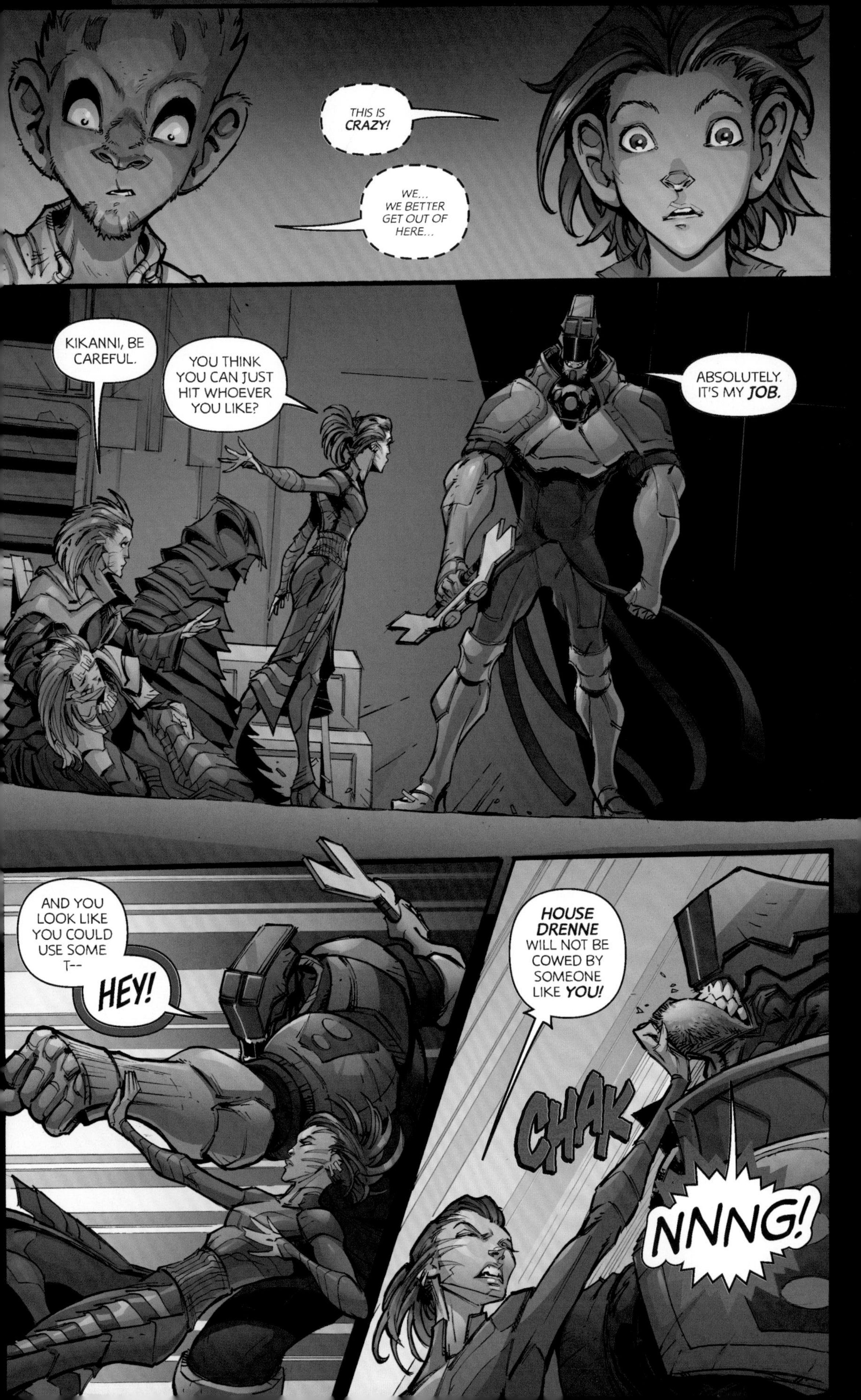

THIS IS CRAZY!
WE... WE BETTER GET OUT OF HERE...
KIKANNI, BE CAREFUL.
YOU THINK YOU CAN JUST HIT WHOEVER YOU LIKE?
ABSOLUTELY. IT'S MY JOB.
AND YOU LOOK LIKE YOU COULD USE SOME T--
HEY!
HOUSE DRENNE WILL NOT BE COWED BY SOMEONE LIKE YOU!
CHAK
NNNG!

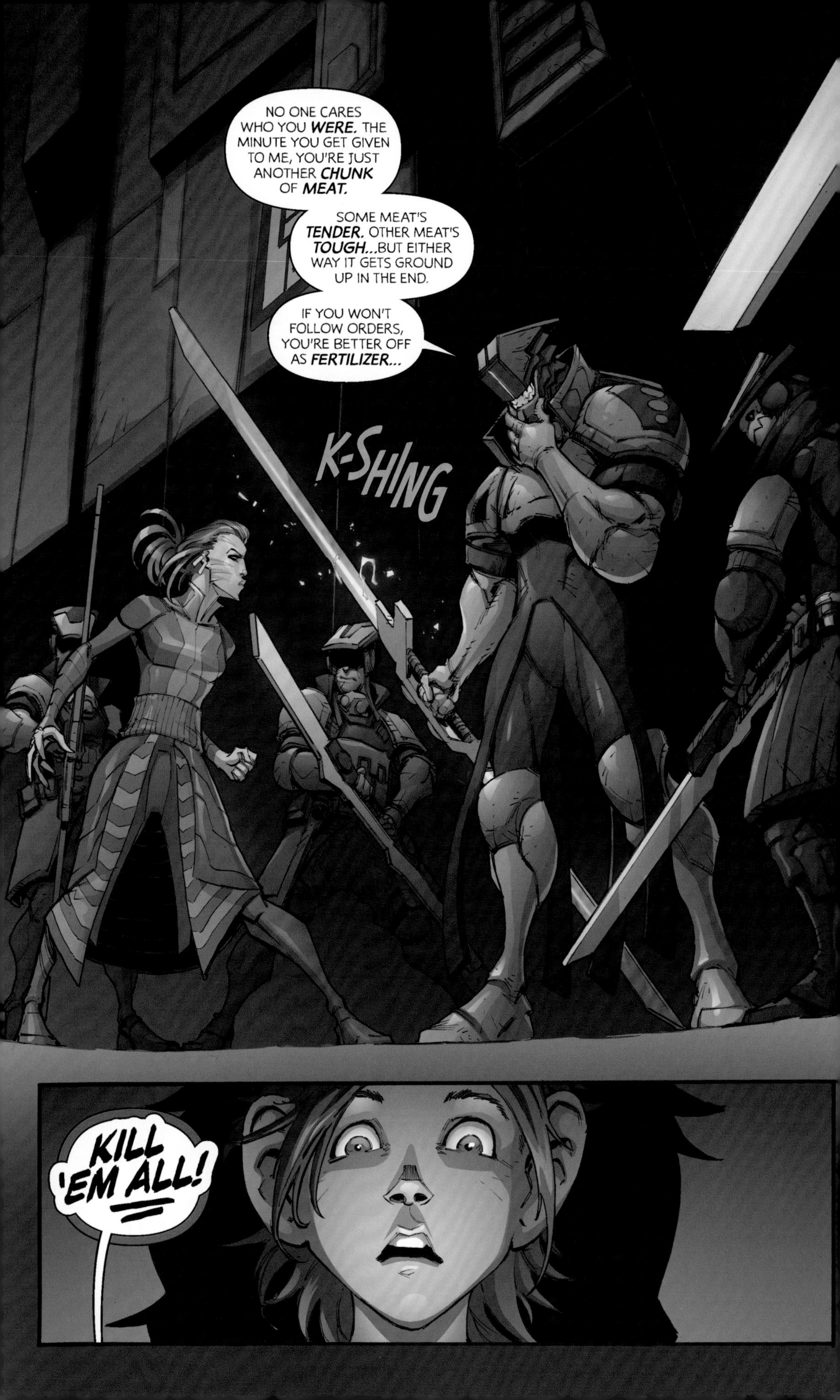

NO ONE CARES WHO YOU WERE. THE MINUTE YOU GET GIVEN TO ME, YOU'RE JUST ANOTHER CHUNK OF MEAT.
SOME MEAT'S TENDER. OTHER MEAT'S TOUGH...BUT EITHER WAY IT GETS GROUND UP IN THE END.
IF YOU WON'T FOLLOW ORDERS, YOU'RE BETTER OFF AS FERTILIZER...
K-SHING
KILL 'EM ALL!

Chapter 2: Hide and Seek

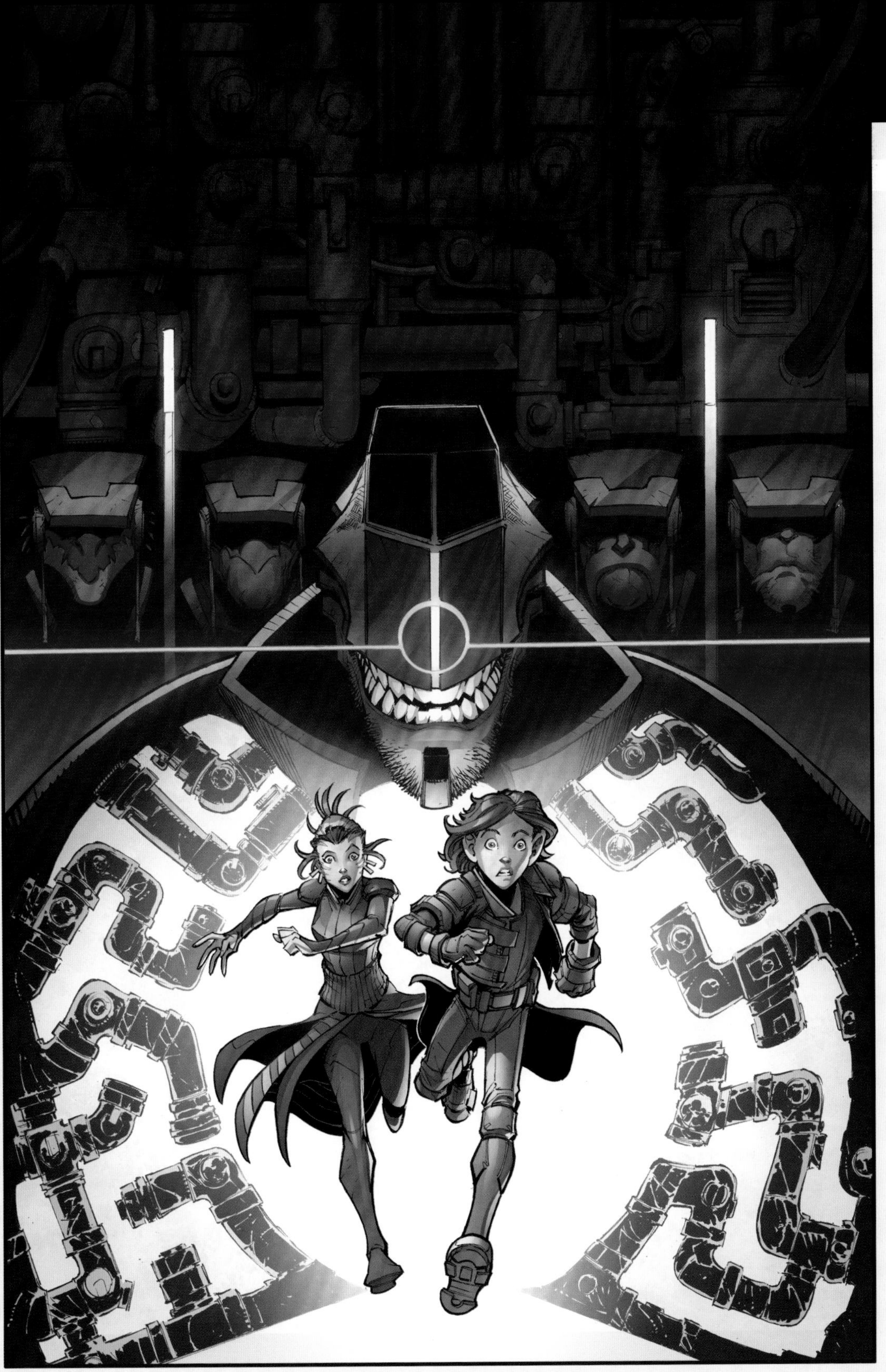

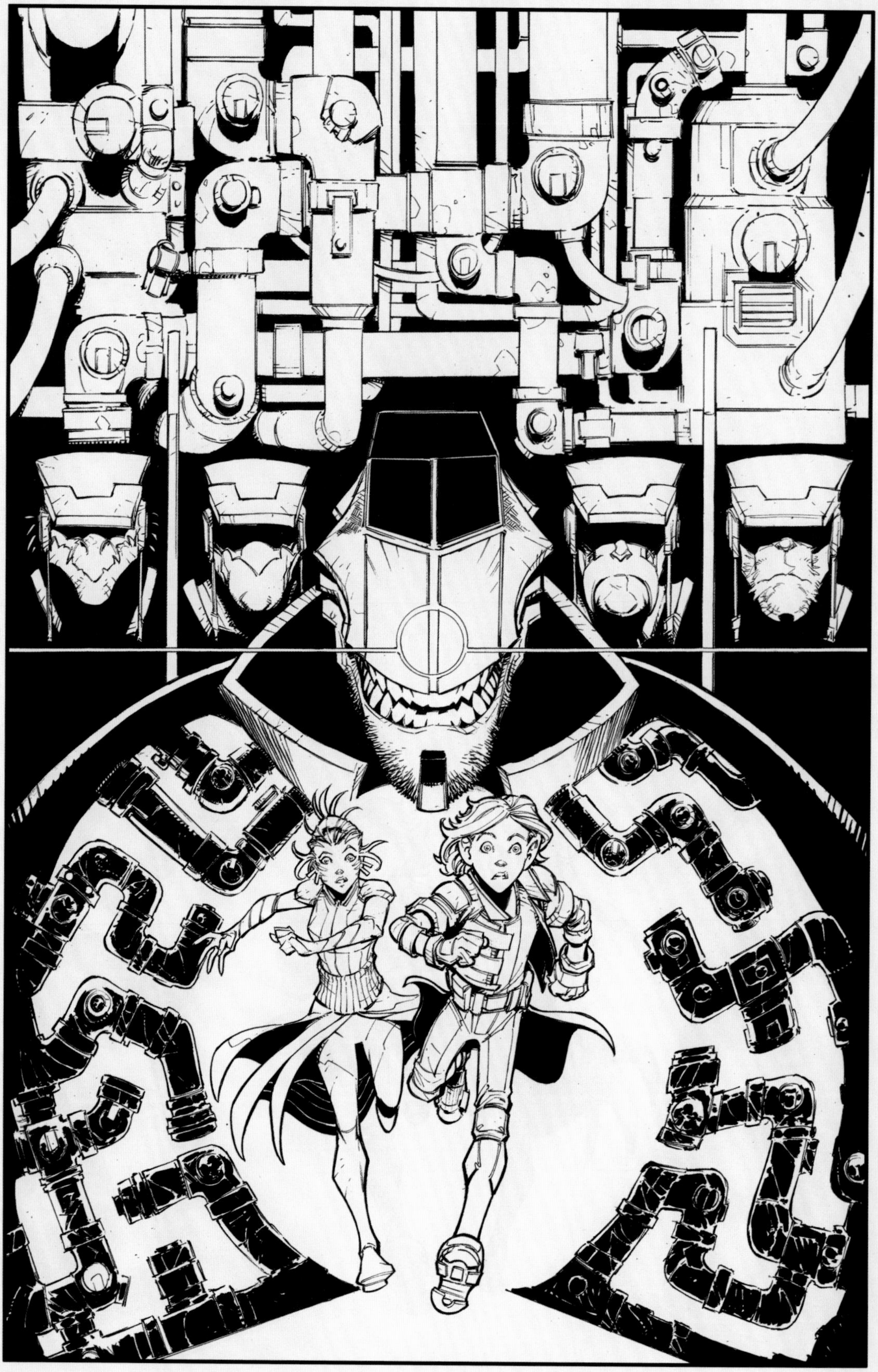

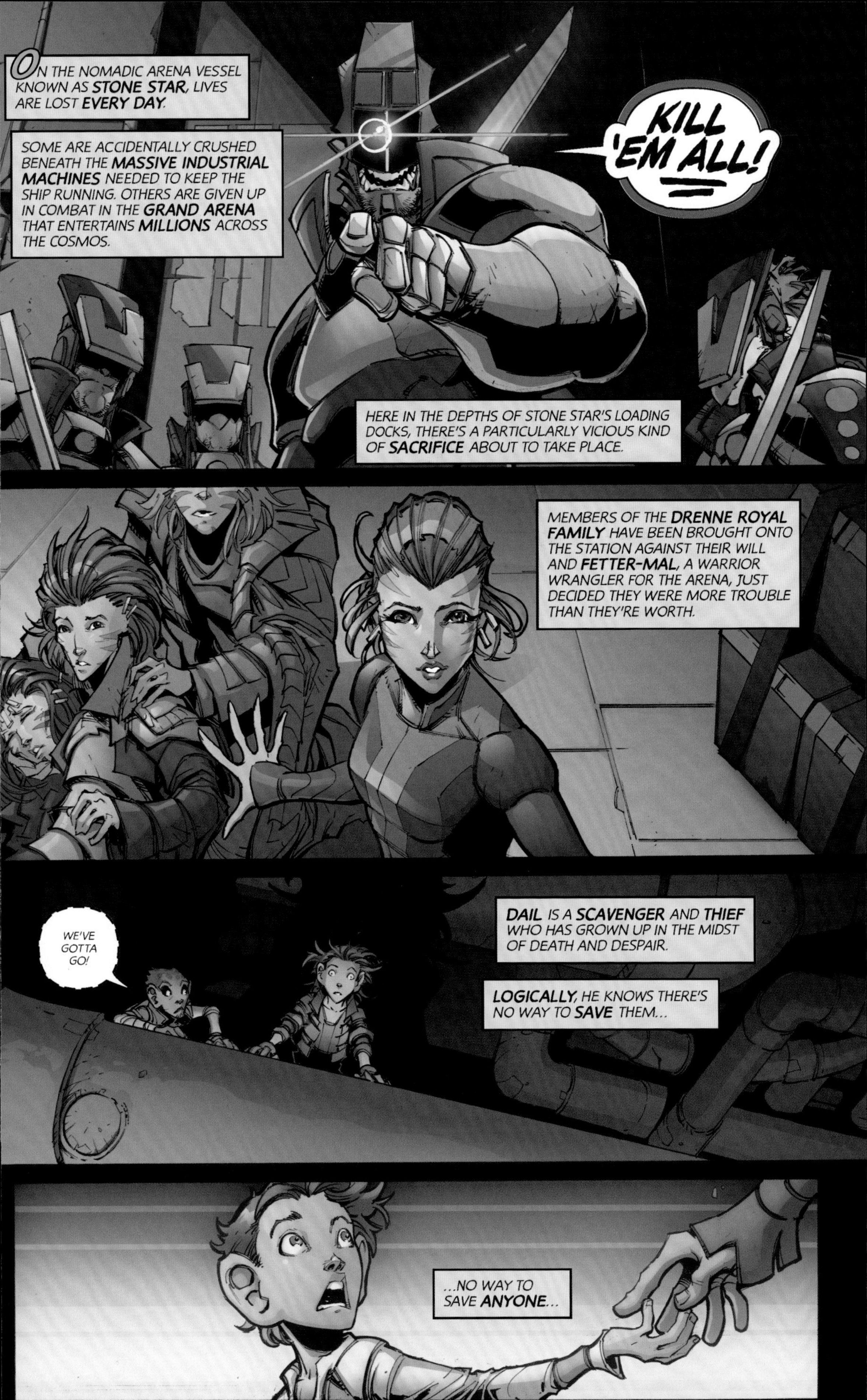
ON THE NOMADIC ARENA VESSEL KNOWN AS STONE STAR, LIVES ARE LOST EVERY DAY.
SOME ARE ACCIDENTALLY CRUSHED BENEATH THE MASSIVE INDUSTRIAL MACHINES NEEDED TO KEEP THE SHIP RUNNING. OTHERS ARE GIVEN UP IN COMBAT IN THE GRAND ARENA THAT ENTERTAINS MILLIONS ACROSS THE COSMOS.
KILL 'EM ALL!
HERE IN THE DEPTHS OF STONE STAR'S LOADING DOCKS, THERE'S A PARTICULARLY VICIOUS KIND OF SACRIFICE ABOUT TO TAKE PLACE.
MEMBERS OF THE DRENNE ROYAL FAMILY HAVE BEEN BROUGHT ONTO THE STATION AGAINST THEIR WILL AND FETTER-MAL, A WARRIOR WRANGLER FOR THE ARENA, JUST DECIDED THEY WERE MORE TROUBLE THAN THEY'RE WORTH.
WE'VE GOTTA GO!
DAIL IS A SCAVENGER AND THIEF WHO HAS GROWN UP IN THE MIDST OF DEATH AND DESPAIR.
LOGICALLY, HE KNOWS THERE'S NO WAY TO SAVE THEM...
...NO WAY TO SAVE ANYONE...

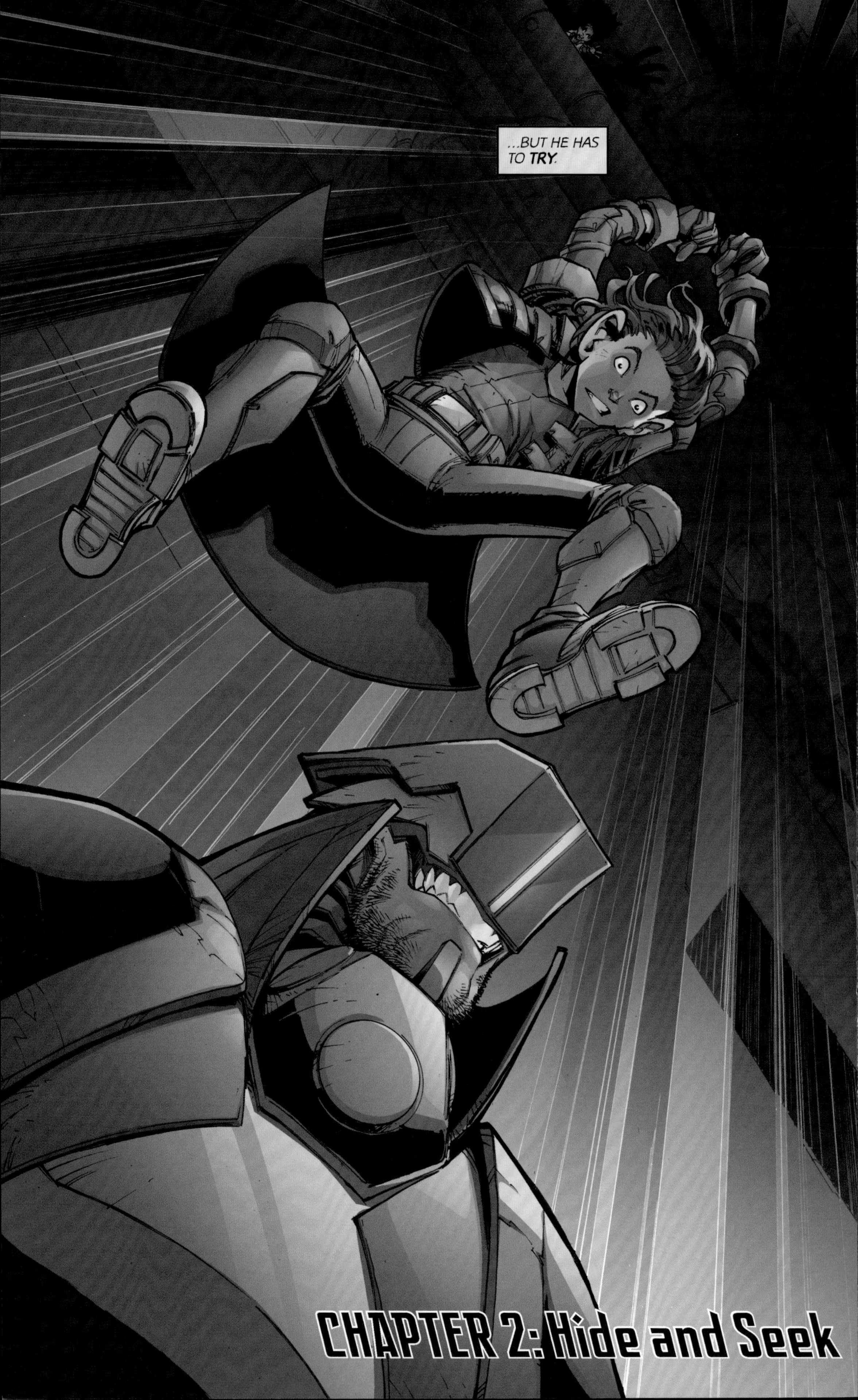
...BUT HE HAS
TO TRY.
CHAPTER 2: Hide and Seek

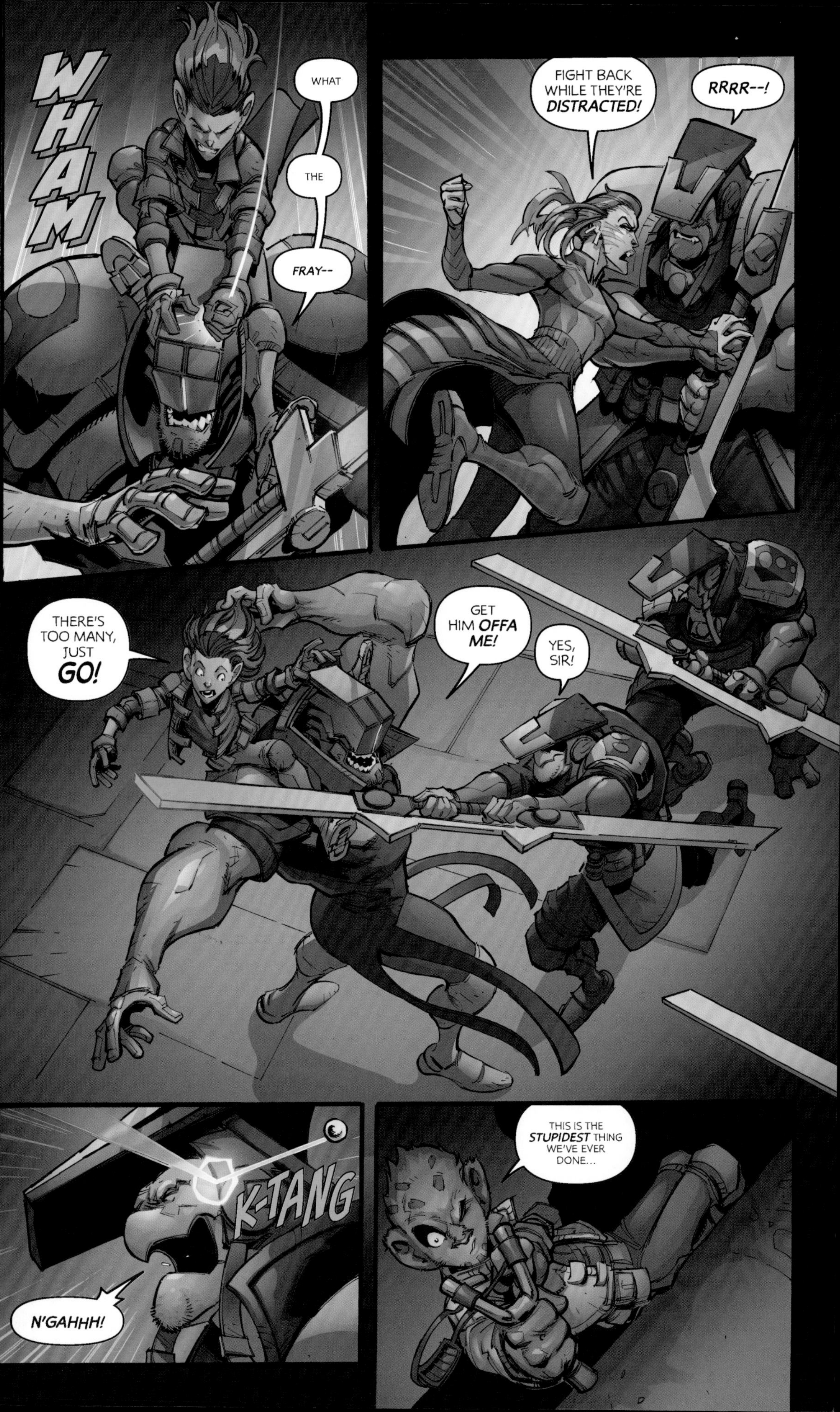
WHAM
WHAT
THE
FRAY--
FIGHT BACK WHILE THEY'RE DISTRACTED!
RRRR--!
THERE'S TOO MANY, JUST GO!
GET HIM OFFA ME!
YES, SIR!
K-TANG
N'GAHHH!
THIS IS THE STUPIDEST THING WE'VE EVER DONE...

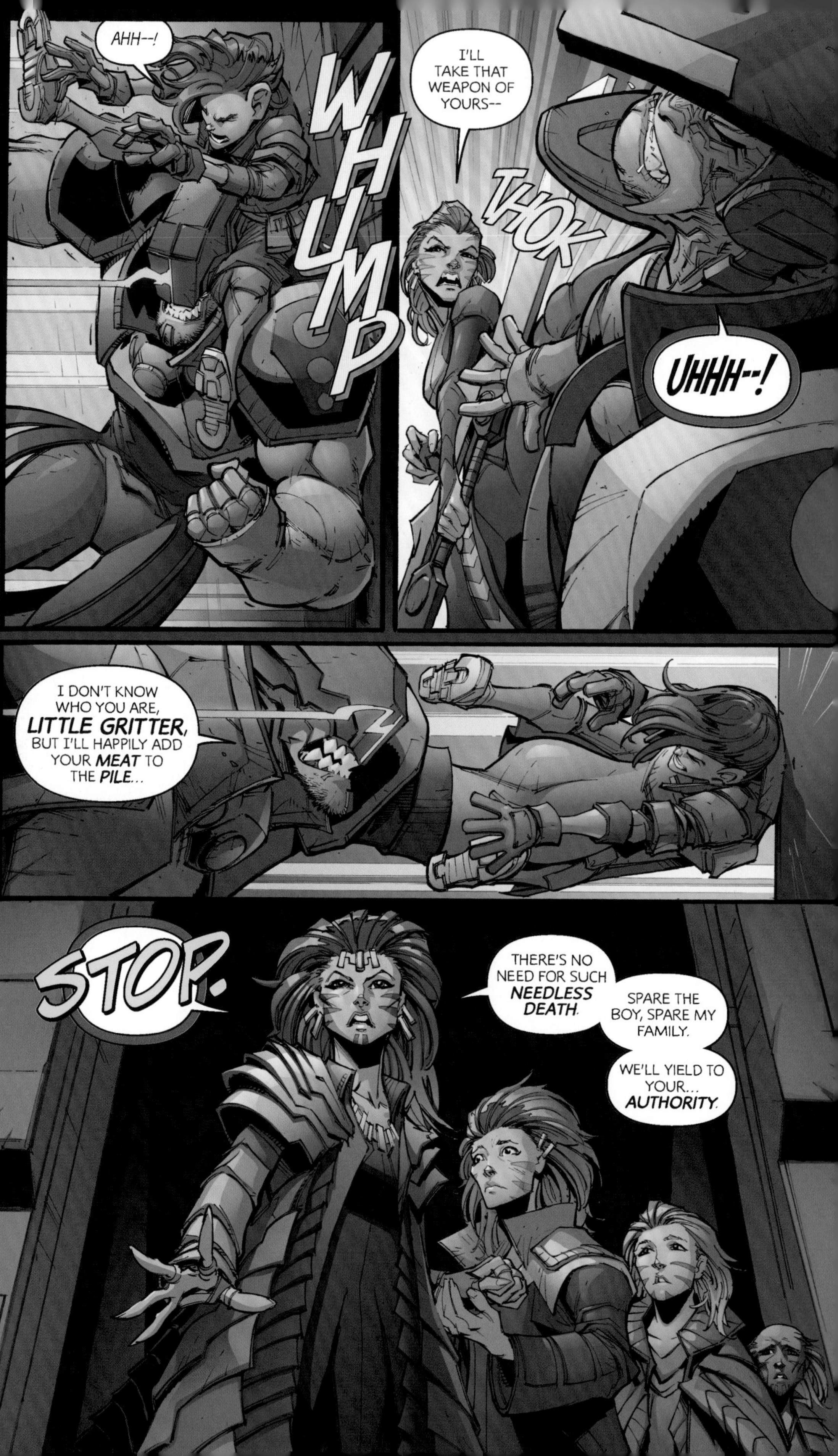

AHH--!
WHUMP
I'LL TAKE THAT WEAPON OF YOURS--
THOK
UHHH--!
I DON'T KNOW WHO YOU ARE, **LITTLE GRITTER,** BUT I'LL HAPPILY ADD YOUR **MEAT** TO THE **PILE**...
STOP.
THERE'S NO NEED FOR SUCH **NEEDLESS DEATH**.
SPARE THE BOY, SPARE MY FAMILY.
WE'LL YIELD TO YOUR... **AUTHORITY**.

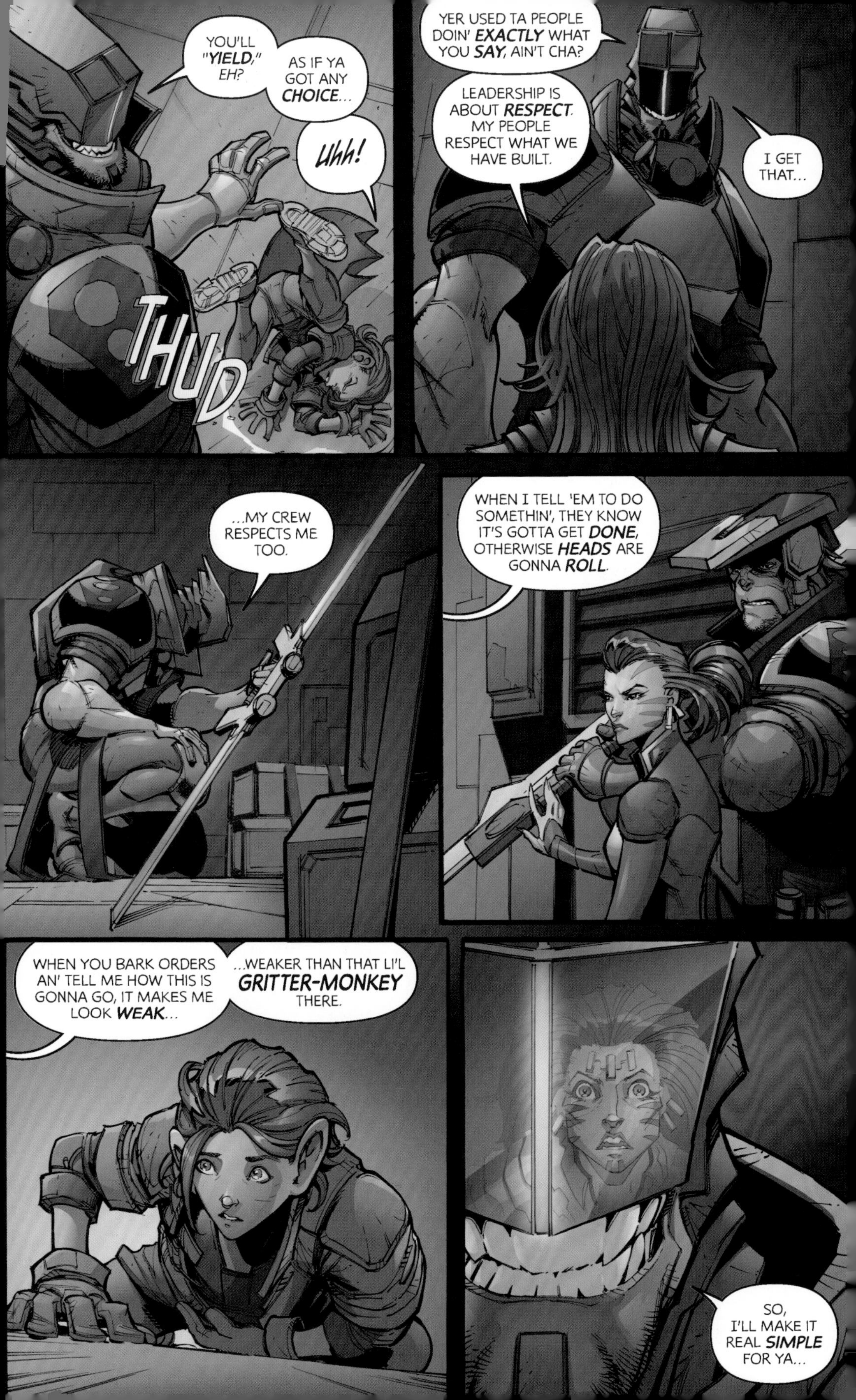

YOU'LL "YIELD," EH?
AS IF YA GOT ANY CHOICE...
Uhh!
THUD
YER USED TA PEOPLE DOIN' EXACTLY WHAT YOU SAY, AIN'T CHA?
LEADERSHIP IS ABOUT RESPECT. MY PEOPLE RESPECT WHAT WE HAVE BUILT.
I GET THAT...
...MY CREW RESPECTS ME TOO.
WHEN I TELL 'EM TO DO SOMETHIN', THEY KNOW IT'S GOTTA GET DONE, OTHERWISE HEADS ARE GONNA ROLL.
WHEN YOU BARK ORDERS AN' TELL ME HOW THIS IS GONNA GO, IT MAKES ME LOOK WEAK...
...WEAKER THAN THAT LI'L GRITTER-MONKEY THERE.
SO, I'LL MAKE IT REAL SIMPLE FOR YA...

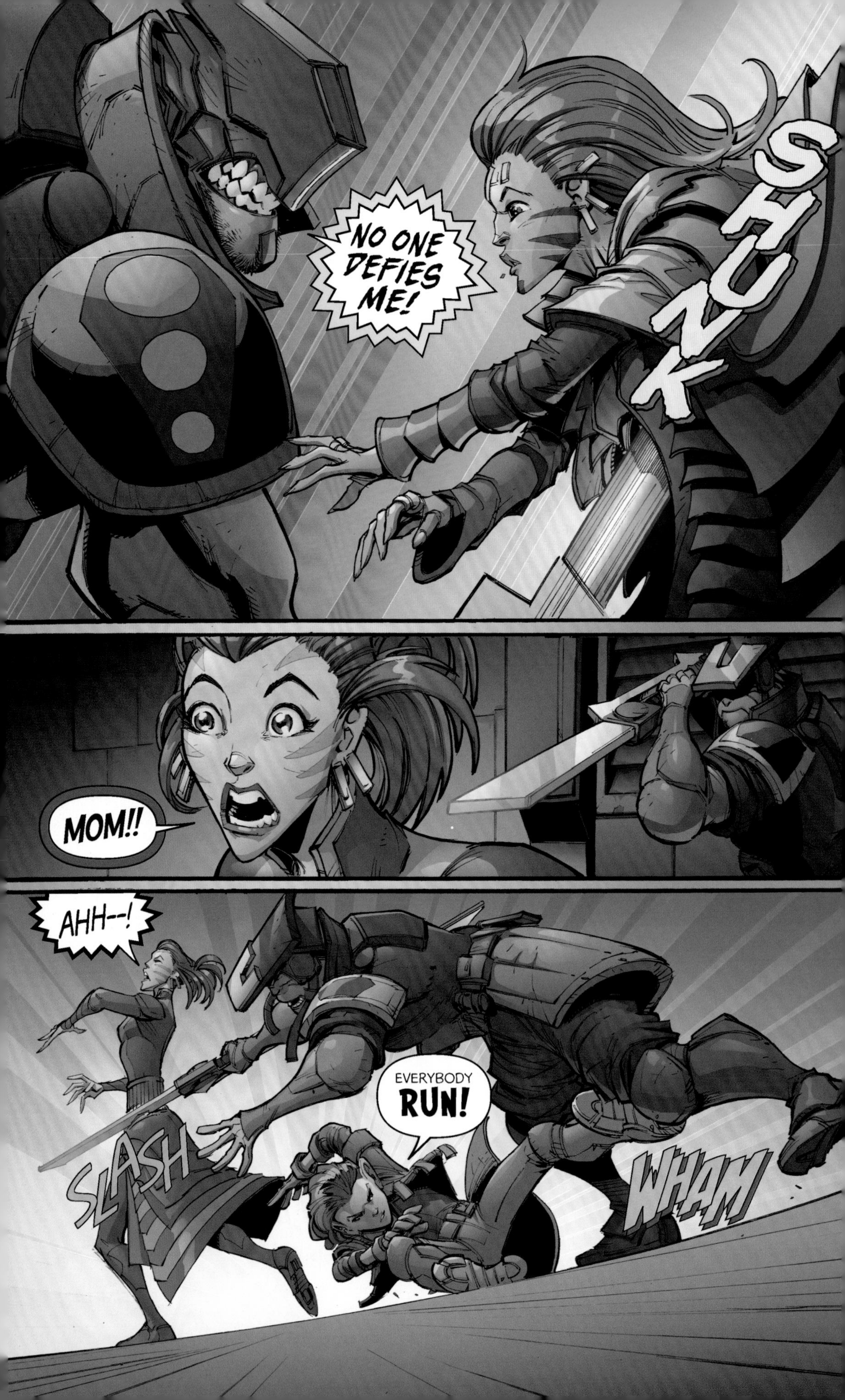
NO ONE DEFIES ME!
SHUNK
MOM!!
AHH--!
EVERYBODY RUN!
SLASH
WHAM

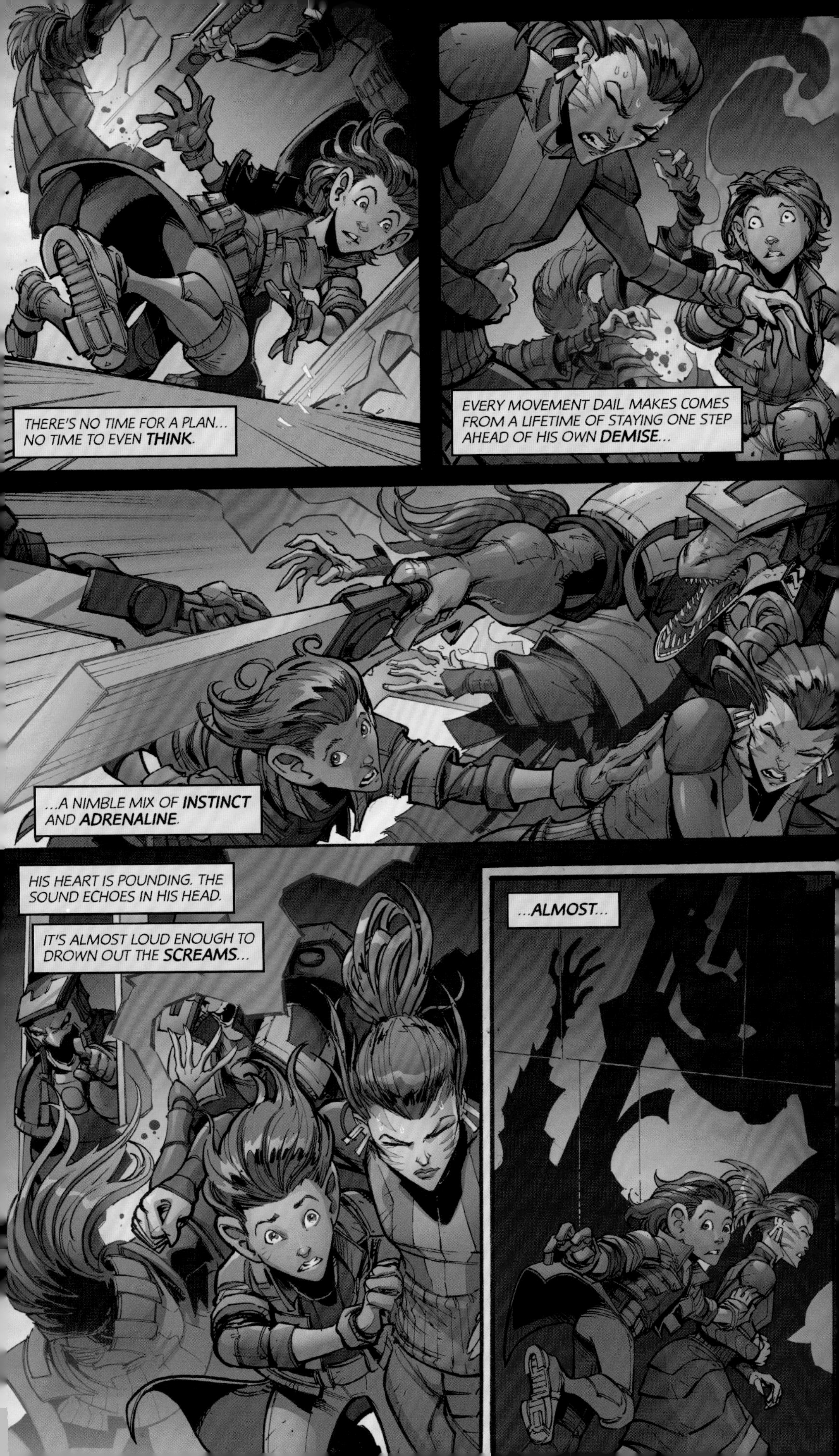
THERE'S NO TIME FOR A PLAN... NO TIME TO EVEN THINK.
EVERY MOVEMENT DAIL MAKES COMES FROM A LIFETIME OF STAYING ONE STEP AHEAD OF HIS OWN DEMISE...
...A NIMBLE MIX OF INSTINCT AND ADRENALINE.
HIS HEART IS POUNDING. THE SOUND ECHOES IN HIS HEAD.
IT'S ALMOST LOUD ENOUGH TO DROWN OUT THE SCREAMS...
...ALMOST...

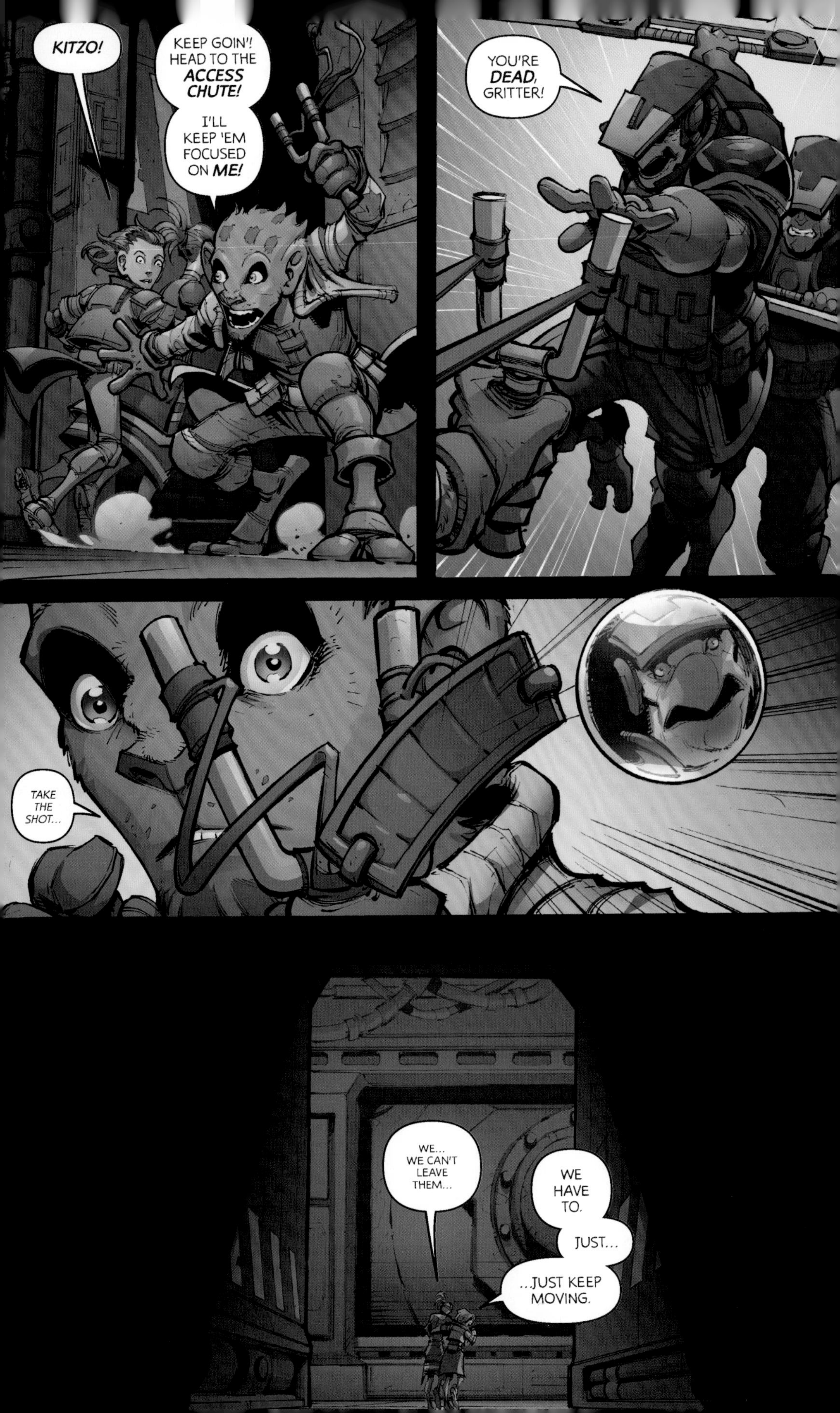
KITZO!
KEEP GOIN'! HEAD TO THE ACCESS CHUTE!
I'LL KEEP 'EM FOCUSED ON ME!
YOU'RE DEAD, GRITTER!
TAKE THE SHOT...
WE... WE CAN'T LEAVE THEM...
WE HAVE TO.
JUST...
...JUST KEEP MOVING.

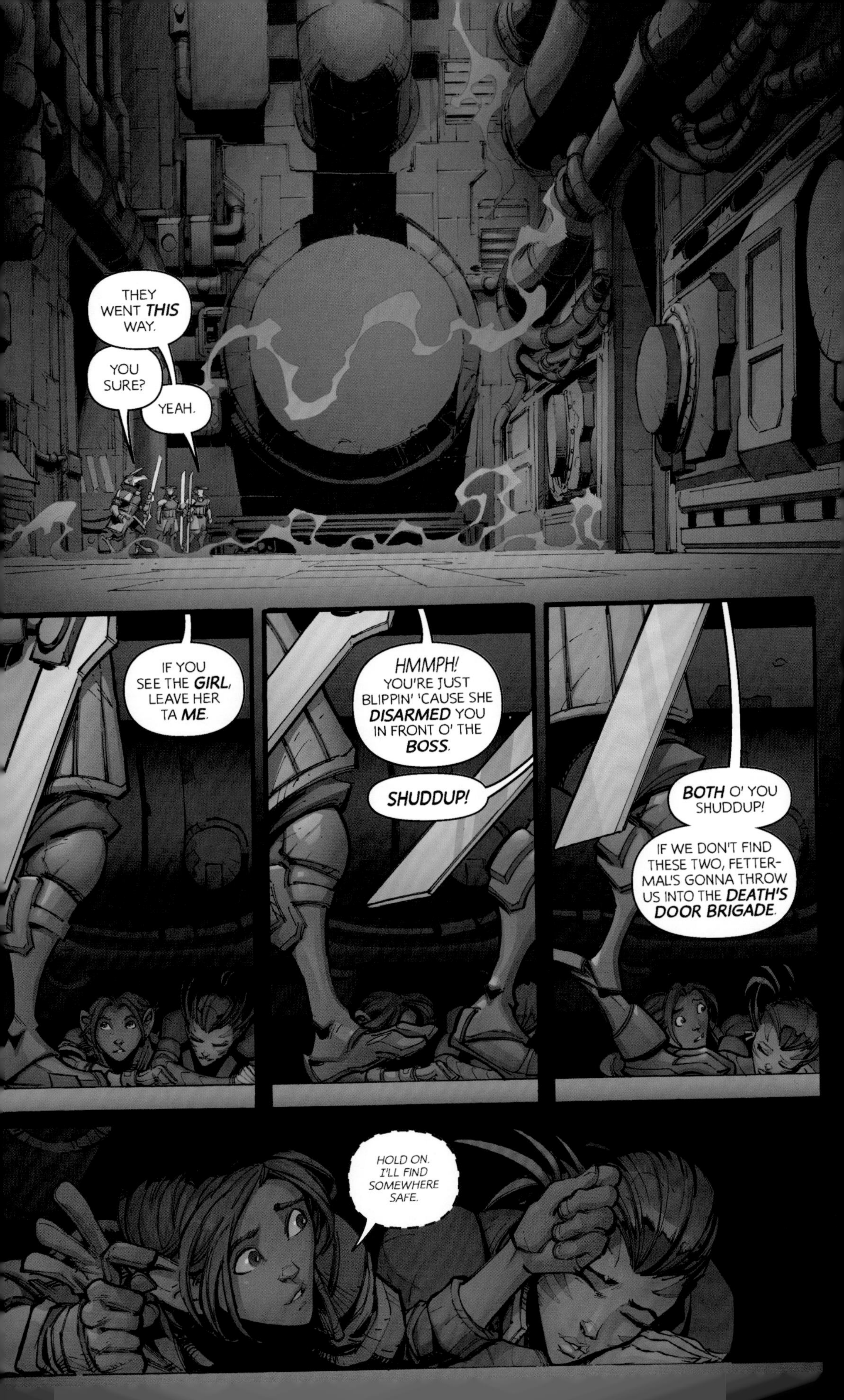
THEY WENT THIS WAY.
YOU SURE?
YEAH.
IF YOU SEE THE GIRL, LEAVE HER TA ME.
HMMPH! YOU'RE JUST BLIPPIN' 'CAUSE SHE DISARMED YOU IN FRONT O' THE BOSS.
SHUDDUP!
BOTH O' YOU SHUDDUP!
IF WE DON'T FIND THESE TWO, FETTERMAL'S GONNA THROW US INTO THE DEATH'S DOOR BRIGADE.
HOLD ON. I'LL FIND SOMEWHERE SAFE.

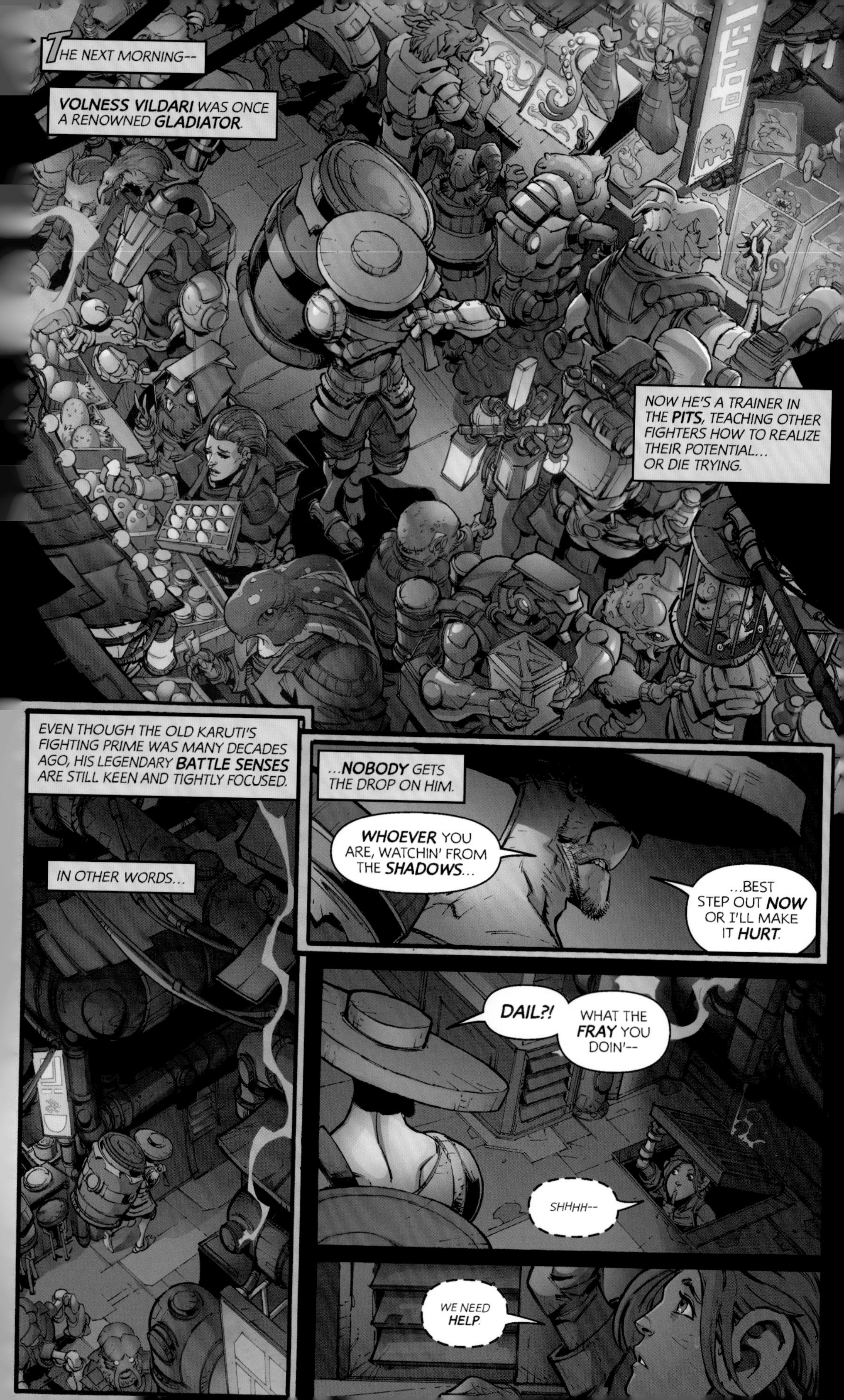
THE NEXT MORNING--
VOLNESS VILDARI WAS ONCE A RENOWNED GLADIATOR.
NOW HE'S A TRAINER IN THE PITS, TEACHING OTHER FIGHTERS HOW TO REALIZE THEIR POTENTIAL... OR DIE TRYING.
EVEN THOUGH THE OLD KARUTI'S FIGHTING PRIME WAS MANY DECADES AGO, HIS LEGENDARY BATTLE SENSES ARE STILL KEEN AND TIGHTLY FOCUSED.
IN OTHER WORDS...
...NOBODY GETS THE DROP ON HIM.
WHOEVER YOU ARE, WATCHIN' FROM THE SHADOWS...
...BEST STEP OUT NOW OR I'LL MAKE IT HURT.
DAIL?!
WHAT THE FRAY YOU DOIN'--
SHHHH--
WE NEED HELP.

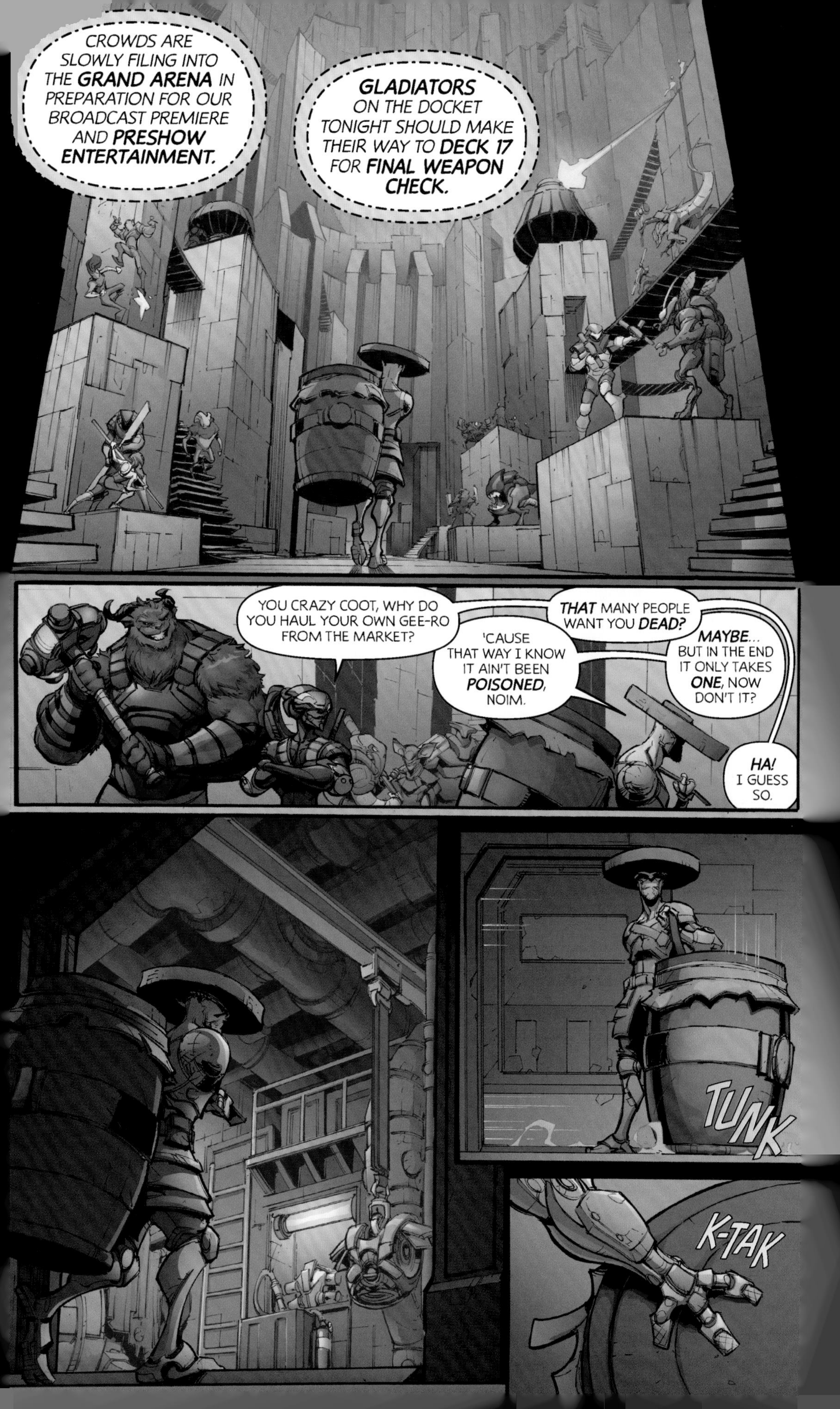

CROWDS ARE SLOWLY FILING INTO THE GRAND ARENA IN PREPARATION FOR OUR BROADCAST PREMIERE AND PRESHOW ENTERTAINMENT.
GLADIATORS ON THE DOCKET TONIGHT SHOULD MAKE THEIR WAY TO DECK 17 FOR FINAL WEAPON CHECK.
YOU CRAZY COOT, WHY DO YOU HAUL YOUR OWN GEE-RO FROM THE MARKET?
'CAUSE THAT WAY I KNOW IT AIN'T BEEN POISONED, NOIM.
THAT MANY PEOPLE WANT YOU DEAD?
MAYBE... BUT IN THE END IT ONLY TAKES ONE, NOW DON'T IT?
HA! I GUESS SO.
TUNK
K-TAK

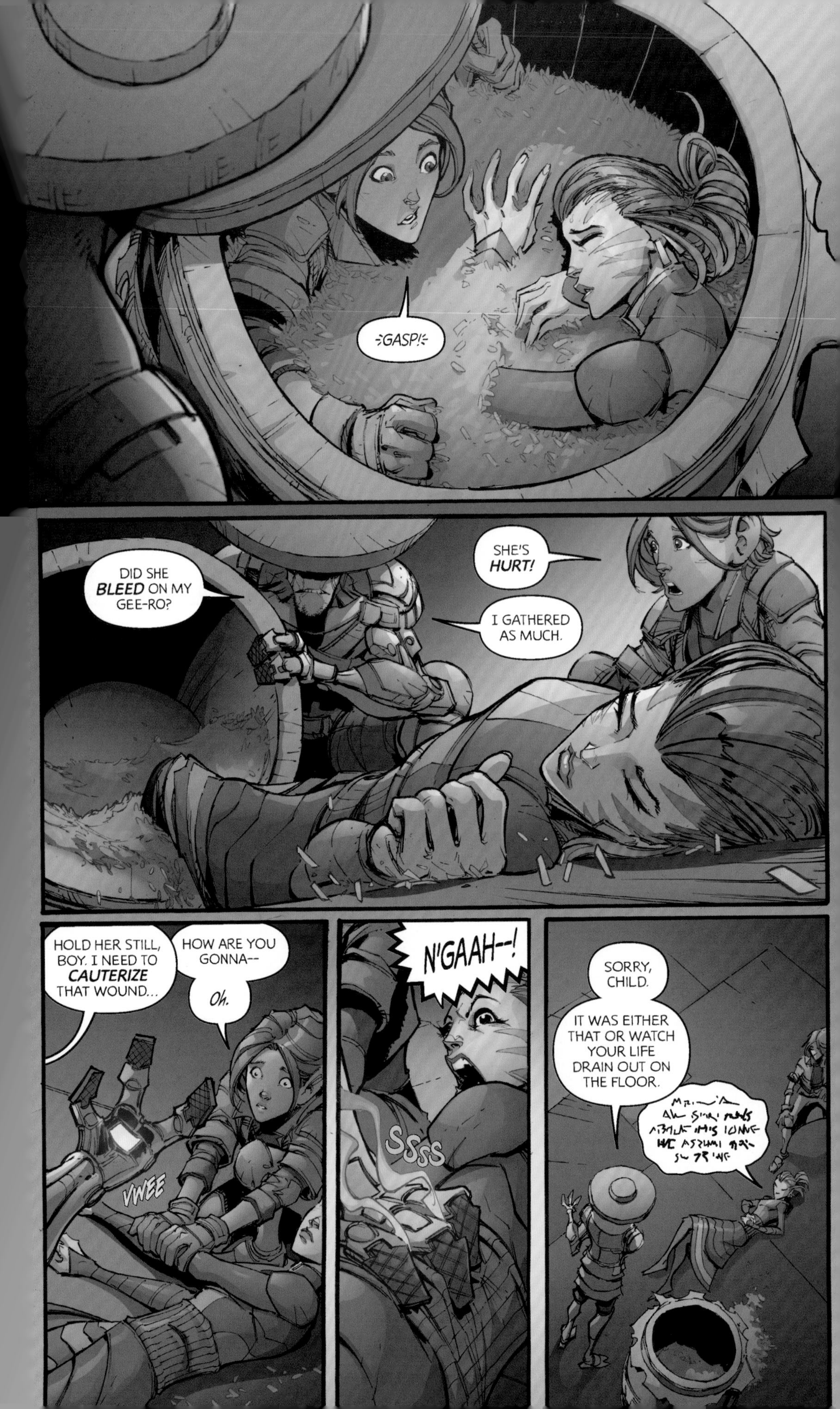

GASP!
DID SHE BLEED ON MY GEE-RO?
SHE'S HURT!
I GATHERED AS MUCH.
HOLD HER STILL, BOY. I NEED TO CAUTERIZE THAT WOUND...
HOW ARE YOU GONNA--
Oh.
VWEE
N'GAAH--!
SSSS
SORRY, CHILD.
IT WAS EITHER THAT OR WATCH YOUR LIFE DRAIN OUT ON THE FLOOR.

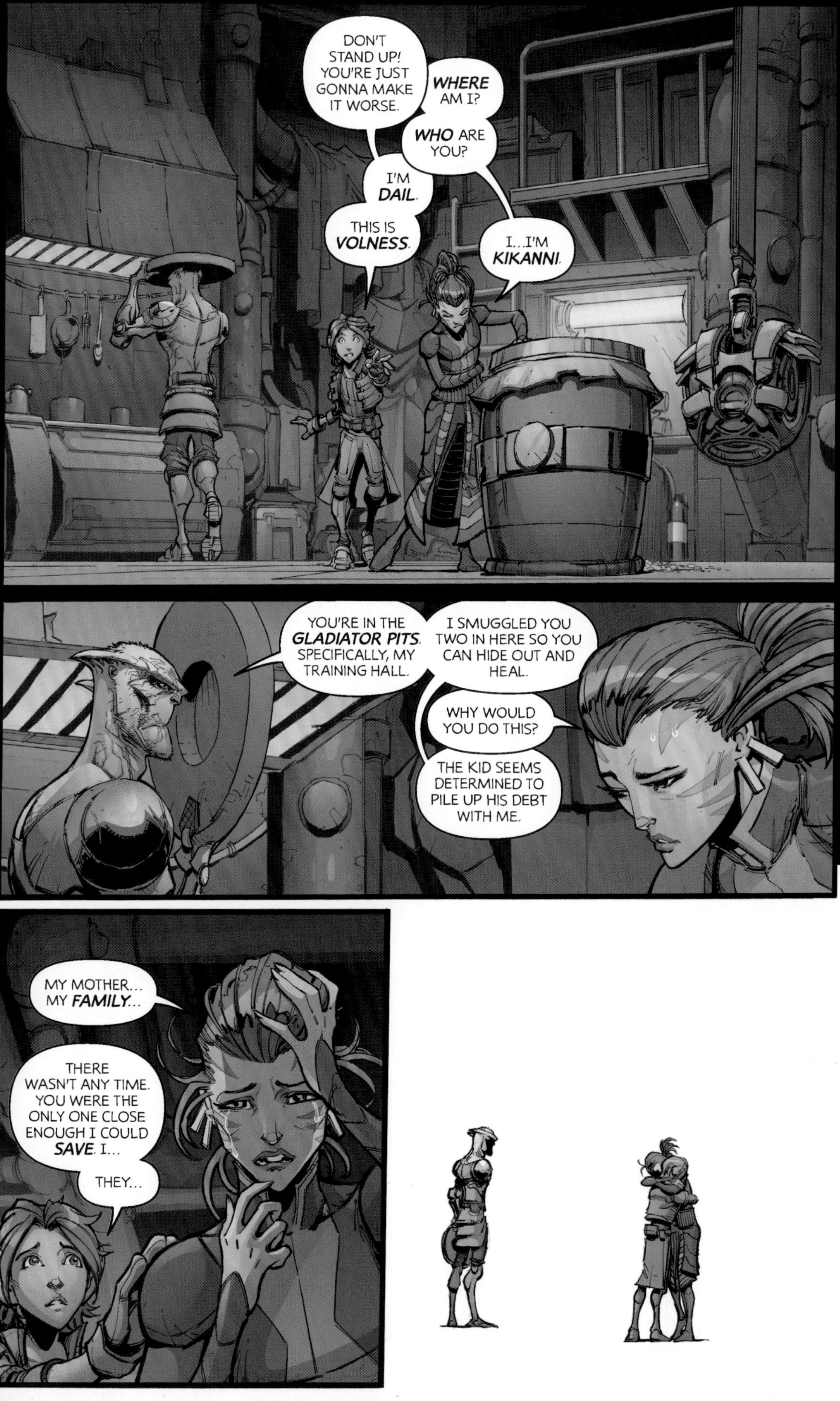
DON'T STAND UP! YOU'RE JUST GONNA MAKE IT WORSE.
WHERE AM I?
WHO ARE YOU?
I'M DAIL.
THIS IS VOLNESS.
I...I'M KIKANNI.
YOU'RE IN THE GLADIATOR PITS. SPECIFICALLY, MY TRAINING HALL.
I SMUGGLED YOU TWO IN HERE SO YOU CAN HIDE OUT AND HEAL.
WHY WOULD YOU DO THIS?
THE KID SEEMS DETERMINED TO PILE UP HIS DEBT WITH ME.
MY MOTHER... MY FAMILY...
THERE WASN'T ANY TIME. YOU WERE THE ONLY ONE CLOSE ENOUGH I COULD SAVE. I...
THEY...

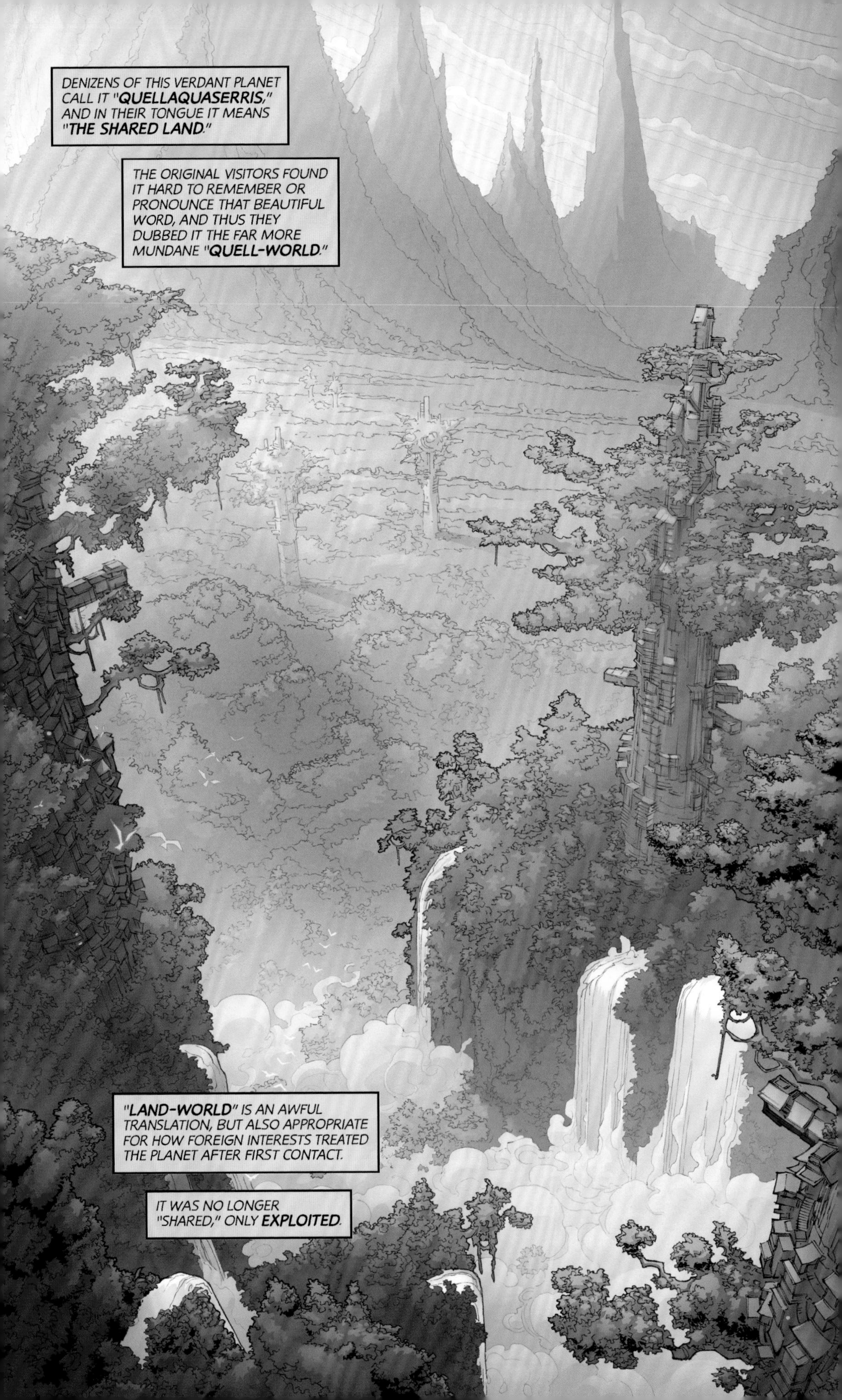
DENIZENS OF THIS VERDANT PLANET CALL IT "QUELLAQUASERRIS," AND IN THEIR TONGUE IT MEANS "THE SHARED LAND."
THE ORIGINAL VISITORS FOUND IT HARD TO REMEMBER OR PRONOUNCE THAT BEAUTIFUL WORD, AND THUS THEY DUBBED IT THE FAR MORE MUNDANE "QUELL-WORLD."
"LAND-WORLD" IS AN AWFUL TRANSLATION, BUT ALSO APPROPRIATE FOR HOW FOREIGN INTERESTS TREATED THE PLANET AFTER FIRST CONTACT.
IT WAS NO LONGER "SHARED," ONLY EXPLOITED.

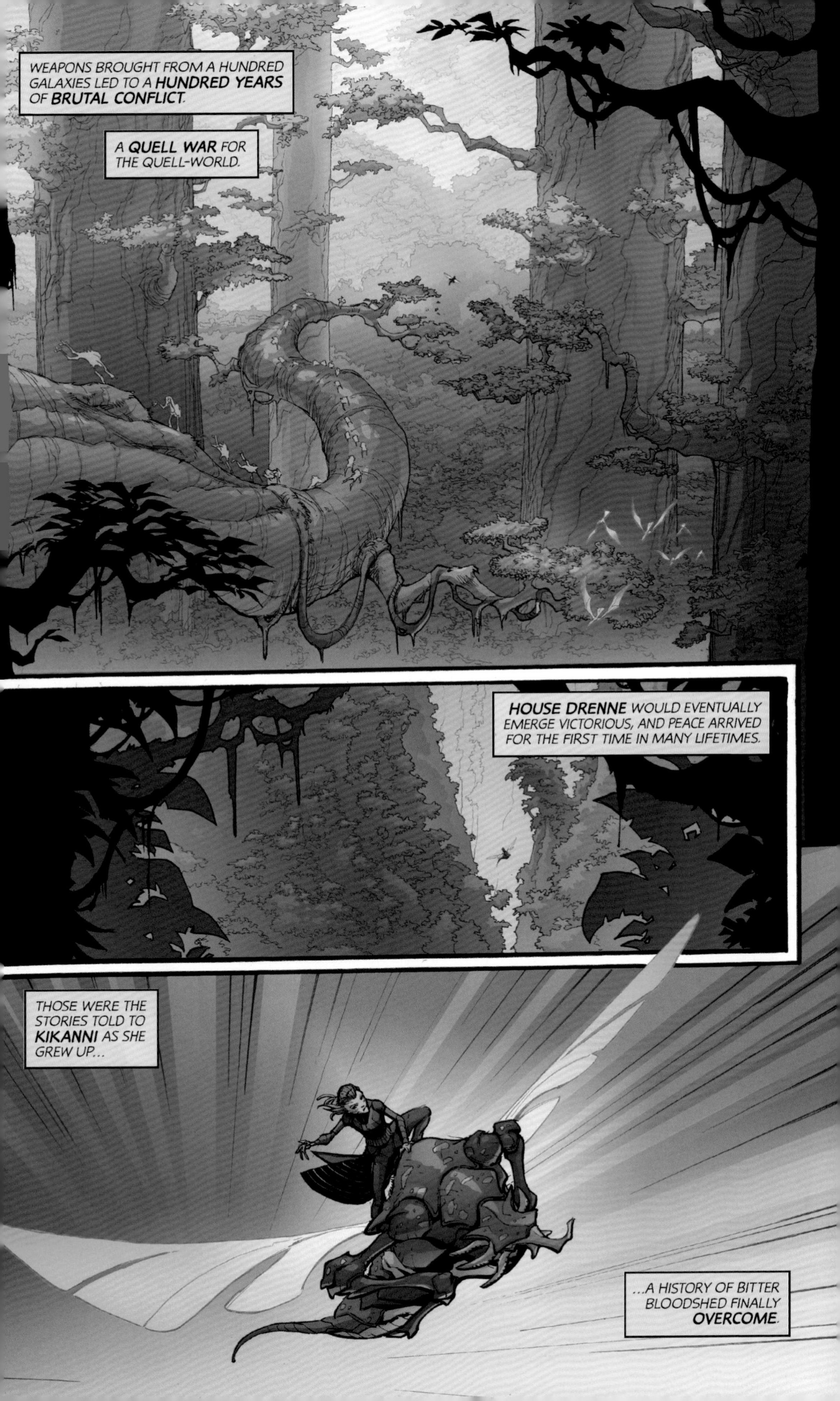
WEAPONS BROUGHT FROM A HUNDRED GALAXIES LED TO A HUNDRED YEARS OF BRUTAL CONFLICT.
A QUELL WAR FOR THE QUELL-WORLD.
HOUSE DRENNE WOULD EVENTUALLY EMERGE VICTORIOUS, AND PEACE ARRIVED FOR THE FIRST TIME IN MANY LIFETIMES.
THOSE WERE THE STORIES TOLD TO KIKANNI AS SHE GREW UP...
...A HISTORY OF BITTER BLOODSHED FINALLY OVERCOME.

THE THIRD PRINCESS OF DRENNE IMAGINED A FUTURE WHERE SHE WOULD HELP BUILD A NEW AGE OF PROSPERITY FOR ALL.

A RETURN TO THE ETHOS OF THE "*SHARED,*" THE CONCEPT WOVEN INTO THE NAME AND HEART OF THOSE WHO CALL QUELL-WORLD THEIR *HOME*...

...THE FUTURE HAD *OTHER PLANS*.

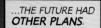

÷GASP!÷

HOW'S SHE DOING?

KIKANNI'S RESTING. THE WOUND LOOKS BAD, BUT I THINK SHE'LL RECOVER.

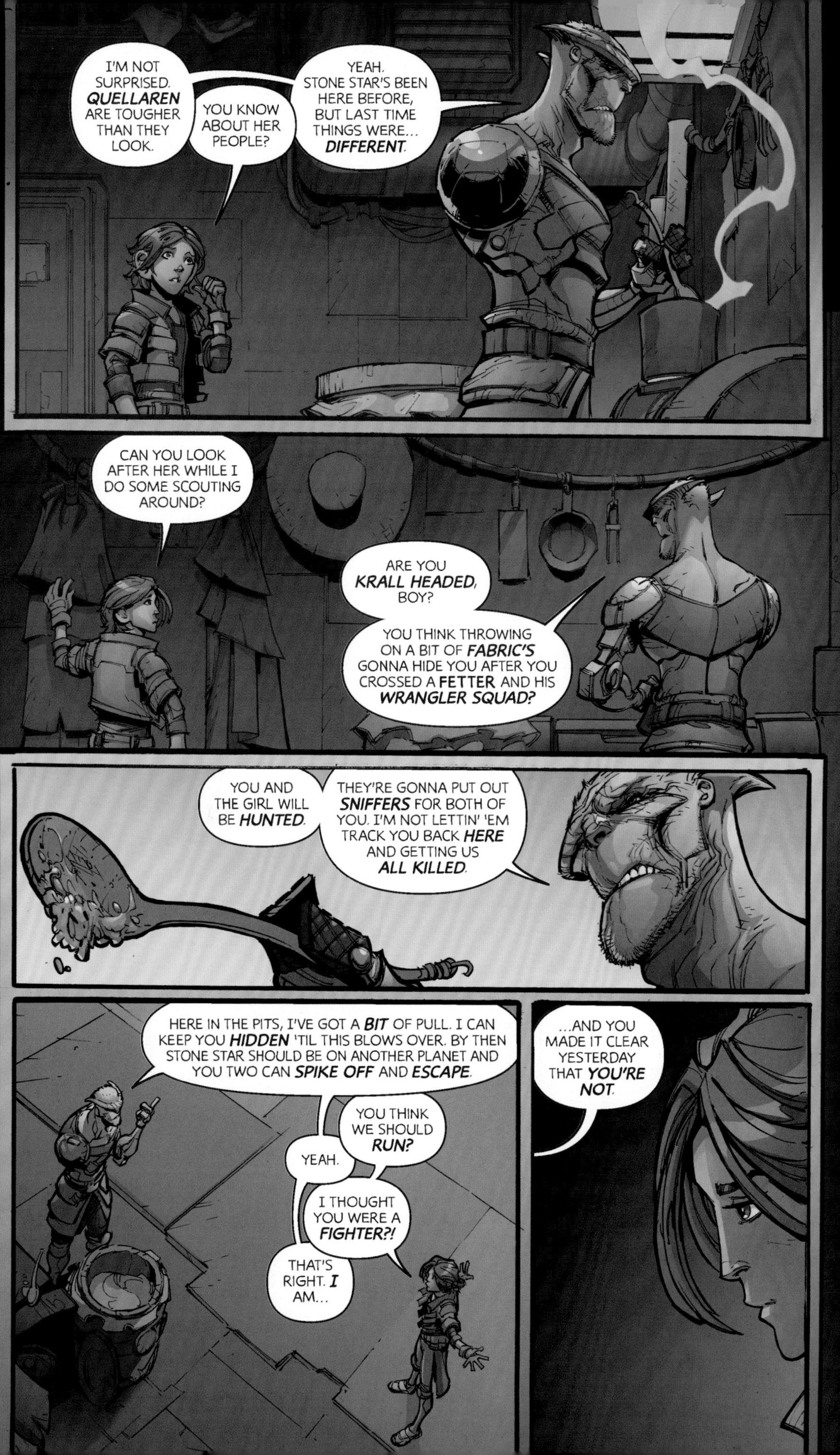
I'M NOT SURPRISED. QUELLAREN ARE TOUGHER THAN THEY LOOK.
YOU KNOW ABOUT HER PEOPLE?
YEAH. STONE STAR'S BEEN HERE BEFORE, BUT LAST TIME THINGS WERE... DIFFERENT.
CAN YOU LOOK AFTER HER WHILE I DO SOME SCOUTING AROUND?
ARE YOU KRALL HEADED, BOY?
YOU THINK THROWING ON A BIT OF FABRIC'S GONNA HIDE YOU AFTER YOU CROSSED A FETTER AND HIS WRANGLER SQUAD?
YOU AND THE GIRL WILL BE HUNTED.
THEY'RE GONNA PUT OUT SNIFFERS FOR BOTH OF YOU. I'M NOT LETTIN' 'EM TRACK YOU BACK HERE AND GETTING US ALL KILLED.
HERE IN THE PITS, I'VE GOT A BIT OF PULL. I CAN KEEP YOU HIDDEN 'TIL THIS BLOWS OVER. BY THEN STONE STAR SHOULD BE ON ANOTHER PLANET AND YOU TWO CAN SPIKE OFF AND ESCAPE.
YOU THINK WE SHOULD RUN?
YEAH.
I THOUGHT YOU WERE A FIGHTER?!
THAT'S RIGHT. I AM...
...AND YOU MADE IT CLEAR YESTERDAY THAT YOU'RE NOT.

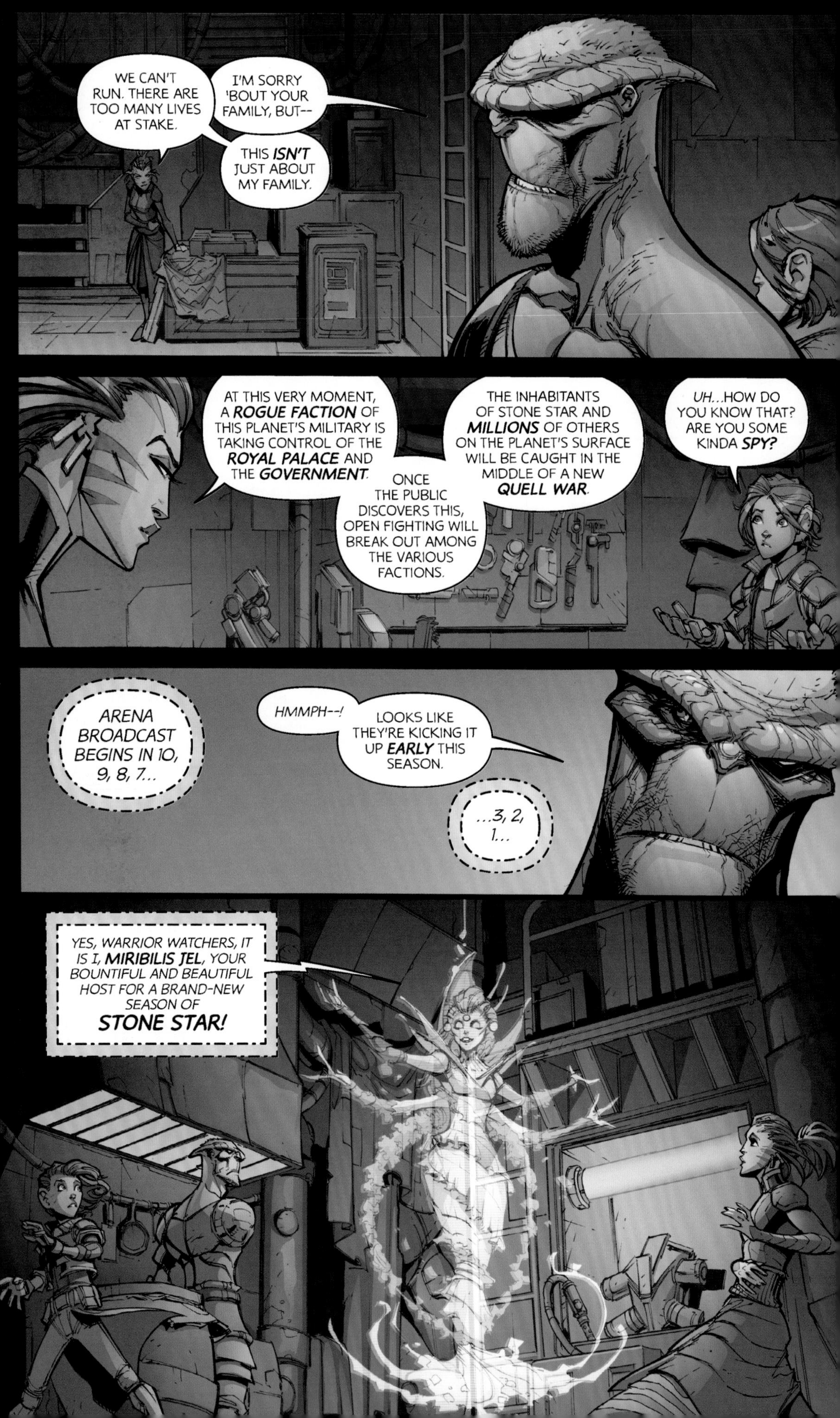
WE CAN'T RUN. THERE ARE TOO MANY LIVES AT STAKE.
I'M SORRY 'BOUT YOUR FAMILY, BUT--
THIS ISN'T JUST ABOUT MY FAMILY.
AT THIS VERY MOMENT, A ROGUE FACTION OF THIS PLANET'S MILITARY IS TAKING CONTROL OF THE ROYAL PALACE AND THE GOVERNMENT.
ONCE THE PUBLIC DISCOVERS THIS, OPEN FIGHTING WILL BREAK OUT AMONG THE VARIOUS FACTIONS.
THE INHABITANTS OF STONE STAR AND MILLIONS OF OTHERS ON THE PLANET'S SURFACE WILL BE CAUGHT IN THE MIDDLE OF A NEW QUELL WAR.
UH...HOW DO YOU KNOW THAT? ARE YOU SOME KINDA SPY?
ARENA BROADCAST BEGINS IN 10, 9, 8, 7...
HMMPH--!
LOOKS LIKE THEY'RE KICKING IT UP EARLY THIS SEASON.
...3, 2, 1...
YES, WARRIOR WATCHERS, IT IS I, MIRIBILIS JEL, YOUR BOUNTIFUL AND BEAUTIFUL HOST FOR A BRAND-NEW SEASON OF STONE STAR!

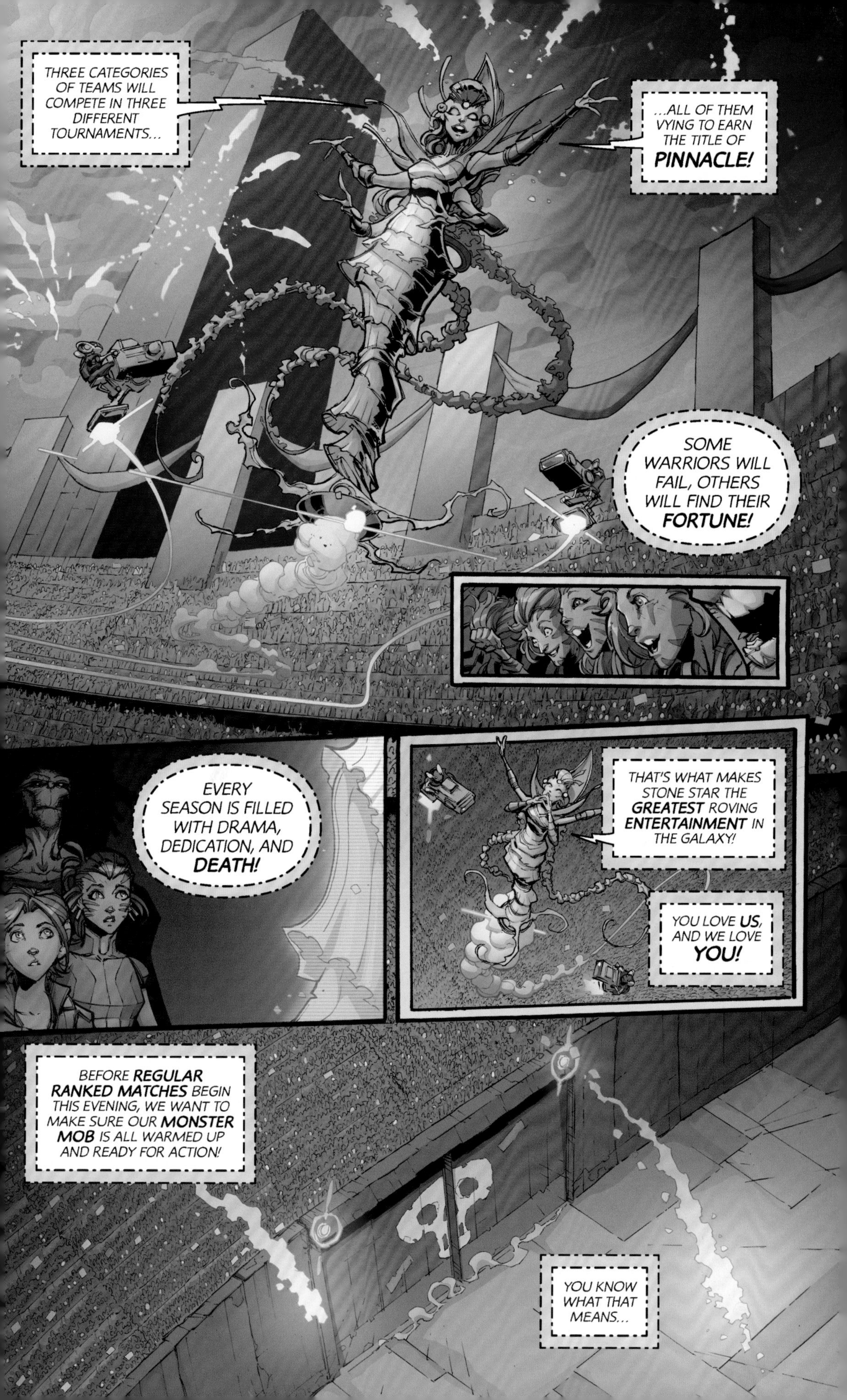

THREE CATEGORIES OF TEAMS WILL COMPETE IN THREE DIFFERENT TOURNAMENTS...
...ALL OF THEM VYING TO EARN THE TITLE OF PINNACLE!
SOME WARRIORS WILL FAIL, OTHERS WILL FIND THEIR FORTUNE!
EVERY SEASON IS FILLED WITH DRAMA, DEDICATION, AND DEATH!
THAT'S WHAT MAKES STONE STAR THE GREATEST ROVING ENTERTAINMENT IN THE GALAXY!
YOU LOVE US, AND WE LOVE YOU!
BEFORE REGULAR RANKED MATCHES BEGIN THIS EVENING, WE WANT TO MAKE SURE OUR MONSTER MOB IS ALL WARMED UP AND READY FOR ACTION!
YOU KNOW WHAT THAT MEANS...

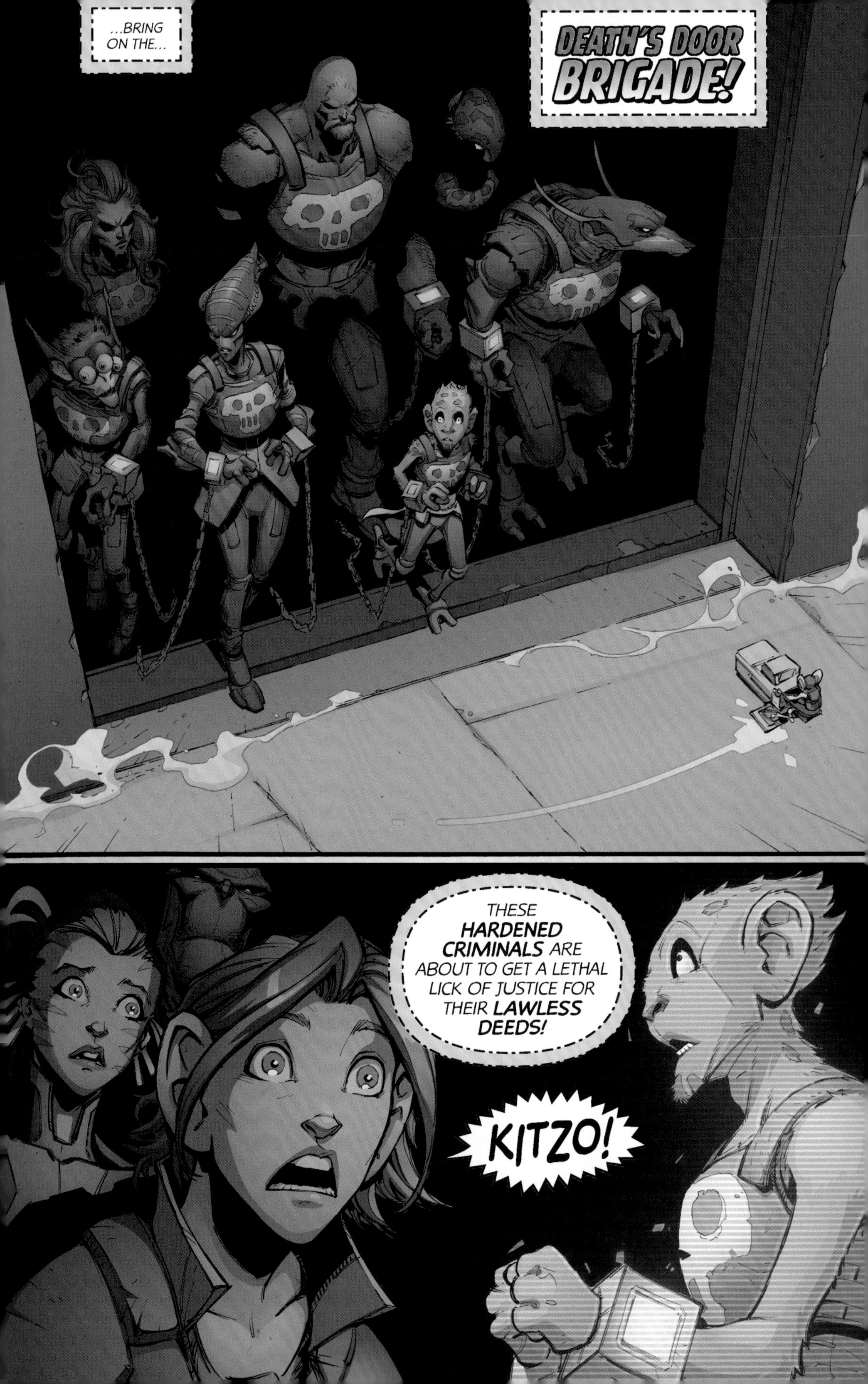
...BRING ON THE...
DEATH'S DOOR BRIGADE!
THESE HARDENED CRIMINALS ARE ABOUT TO GET A LETHAL LICK OF JUSTICE FOR THEIR LAWLESS DEEDS!
KITZO!

Chapter 3: Power and Peril

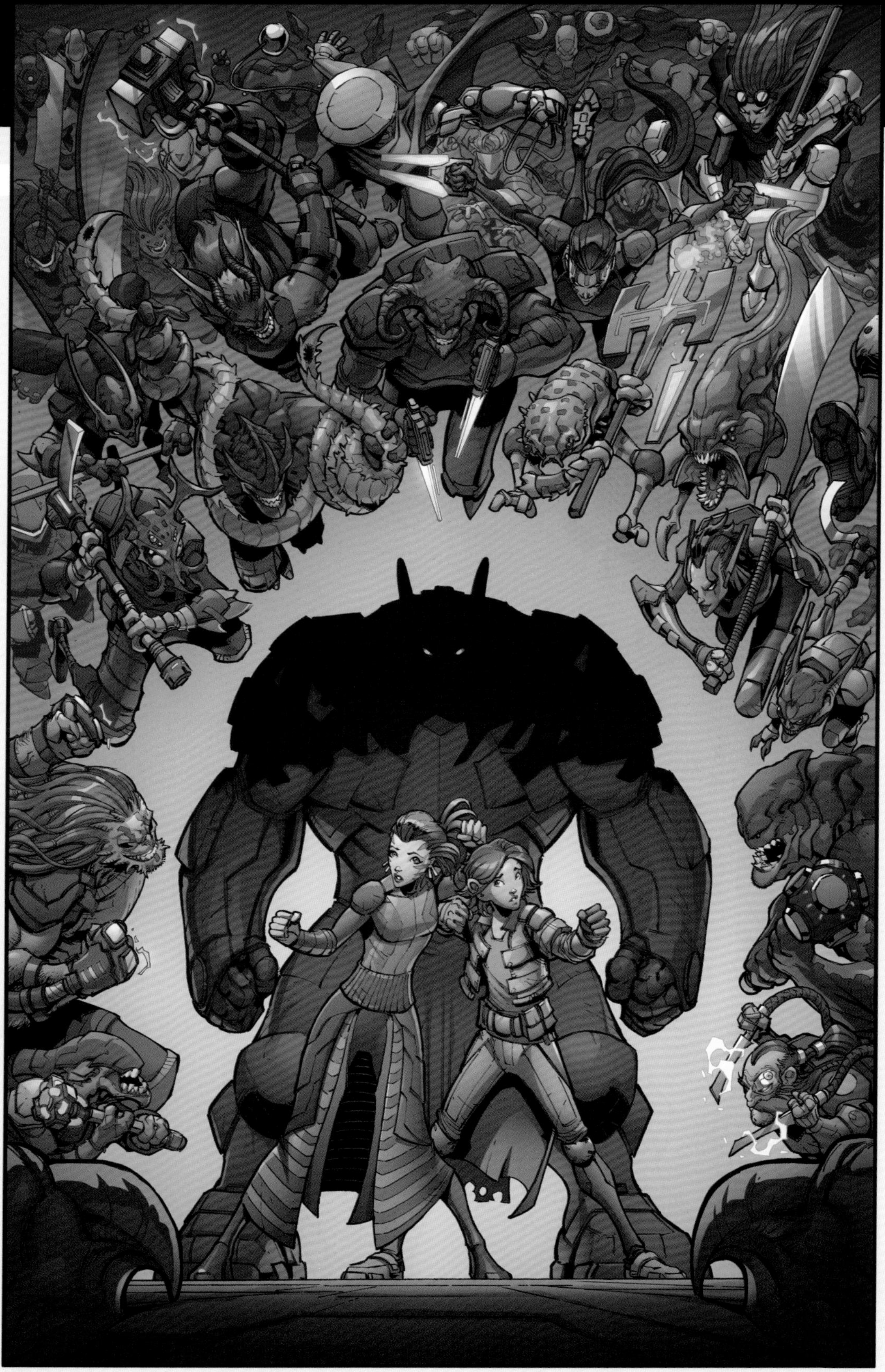

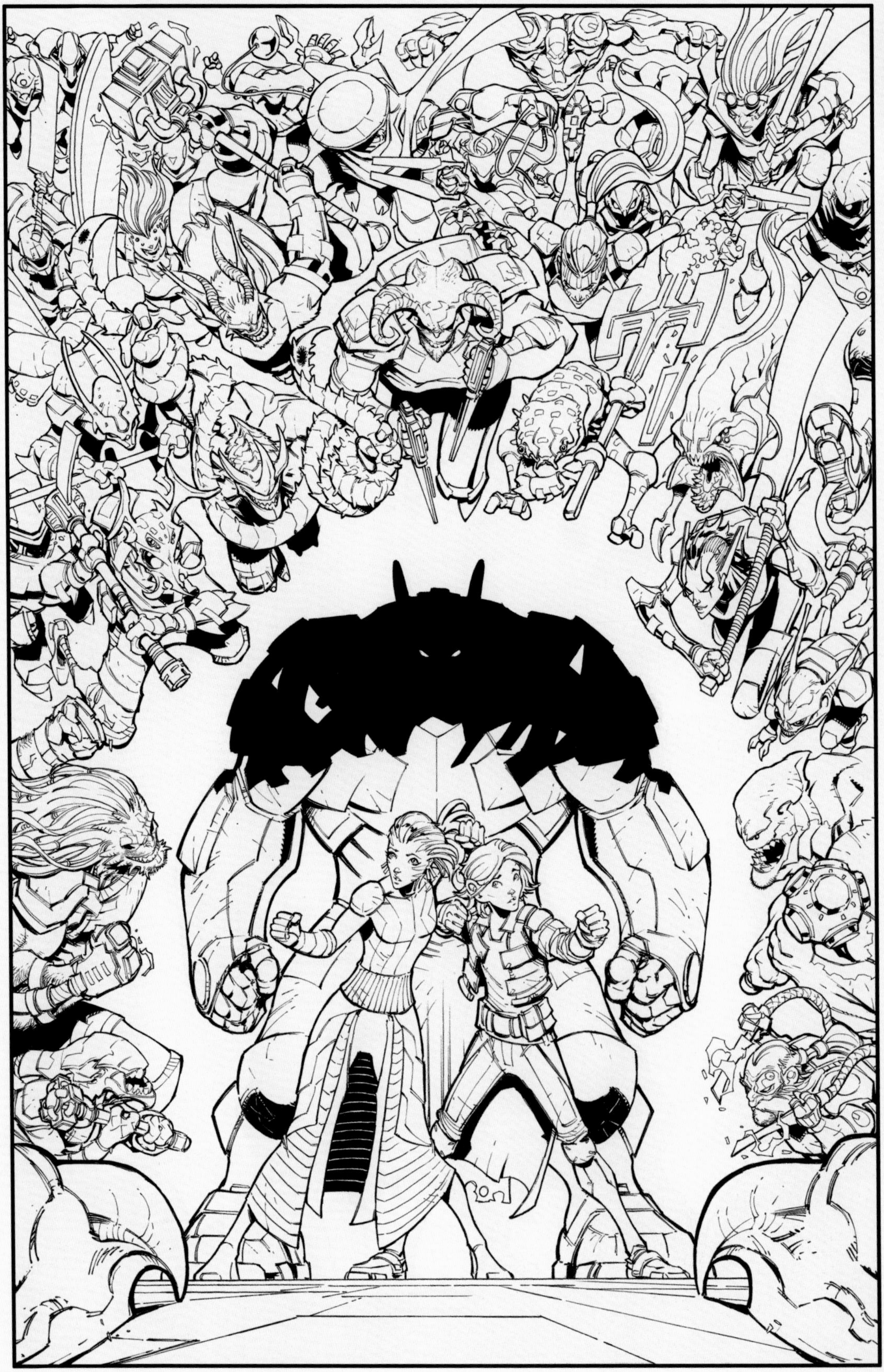

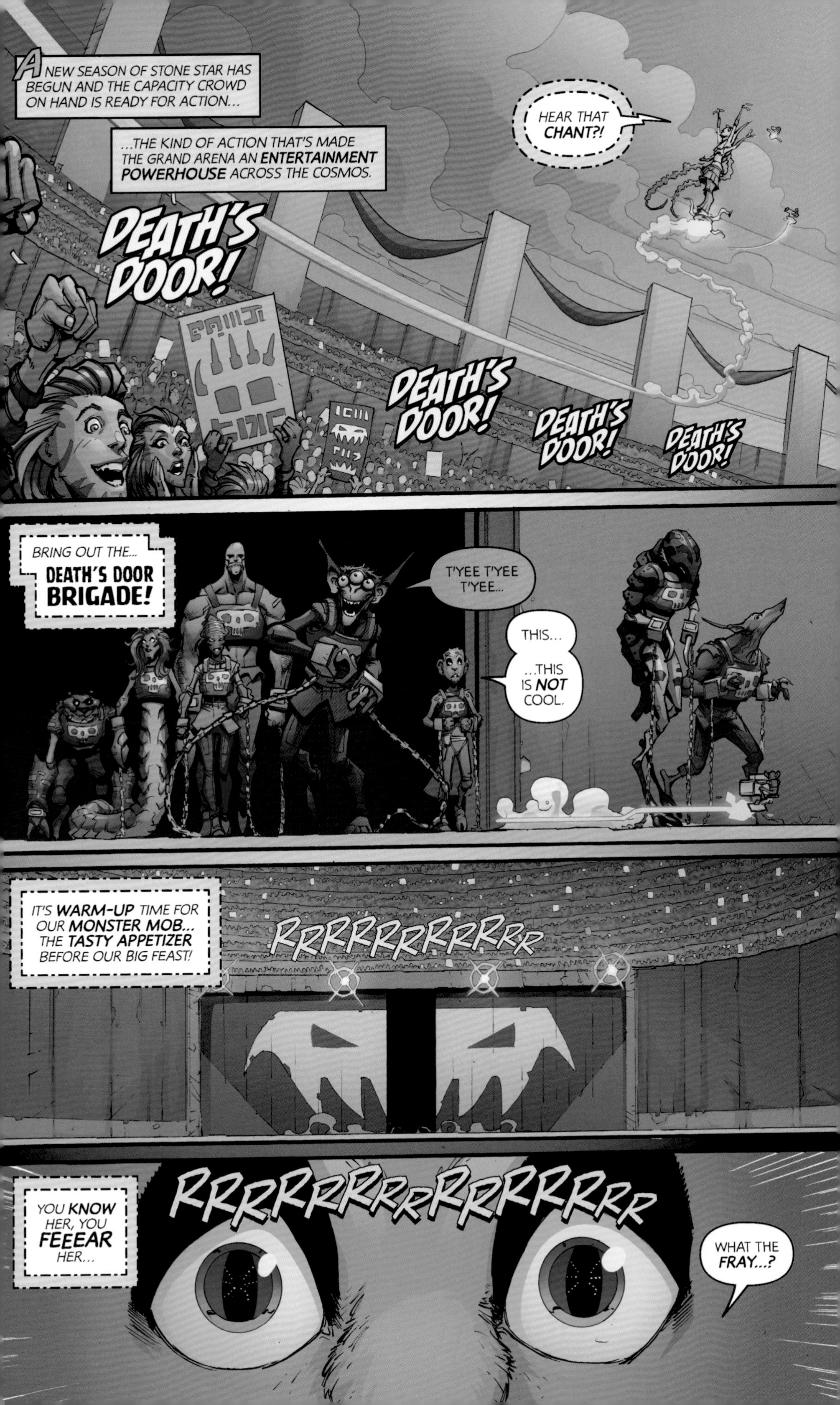
A NEW SEASON OF STONE STAR HAS BEGUN AND THE CAPACITY CROWD ON HAND IS READY FOR ACTION...
...THE KIND OF ACTION THAT'S MADE THE GRAND ARENA AN ENTERTAINMENT POWERHOUSE ACROSS THE COSMOS.
HEAR THAT CHANT?!
DEATH'S DOOR!
DEATH'S DOOR!
DEATH'S DOOR!
DEATH'S DOOR!
BRING OUT THE... DEATH'S DOOR BRIGADE!
T'YEE T'YEE T'YEE...
THIS...
...THIS IS NOT COOL.
IT'S WARM-UP TIME FOR OUR MONSTER MOB... THE TASTY APPETIZER BEFORE OUR BIG FEAST!
RRRRRRRRRRRRR
YOU KNOW HER, YOU FEEEAR HER...
RRRRRRRRRRRRRRRRR
WHAT THE FRAY...?

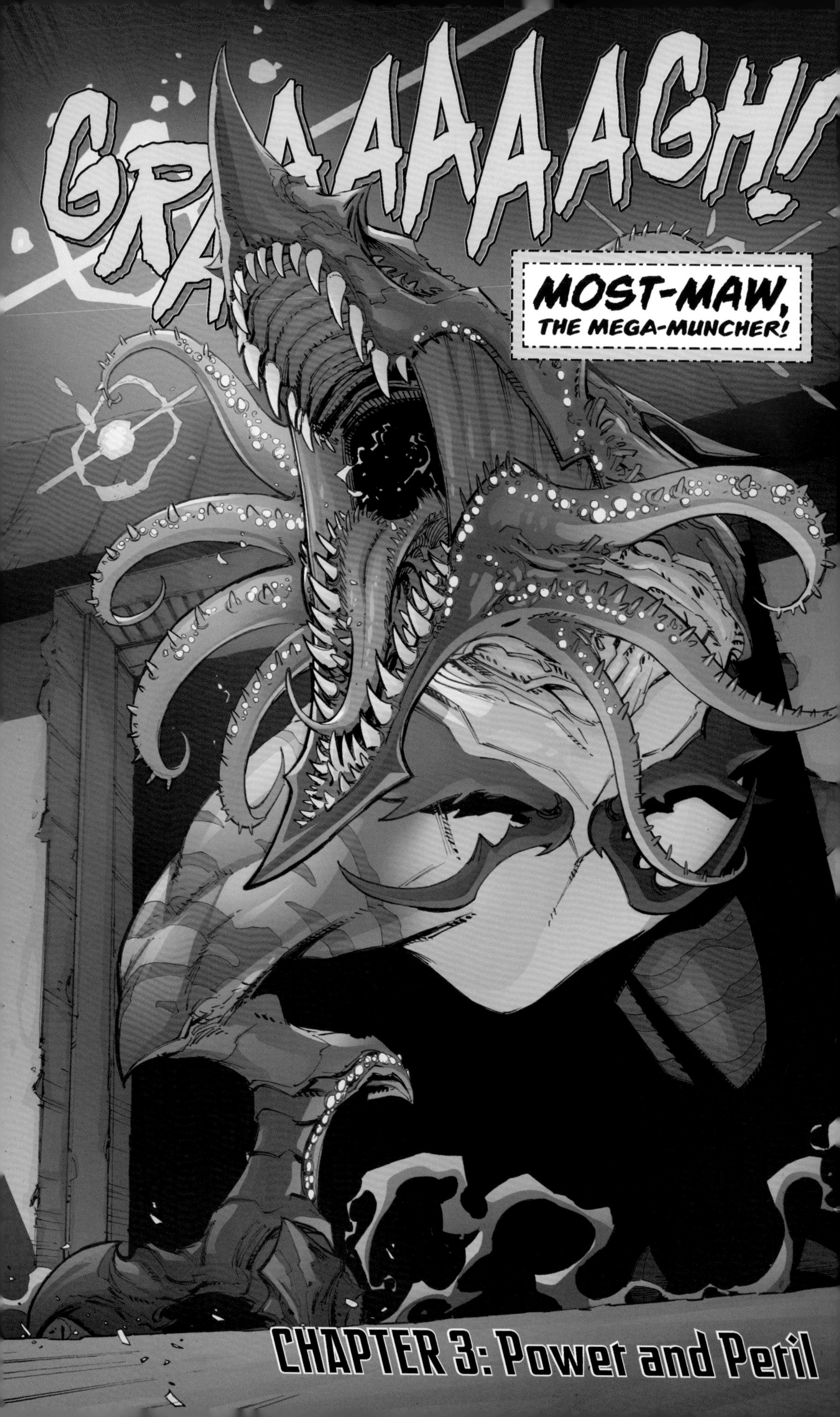

CHAPTER 3: Power and Peril

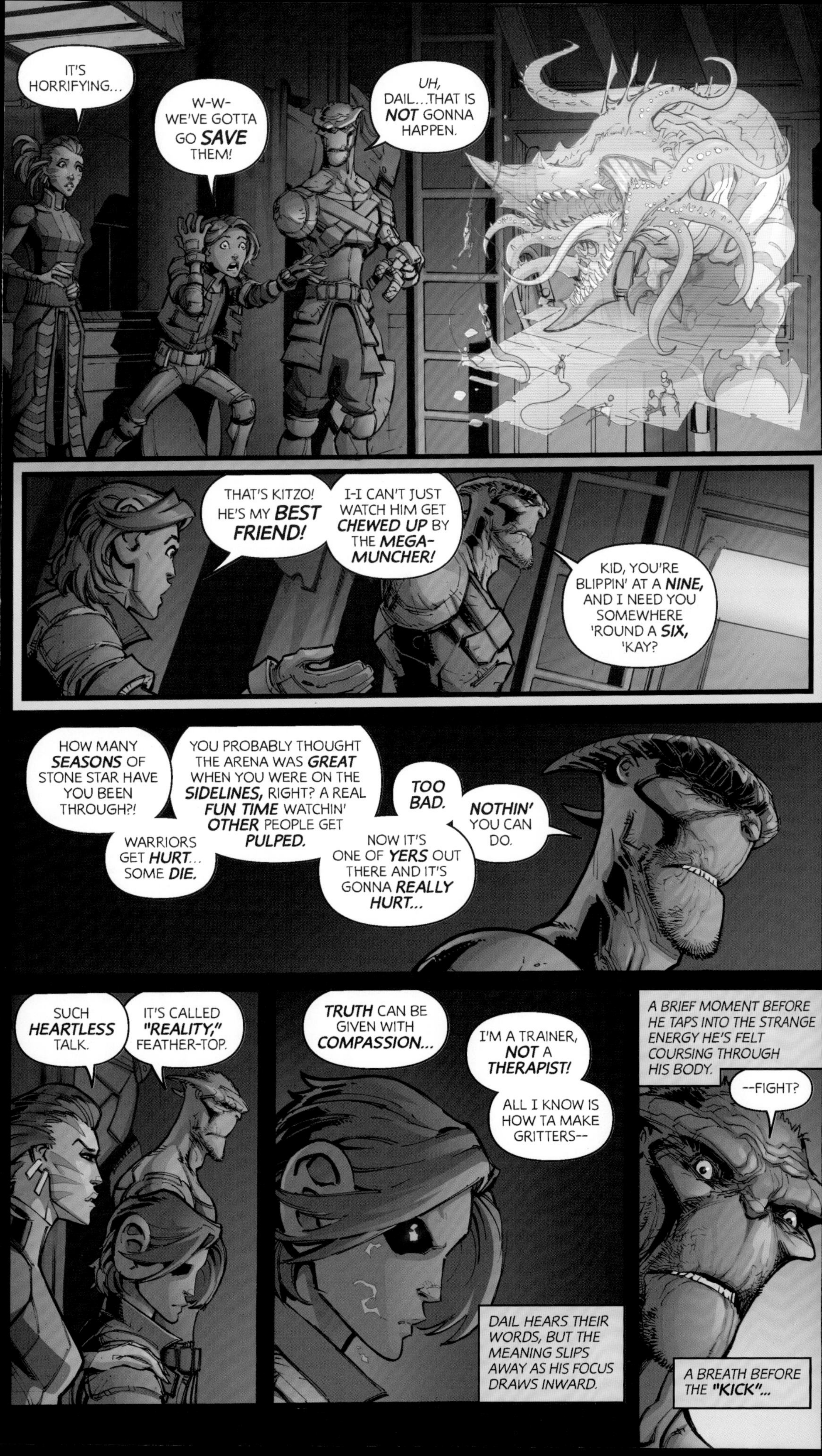
IT'S HORRIFYING...
W-W- WE'VE GOTTA GO SAVE THEM!
UH, DAIL...THAT IS NOT GONNA HAPPEN.
THAT'S KITZO! HE'S MY BEST FRIEND!
I-I CAN'T JUST WATCH HIM GET CHEWED UP BY THE MEGA-MUNCHER!
KID, YOU'RE BLIPPIN' AT A NINE, AND I NEED YOU SOMEWHERE 'ROUND A SIX, 'KAY?
HOW MANY SEASONS OF STONE STAR HAVE YOU BEEN THROUGH?!
WARRIORS GET HURT... SOME DIE.
YOU PROBABLY THOUGHT THE ARENA WAS GREAT WHEN YOU WERE ON THE SIDELINES, RIGHT? A REAL FUN TIME WATCHIN' OTHER PEOPLE GET PULPED.
TOO BAD.
NOW IT'S ONE OF YERS OUT THERE AND IT'S GONNA REALLY HURT...
NOTHIN' YOU CAN DO.
SUCH HEARTLESS TALK.
IT'S CALLED "REALITY," FEATHER-TOP.
TRUTH CAN BE GIVEN WITH COMPASSION...
I'M A TRAINER, NOT A THERAPIST!
ALL I KNOW IS HOW TA MAKE GRITTERS--
DAIL HEARS THEIR WORDS, BUT THE MEANING SLIPS AWAY AS HIS FOCUS DRAWS INWARD.
A BRIEF MOMENT BEFORE HE TAPS INTO THE STRANGE ENERGY HE'S FELT COURSING THROUGH HIS BODY.
--FIGHT?
A BREATH BEFORE THE "KICK"...

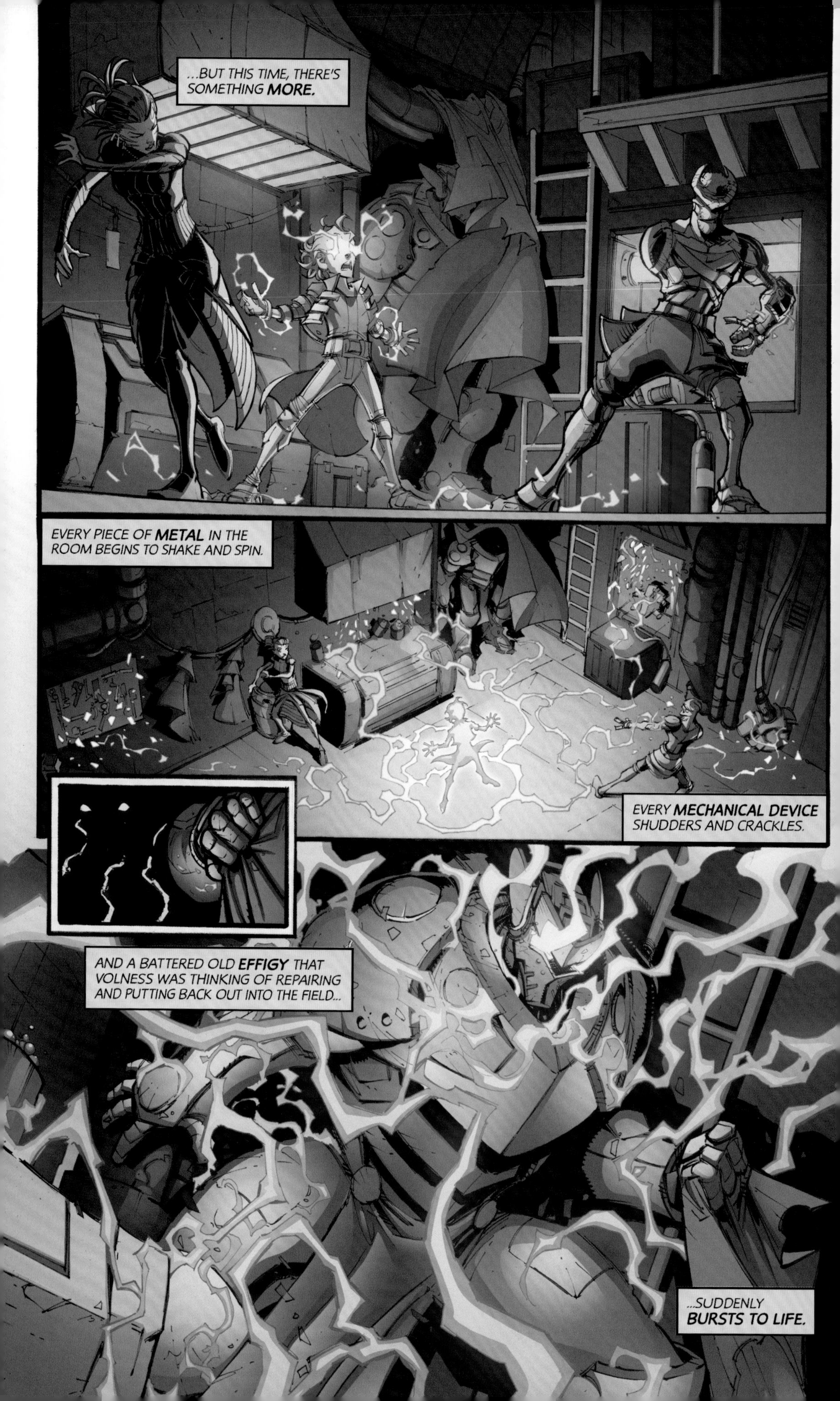

...BUT THIS TIME, THERE'S SOMETHING MORE.
EVERY PIECE OF METAL IN THE ROOM BEGINS TO SHAKE AND SPIN.
EVERY MECHANICAL DEVICE SHUDDERS AND CRACKLES.
AND A BATTERED OLD EFFIGY THAT VOLNESS WAS THINKING OF REPAIRING AND PUTTING BACK OUT INTO THE FIELD...
...SUDDENLY BURSTS TO LIFE.

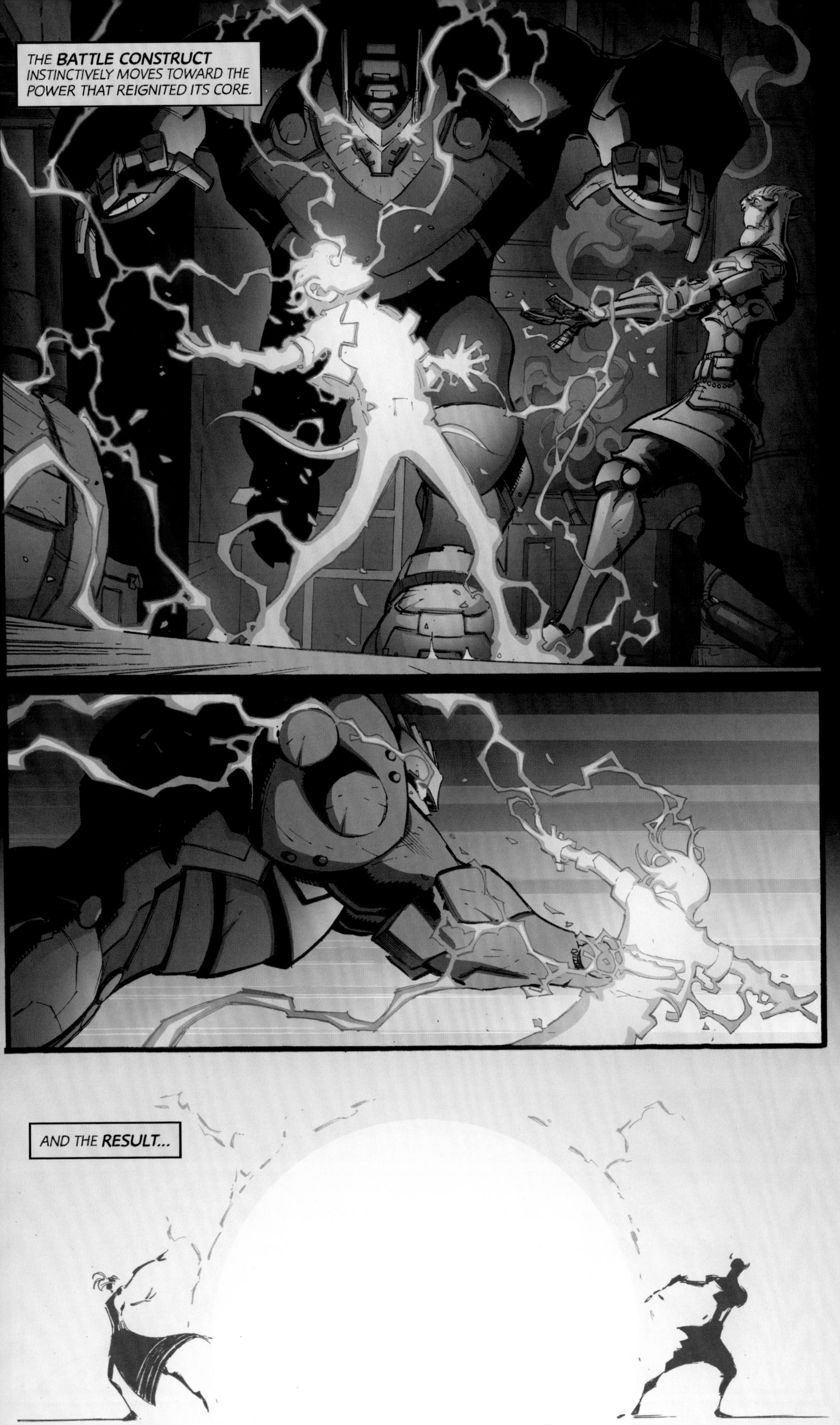
THE BATTLE CONSTRUCT INSTINCTIVELY MOVES TOWARD THE POWER THAT REIGNITED ITS CORE.
AND THE RESULT...

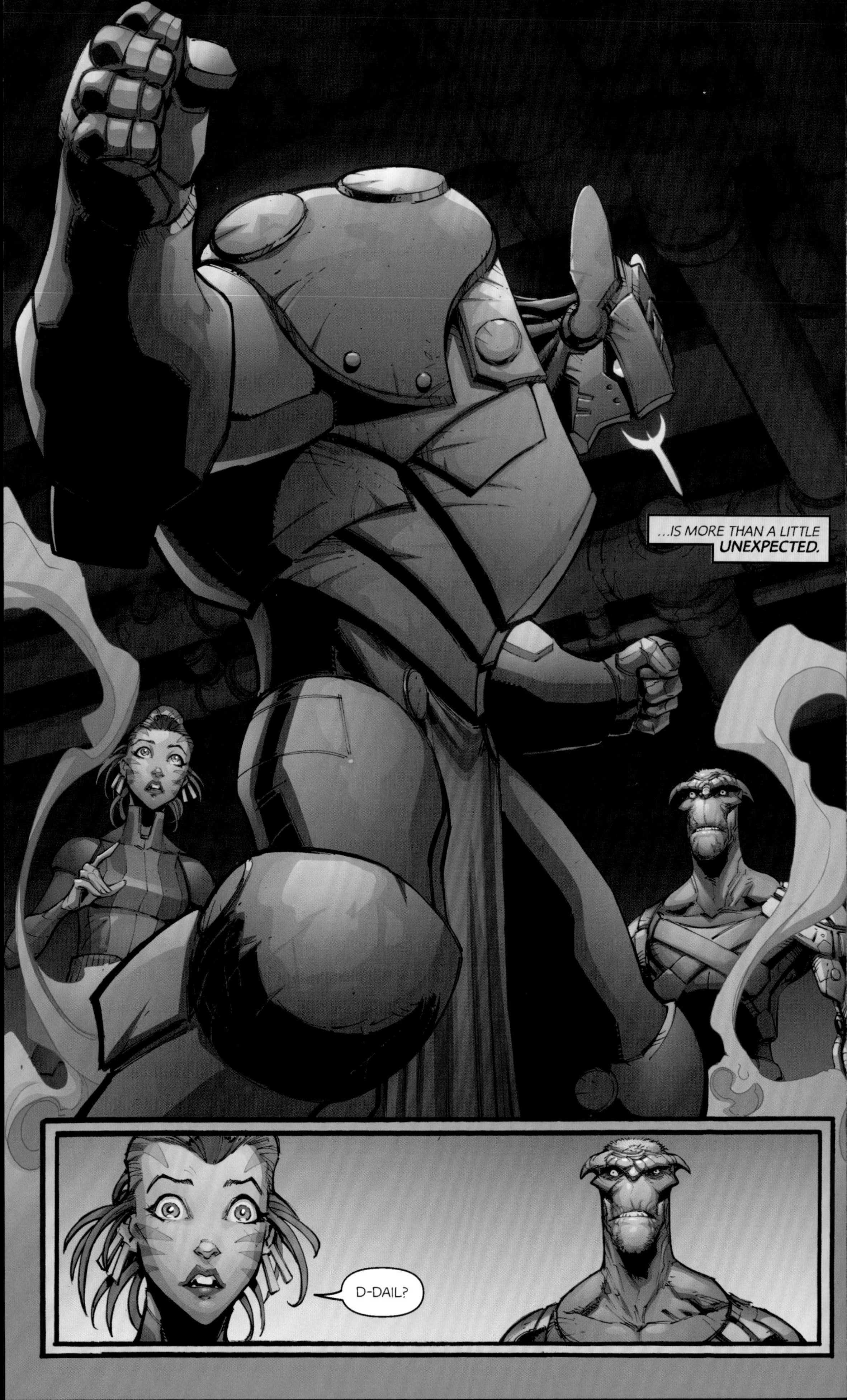
...IS MORE THAN A LITTLE UNEXPECTED.
D-DAIL?

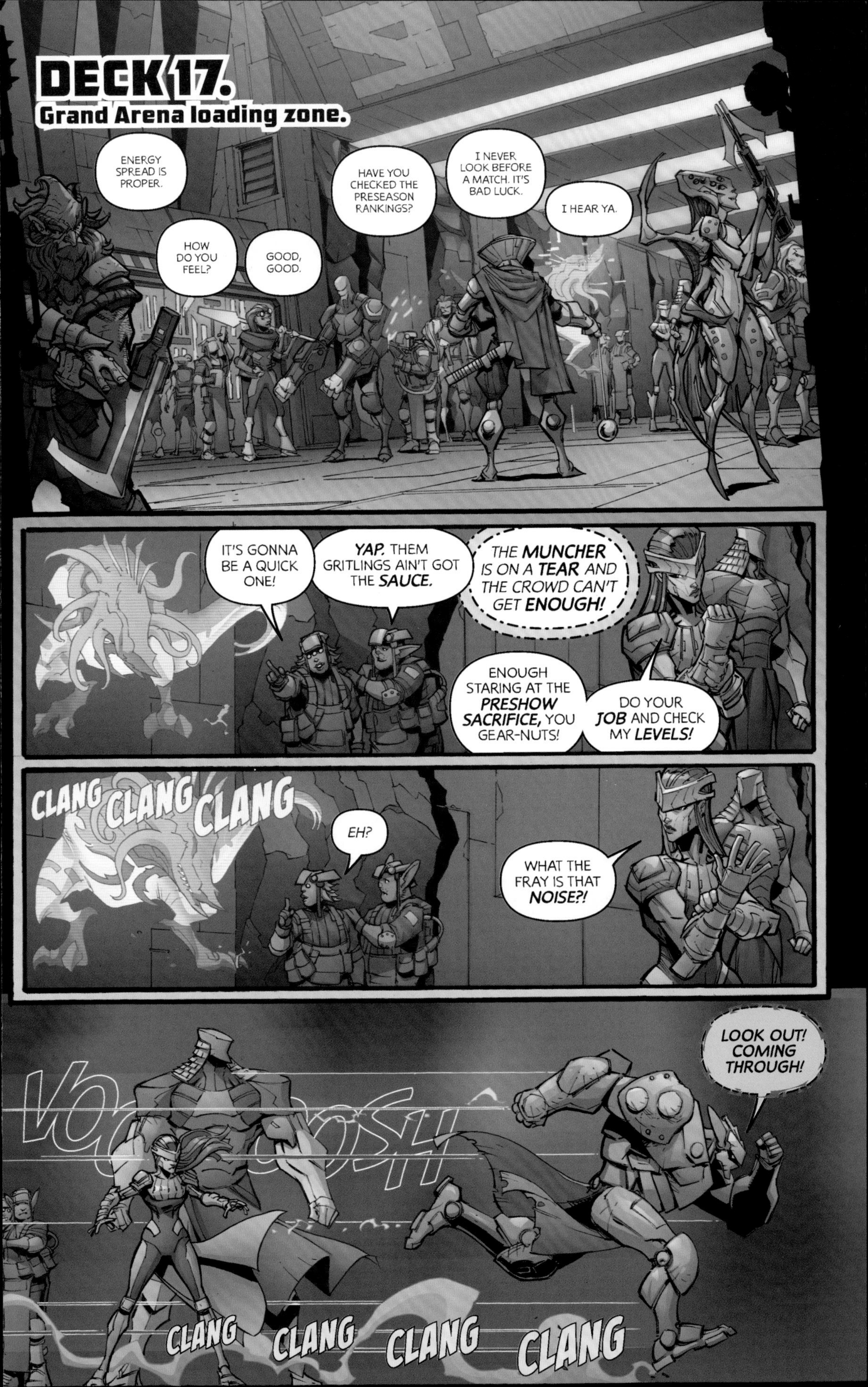
DECK 17.
Grand Arena loading zone.
ENERGY SPREAD IS PROPER.
HOW DO YOU FEEL?
GOOD, GOOD.
HAVE YOU CHECKED THE PRESEASON RANKINGS?
I NEVER LOOK BEFORE A MATCH. IT'S BAD LUCK.
I HEAR YA.
IT'S GONNA BE A QUICK ONE!
YAP. THEM GRITLINGS AIN'T GOT THE SAUCE.
THE MUNCHER IS ON A TEAR AND THE CROWD CAN'T GET ENOUGH!
ENOUGH STARING AT THE PRESHOW SACRIFICE, YOU GEAR-NUTS!
DO YOUR JOB AND CHECK MY LEVELS!
CLANG CLANG CLANG
EH?
WHAT THE FRAY IS THAT NOISE?!
LOOK OUT! COMING THROUGH!
VOOOOOSH
CLANG CLANG CLANG CLANG

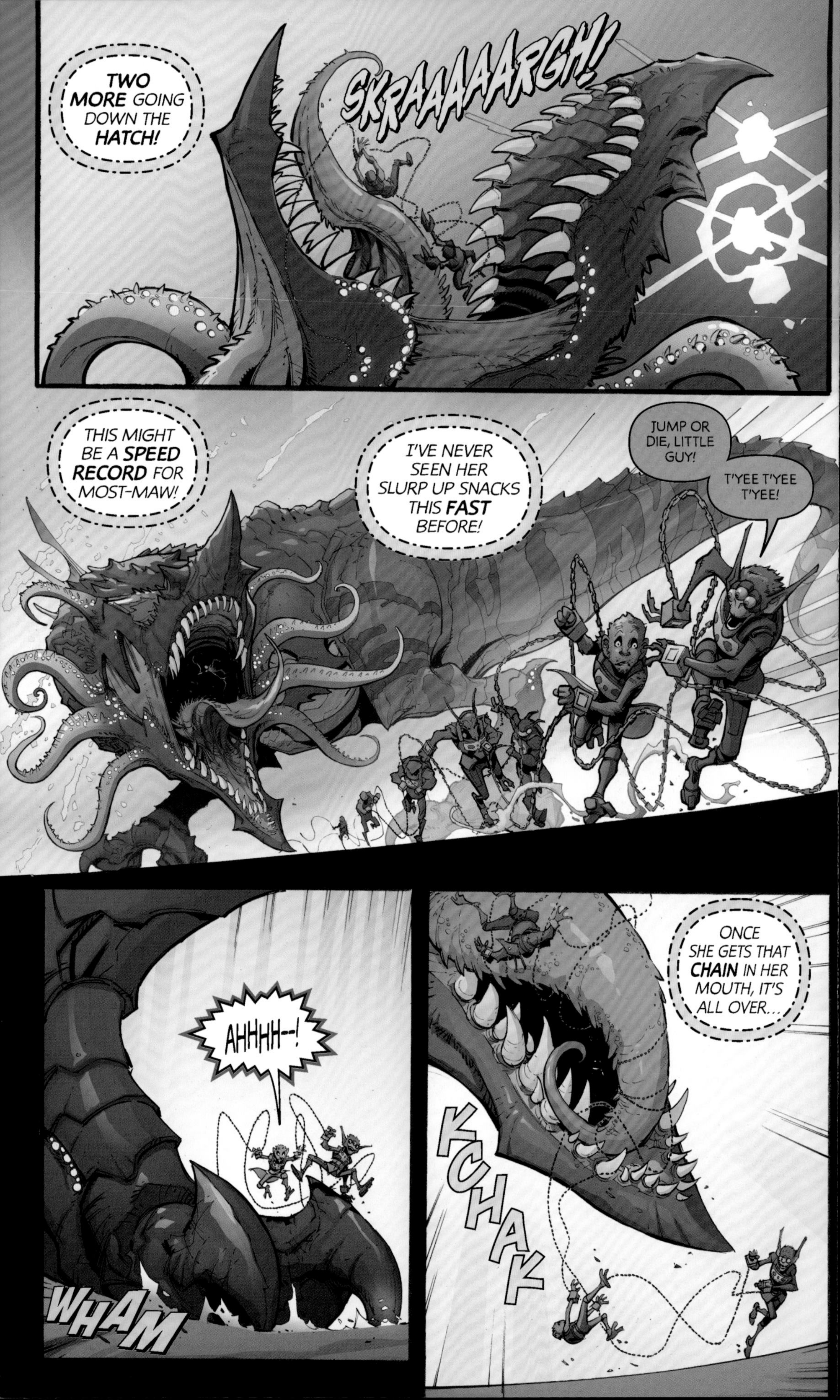
TWO MORE GOING DOWN THE HATCH!
SKRAAAAARGH!
THIS MIGHT BE A SPEED RECORD FOR MOST-MAW!
I'VE NEVER SEEN HER SLURP UP SNACKS THIS FAST BEFORE!
JUMP OR DIE, LITTLE GUY!
T'YEE T'YEE T'YEE!
AHHHH--!
WHAM
ONCE SHE GETS THAT CHAIN IN HER MOUTH, IT'S ALL OVER...
KCHAK

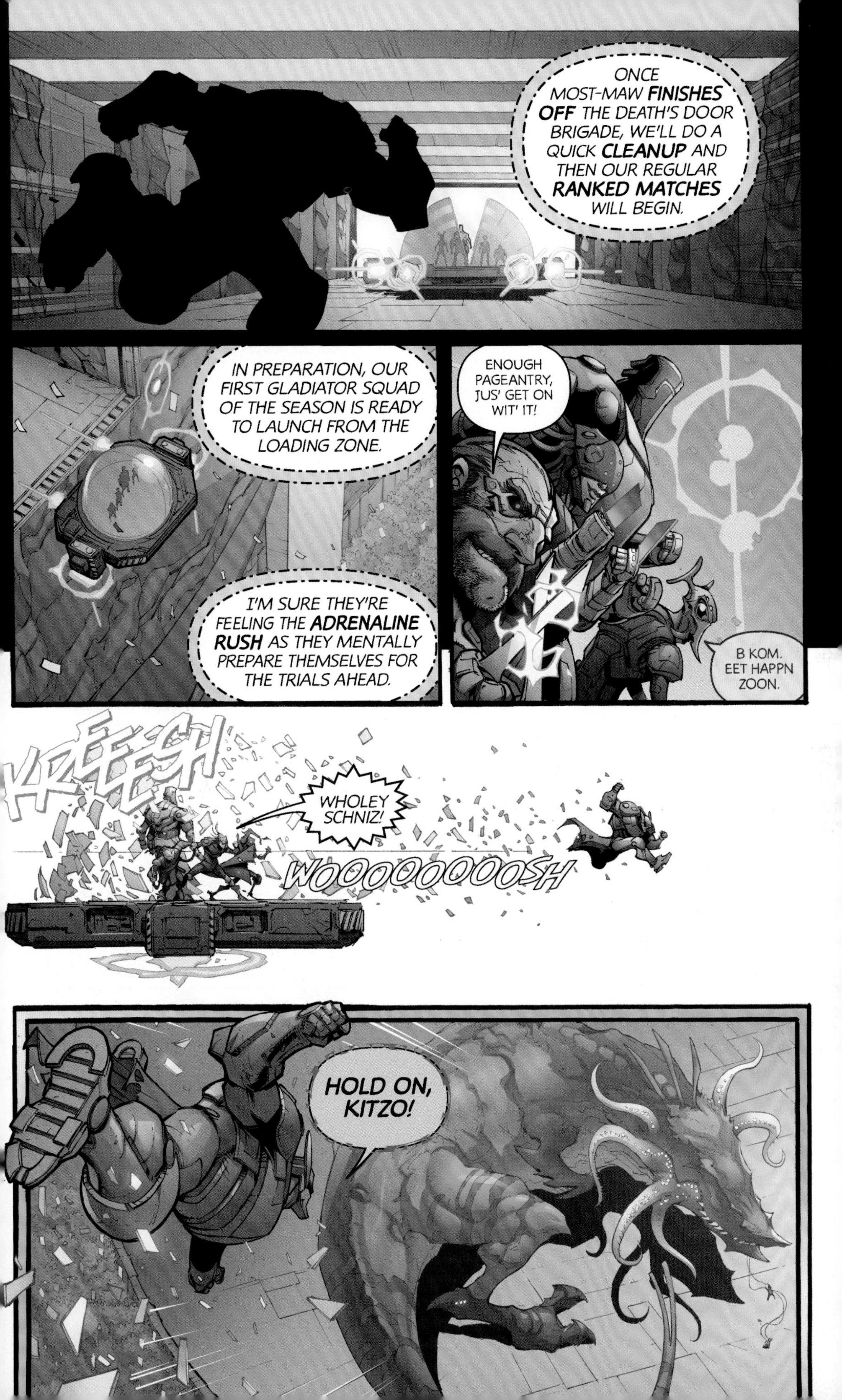

ONCE MOST-MAW **FINISHES OFF** THE DEATH'S DOOR BRIGADE, WE'LL DO A QUICK **CLEANUP** AND THEN OUR REGULAR **RANKED MATCHES** WILL BEGIN.
IN PREPARATION, OUR FIRST GLADIATOR SQUAD OF THE SEASON IS READY TO LAUNCH FROM THE LOADING ZONE.
I'M SURE THEY'RE FEELING THE **ADRENALINE RUSH** AS THEY MENTALLY PREPARE THEMSELVES FOR THE TRIALS AHEAD.
ENOUGH PAGEANTRY, JUS' GET ON WIT' IT!
B KOM. EET HAPPN ZOON.
KREEESH
WHOLEY SCHNIZ!
WOOOOOOOOOSH
HOLD ON, KITZO!

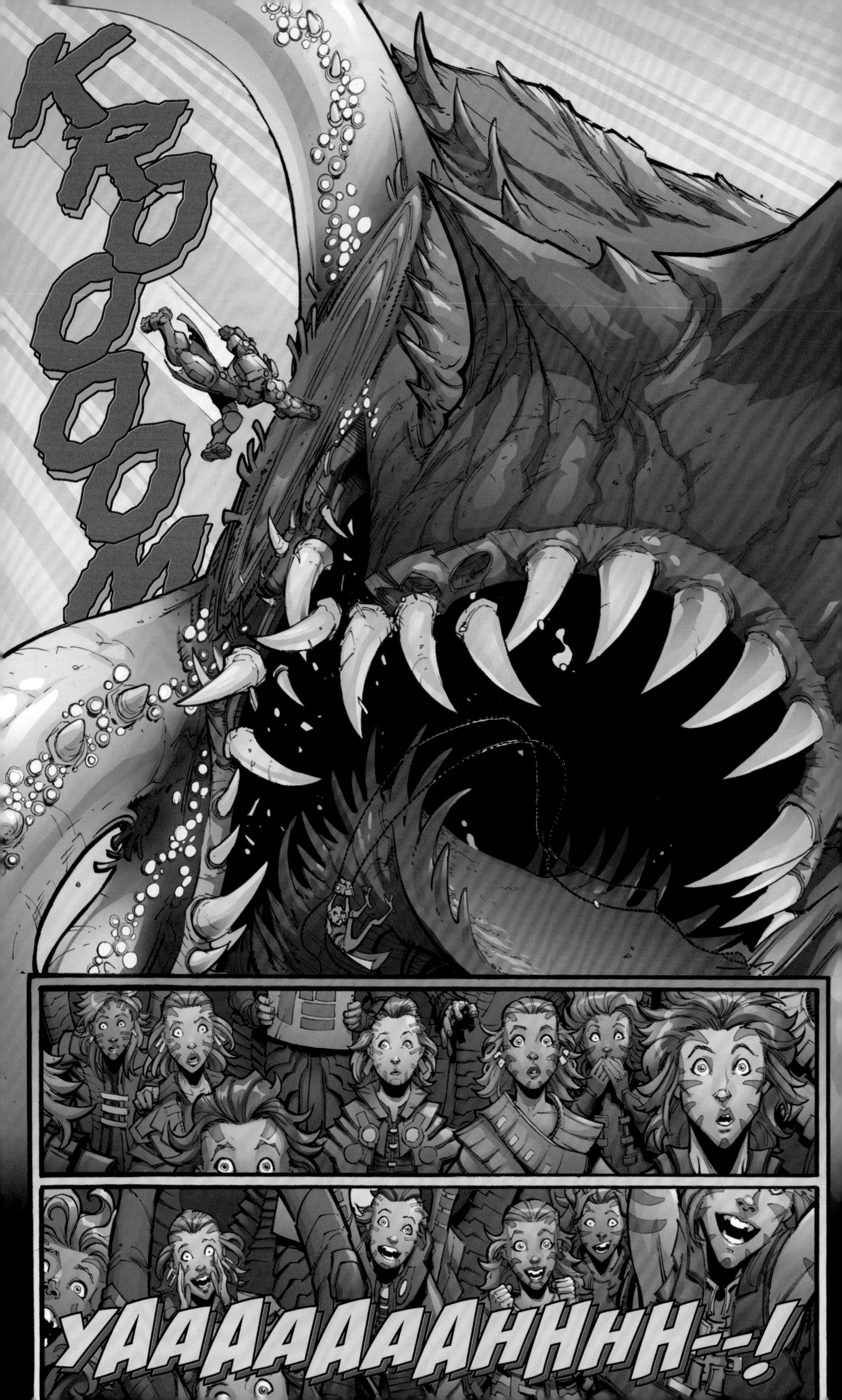
KROOOOOM
YAAAAAAAHHHH--!

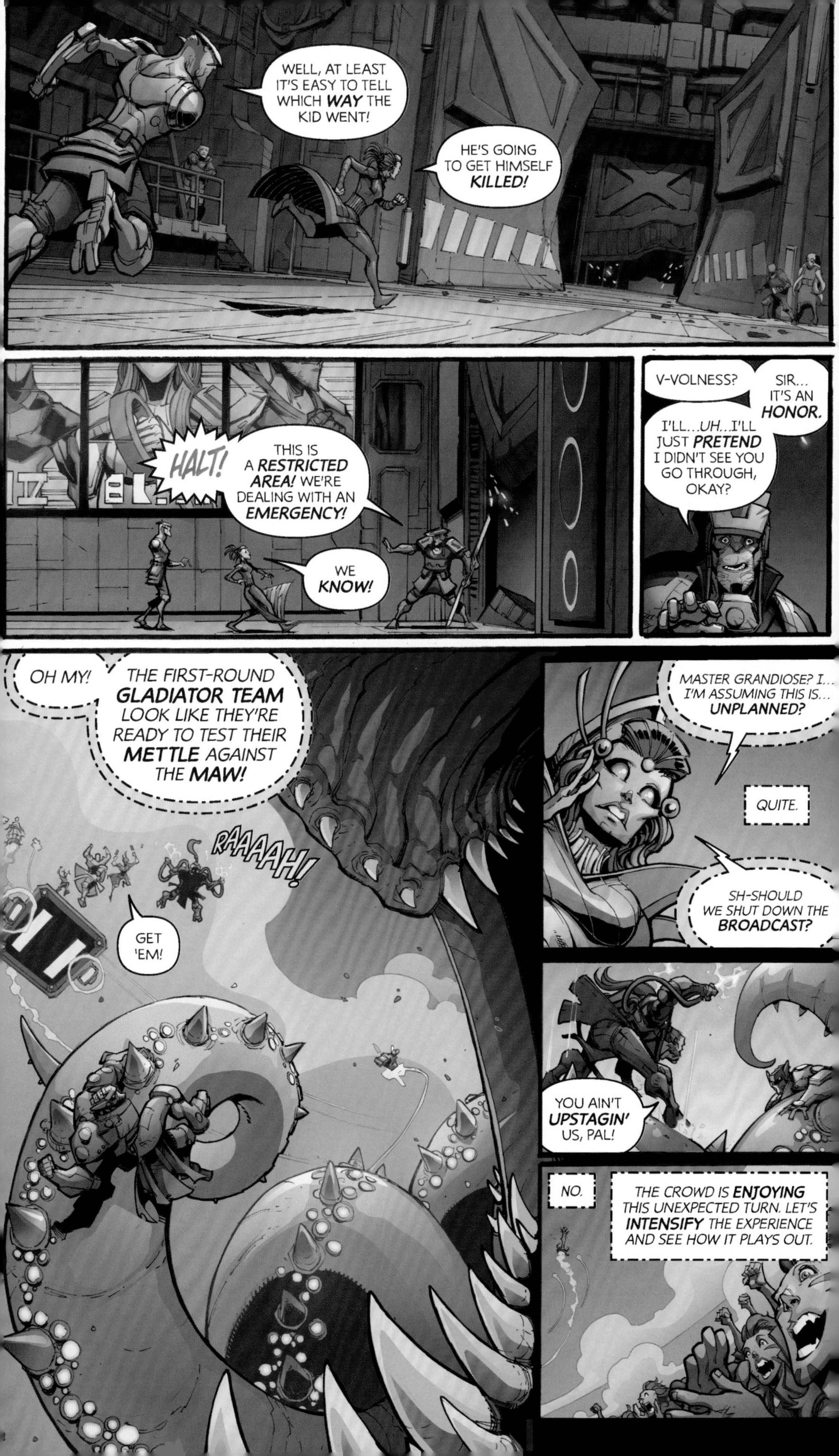
WELL, AT LEAST IT'S EASY TO TELL WHICH **WAY** THE KID WENT!
HE'S GOING TO GET HIMSELF **KILLED!**
HALT!
THIS IS A **RESTRICTED AREA!** WE'RE DEALING WITH AN **EMERGENCY!**
WE **KNOW!**
V-VOLNESS?
SIR... IT'S AN **HONOR.**
I'LL...*UH*...I'LL JUST **PRETEND** I DIDN'T SEE YOU GO THROUGH, OKAY?
OH MY!
THE FIRST-ROUND **GLADIATOR TEAM** LOOK LIKE THEY'RE READY TO TEST THEIR **METTLE** AGAINST THE **MAW!**
RAAAAH!
GET 'EM!
MASTER GRANDIOSE? I... I'M ASSUMING THIS IS... **UNPLANNED?**
QUITE.
SH-SHOULD WE SHUT DOWN THE **BROADCAST?**
YOU AIN'T **UPSTAGIN'** US, PAL!
NO.
THE CROWD IS **ENJOYING** THIS UNEXPECTED TURN. LET'S **INTENSIFY** THE EXPERIENCE AND SEE HOW IT PLAYS OUT.

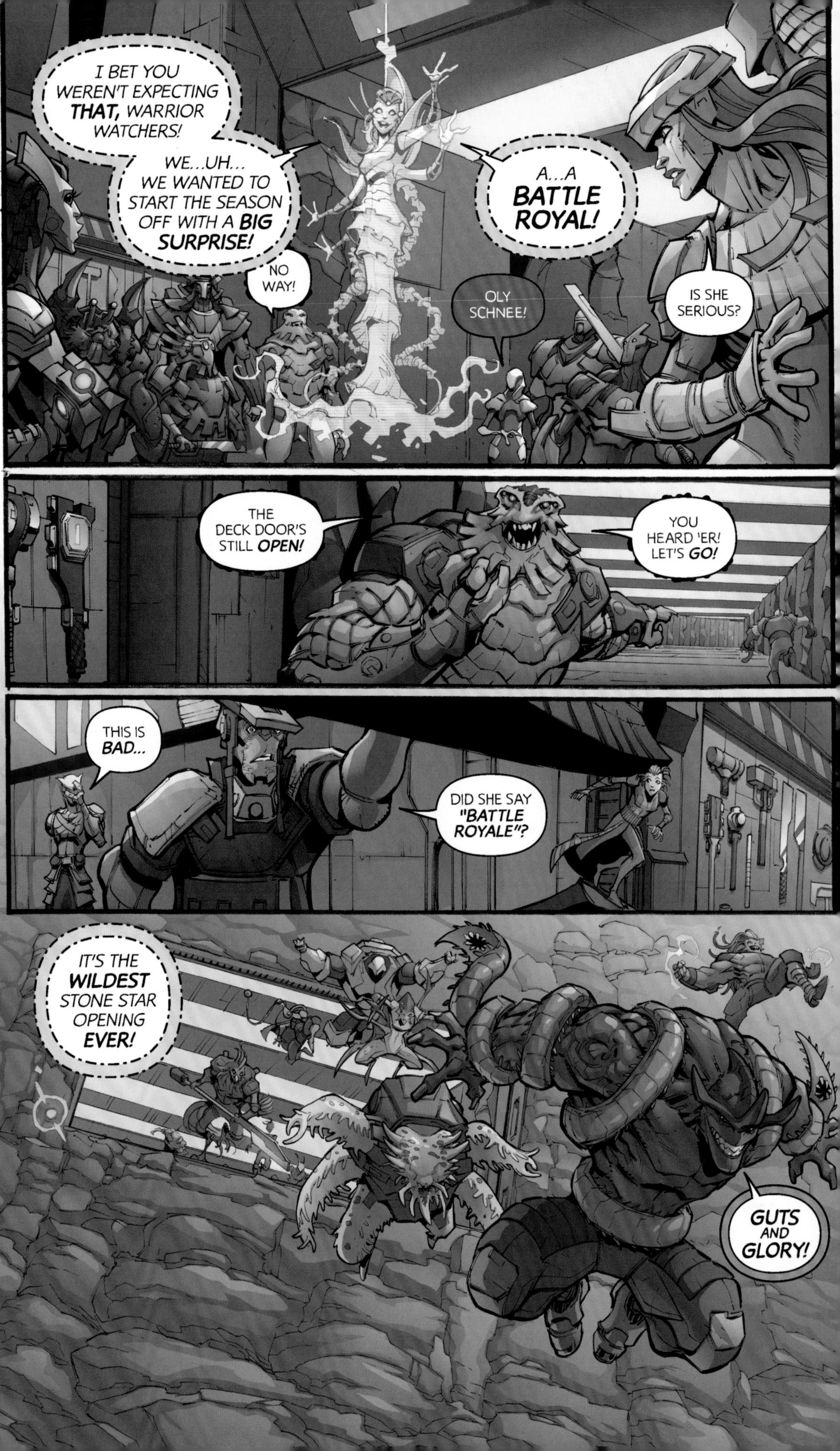
I BET YOU WEREN'T EXPECTING THAT, WARRIOR WATCHERS!
WE...UH... WE WANTED TO START THE SEASON OFF WITH A BIG SURPRISE!
A...A BATTLE ROYAL!
NO WAY!
OLY SCHNEE!
IS SHE SERIOUS?
THE DECK DOOR'S STILL OPEN!
YOU HEARD 'ER! LET'S GO!
THIS IS BAD...
DID SHE SAY "BATTLE ROYALE"?
IT'S THE WILDEST STONE STAR OPENING EVER!
GUTS AND GLORY!

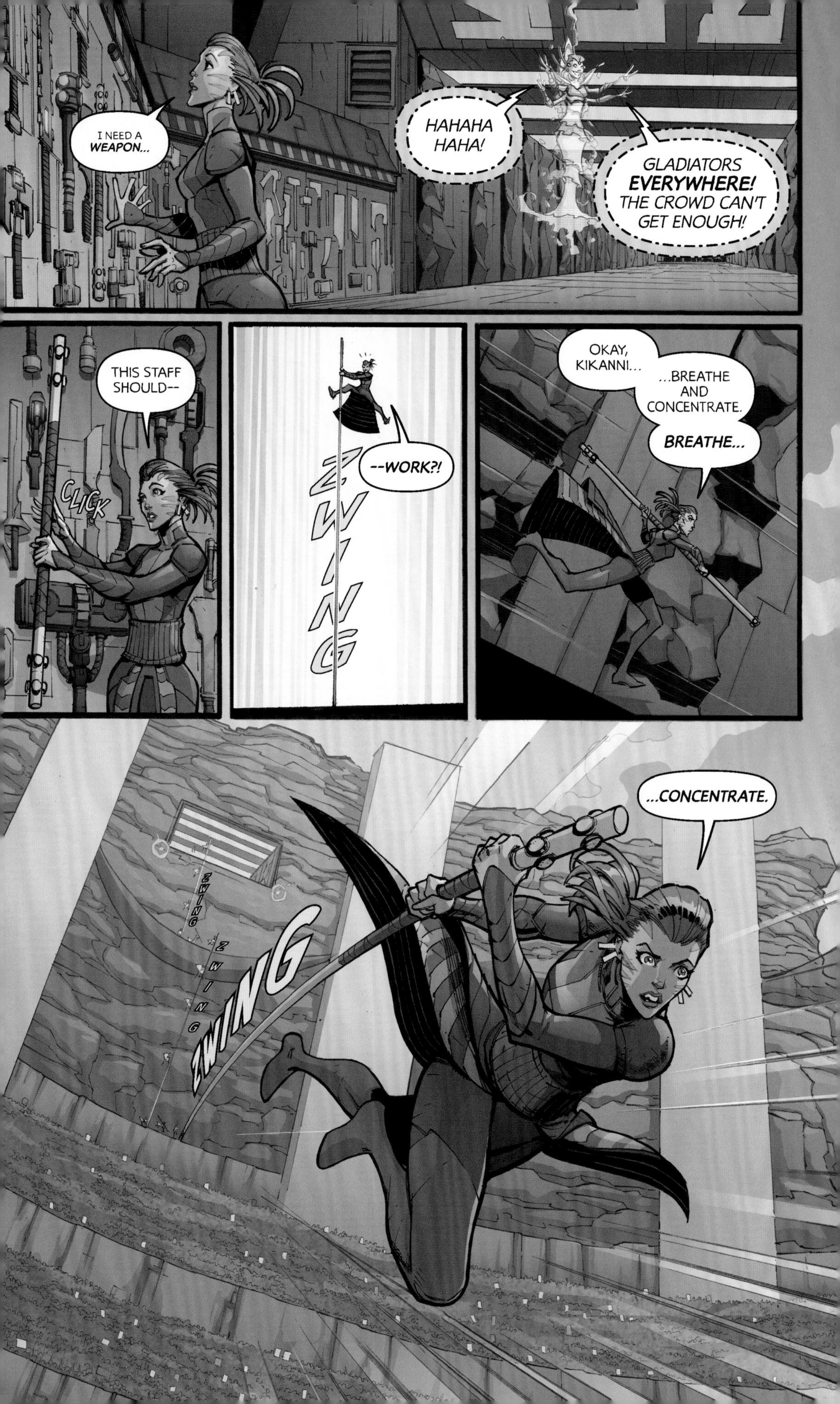
I NEED A WEAPON...
HAHAHA HAHA!
GLADIATORS EVERYWHERE! THE CROWD CAN'T GET ENOUGH!
THIS STAFF SHOULD--
CLICK
--WORK?!
ZWING
OKAY, KIKANNI...
...BREATHE AND CONCENTRATE.
BREATHE...
...CONCENTRATE.
ZWING
ZWING
ZWING

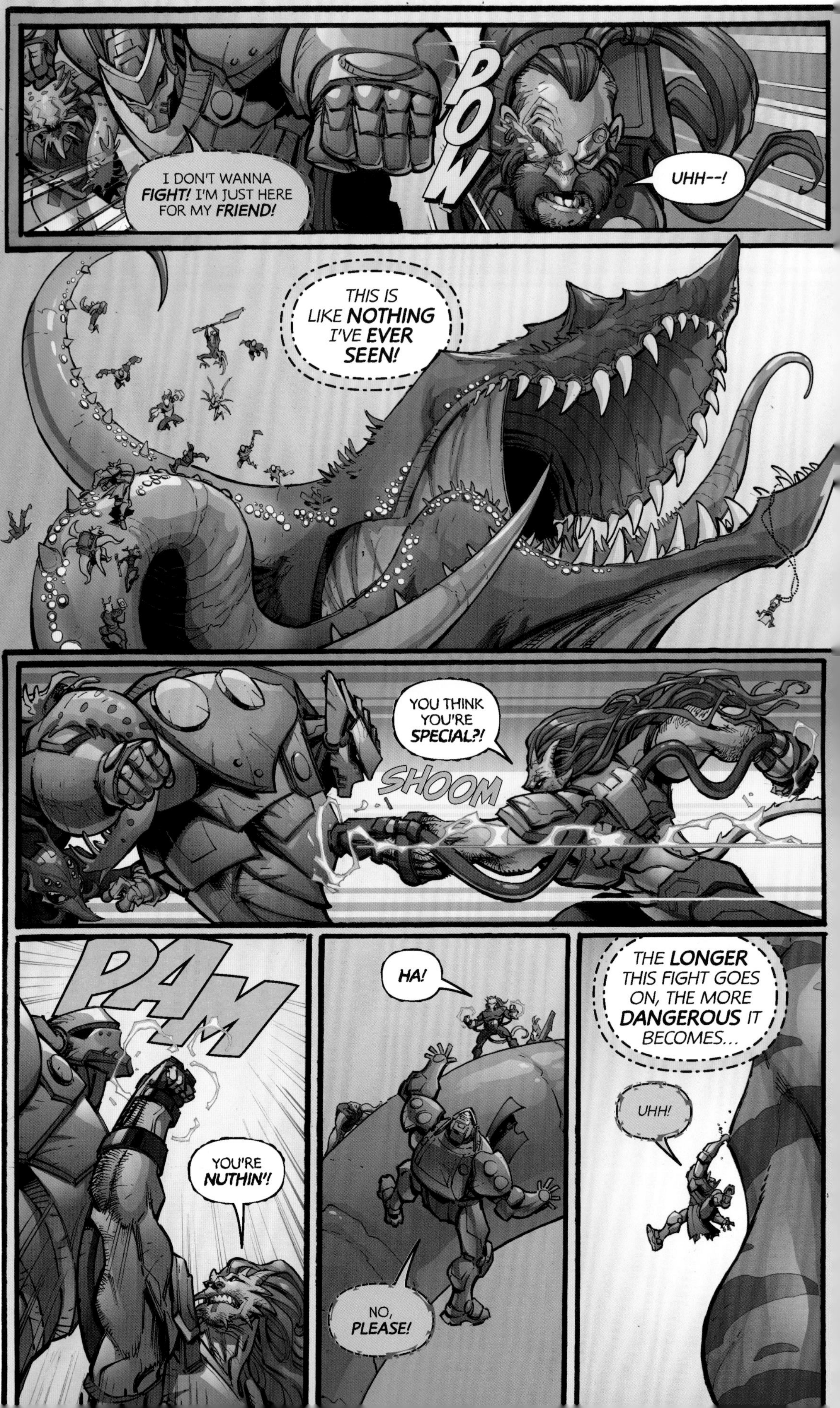
I DON'T WANNA FIGHT! I'M JUST HERE FOR MY FRIEND!
POW
UHH--!
THIS IS LIKE NOTHING I'VE EVER SEEN!
YOU THINK YOU'RE SPECIAL?!
SHOOM
PAM
YOU'RE NUTHIN'!
HA!
NO, PLEASE!
THE LONGER THIS FIGHT GOES ON, THE MORE DANGEROUS IT BECOMES...
UHH!

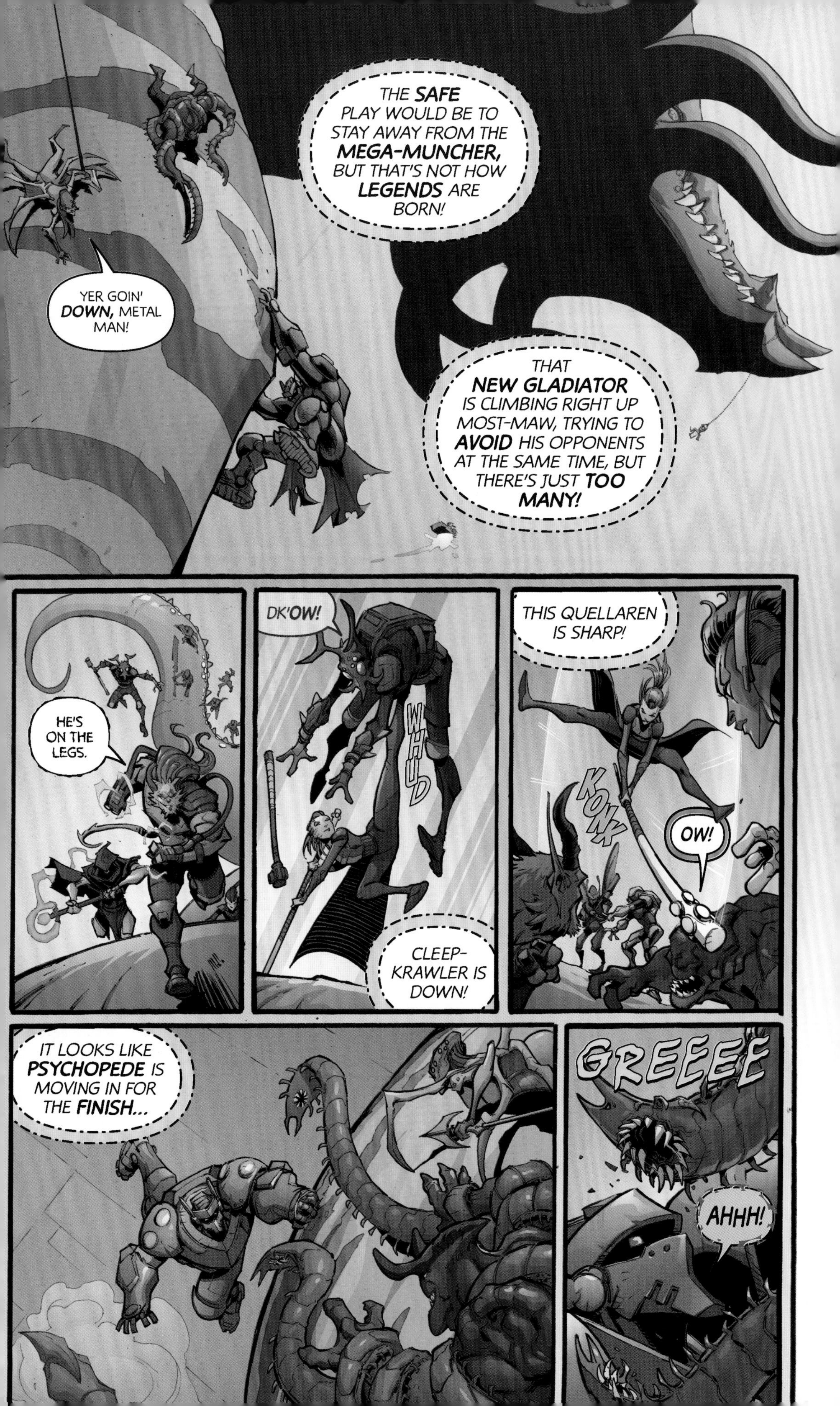
THE SAFE PLAY WOULD BE TO STAY AWAY FROM THE MEGA-MUNCHER, BUT THAT'S NOT HOW LEGENDS ARE BORN!
YER GOIN' DOWN, METAL MAN!
THAT NEW GLADIATOR IS CLIMBING RIGHT UP MOST-MAW, TRYING TO AVOID HIS OPPONENTS AT THE SAME TIME, BUT THERE'S JUST TOO MANY!
HE'S ON THE LEGS.
DK'OW!
WHUD
CLEEP-KRAWLER IS DOWN!
THIS QUELLAREN IS SHARP!
KONK
OW!
IT LOOKS LIKE PSYCHOPEDE IS MOVING IN FOR THE FINISH...
GREEEEE
AHHH!

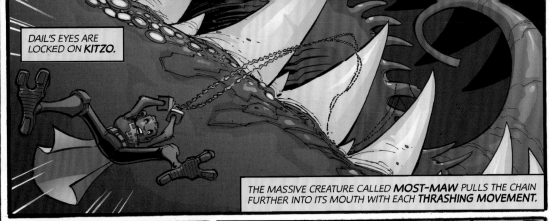

DAIL'S EYES ARE LOCKED ON **KITZO.**

THE MASSIVE CREATURE CALLED **MOST-MAW** PULLS THE CHAIN FURTHER INTO ITS MOUTH WITH EACH *THRASHING MOVEMENT.*

THE END IS **CLOSE...**

...AND HELP **TOO FAR AWAY.**

BUT DAIL IS NO LONGER JUST A SCARED **SCAVENGER** AND **THIEF.**

THE **ARMORED FORM** HE INHABITS CAN **DO** MORE...

...BE MORE...

...AND CARRY HIM **FURTHER.**

WHILE THE GRIZZLED OLD **TRAINER** WHO TOLD HIM HE DIDN'T HAVE THE **GRIT...**

...WATCHES AND WONDERS WHERE HIS OWN **COURAGE** HAS FLED.

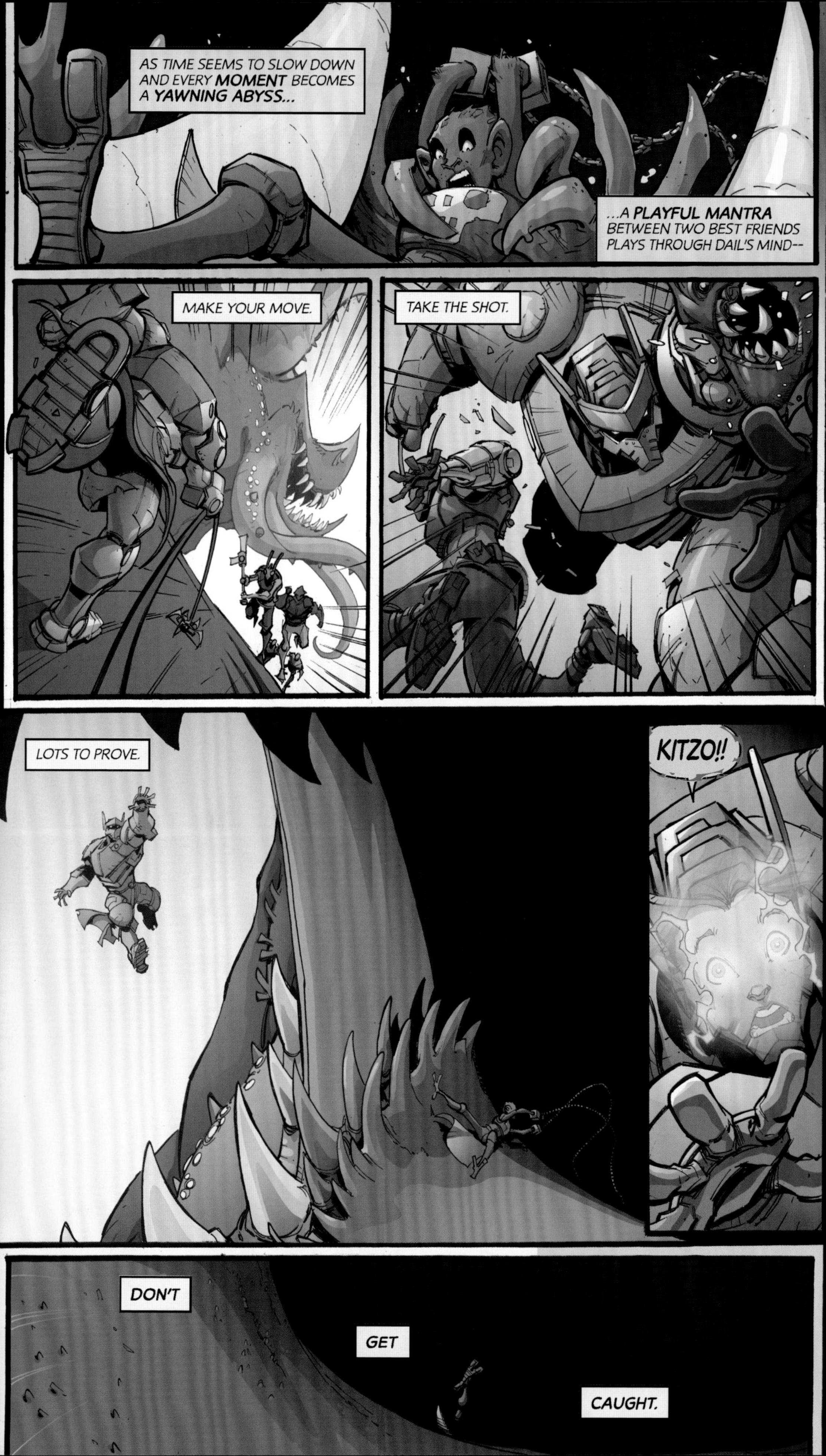
AS TIME SEEMS TO SLOW DOWN AND EVERY MOMENT BECOMES A YAWNING ABYSS...
...A PLAYFUL MANTRA BETWEEN TWO BEST FRIENDS PLAYS THROUGH DAIL'S MIND--
MAKE YOUR MOVE.
TAKE THE SHOT.
LOTS TO PROVE.
KITZO!!
DON'T
GET
CAUGHT.

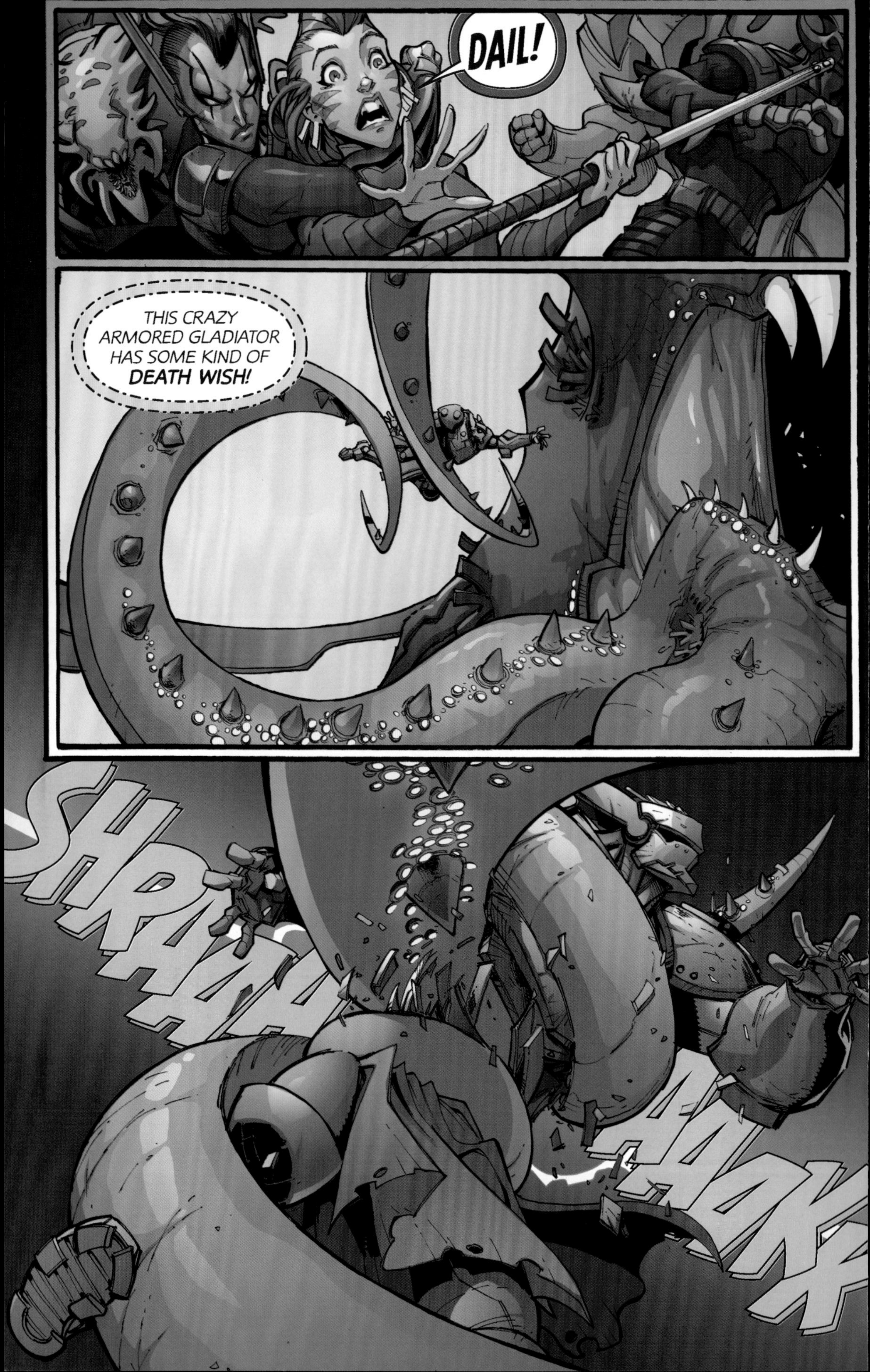
DAIL!
THIS CRAZY ARMORED GLADIATOR HAS SOME KIND OF **DEATH WISH!**
SHRAAA
AAKK

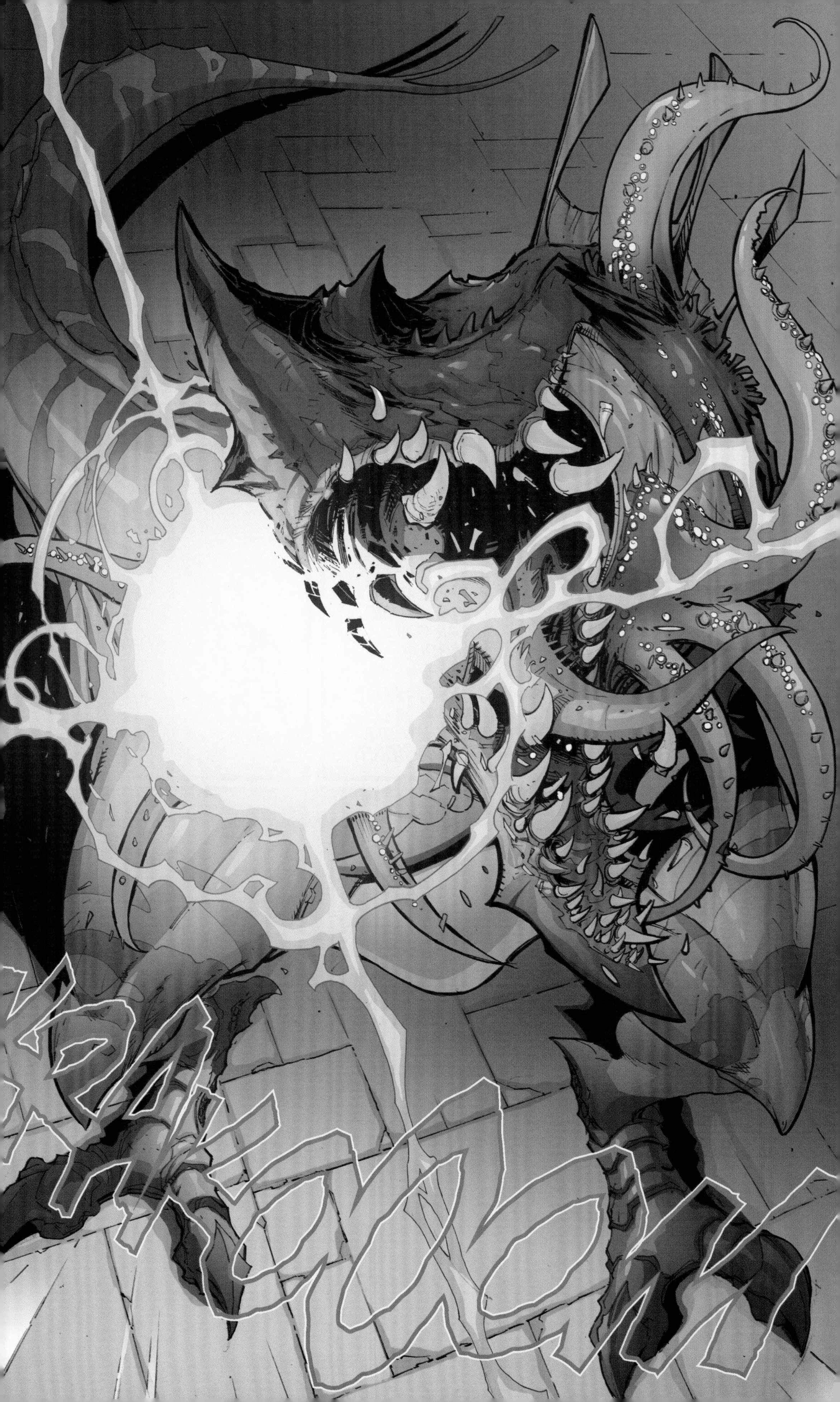
KRAKOOOM!!

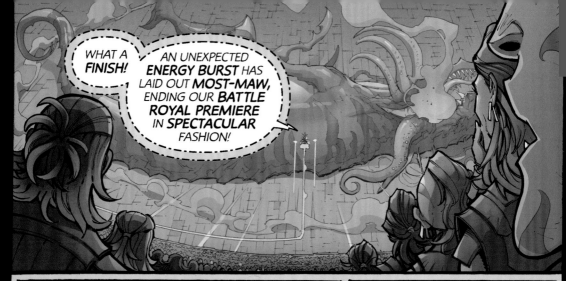

WHAT A **FINISH!**

AN UNEXPECTED **ENERGY BURST** HAS LAID OUT **MOST-MAW,** ENDING OUR **BATTLE ROYAL** PREMIERE IN *SPECTACULAR FASHION!*

HEH HEH HEH-- AH, YES!

TH-**THAT** IS WHAT **STONE STAR** IS ALL ABOUT!

UNFORGETTABLE MOMENTS AND LARGER-THAN-LIFE **ENTERTAINMENT!**

GLADIATORS, CLEAR THE FIELD...

...WHILE WE **TIDY UP** THE **DEBRIS** AND TAKE A **SHORT BREAK** FOR A **WORD** FROM OUR SPONSORS...

Chapter 4: Past and Present

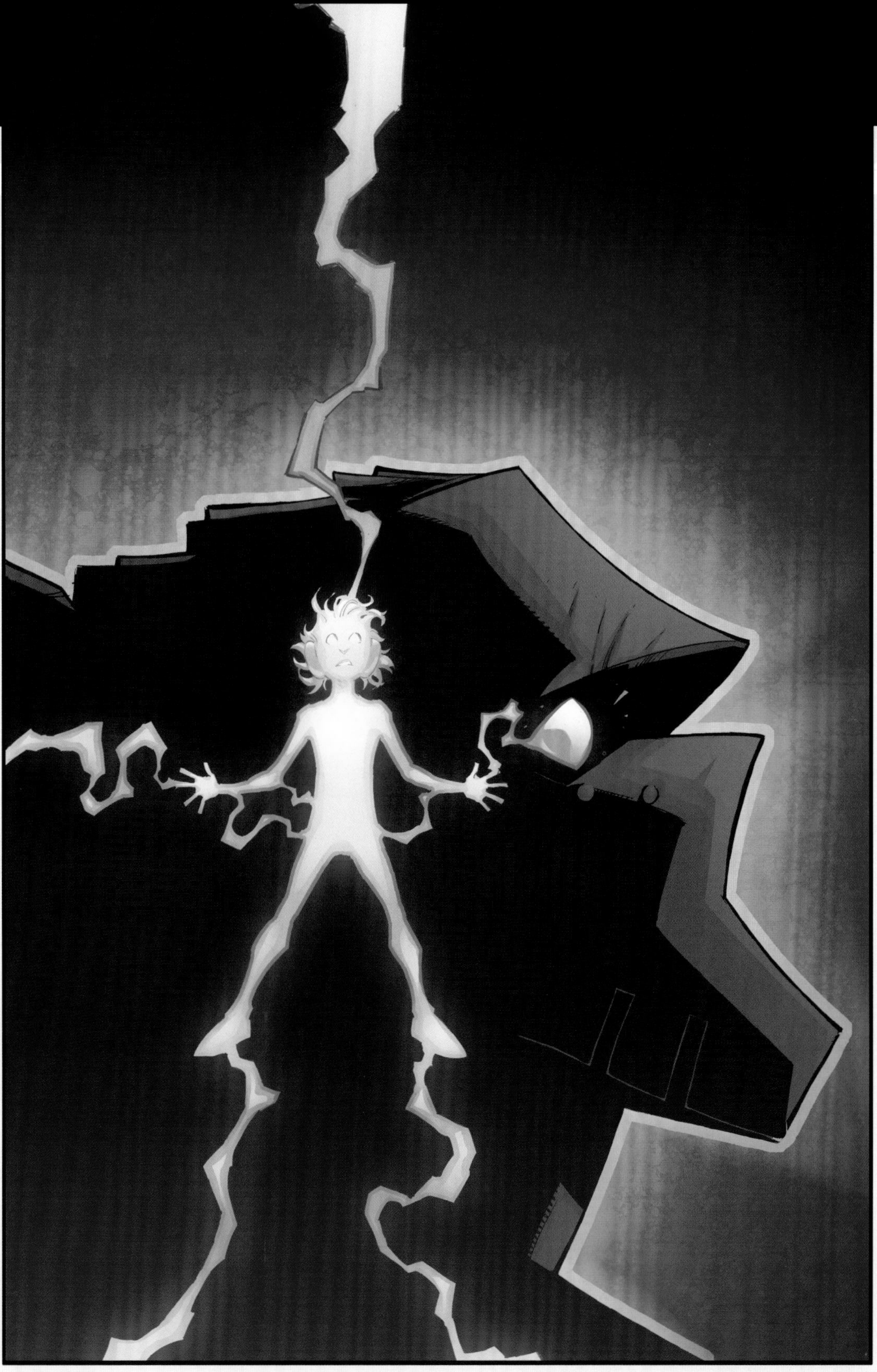

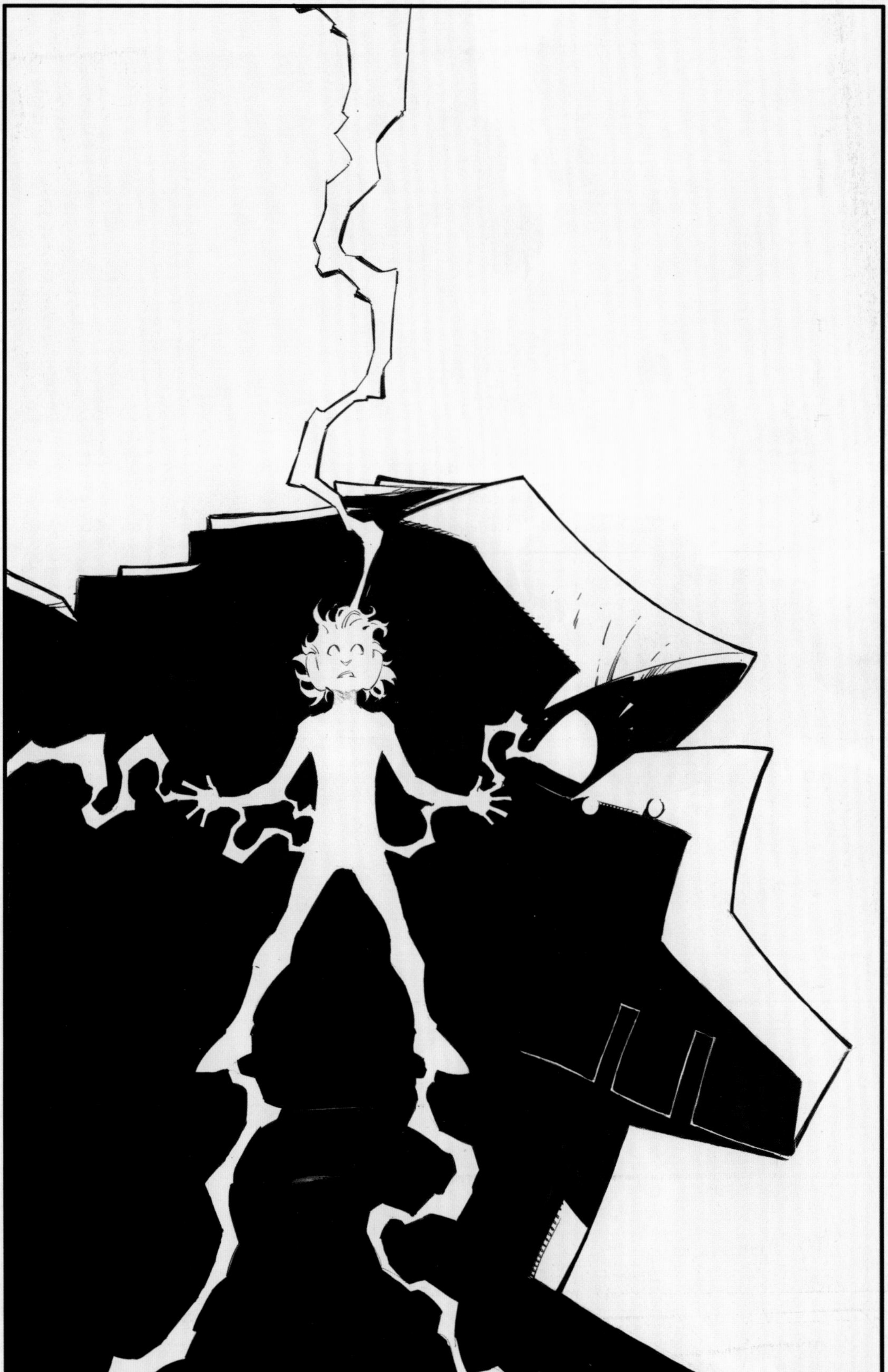

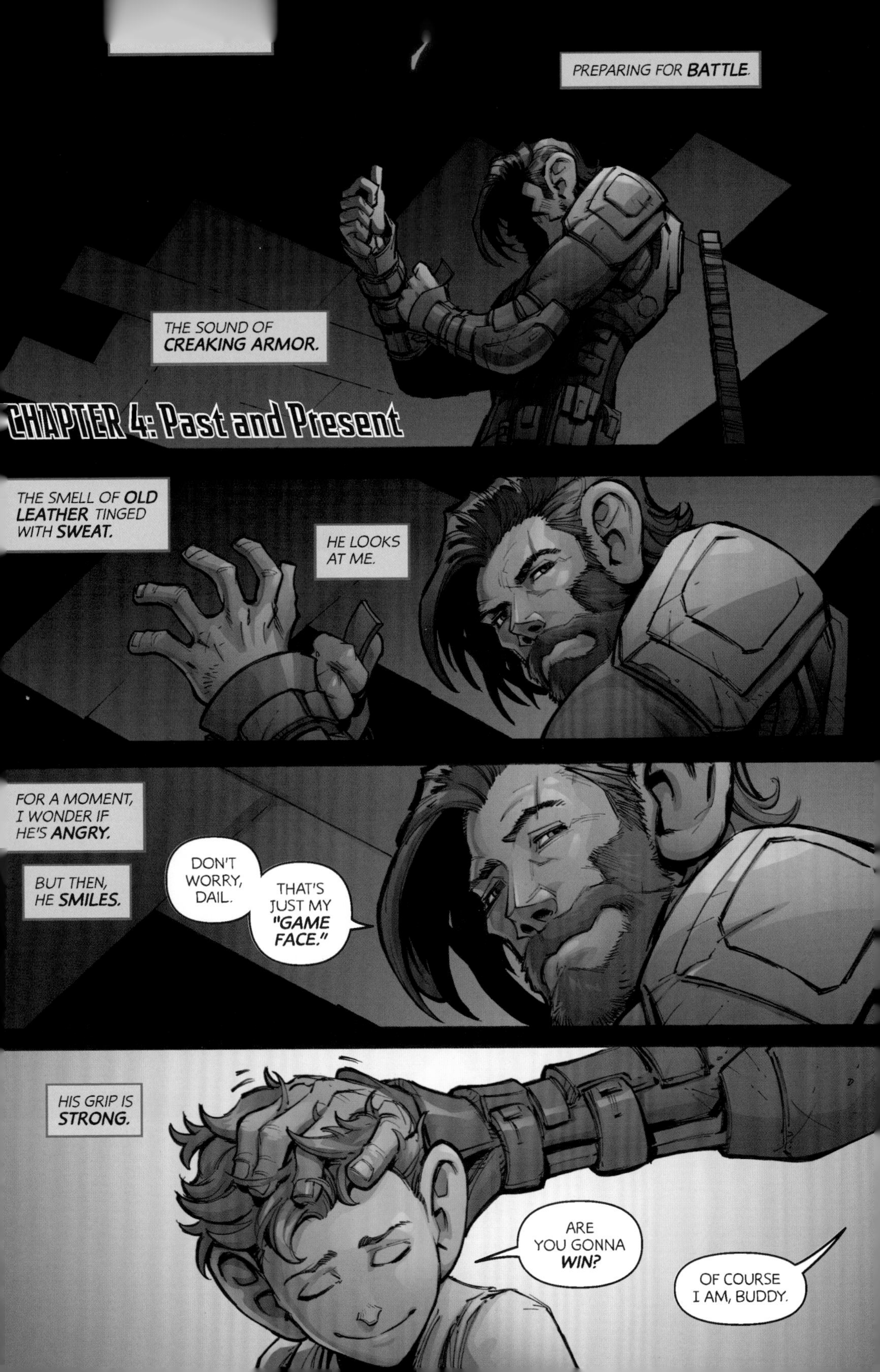
PREPARING FOR BATTLE.
THE SOUND OF CREAKING ARMOR.
CHAPTER 4: Past and Present
THE SMELL OF OLD LEATHER TINGED WITH SWEAT.
HE LOOKS AT ME.
FOR A MOMENT, I WONDER IF HE'S ANGRY.
BUT THEN, HE SMILES.
DON'T WORRY, DAIL.
THAT'S JUST MY "GAME FACE."
HIS GRIP IS STRONG.
ARE YOU GONNA WIN?
OF COURSE I AM, BUDDY.

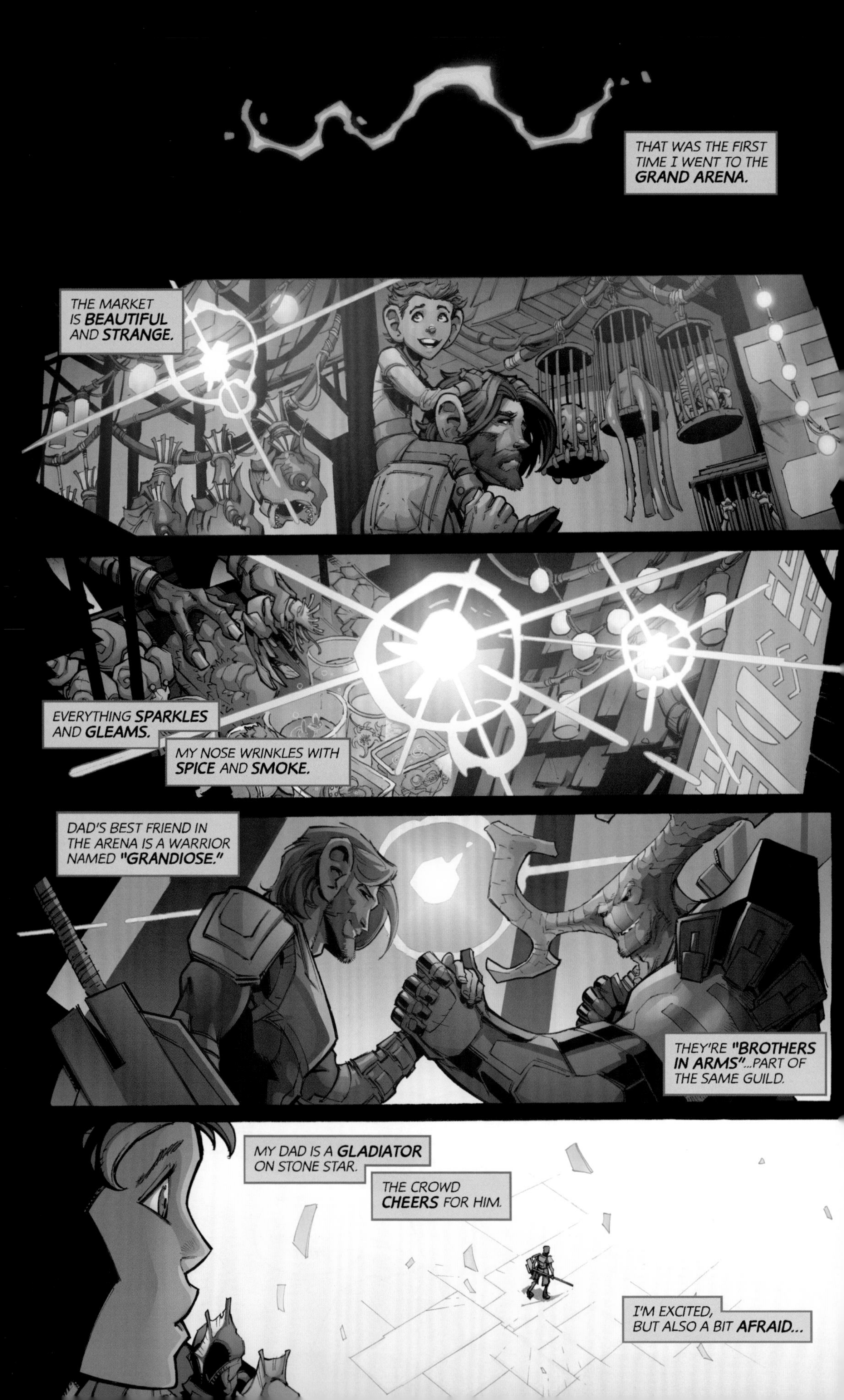
THAT WAS THE FIRST TIME I WENT TO THE GRAND ARENA.
THE MARKET IS BEAUTIFUL AND STRANGE.
EVERYTHING SPARKLES AND GLEAMS.
MY NOSE WRINKLES WITH SPICE AND SMOKE.
DAD'S BEST FRIEND IN THE ARENA IS A WARRIOR NAMED "GRANDIOSE."
THEY'RE "BROTHERS IN ARMS"...PART OF THE SAME GUILD.
MY DAD IS A GLADIATOR ON STONE STAR.
THE CROWD CHEERS FOR HIM.
I'M EXCITED, BUT ALSO A BIT AFRAID...

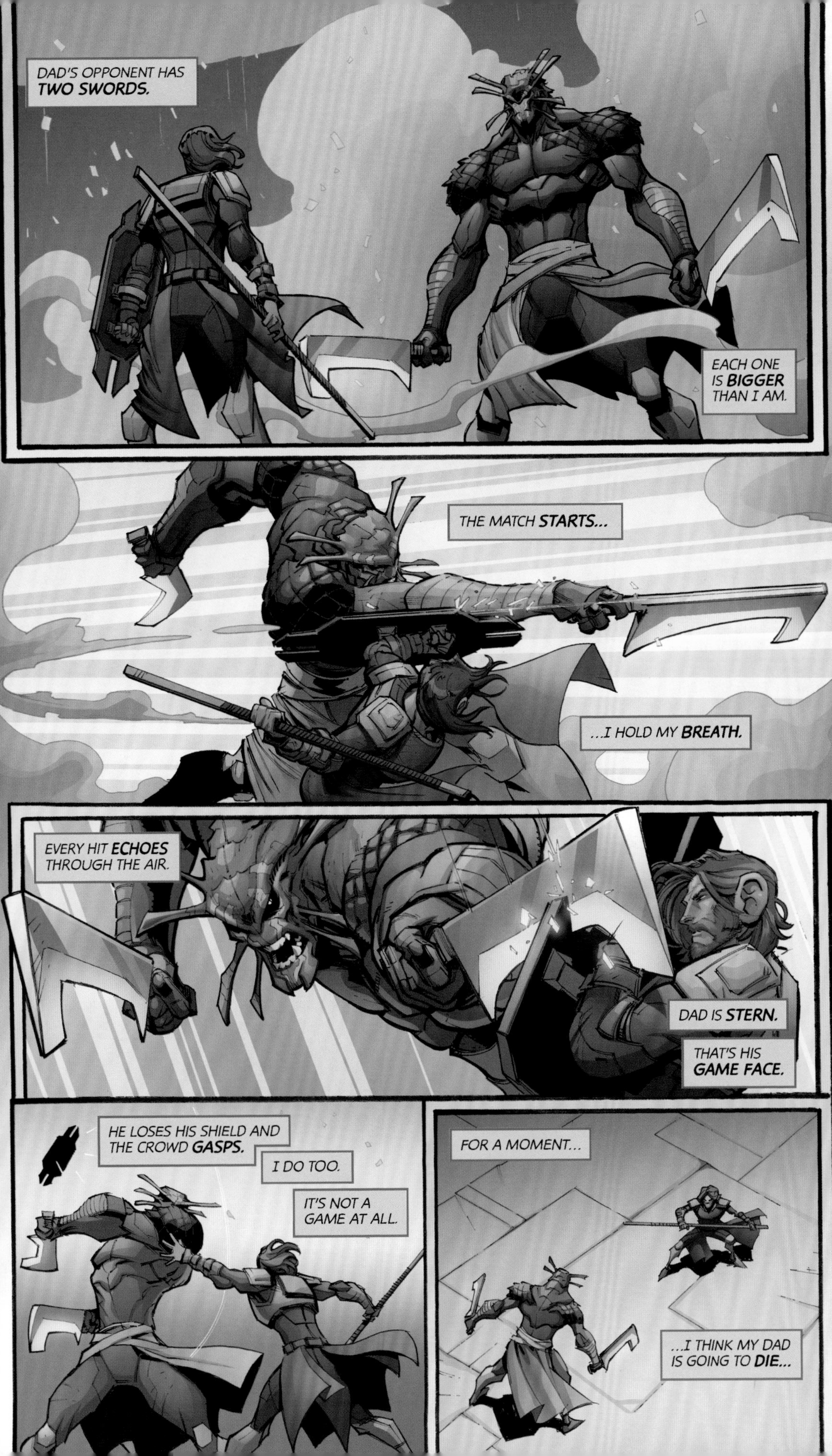
DAD'S OPPONENT HAS TWO SWORDS.
EACH ONE IS BIGGER THAN I AM.
THE MATCH STARTS...
...I HOLD MY BREATH.
EVERY HIT ECHOES THROUGH THE AIR.
DAD IS STERN.
THAT'S HIS GAME FACE.
HE LOSES HIS SHIELD AND THE CROWD GASPS.
I DO TOO.
IT'S NOT A GAME AT ALL.
FOR A MOMENT...
...I THINK MY DAD IS GOING TO DIE...

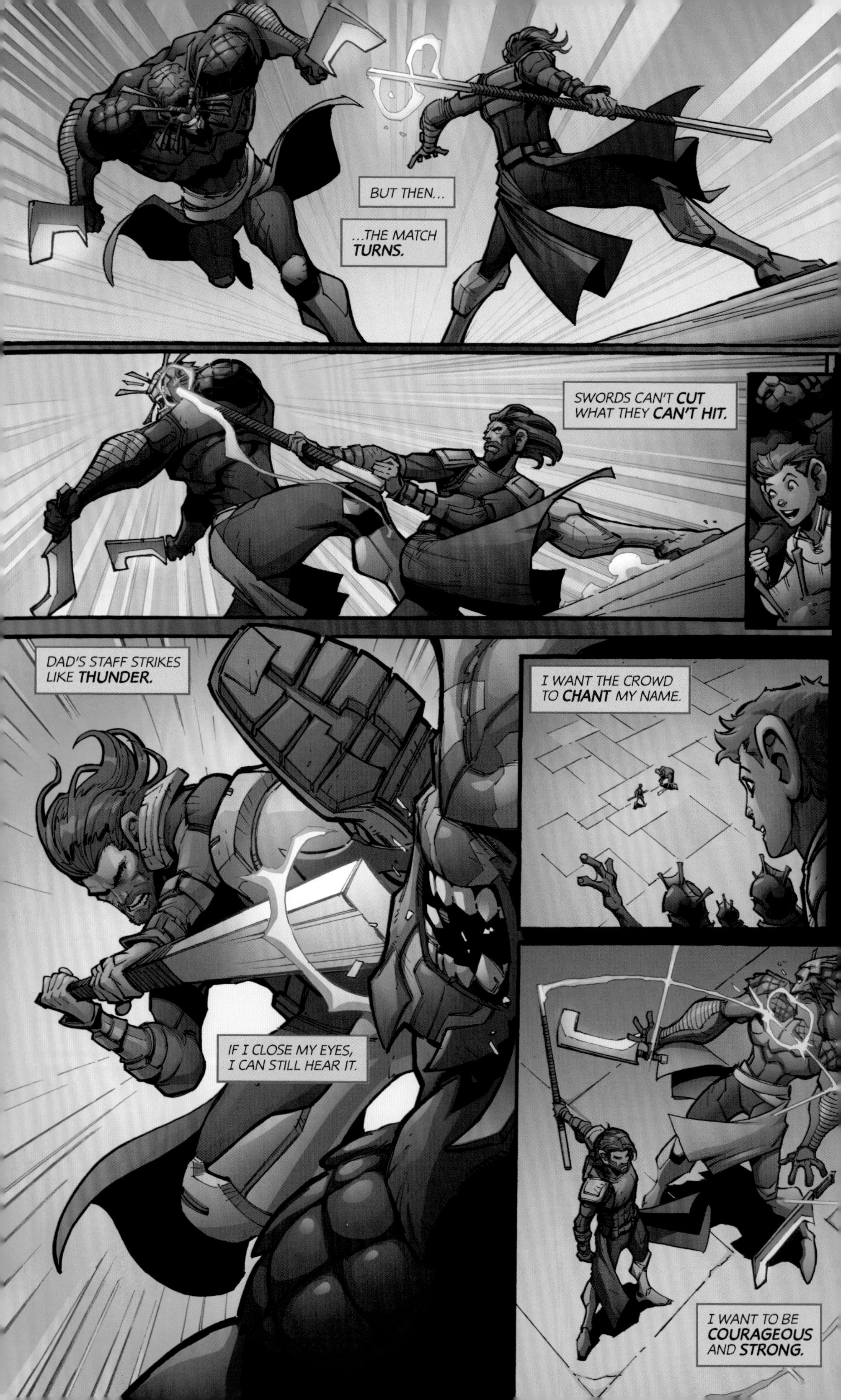
BUT THEN...
...THE MATCH TURNS.
SWORDS CAN'T CUT WHAT THEY CAN'T HIT.
DAD'S STAFF STRIKES LIKE THUNDER.
I WANT THE CROWD TO CHANT MY NAME.
IF I CLOSE MY EYES, I CAN STILL HEAR IT.
I WANT TO BE COURAGEOUS AND STRONG.

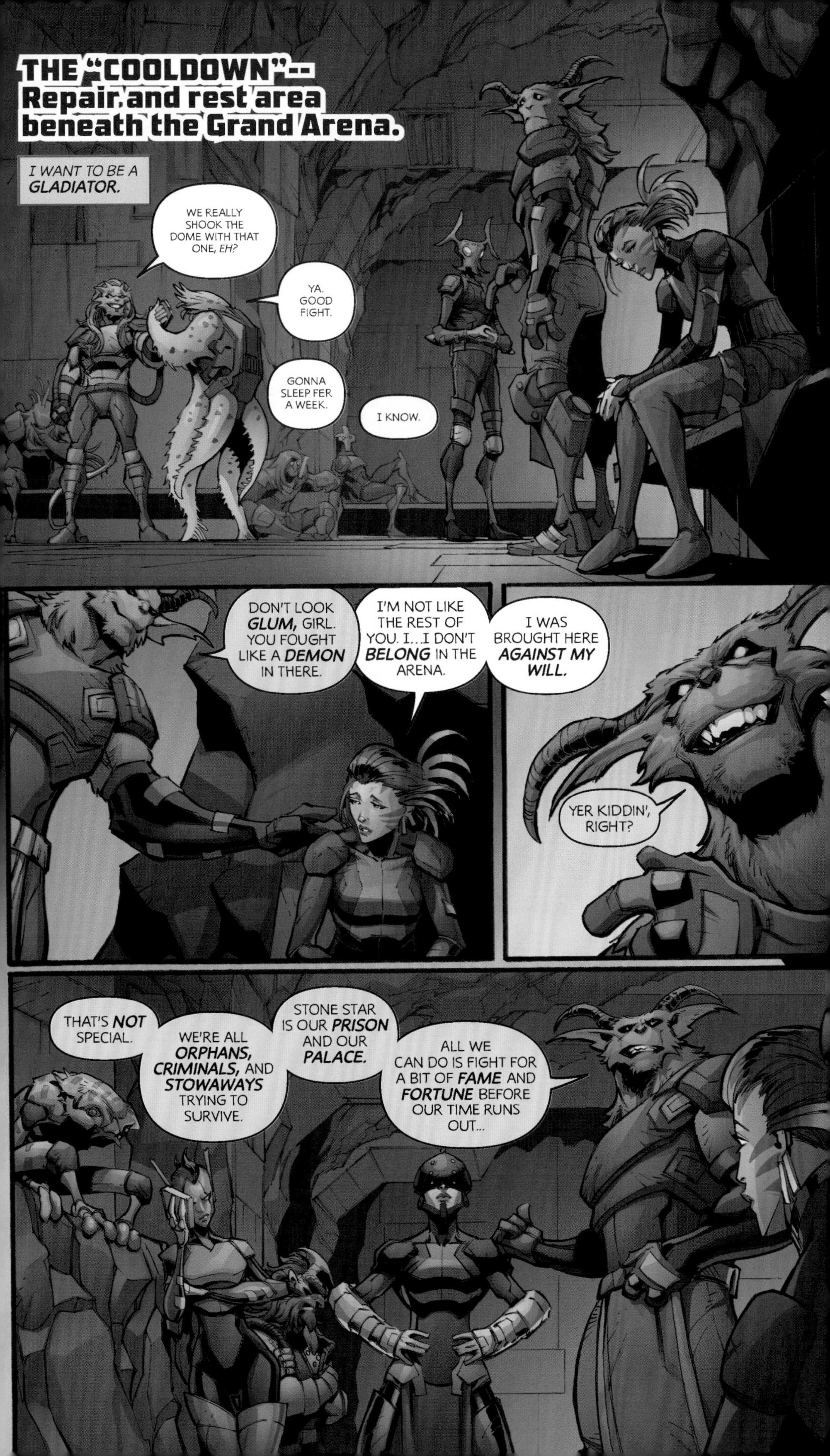

THE "COOLDOWN"-- Repair and rest area beneath the Grand Arena.
I WANT TO BE A GLADIATOR.
WE REALLY SHOOK THE DOME WITH THAT ONE, EH?
YA. GOOD FIGHT.
GONNA SLEEP FER A WEEK.
I KNOW.
DON'T LOOK GLUM, GIRL. YOU FOUGHT LIKE A DEMON IN THERE.
I'M NOT LIKE THE REST OF YOU. I...I DON'T BELONG IN THE ARENA.
I WAS BROUGHT HERE AGAINST MY WILL.
YER KIDDIN', RIGHT?
THAT'S NOT SPECIAL.
WE'RE ALL ORPHANS, CRIMINALS, AND STOWAWAYS TRYING TO SURVIVE.
STONE STAR IS OUR PRISON AND OUR PALACE.
ALL WE CAN DO IS FIGHT FOR A BIT OF FAME AND FORTUNE BEFORE OUR TIME RUNS OUT...

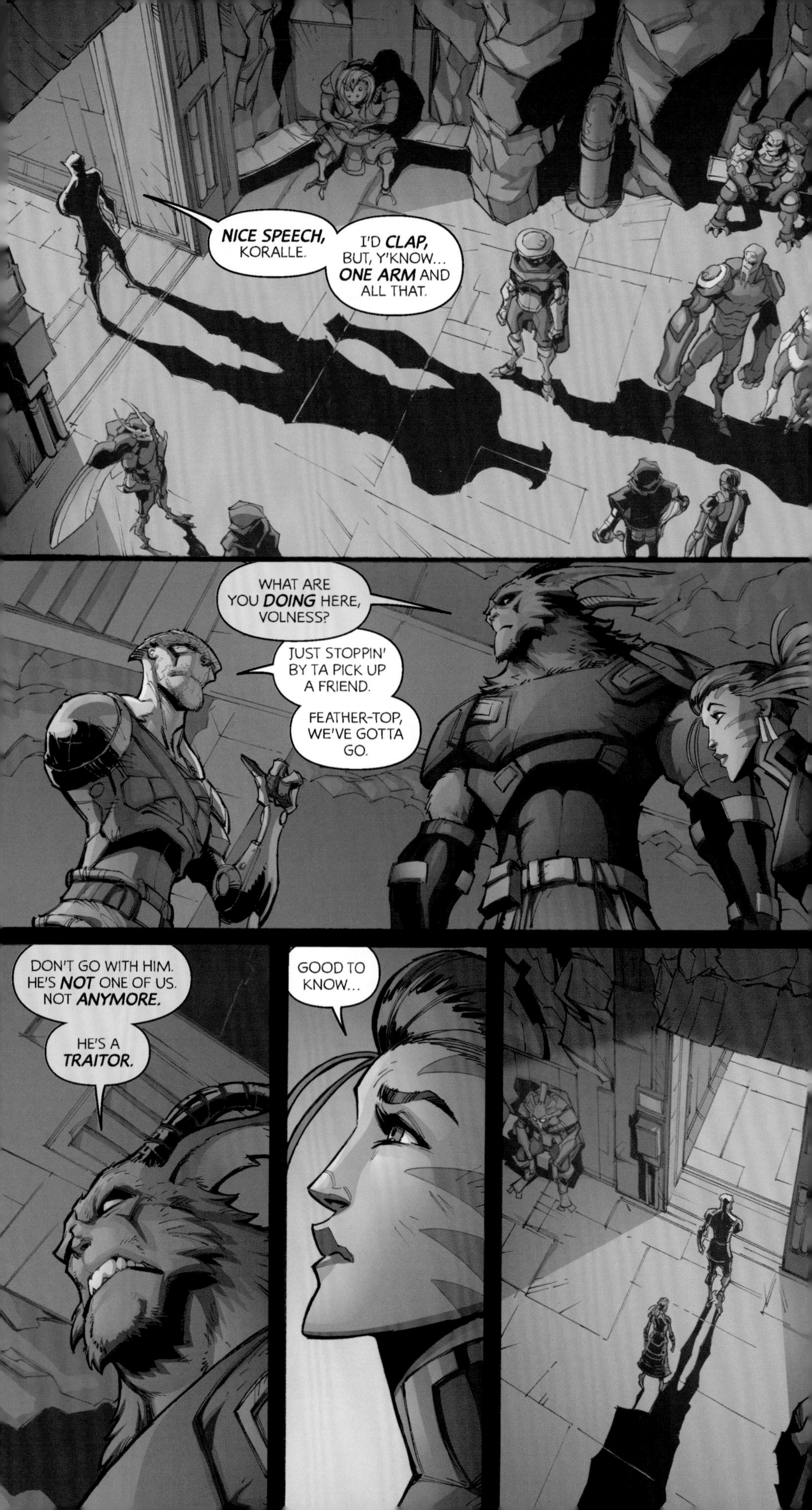
NICE SPEECH, KORALLE.
I'D CLAP, BUT, Y'KNOW... ONE ARM AND ALL THAT.
WHAT ARE YOU DOING HERE, VOLNESS?
JUST STOPPIN' BY TA PICK UP A FRIEND.
FEATHER-TOP, WE'VE GOTTA GO.
DON'T GO WITH HIM. HE'S NOT ONE OF US. NOT ANYMORE.
HE'S A TRAITOR.
GOOD TO KNOW...

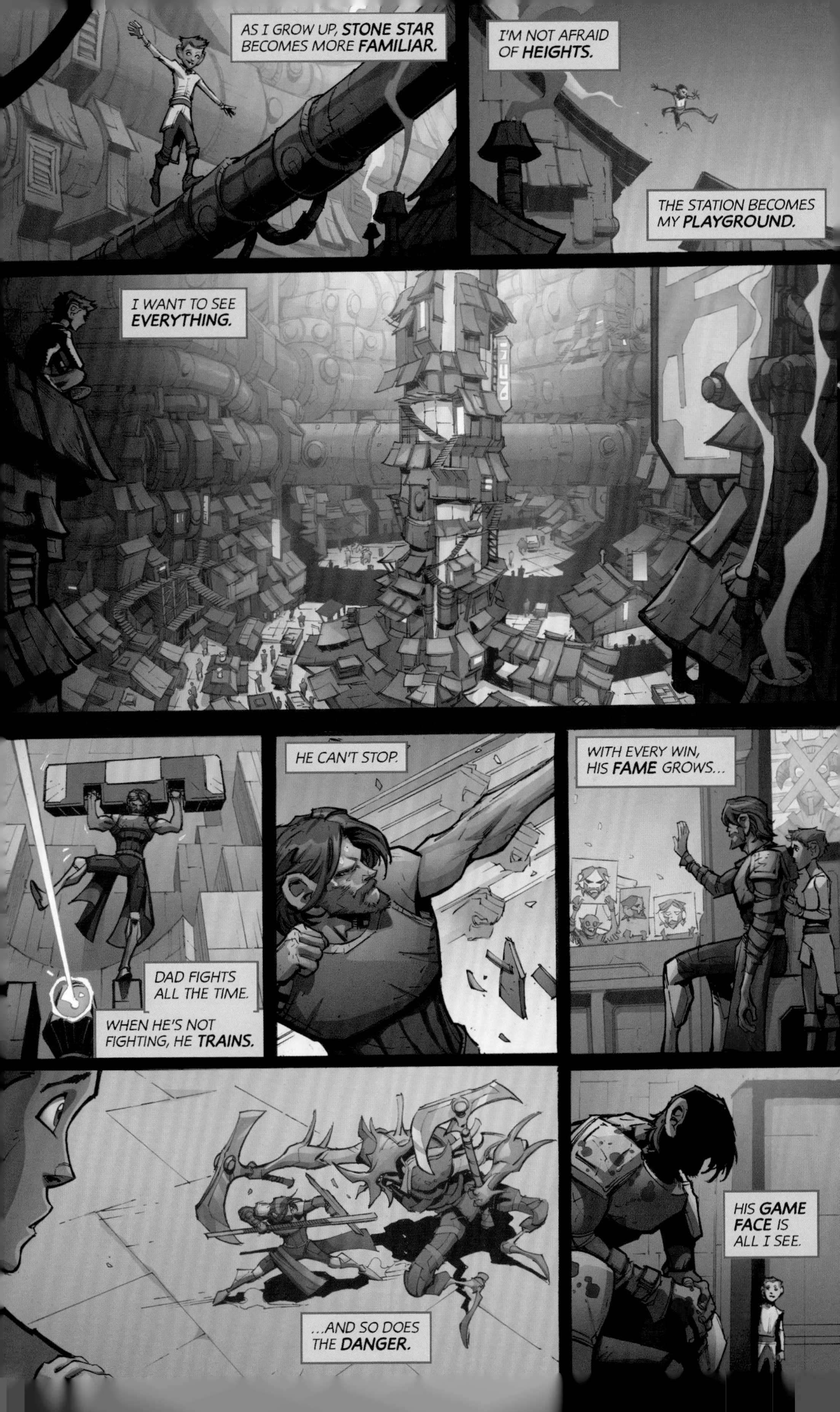

AS I GROW UP, STONE STAR BECOMES MORE FAMILIAR.
I'M NOT AFRAID OF HEIGHTS.
THE STATION BECOMES MY PLAYGROUND.
I WANT TO SEE EVERYTHING.
DAD FIGHTS ALL THE TIME.
WHEN HE'S NOT FIGHTING, HE TRAINS.
HE CAN'T STOP.
WITH EVERY WIN, HIS FAME GROWS...
...AND SO DOES THE DANGER.
HIS GAME FACE IS ALL I SEE.

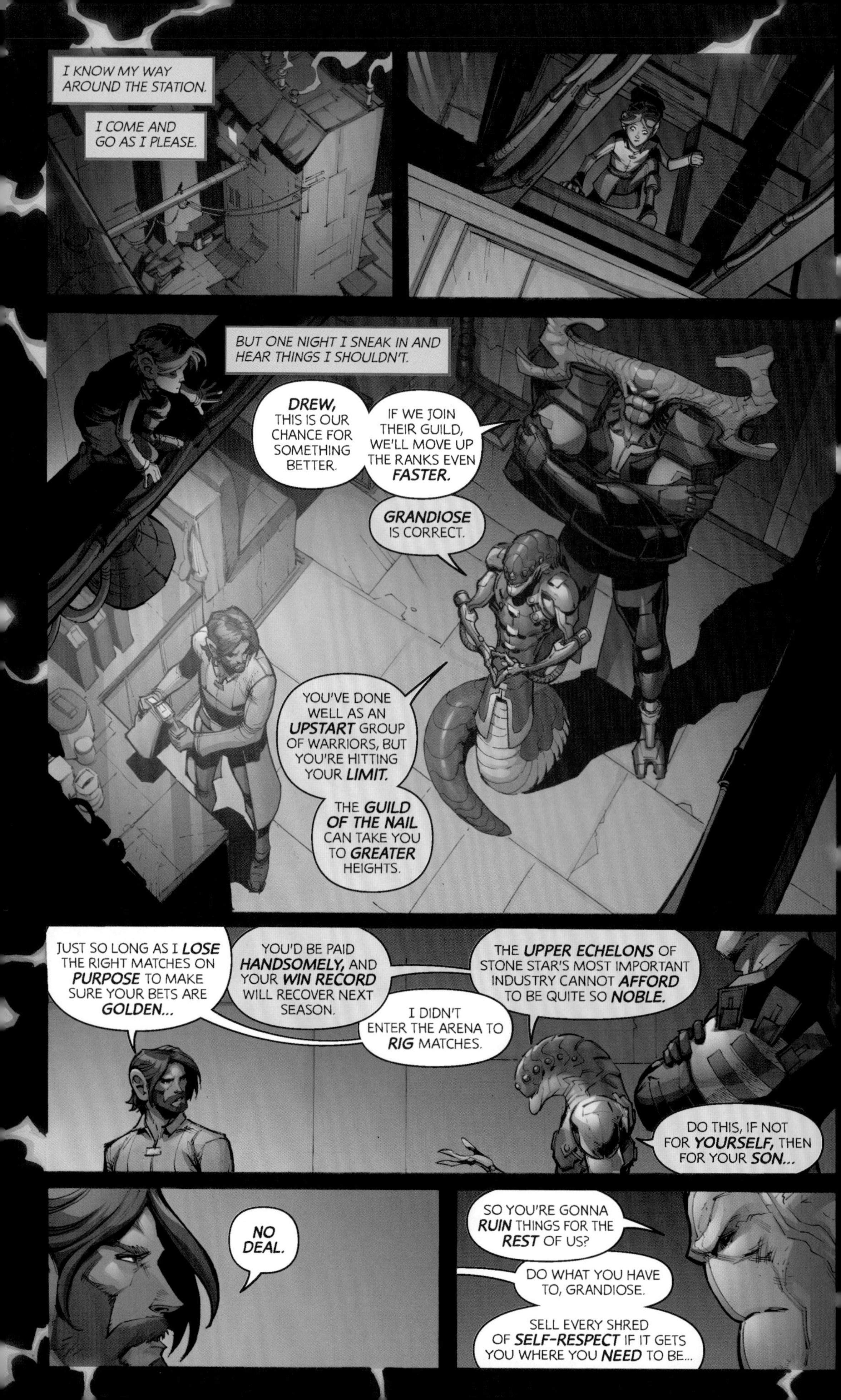

I KNOW MY WAY AROUND THE STATION.
I COME AND GO AS I PLEASE.
BUT ONE NIGHT I SNEAK IN AND HEAR THINGS I SHOULDN'T.
DREW, THIS IS OUR CHANCE FOR SOMETHING BETTER.
IF WE JOIN THEIR GUILD, WE'LL MOVE UP THE RANKS EVEN FASTER.
GRANDIOSE IS CORRECT.
YOU'VE DONE WELL AS AN UPSTART GROUP OF WARRIORS, BUT YOU'RE HITTING YOUR LIMIT.
THE GUILD OF THE NAIL CAN TAKE YOU TO GREATER HEIGHTS.
JUST SO LONG AS I LOSE THE RIGHT MATCHES ON PURPOSE TO MAKE SURE YOUR BETS ARE GOLDEN...
YOU'D BE PAID HANDSOMELY, AND YOUR WIN RECORD WILL RECOVER NEXT SEASON.
I DIDN'T ENTER THE ARENA TO RIG MATCHES.
THE UPPER ECHELONS OF STONE STAR'S MOST IMPORTANT INDUSTRY CANNOT AFFORD TO BE QUITE SO NOBLE.
DO THIS, IF NOT FOR YOURSELF, THEN FOR YOUR SON...
NO DEAL.
SO YOU'RE GONNA RUIN THINGS FOR THE REST OF US?
DO WHAT YOU HAVE TO, GRANDIOSE.
SELL EVERY SHRED OF SELF-RESPECT IF IT GETS YOU WHERE YOU NEED TO BE...

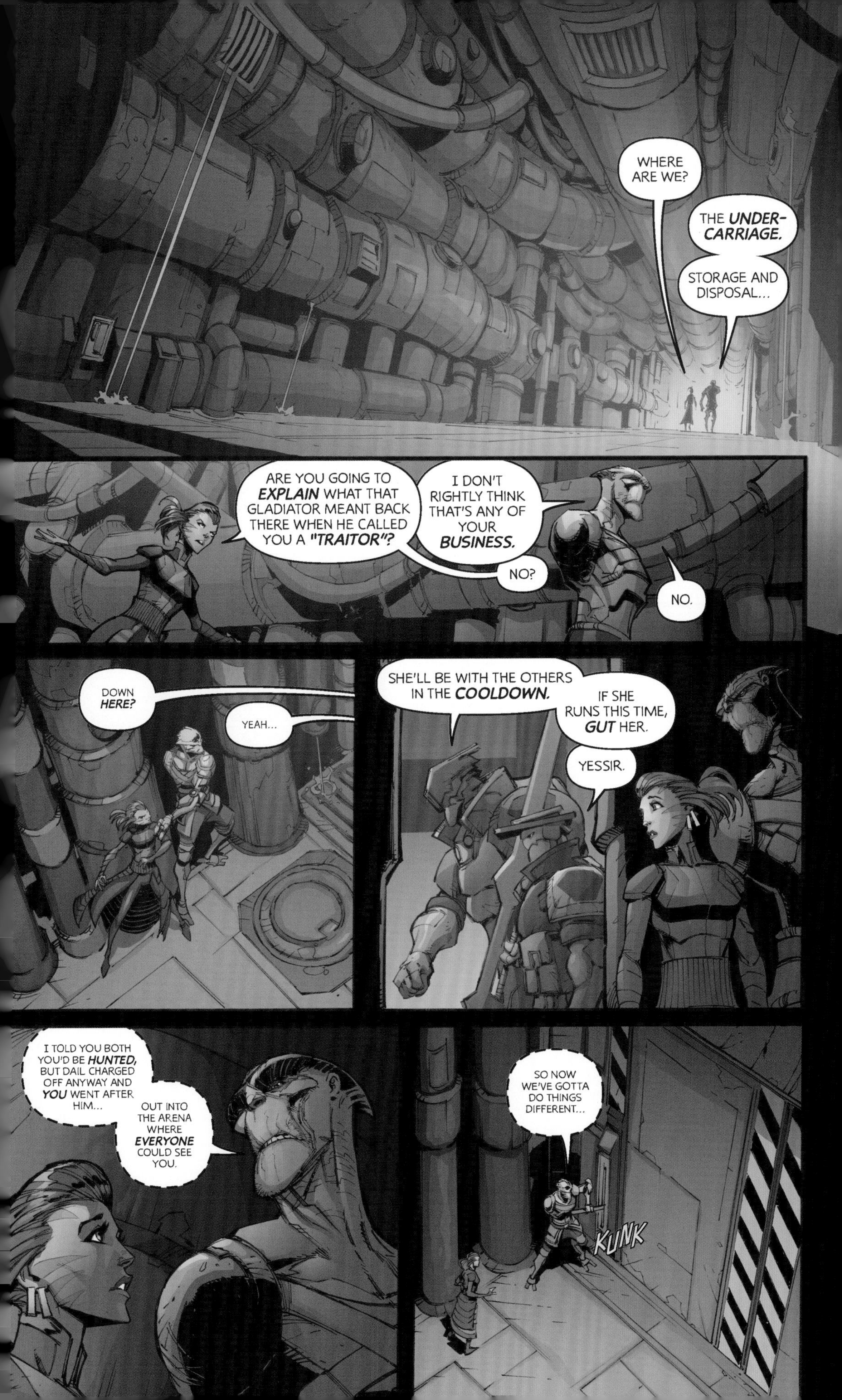
WHERE ARE WE?
THE UNDER-CARRIAGE.
STORAGE AND DISPOSAL...
ARE YOU GOING TO EXPLAIN WHAT THAT GLADIATOR MEANT BACK THERE WHEN HE CALLED YOU A "TRAITOR"?
I DON'T RIGHTLY THINK THAT'S ANY OF YOUR BUSINESS.
NO?
NO.
DOWN HERE?
YEAH...
SHE'LL BE WITH THE OTHERS IN THE COOLDOWN.
IF SHE RUNS THIS TIME, GUT HER.
YESSIR.
I TOLD YOU BOTH YOU'D BE HUNTED, BUT DAIL CHARGED OFF ANYWAY AND YOU WENT AFTER HIM...
OUT INTO THE ARENA WHERE EVERYONE COULD SEE YOU.
SO NOW WE'VE GOTTA DO THINGS DIFFERENT...
KUNK

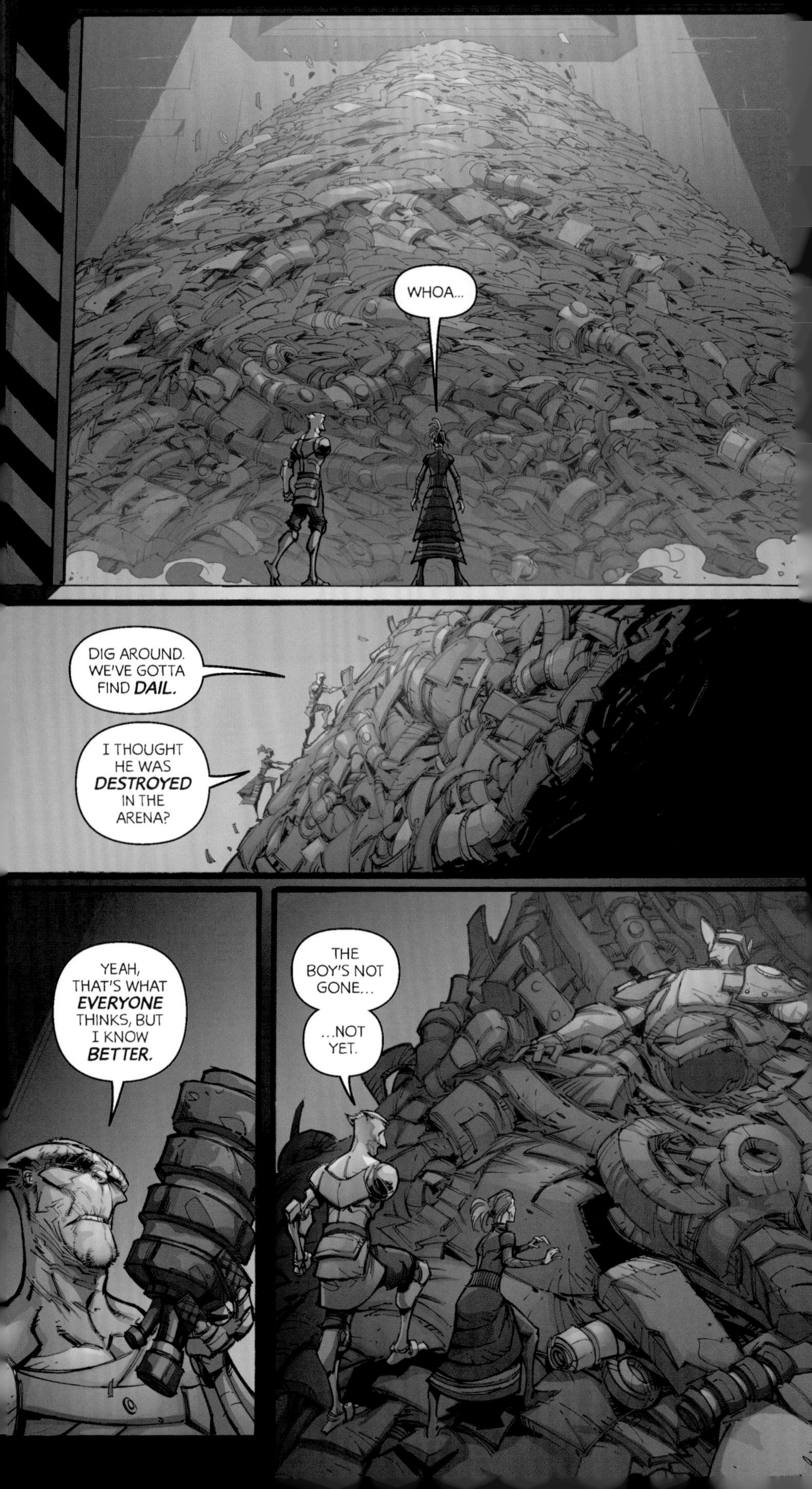
WHOA...
DIG AROUND. WE'VE GOTTA FIND DAIL.
I THOUGHT HE WAS DESTROYED IN THE ARENA?
YEAH, THAT'S WHAT EVERYONE THINKS, BUT I KNOW BETTER.
THE BOY'S NOT GONE...
...NOT YET.

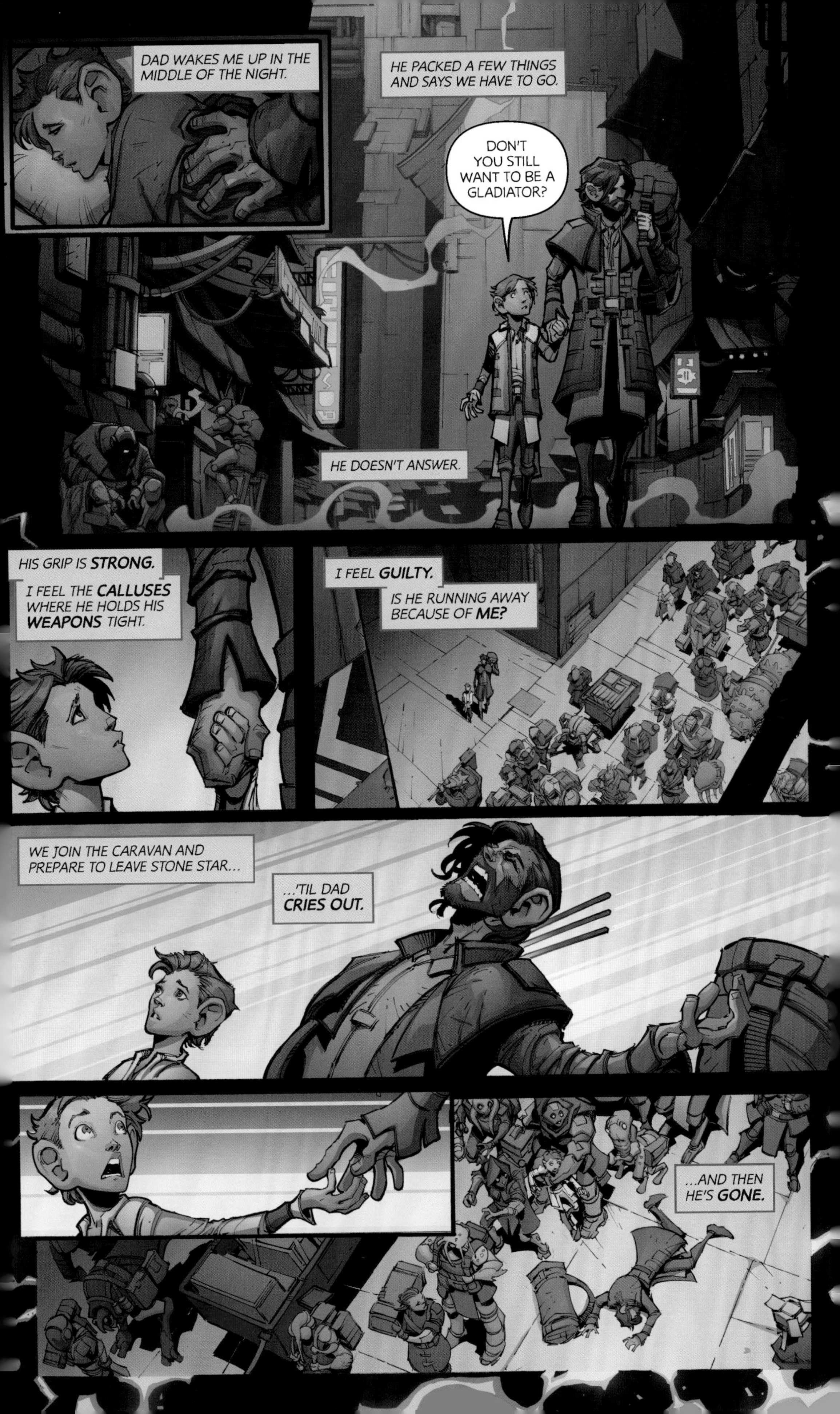

DAD WAKES ME UP IN THE MIDDLE OF THE NIGHT.
HE PACKED A FEW THINGS AND SAYS WE HAVE TO GO.
DON'T YOU STILL WANT TO BE A GLADIATOR?
HE DOESN'T ANSWER.
HIS GRIP IS **STRONG.**
I FEEL THE **CALLUSES** WHERE HE HOLDS HIS **WEAPONS** TIGHT.
I FEEL **GUILTY.**
IS HE RUNNING AWAY BECAUSE OF **ME?**
WE JOIN THE CARAVAN AND PREPARE TO LEAVE STONE STAR...
...'TIL DAD **CRIES OUT.**
...AND THEN HE'S **GONE.**

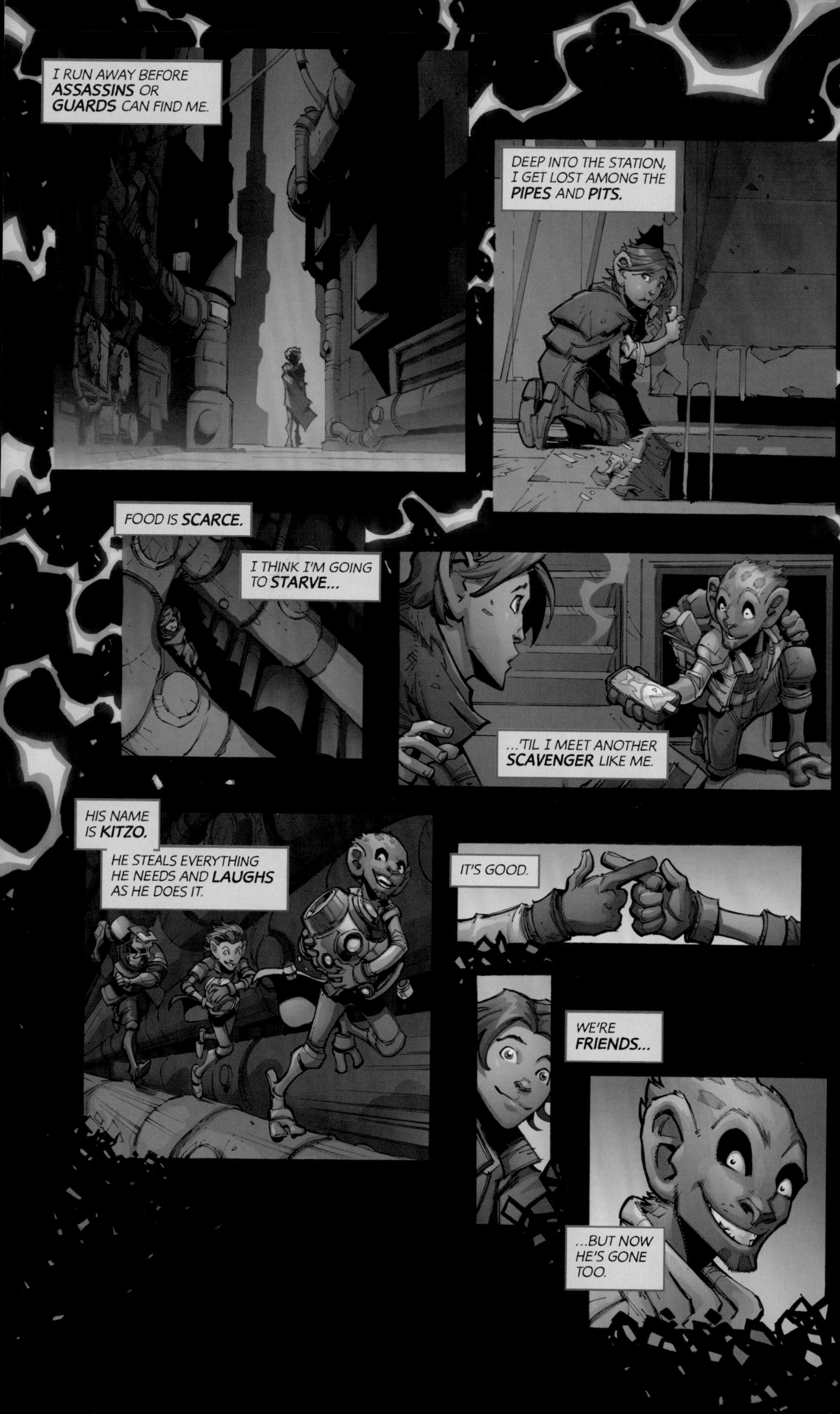
I RUN AWAY BEFORE ASSASSINS OR GUARDS CAN FIND ME.
DEEP INTO THE STATION, I GET LOST AMONG THE PIPES AND PITS.
FOOD IS SCARCE.
I THINK I'M GOING TO STARVE...
...'TIL I MEET ANOTHER SCAVENGER LIKE ME.
HIS NAME IS KITZO.
HE STEALS EVERYTHING HE NEEDS AND LAUGHS AS HE DOES IT.
IT'S GOOD.
WE'RE FRIENDS...
...BUT NOW HE'S GONE TOO.

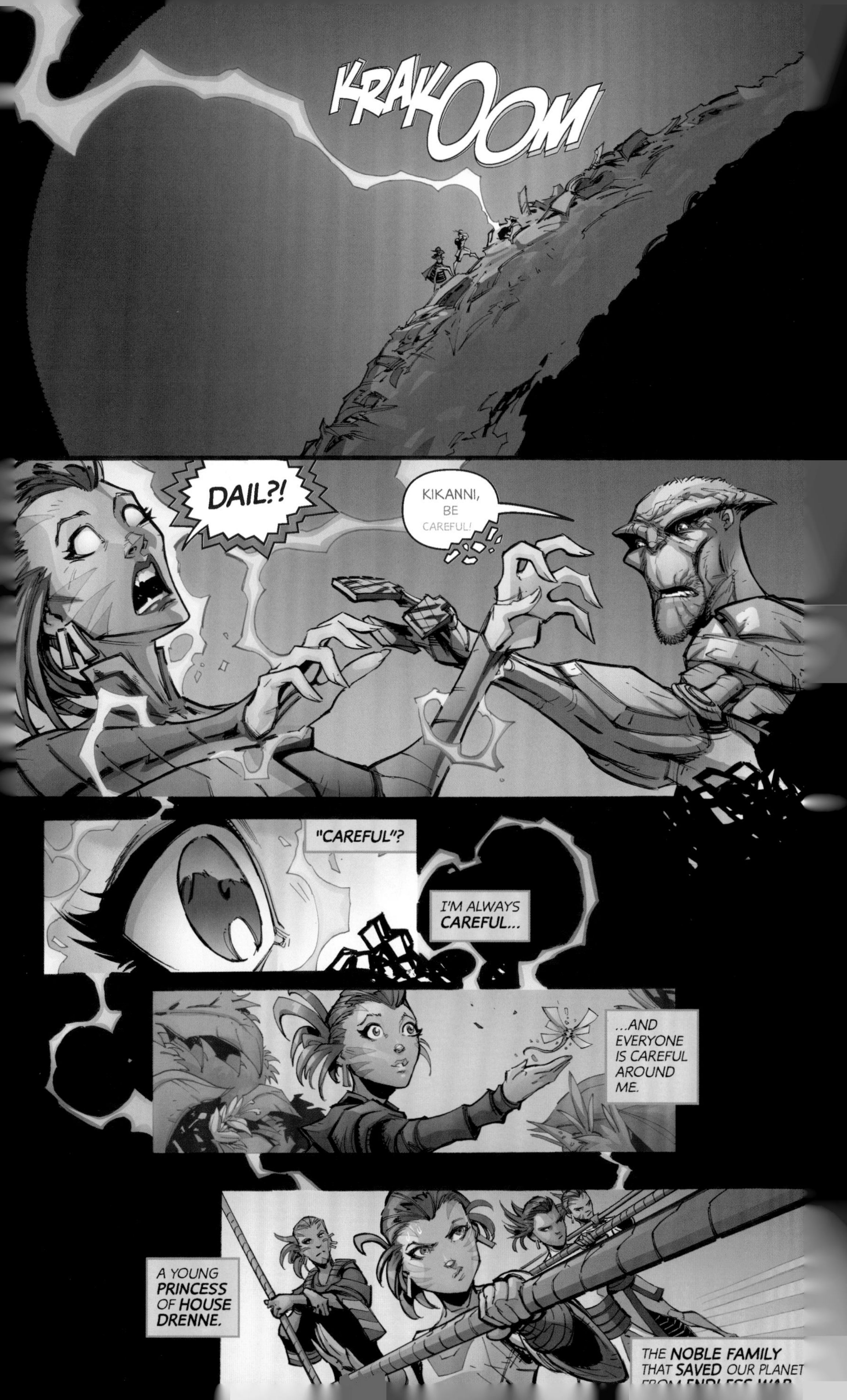
KRAKOOOM
DAIL?!
KIKANNI, BE CAREFUL!
"CAREFUL"?
I'M ALWAYS CAREFUL...
...AND EVERYONE IS CAREFUL AROUND ME.
A YOUNG PRINCESS OF HOUSE DRENNE.
THE NOBLE FAMILY THAT SAVED OUR PLANET

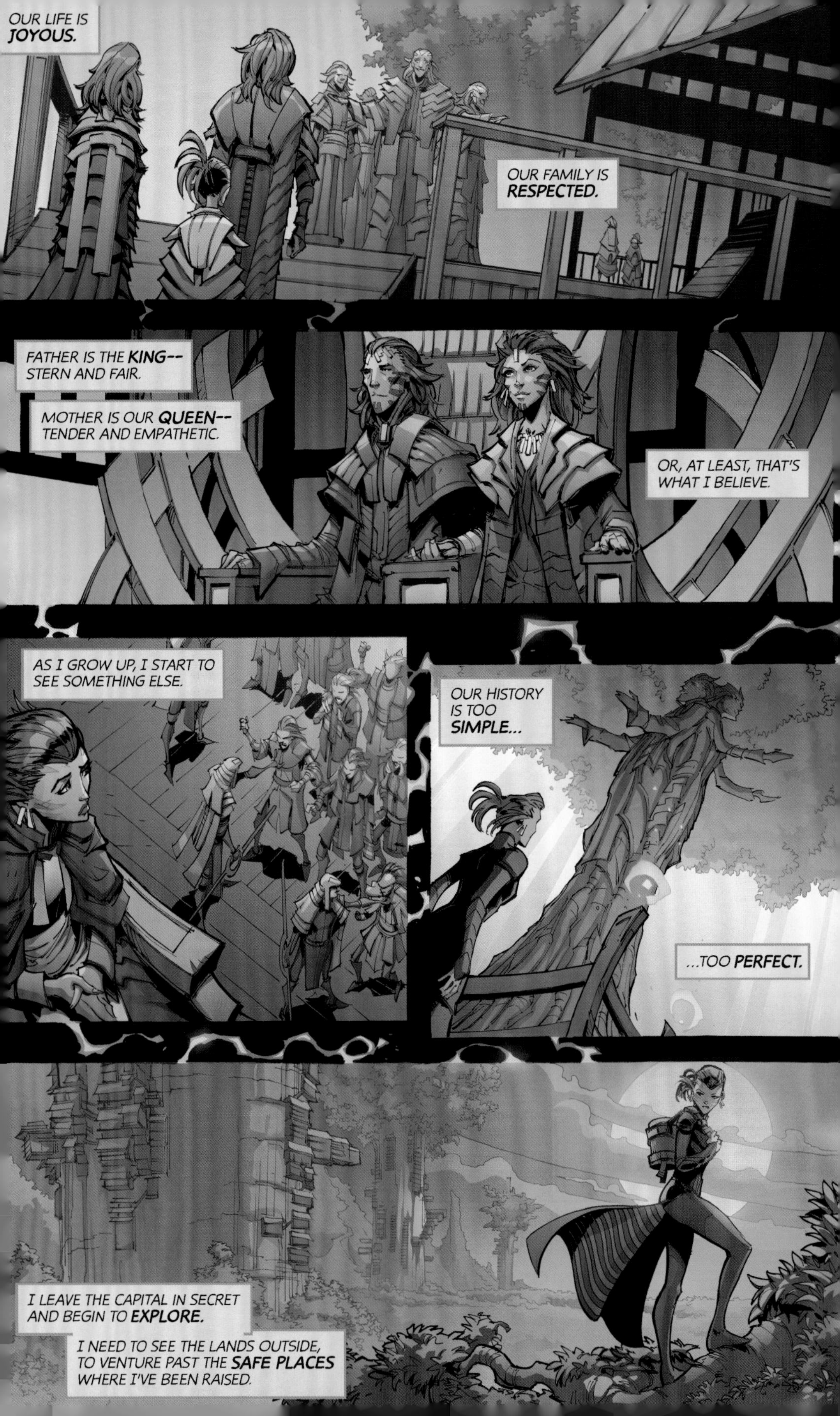
OUR LIFE IS **JOYOUS.**
OUR FAMILY IS **RESPECTED.**
FATHER IS THE **KING--** STERN AND FAIR.
MOTHER IS OUR **QUEEN--** TENDER AND EMPATHETIC.
OR, AT LEAST, THAT'S WHAT I BELIEVE.
AS I GROW UP, I START TO SEE SOMETHING ELSE.
OUR HISTORY IS TOO **SIMPLE...**
...TOO **PERFECT.**
I LEAVE THE CAPITAL IN SECRET AND BEGIN TO **EXPLORE.**
I NEED TO SEE THE LANDS OUTSIDE, TO VENTURE PAST THE **SAFE PLACES** WHERE I'VE BEEN RAISED.

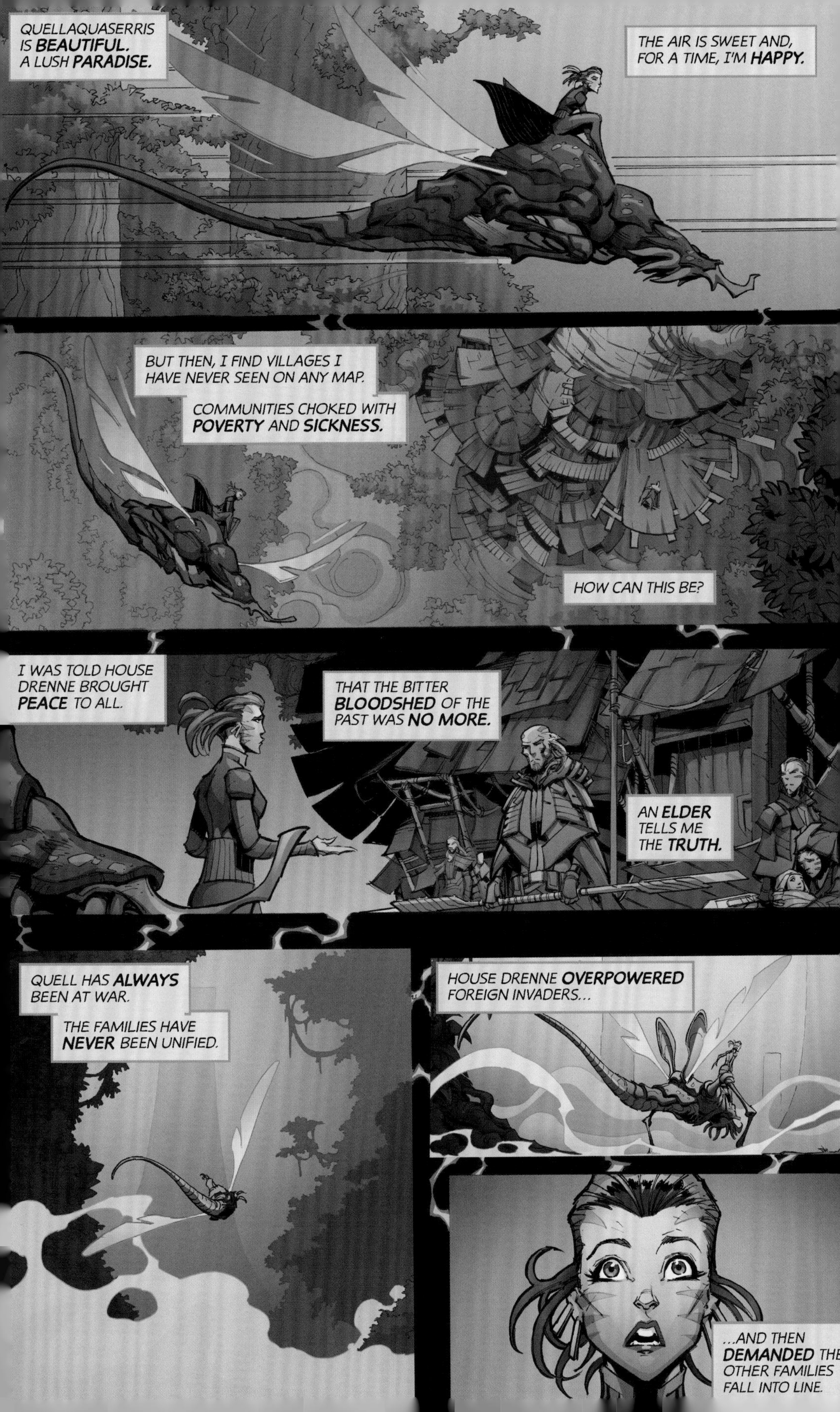
QUELLAQUASERRIS IS BEAUTIFUL. A LUSH PARADISE.
THE AIR IS SWEET AND, FOR A TIME, I'M HAPPY.
BUT THEN, I FIND VILLAGES I HAVE NEVER SEEN ON ANY MAP.
COMMUNITIES CHOKED WITH POVERTY AND SICKNESS.
HOW CAN THIS BE?
I WAS TOLD HOUSE DRENNE BROUGHT PEACE TO ALL.
THAT THE BITTER BLOODSHED OF THE PAST WAS NO MORE.
AN ELDER TELLS ME THE TRUTH.
QUELL HAS ALWAYS BEEN AT WAR.
THE FAMILIES HAVE NEVER BEEN UNIFIED.
HOUSE DRENNE OVERPOWERED FOREIGN INVADERS...
...AND THEN DEMANDED THE OTHER FAMILIES FALL INTO LINE.

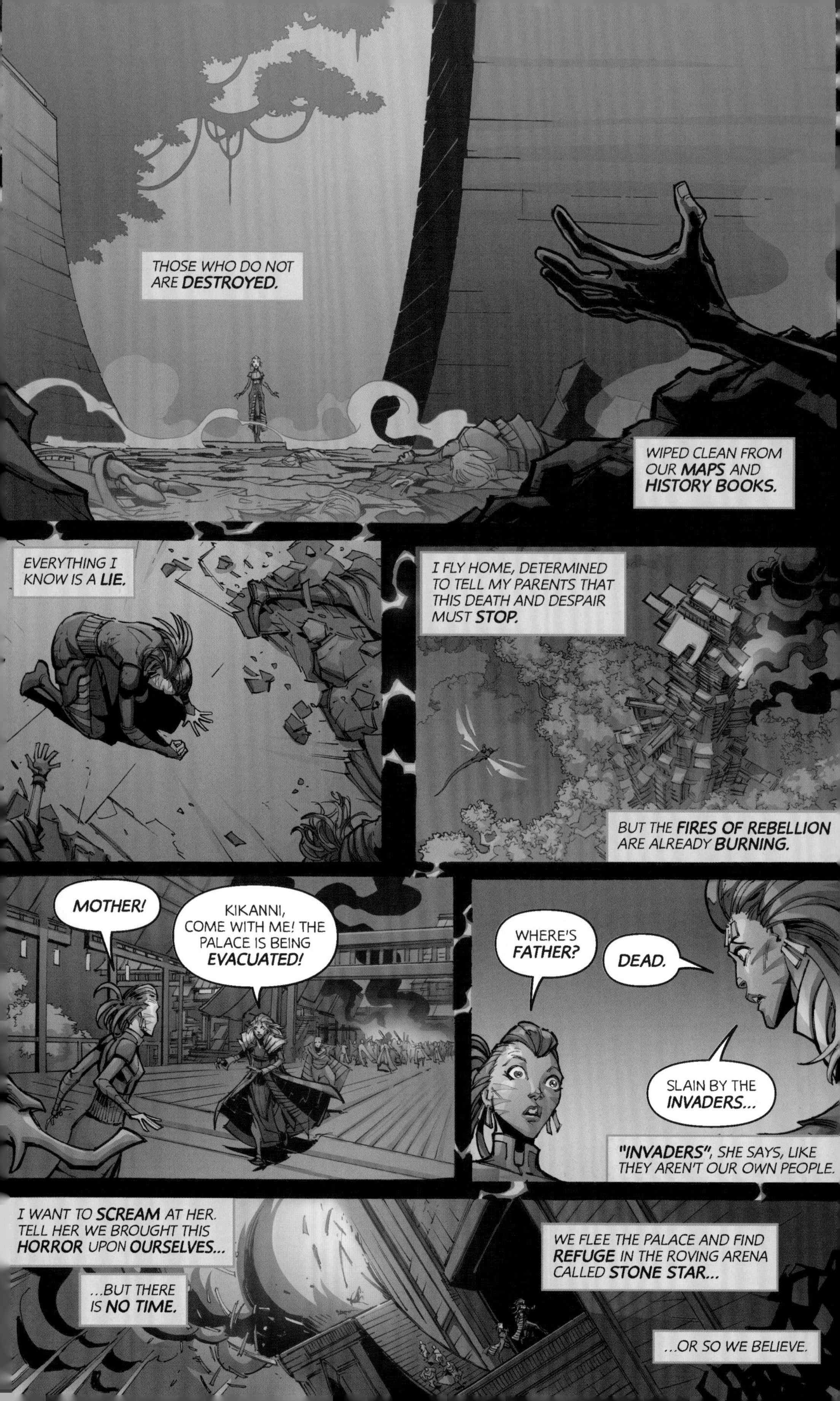
THOSE WHO DO NOT ARE DESTROYED.
WIPED CLEAN FROM OUR MAPS AND HISTORY BOOKS.
EVERYTHING I KNOW IS A LIE.
I FLY HOME, DETERMINED TO TELL MY PARENTS THAT THIS DEATH AND DESPAIR MUST STOP.
BUT THE FIRES OF REBELLION ARE ALREADY BURNING.
MOTHER!
KIKANNI, COME WITH ME! THE PALACE IS BEING EVACUATED!
WHERE'S FATHER?
DEAD.
SLAIN BY THE INVADERS...
"INVADERS", SHE SAYS, LIKE THEY AREN'T OUR OWN PEOPLE.
I WANT TO SCREAM AT HER. TELL HER WE BROUGHT THIS HORROR UPON OURSELVES...
...BUT THERE IS NO TIME.
WE FLEE THE PALACE AND FIND REFUGE IN THE ROVING ARENA CALLED STONE STAR...
...OR SO WE BELIEVE.

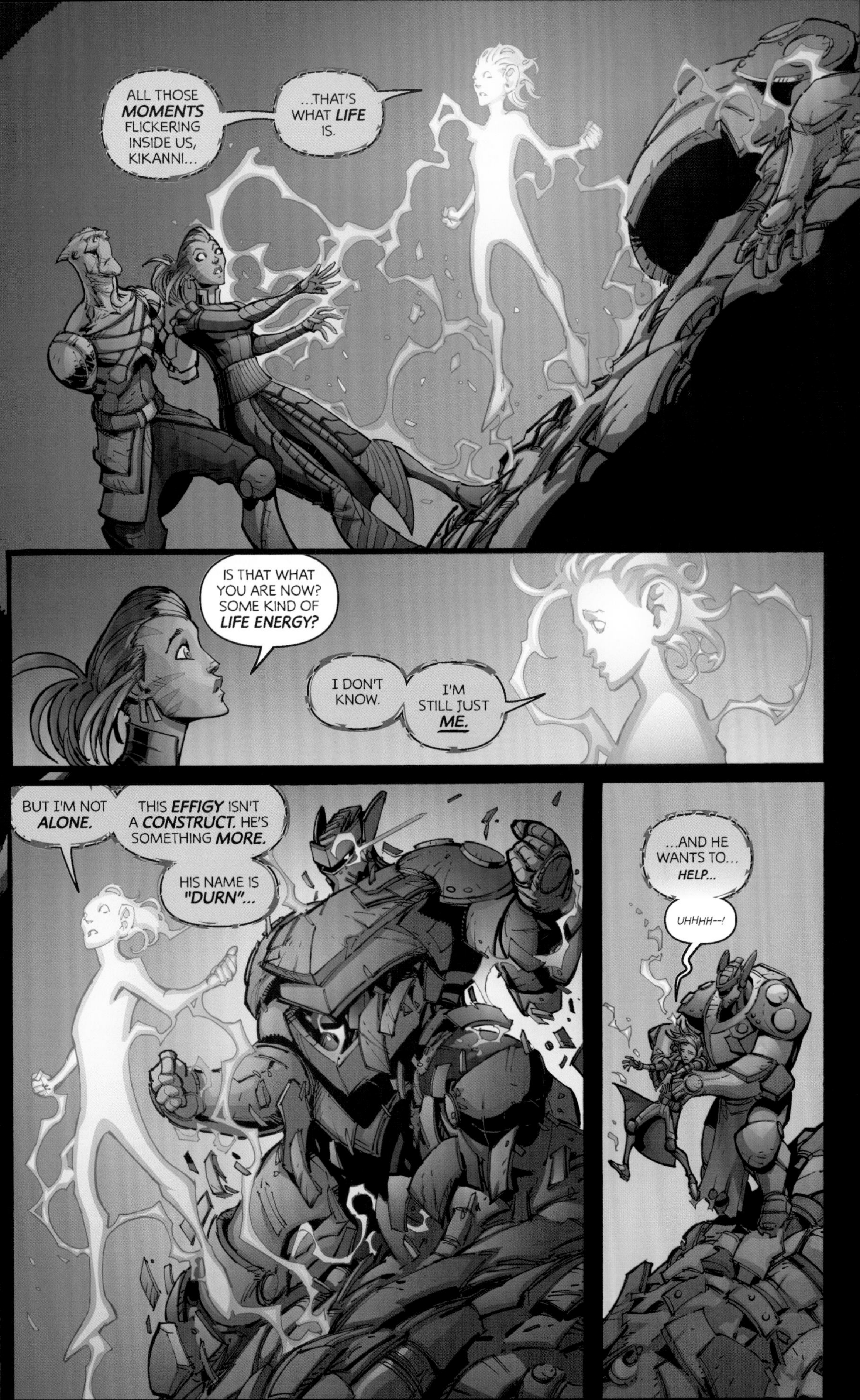
ALL THOSE MOMENTS FLICKERING INSIDE US, KIKANNI...
...THAT'S WHAT LIFE IS.
IS THAT WHAT YOU ARE NOW? SOME KIND OF LIFE ENERGY?
I DON'T KNOW.
I'M STILL JUST ME.
BUT I'M NOT ALONE.
THIS EFFIGY ISN'T A CONSTRUCT. HE'S SOMETHING MORE.
HIS NAME IS "DURN"...
...AND HE WANTS TO... HELP...
UHHHH--!

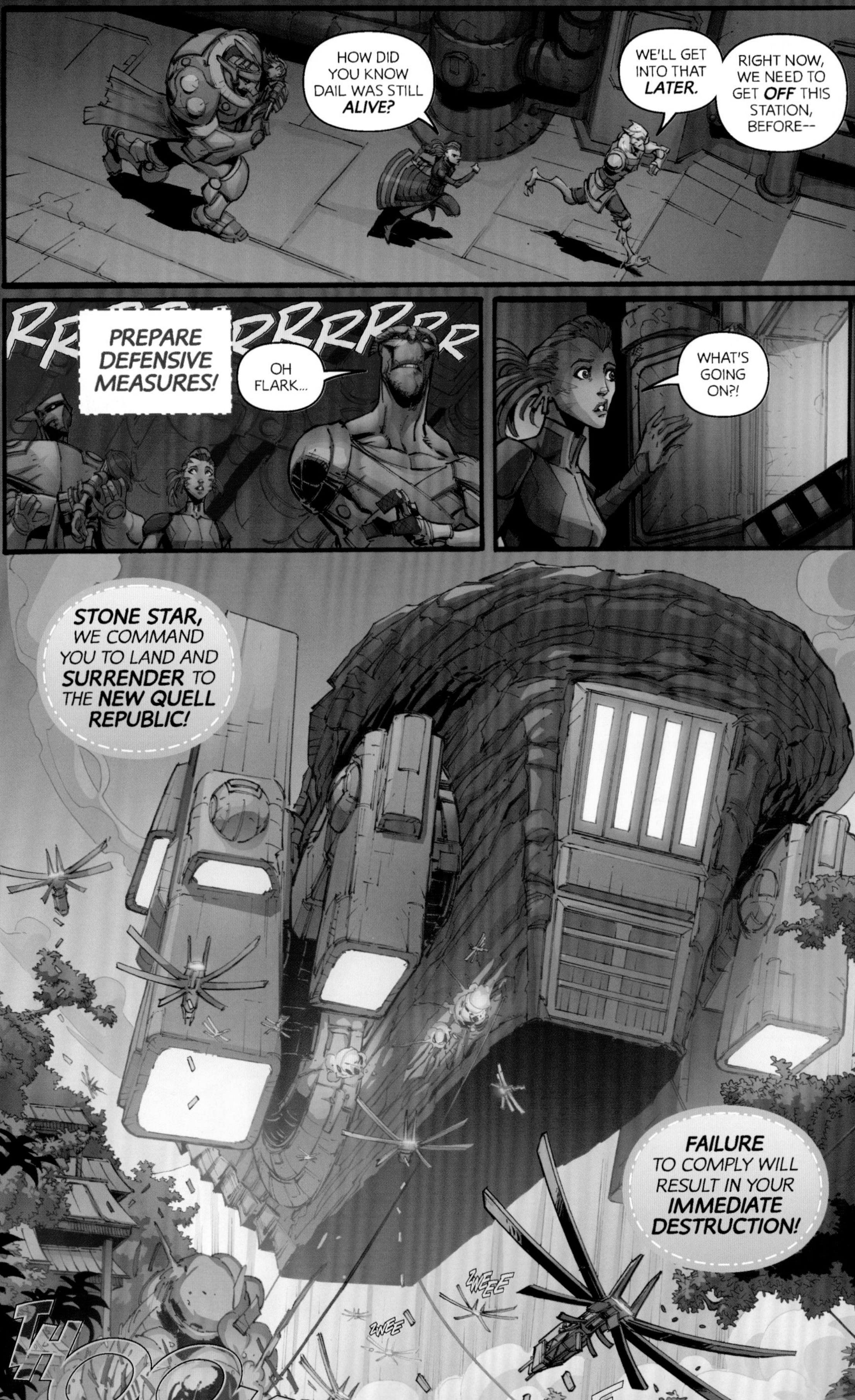

HOW DID YOU KNOW DAIL WAS STILL ALIVE?
WE'LL GET INTO THAT LATER.
RIGHT NOW, WE NEED TO GET OFF THIS STATION, BEFORE--
RRRRRRRRRRRr
PREPARE DEFENSIVE MEASURES!
OH FLARK...
WHAT'S GOING ON?!
STONE STAR, WE COMMAND YOU TO LAND AND SURRENDER TO THE NEW QUELL REPUBLIC!
FAILURE TO COMPLY WILL RESULT IN YOUR IMMEDIATE DESTRUCTION!
ZWEEE
ZWEE
THOOOM
ZWEE
ZWEEEE

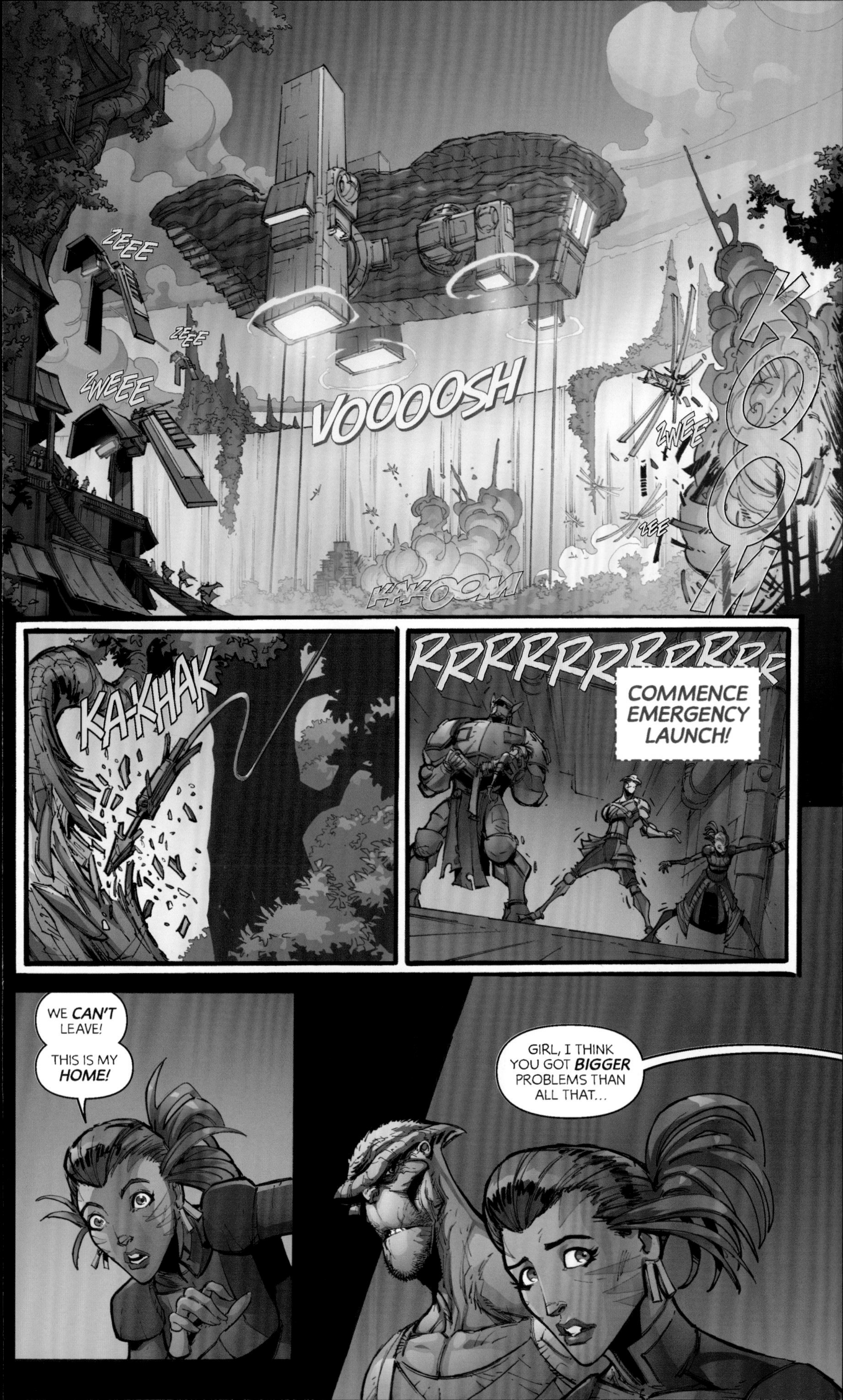
ZEEE
ZEEE
ZWEEE
VOOOOSH
ZWEE
ZEE
KABOOM
KAKOOM
KA-KHAK
RRRRRRRRRRR
COMMENCE EMERGENCY LAUNCH!
WE CAN'T LEAVE!
THIS IS MY HOME!
GIRL, I THINK YOU GOT BIGGER PROBLEMS THAN ALL THAT...

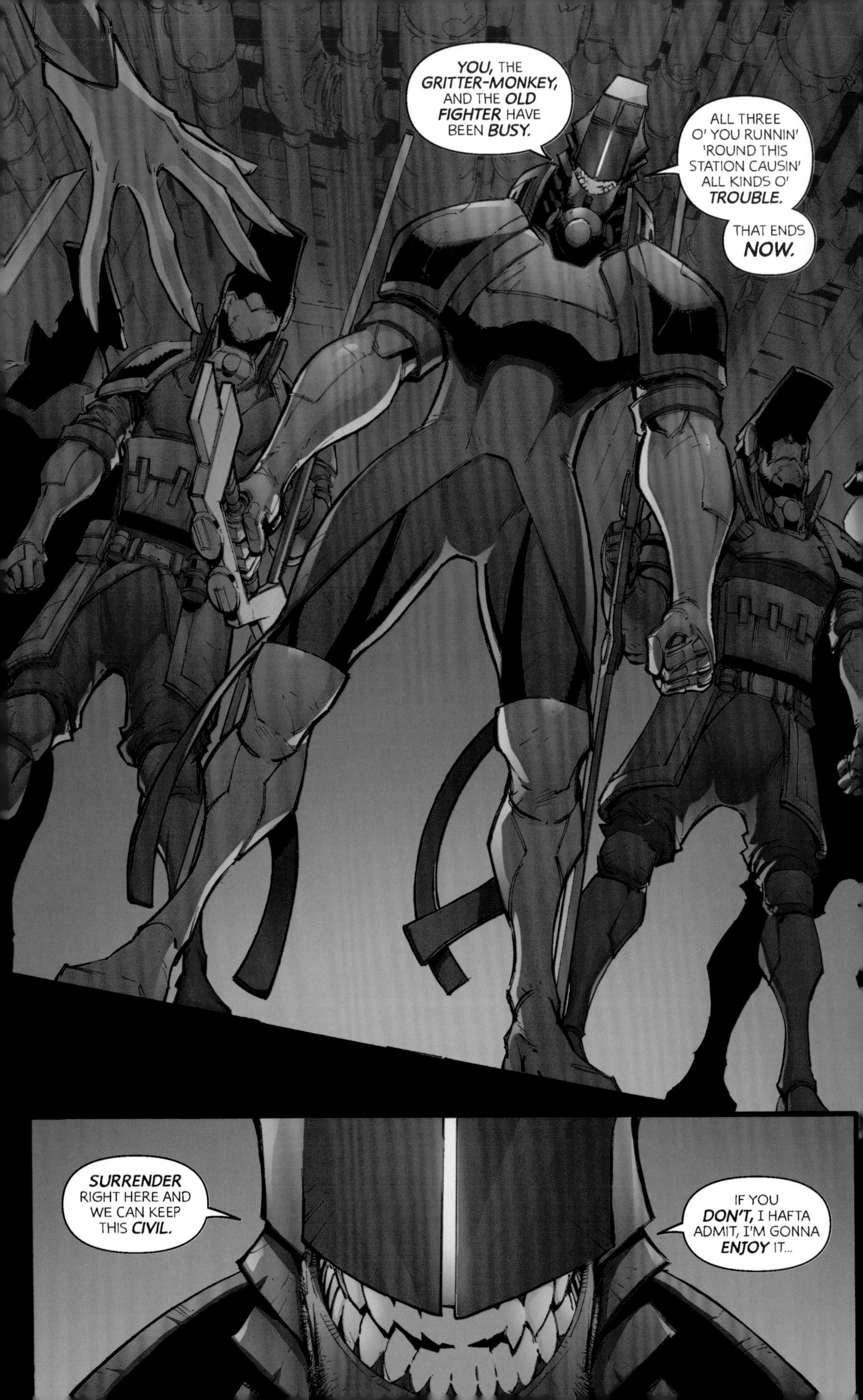

YOU, THE GRITTER-MONKEY, AND THE OLD FIGHTER HAVE BEEN BUSY.
ALL THREE O' YOU RUNNIN' 'ROUND THIS STATION CAUSIN' ALL KINDS O' TROUBLE.
THAT ENDS NOW.
SURRENDER RIGHT HERE AND WE CAN KEEP THIS CIVIL.
IF YOU DON'T, I HAFTA ADMIT, I'M GONNA ENJOY IT...

Chapter 5: Fight or Flight

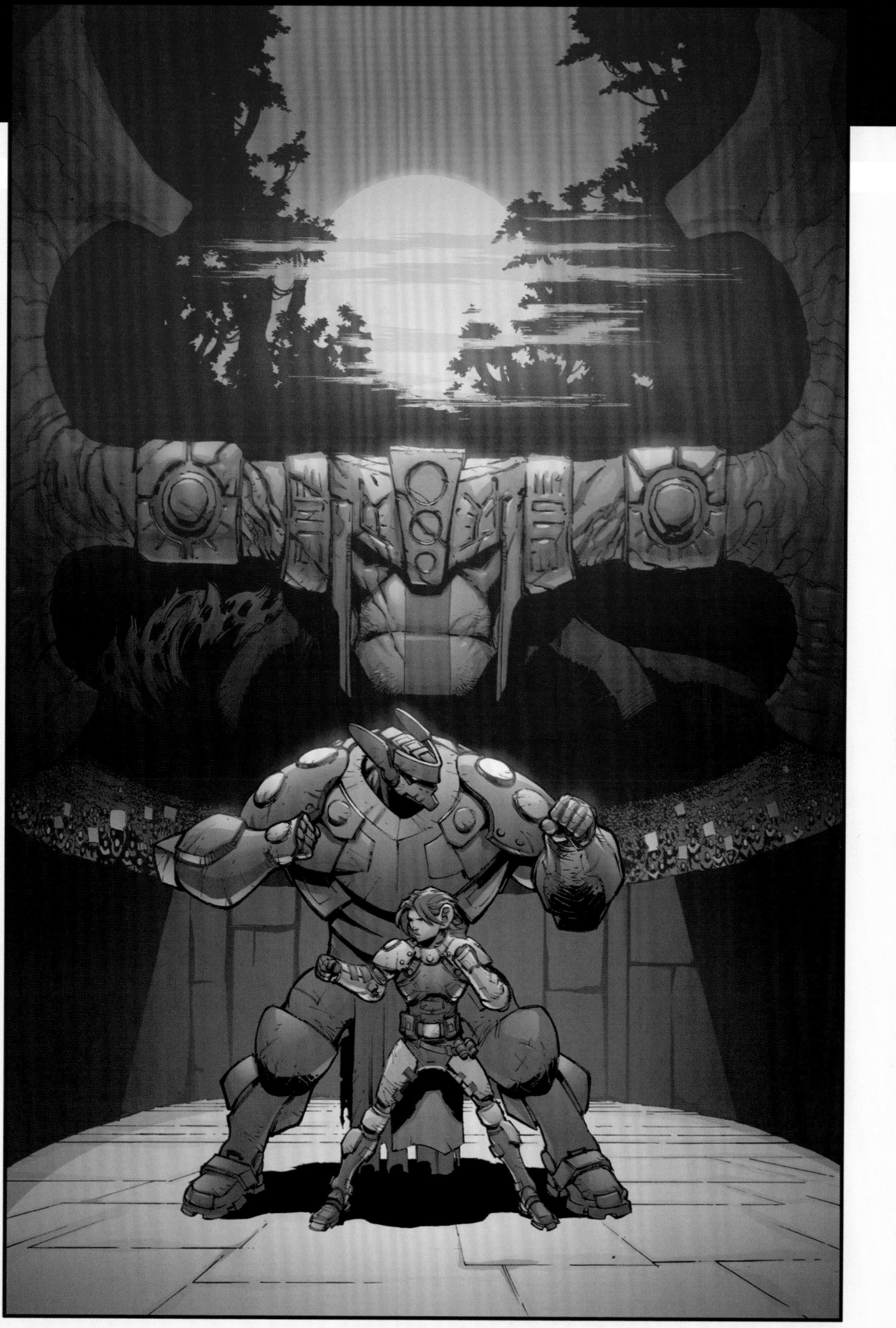

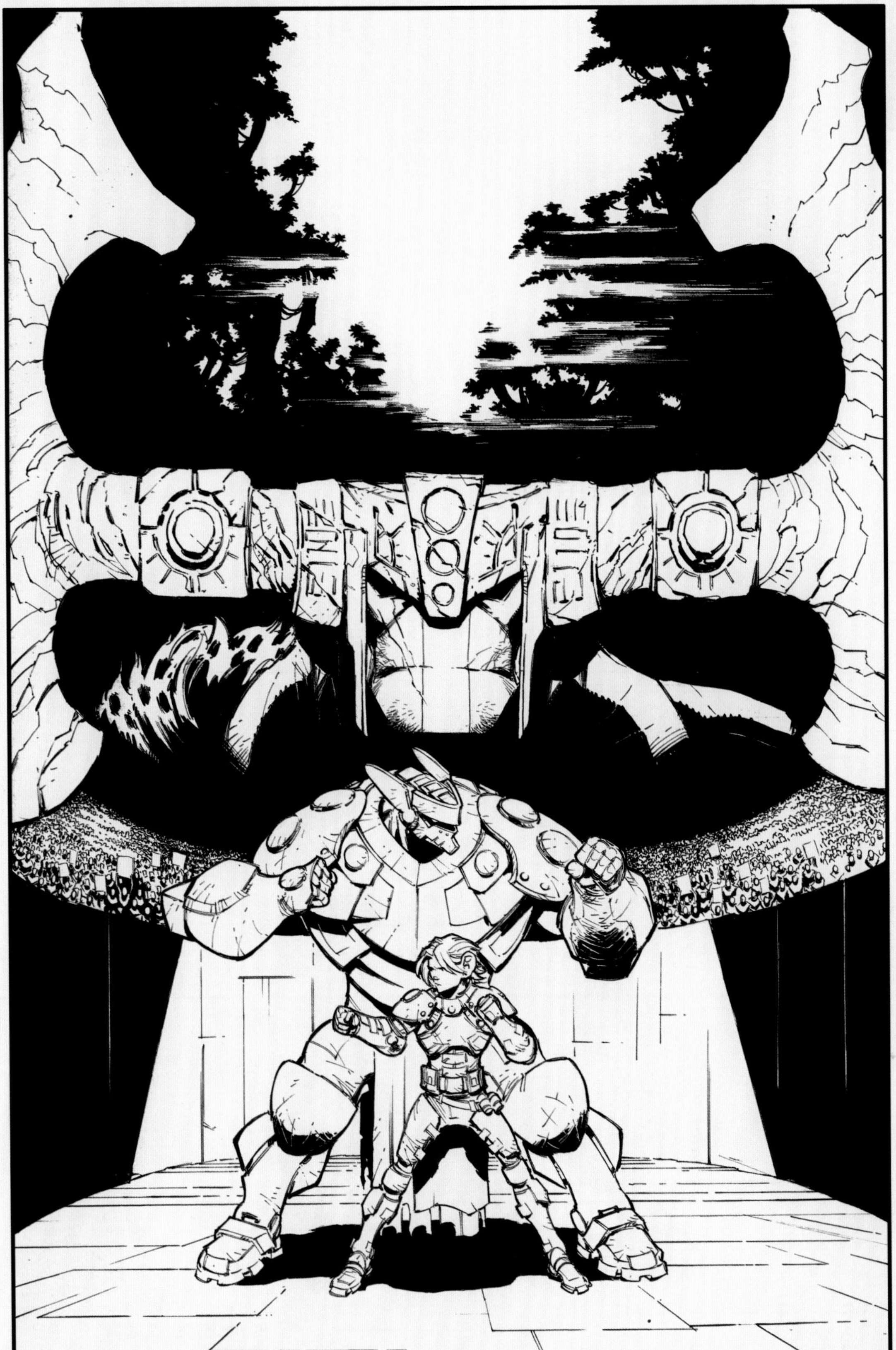

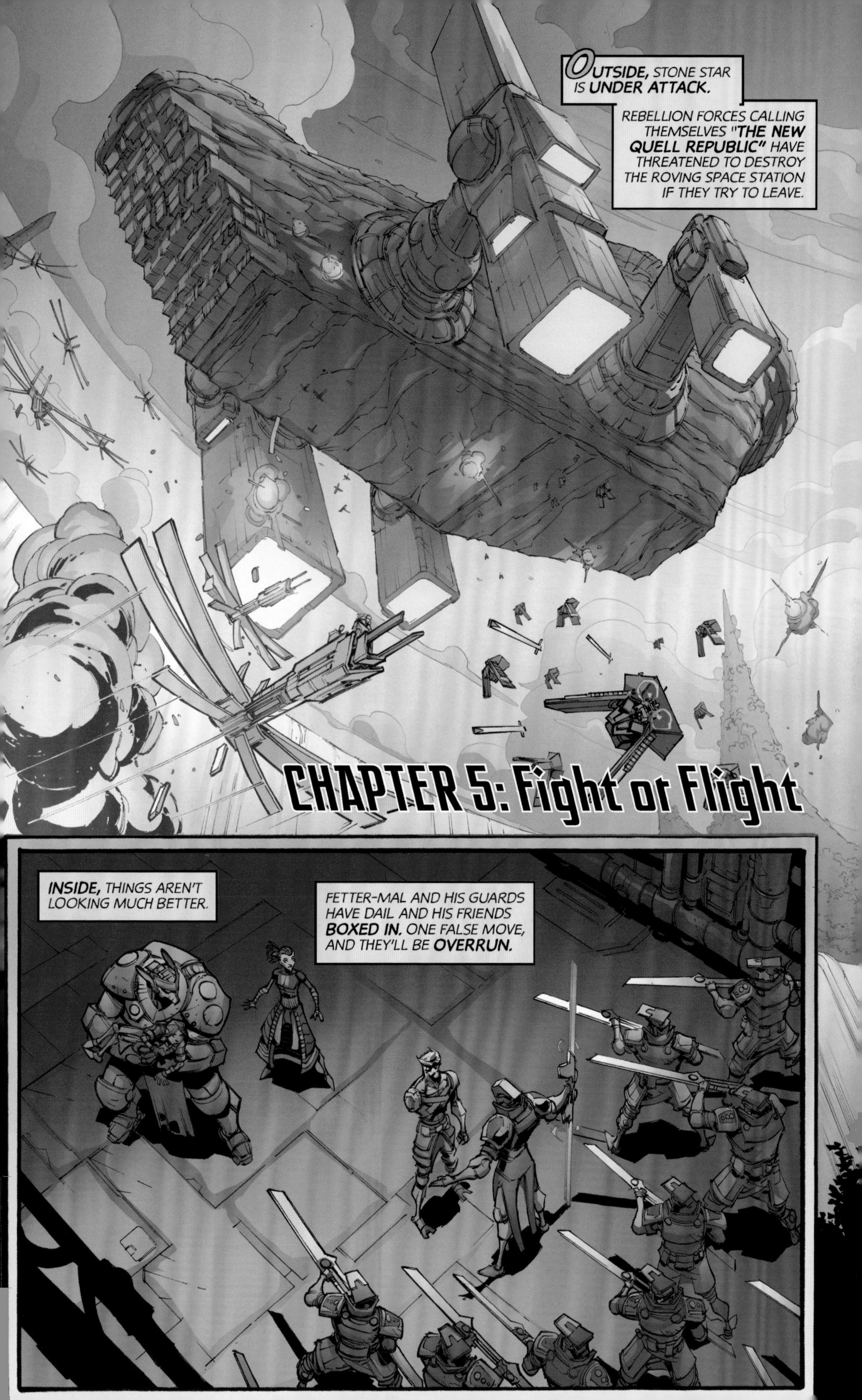
OUTSIDE, STONE STAR IS UNDER ATTACK.
REBELLION FORCES CALLING THEMSELVES "THE NEW QUELL REPUBLIC" HAVE THREATENED TO DESTROY THE ROVING SPACE STATION IF THEY TRY TO LEAVE.
CHAPTER 5: Fight or Flight
INSIDE, THINGS AREN'T LOOKING MUCH BETTER.
FETTER-MAL AND HIS GUARDS HAVE DAIL AND HIS FRIENDS BOXED IN. ONE FALSE MOVE, AND THEY'LL BE OVERRUN.

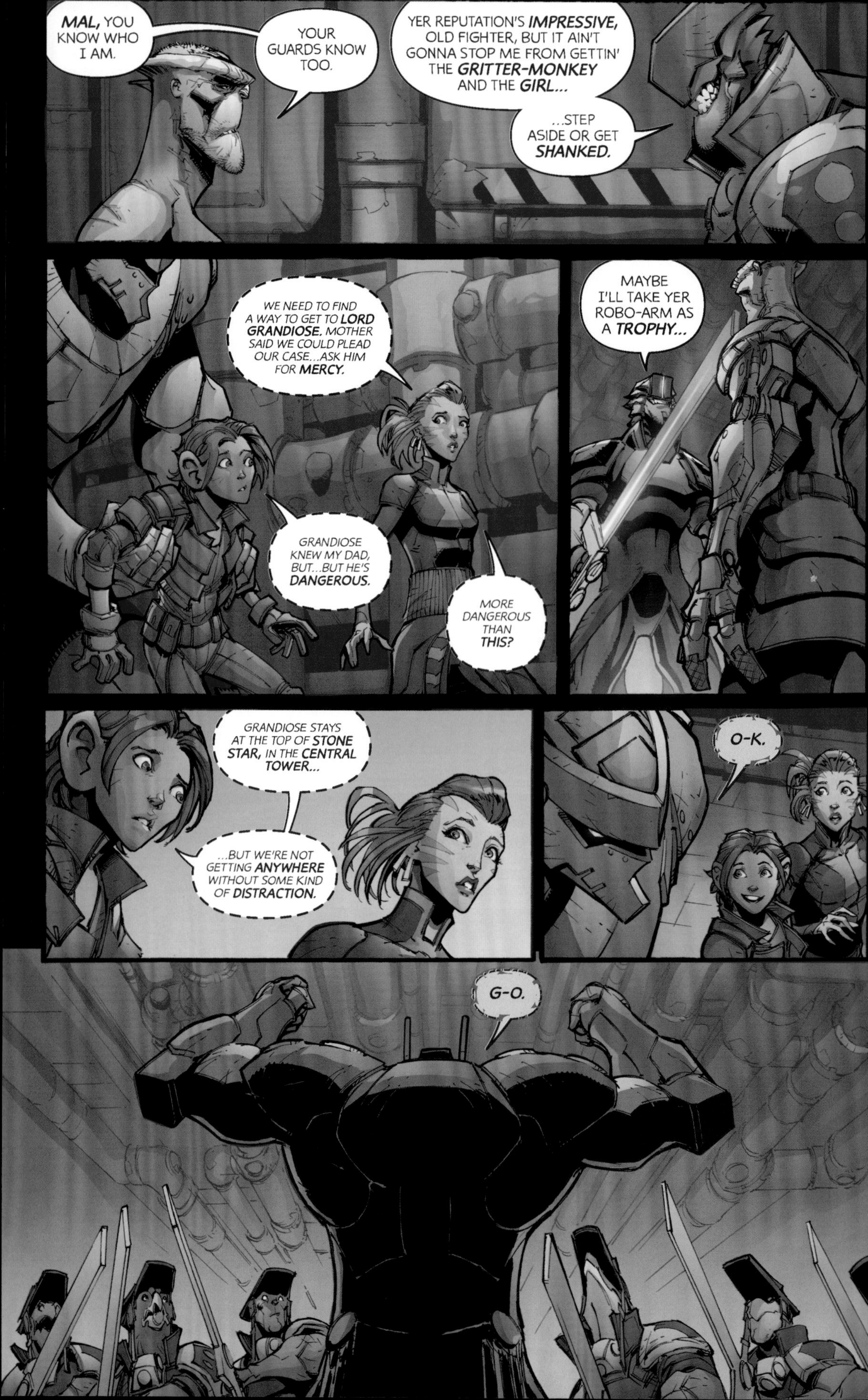
MAL, YOU KNOW WHO I AM.
YOUR GUARDS KNOW TOO.
YER REPUTATION'S IMPRESSIVE, OLD FIGHTER, BUT IT AIN'T GONNA STOP ME FROM GETTIN' THE GRITTER-MONKEY AND THE GIRL...
...STEP ASIDE OR GET SHANKED.
WE NEED TO FIND A WAY TO GET TO LORD GRANDIOSE. MOTHER SAID WE COULD PLEAD OUR CASE...ASK HIM FOR MERCY.
GRANDIOSE KNEW MY DAD, BUT...BUT HE'S DANGEROUS.
MORE DANGEROUS THAN THIS?
MAYBE I'LL TAKE YER ROBO-ARM AS A TROPHY...
GRANDIOSE STAYS AT THE TOP OF STONE STAR, IN THE CENTRAL TOWER...
...BUT WE'RE NOT GETTING ANYWHERE WITHOUT SOME KIND OF DISTRACTION.
O-K.
G-O.

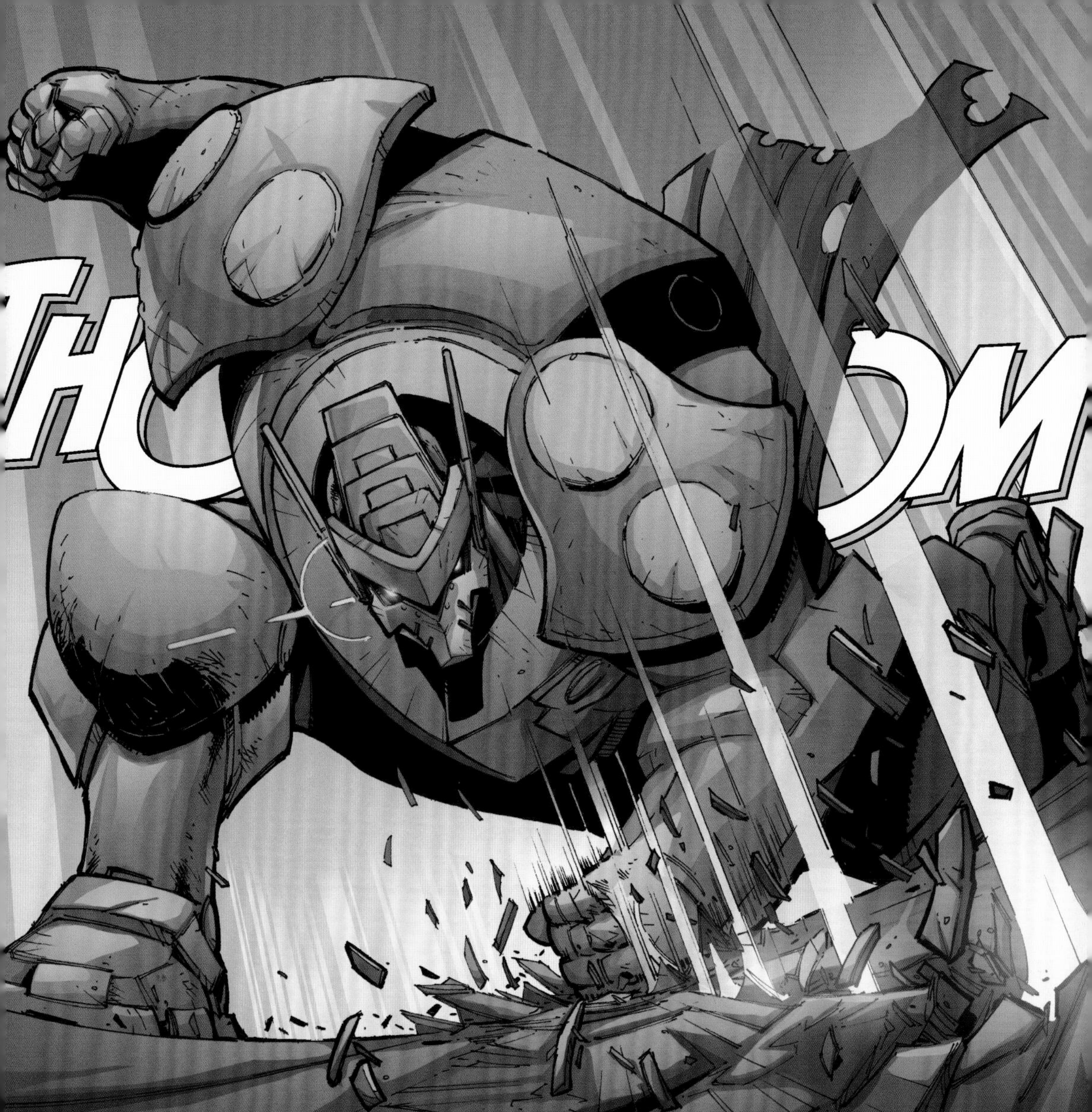

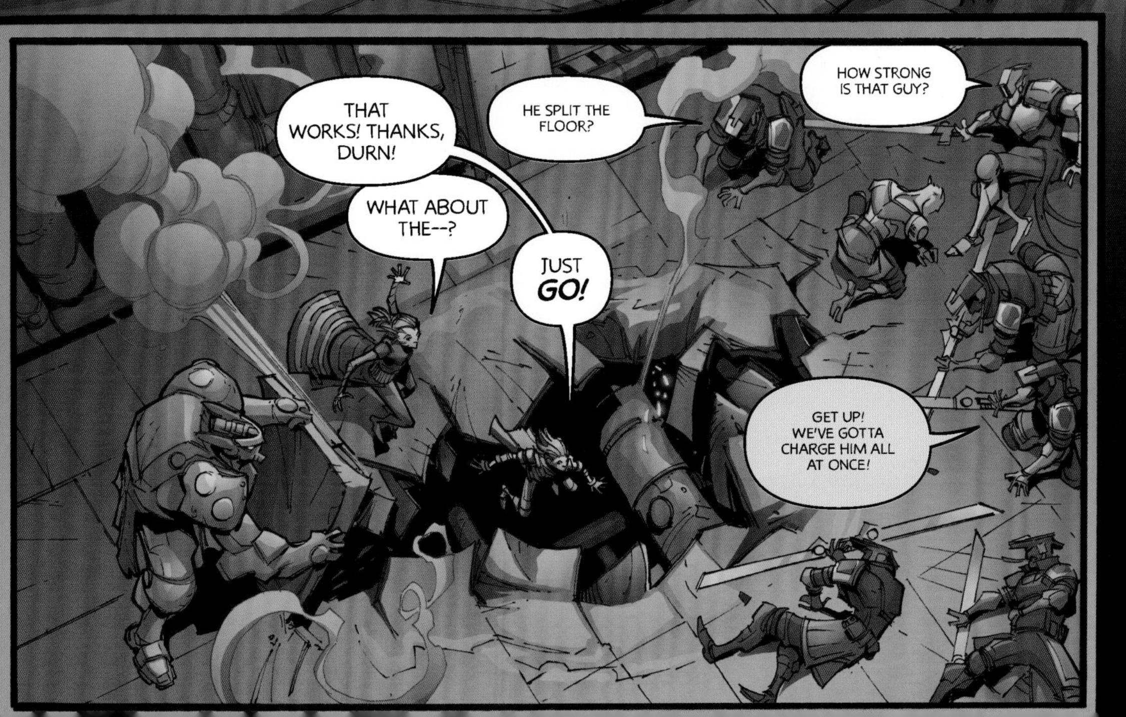
THAT WORKS! THANKS, DURN!
HE SPLIT THE FLOOR?
HOW STRONG IS THAT GUY?
WHAT ABOUT THE--?
JUST *GO!*
GET UP! WE'VE GOTTA CHARGE HIM ALL AT ONCE!

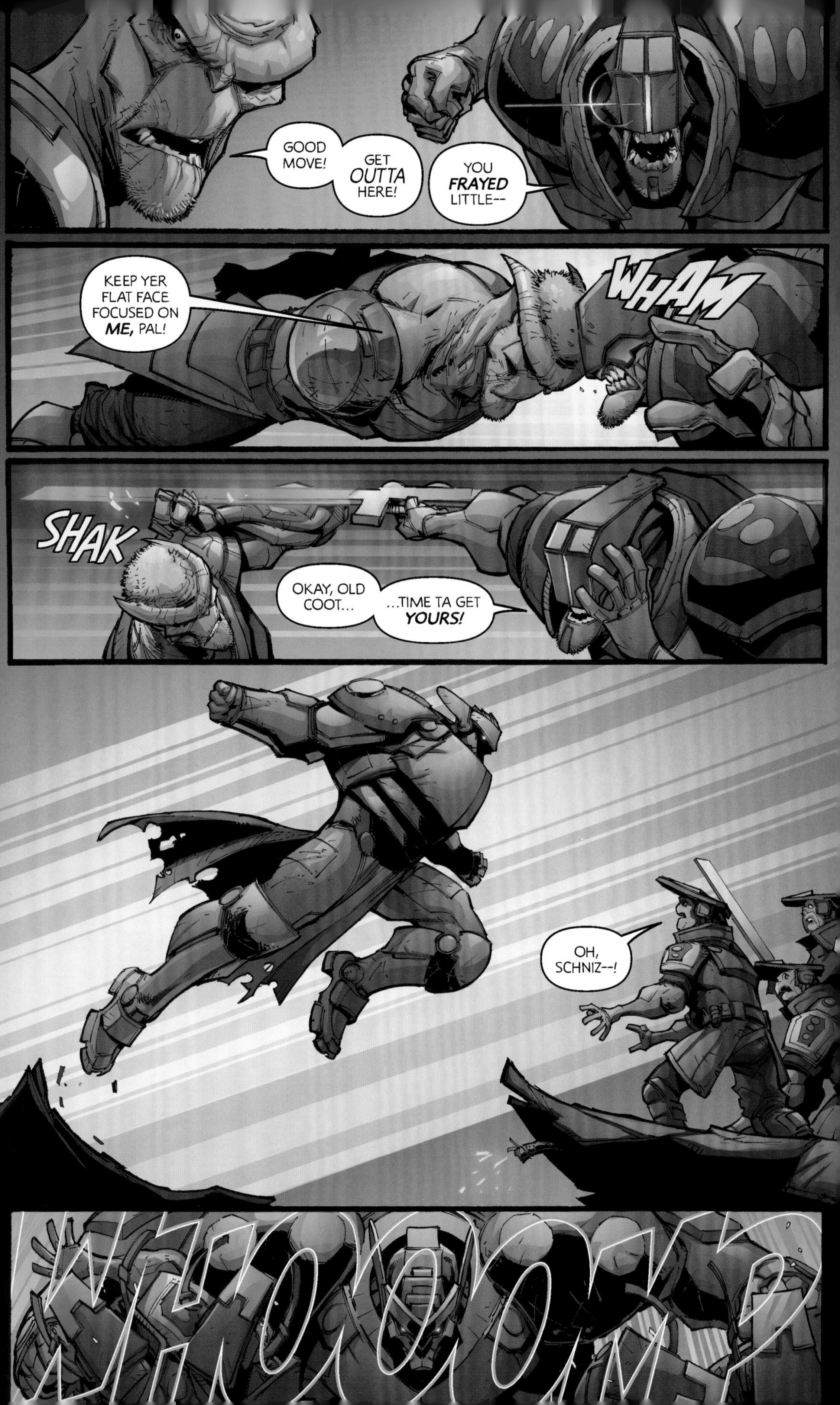
GOOD MOVE!
GET OUTTA HERE!
YOU FRAYED LITTLE--
KEEP YER FLAT FACE FOCUSED ON ME, PAL!
WHAM
SHAK
OKAY, OLD COOT...
...TIME TA GET YOURS!
OH, SCHNIZ--!

DON'T LET 'EM GET AWAY!

DAIL, WH-WHERE ARE WE GOING?!

DON'T WORRY, KIKANNI!

I KNOW MY WAY AROUND ALL THESE PIPES!

WE'LL HEAD TO AN ACCESS SPOUT BEFORE THEY CAN EVEN--

KER-THAAAA-

THOOM

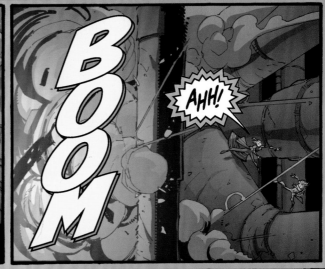

BOOM

AHH!

DAIL!

UH...

NICE *GRAB!*

DAIL, I CAN'T KEEP... HOLD...

THOSE *FIGHTERS...*

...THEY'RE HEADING RIGHT AT US!

ZARK ZARK ZARK

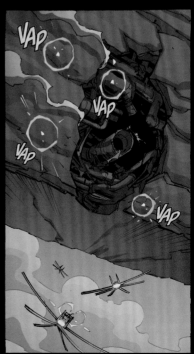

VAP
VAP
VAP
VAP

THE SOUND OF CREAKING METAL GIVING WAY IS DROWNED OUT BY THE **ROAR** OF THE APPROACHING **FIGHTERS.**

JUST LIKE BEFORE...

...THERE'S NO TIME TO THINK.

INSTINCT AND ADRENALINE...

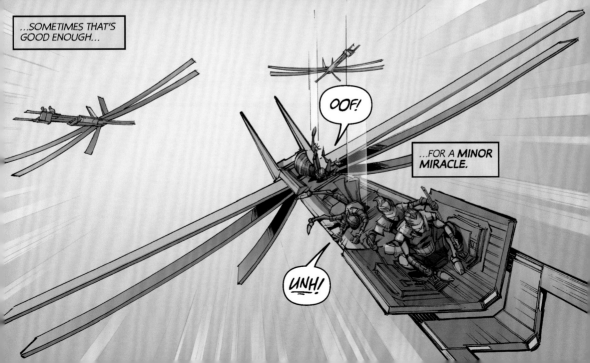

...SOMETIMES THAT'S GOOD ENOUGH...

OOF!

...FOR A **MINOR MIRACLE.**

UNH!

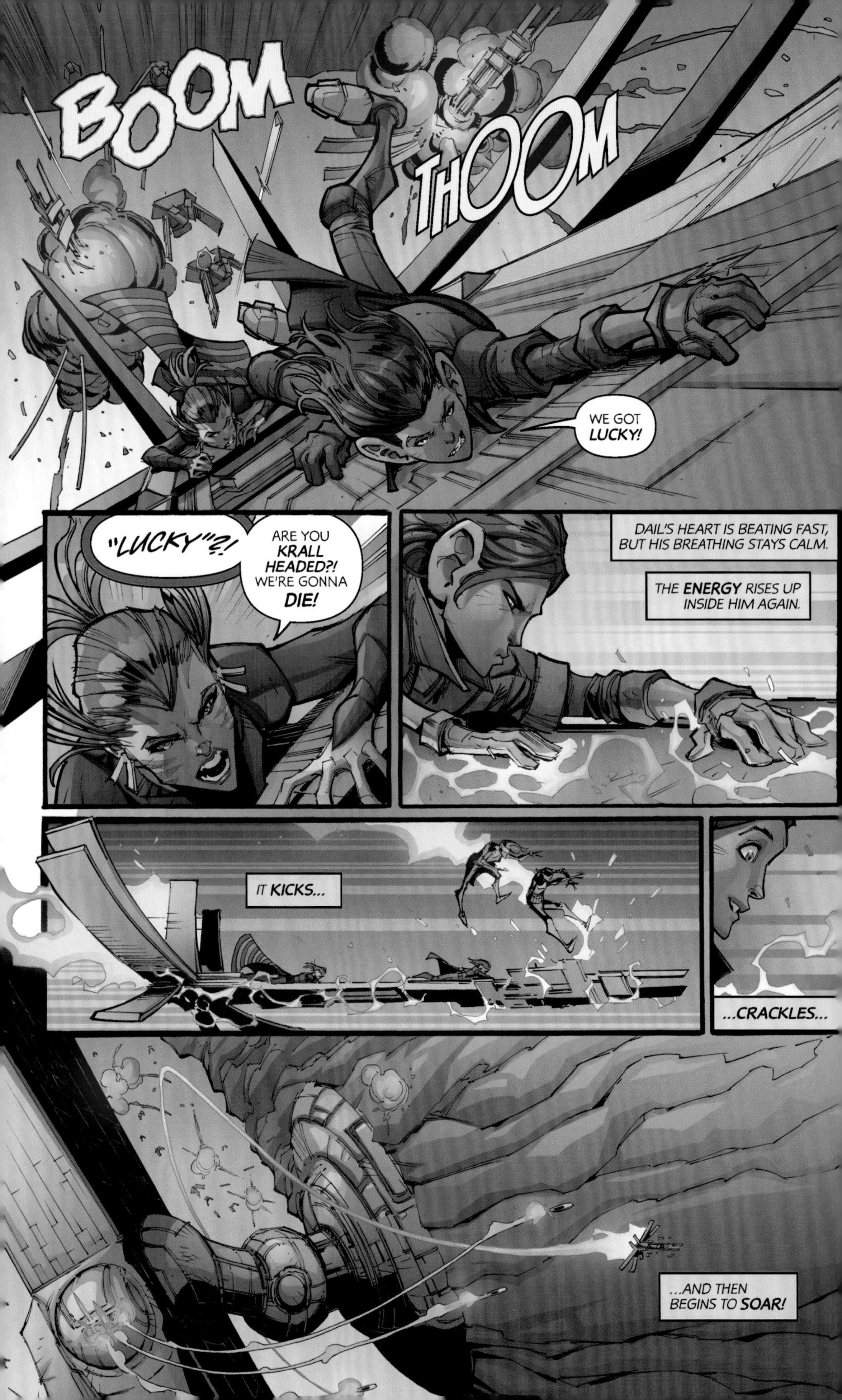
BOOM
THOOM
WE GOT LUCKY!
"LUCKY"?!
ARE YOU KRALL HEADED?! WE'RE GONNA DIE!
DAIL'S HEART IS BEATING FAST, BUT HIS BREATHING STAYS CALM.
THE ENERGY RISES UP INSIDE HIM AGAIN.
IT KICKS...
...CRACKLES...
...AND THEN BEGINS TO SOAR!

MEANWHILE, THE BATTLE CONSTRUCT THAT CALLS ITSELF "DURN" BATTLES ON.

THE GUARDS DO THEIR BEST.

IT'S NOT ENOUGH.

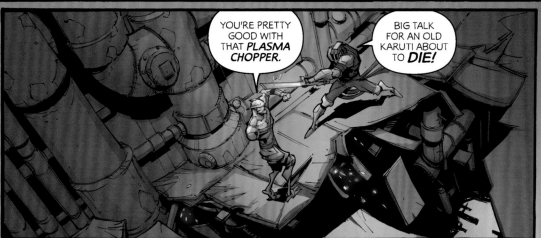

YOU'RE PRETTY GOOD WITH THAT PLASMA CHOPPER.

BIG TALK FOR AN OLD KARUTI ABOUT TO DIE!

SLASH

STRENGTH IS GOOD...

...HITTIN' THE MARK IS EVEN BETTER.

GEK--!

THOK

YOU GOT YER HIT, ONE-ARM, BUT THAT LEFT YOU OPEN!

WHAP

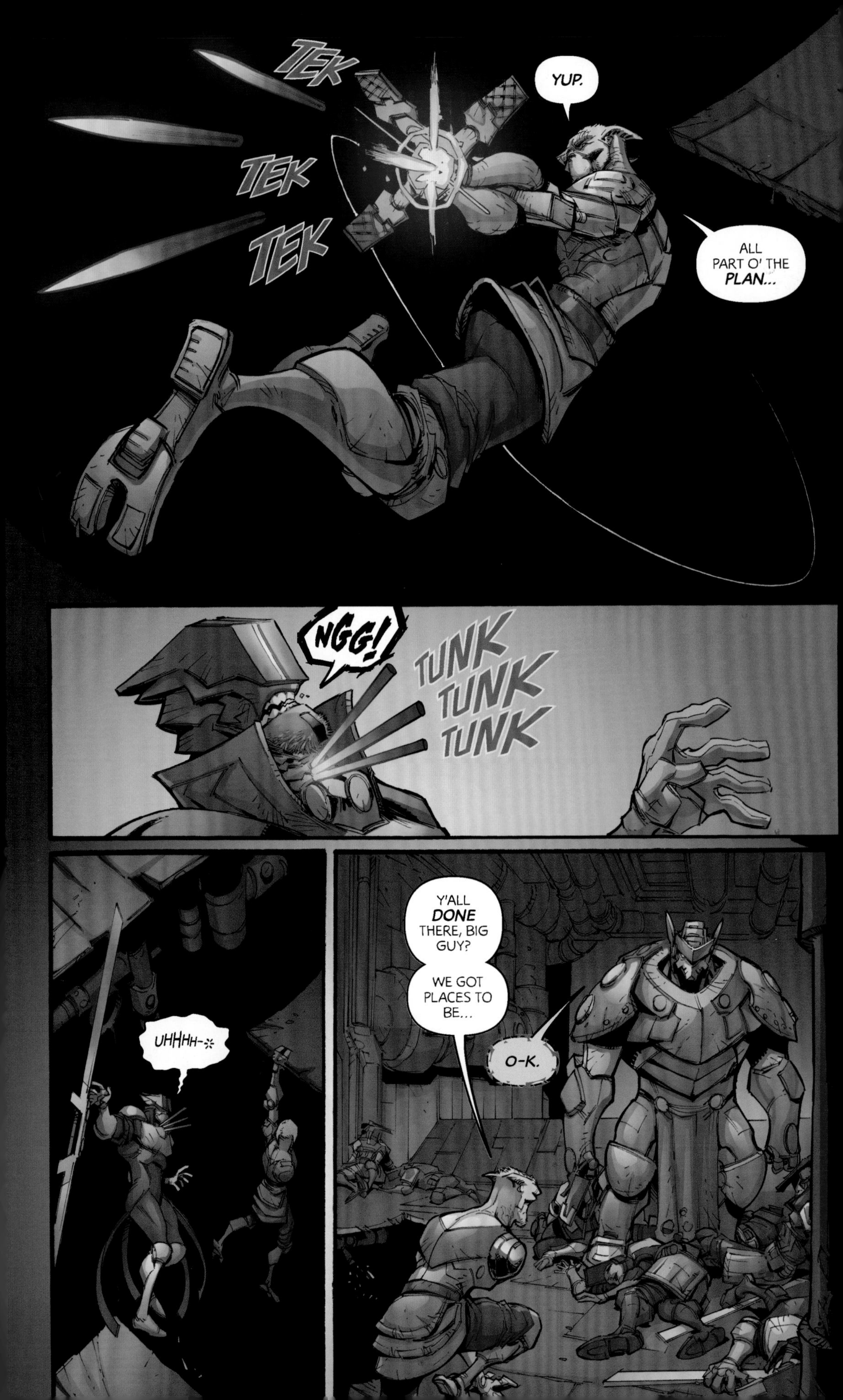
TEK
TEK
TEK
YUP.
ALL PART O' THE PLAN...
NGG!
TUNK TUNK TUNK
UHHHH-
Y'ALL DONE THERE, BIG GUY?
WE GOT PLACES TO BE...
O-K.

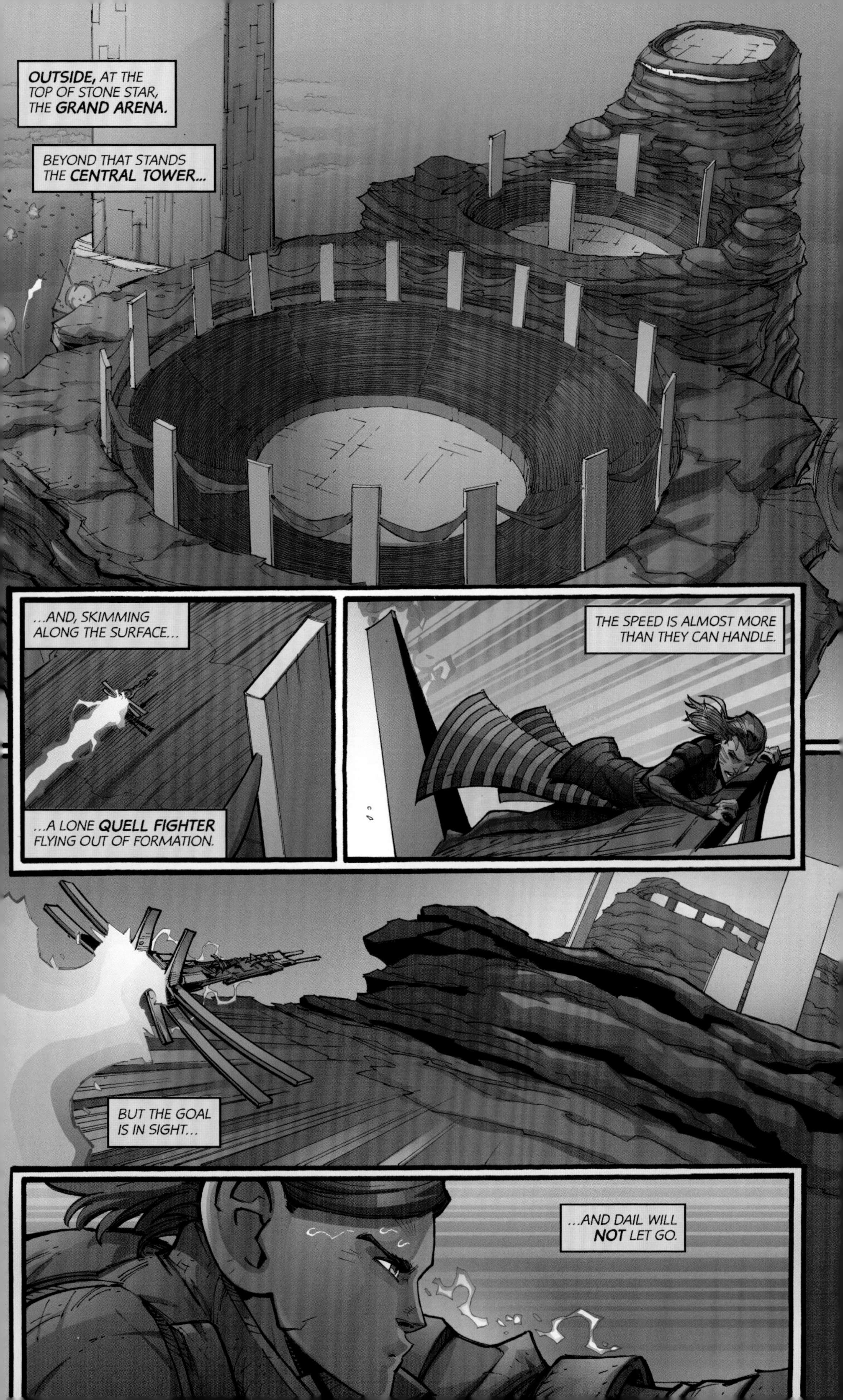
OUTSIDE, AT THE TOP OF STONE STAR, THE GRAND ARENA.
BEYOND THAT STANDS THE CENTRAL TOWER...
...AND, SKIMMING ALONG THE SURFACE...
...A LONE QUELL FIGHTER FLYING OUT OF FORMATION.
THE SPEED IS ALMOST MORE THAN THEY CAN HANDLE.
BUT THE GOAL IS IN SIGHT...
...AND DAIL WILL NOT LET GO.

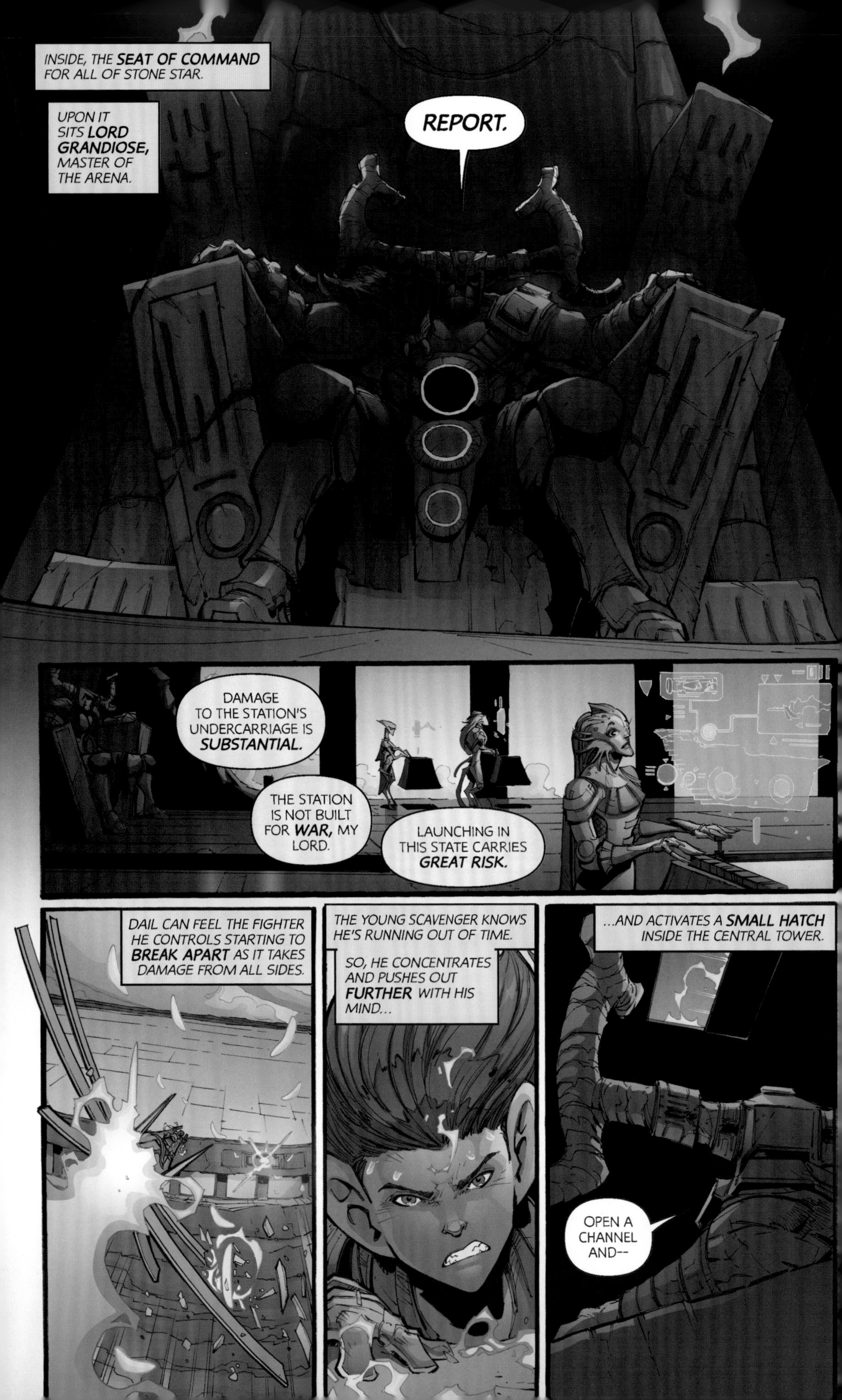

INSIDE, THE **SEAT OF COMMAND** FOR ALL OF STONE STAR.
UPON IT SITS **LORD GRANDIOSE,** MASTER OF THE ARENA.
REPORT.
DAMAGE TO THE STATION'S UNDERCARRIAGE IS ***SUBSTANTIAL.***
THE STATION IS NOT BUILT FOR ***WAR,*** MY LORD.
LAUNCHING IN THIS STATE CARRIES ***GREAT RISK.***
DAIL CAN FEEL THE FIGHTER HE CONTROLS STARTING TO **BREAK APART** AS IT TAKES DAMAGE FROM ALL SIDES.
THE YOUNG SCAVENGER KNOWS HE'S RUNNING OUT OF TIME.
SO, HE CONCENTRATES AND PUSHES OUT **FURTHER** WITH HIS MIND...
...AND ACTIVATES A **SMALL HATCH** INSIDE THE CENTRAL TOWER.
OPEN A CHANNEL AND--

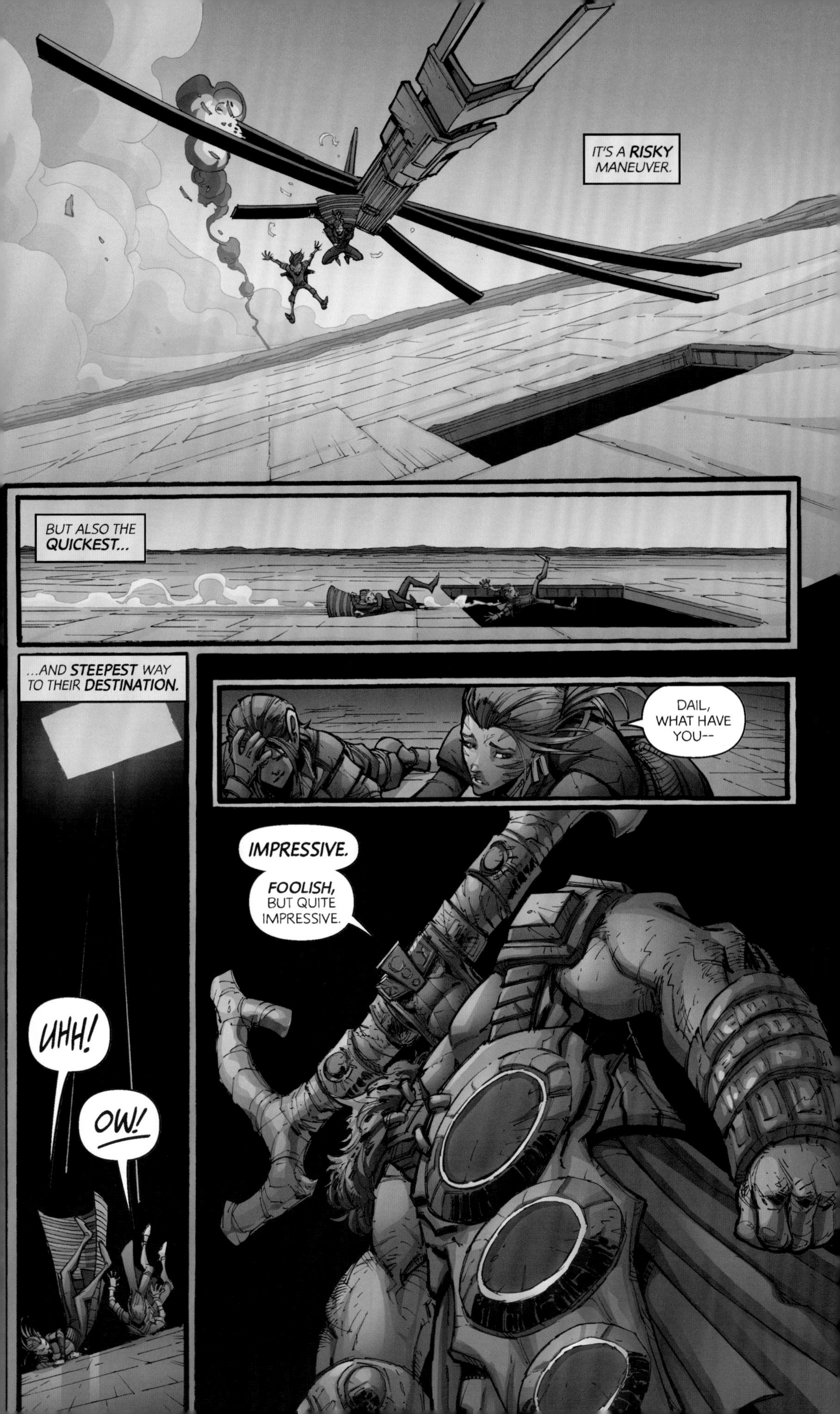
IT'S A RISKY MANEUVER.
BUT ALSO THE QUICKEST...
...AND STEEPEST WAY TO THEIR DESTINATION.
UHH!
OW!
DAIL, WHAT HAVE YOU--
IMPRESSIVE.
FOOLISH, BUT QUITE IMPRESSIVE.

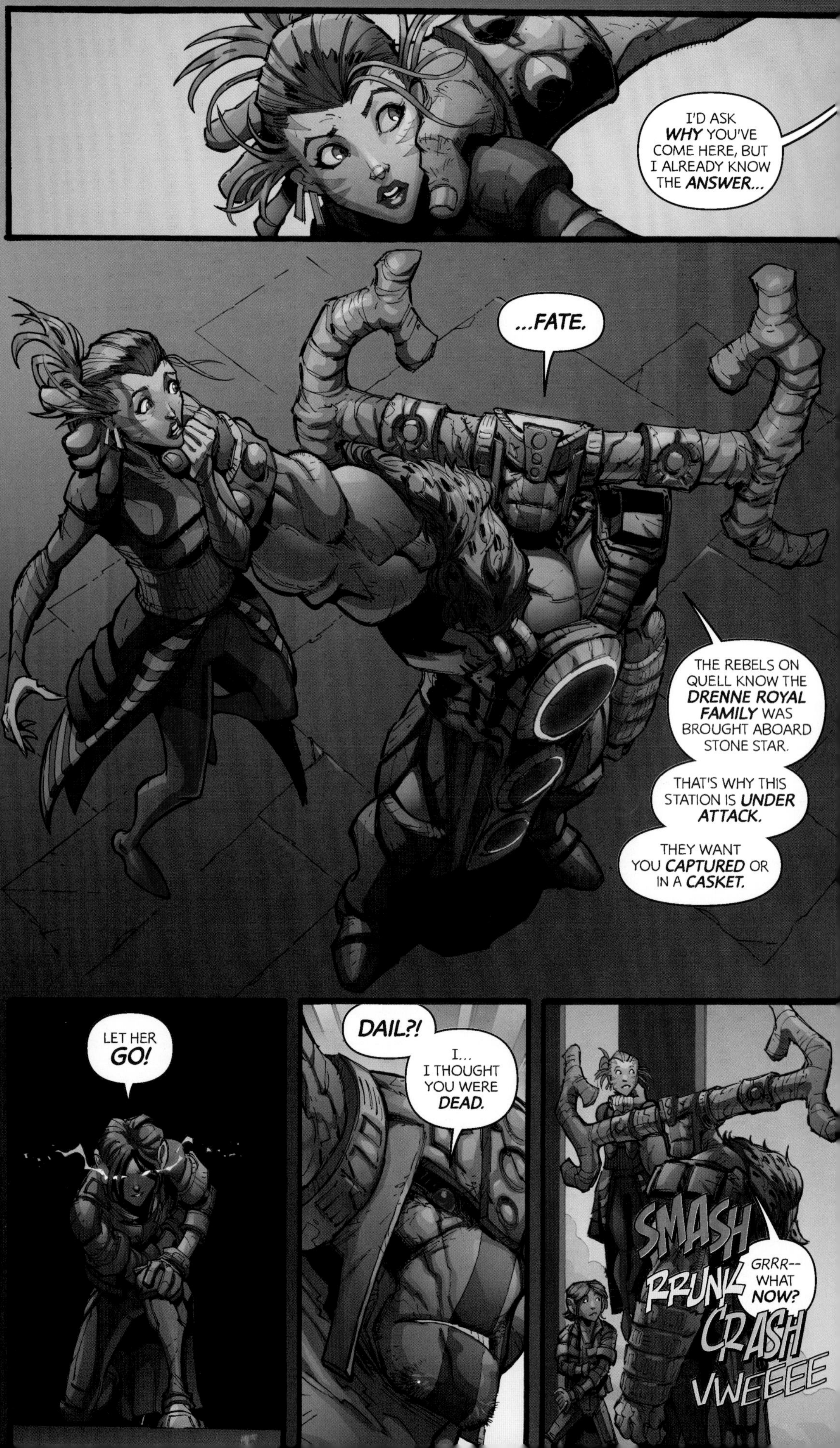
I'D ASK WHY YOU'VE COME HERE, BUT I ALREADY KNOW THE ANSWER...
...FATE.
THE REBELS ON QUELL KNOW THE DRENNE ROYAL FAMILY WAS BROUGHT ABOARD STONE STAR.
THAT'S WHY THIS STATION IS UNDER ATTACK.
THEY WANT YOU CAPTURED OR IN A CASKET.
LET HER GO!
DAIL?!
I... I THOUGHT YOU WERE DEAD.
SMASH
RRUNK
CRASH
VWEEEEE
GRRR-- WHAT NOW?

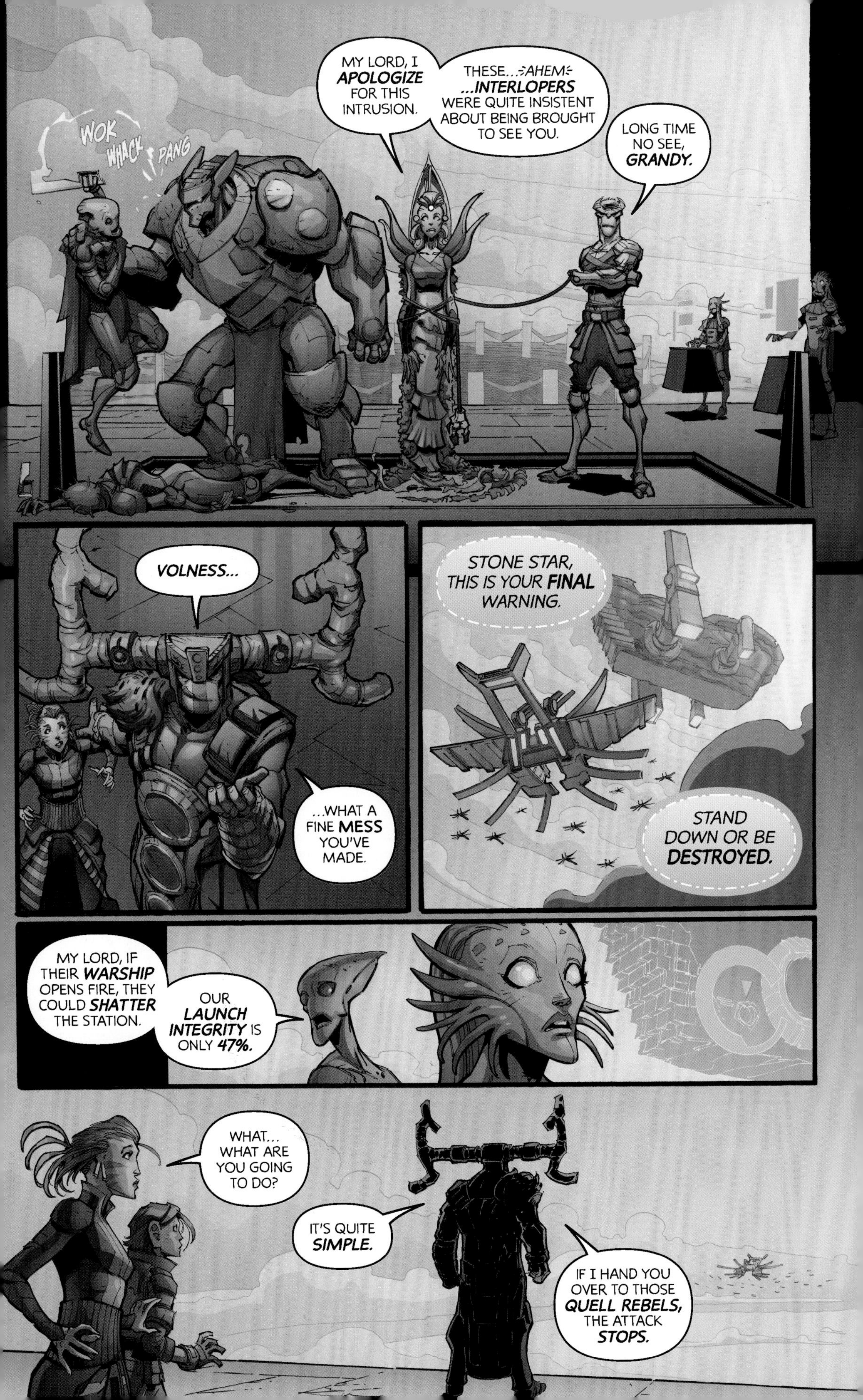
WOK
WHACK
PANG
MY LORD, I APOLOGIZE FOR THIS INTRUSION.
THESE... AHEM ...INTERLOPERS WERE QUITE INSISTENT ABOUT BEING BROUGHT TO SEE YOU.
LONG TIME NO SEE, GRANDY.
VOLNESS...
...WHAT A FINE MESS YOU'VE MADE.
STONE STAR, THIS IS YOUR FINAL WARNING.
STAND DOWN OR BE DESTROYED.
MY LORD, IF THEIR WARSHIP OPENS FIRE, THEY COULD SHATTER THE STATION.
OUR LAUNCH INTEGRITY IS ONLY 47%.
WHAT... WHAT ARE YOU GOING TO DO?
IT'S QUITE SIMPLE.
IF I HAND YOU OVER TO THOSE QUELL REBELS, THE ATTACK STOPS.

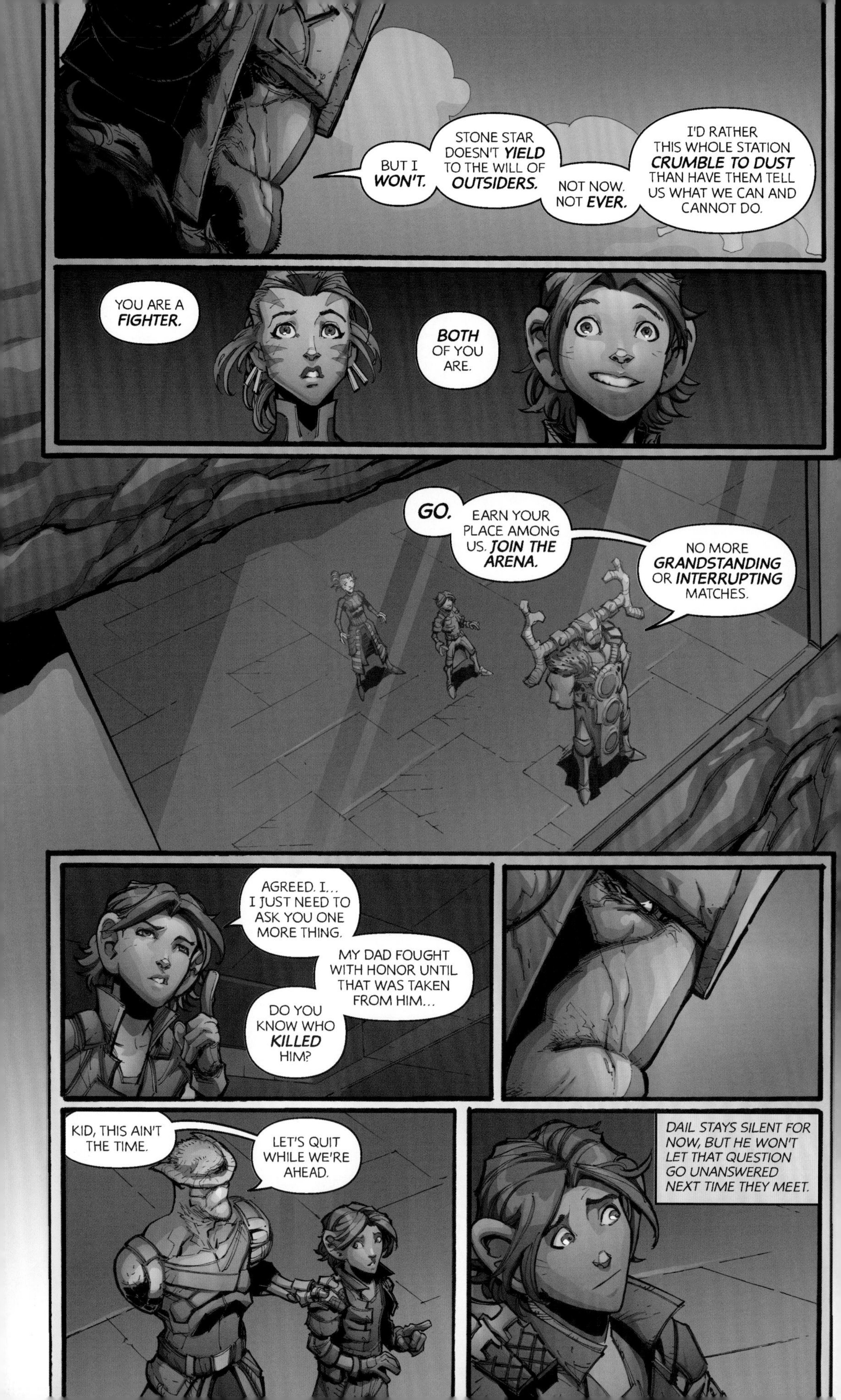
BUT I WON'T.
STONE STAR DOESN'T YIELD TO THE WILL OF OUTSIDERS.
NOT NOW. NOT EVER.
I'D RATHER THIS WHOLE STATION CRUMBLE TO DUST THAN HAVE THEM TELL US WHAT WE CAN AND CANNOT DO.
YOU ARE A FIGHTER.
BOTH OF YOU ARE.
GO.
EARN YOUR PLACE AMONG US. JOIN THE ARENA.
NO MORE GRANDSTANDING OR INTERRUPTING MATCHES.
AGREED. I... I JUST NEED TO ASK YOU ONE MORE THING.
MY DAD FOUGHT WITH HONOR UNTIL THAT WAS TAKEN FROM HIM...
DO YOU KNOW WHO KILLED HIM?
KID, THIS AIN'T THE TIME.
LET'S QUIT WHILE WE'RE AHEAD.
DAIL STAYS SILENT FOR NOW, BUT HE WON'T LET THAT QUESTION GO UNANSWERED NEXT TIME THEY MEET.

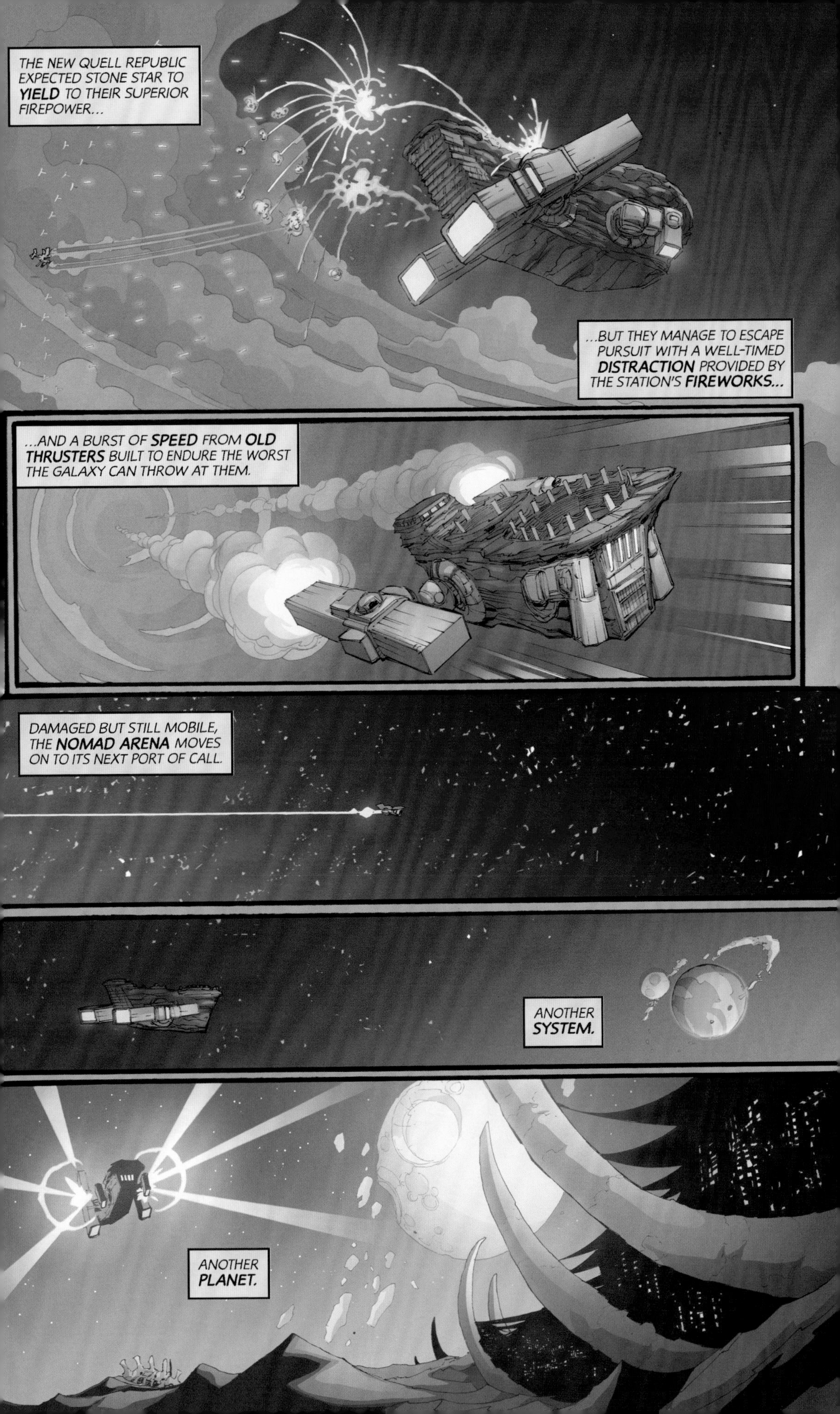
THE NEW QUELL REPUBLIC EXPECTED STONE STAR TO **YIELD** TO THEIR SUPERIOR FIREPOWER...
...BUT THEY MANAGE TO ESCAPE PURSUIT WITH A WELL-TIMED **DISTRACTION** PROVIDED BY THE STATION'S **FIREWORKS...**
...AND A BURST OF **SPEED** FROM **OLD THRUSTERS** BUILT TO ENDURE THE WORST THE GALAXY CAN THROW AT THEM.
DAMAGED BUT STILL MOBILE, THE **NOMAD ARENA** MOVES ON TO ITS NEXT PORT OF CALL.
ANOTHER **SYSTEM.**
ANOTHER **PLANET.**

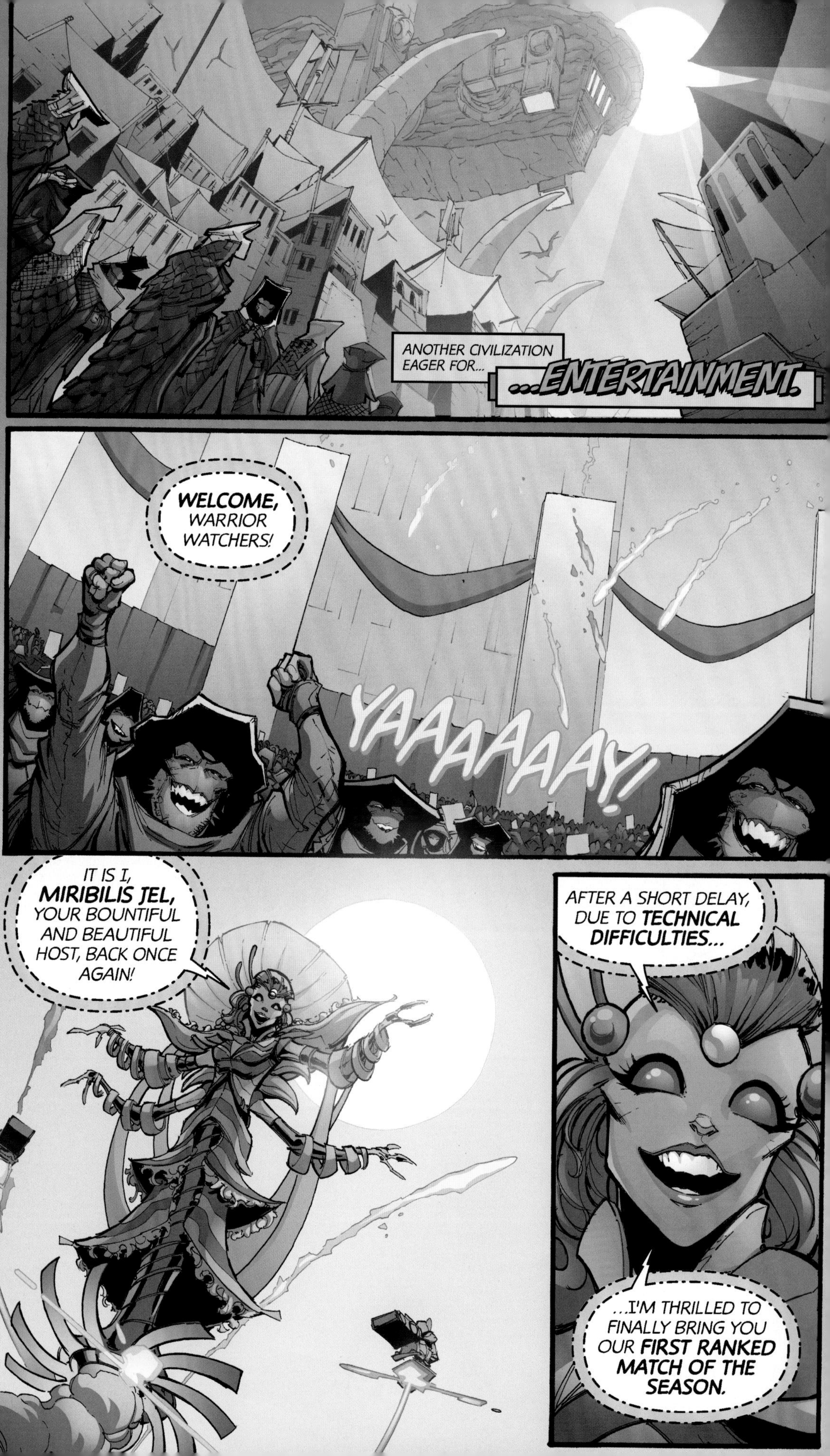

ANOTHER CIVILIZATION EAGER FOR...
...ENTERTAINMENT.
WELCOME, WARRIOR WATCHERS!
YAAAAAAY!
IT IS I, MIRIBILIS JEL, YOUR BOUNTIFUL AND BEAUTIFUL HOST, BACK ONCE AGAIN!
AFTER A SHORT DELAY, DUE TO TECHNICAL DIFFICULTIES...
...I'M THRILLED TO FINALLY BRING YOU OUR FIRST RANKED MATCH OF THE SEASON.

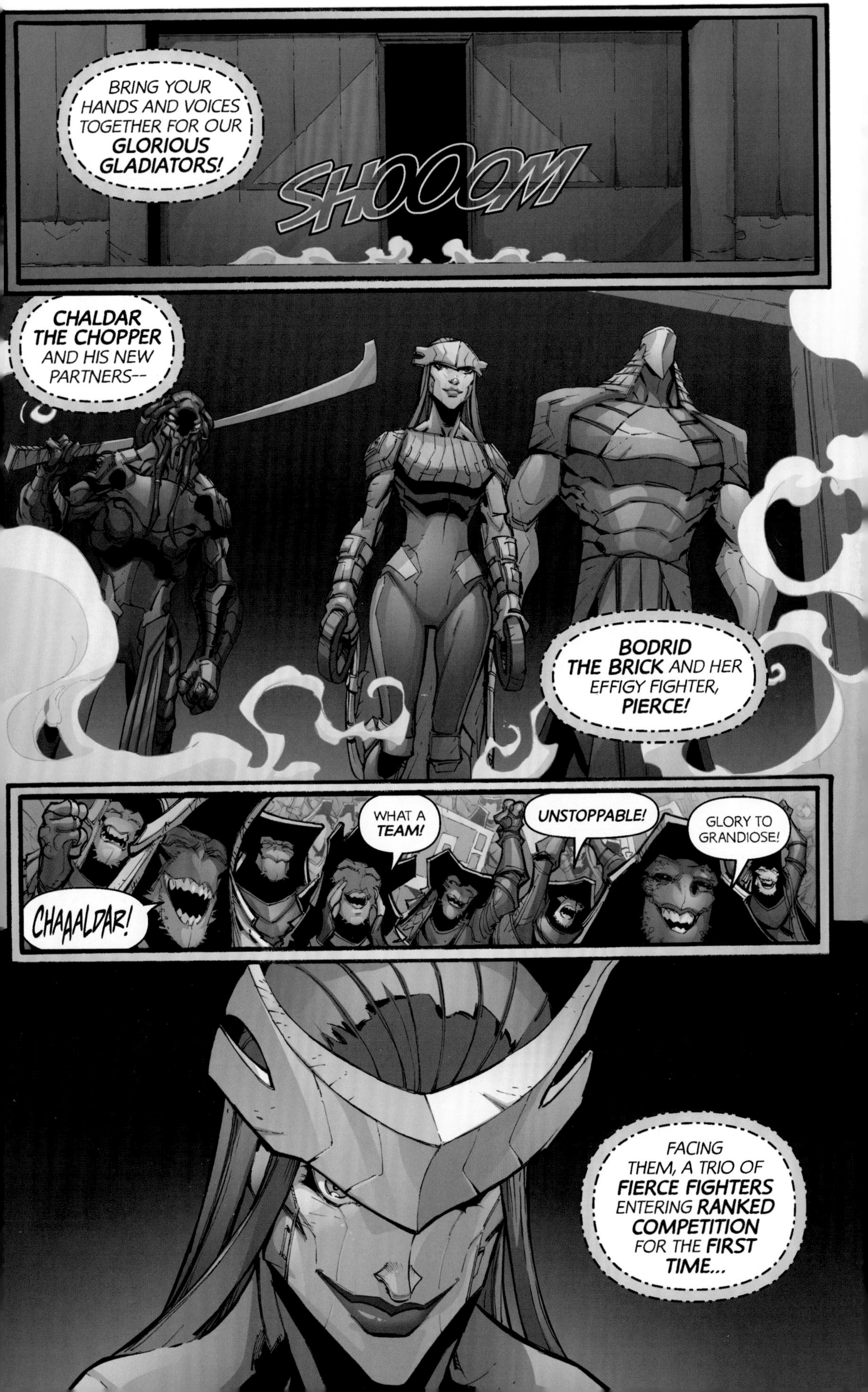
BRING YOUR HANDS AND VOICES TOGETHER FOR OUR GLORIOUS GLADIATORS!
SHOOOM
CHALDAR THE CHOPPER AND HIS NEW PARTNERS--
BODRID THE BRICK AND HER EFFIGY FIGHTER, PIERCE!
CHAAALDAR!
WHAT A TEAM!
UNSTOPPABLE!
GLORY TO GRANDIOSE!
FACING THEM, A TRIO OF FIERCE FIGHTERS ENTERING RANKED COMPETITION FOR THE FIRST TIME...

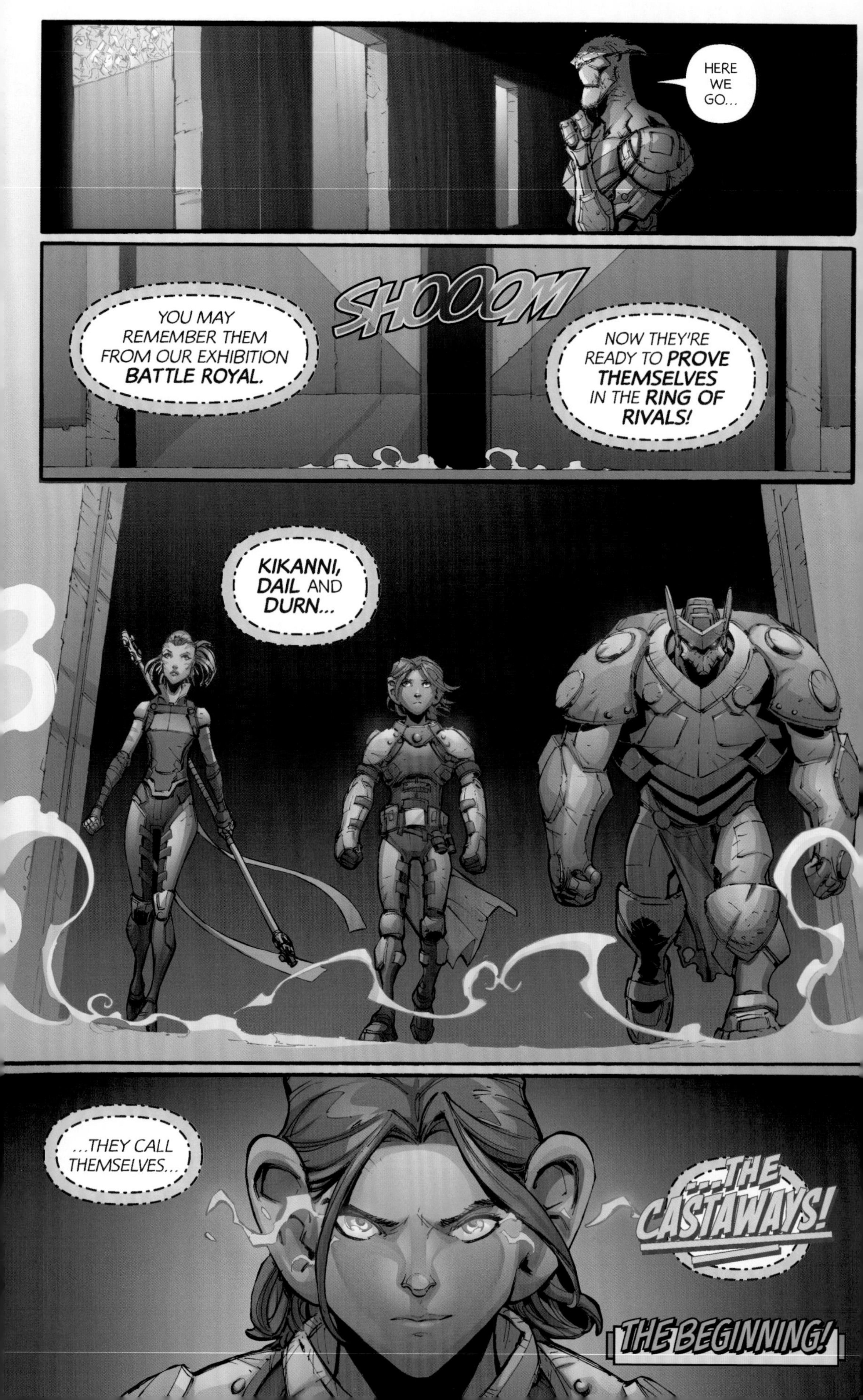
HERE WE GO...
SHOOOM
YOU MAY REMEMBER THEM FROM OUR EXHIBITION BATTLE ROYAL.
NOW THEY'RE READY TO PROVE THEMSELVES IN THE RING OF RIVALS!
KIKANNI, DAIL AND DURN...
...THEY CALL THEMSELVES...
...THE CASTAWAYS!
THE BEGINNING!

Zub • Dunbar • Grundetjern • Dillon

Stone Star

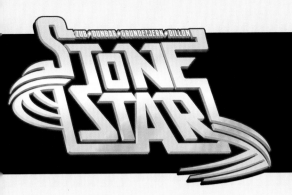

Welcome to the Arena!

Max and I have been talking about working together on a creator-owned project for almost six years. We kept putting it off, but I realized that if we didn't make time and get started, we'd always find an excuse not to do it. At that same time, opportunity came knocking.

Chip Mosher from ComiXology Originals reached out to see what ideas I had on deck. Espen Grundetjern told me he had room in his coloring schedule. Marshall Dillon told me he'd be happy to jump onboard.

I dug into my story notes and found an idea I'd been wanting to build for years and Max started blasting out concept designs that blew my mind.

It was go time.

There's never been a better time to create and share stories. Getting the chance to do that and have people support us is a gift.

We can't wait to show you more in our future chapters!

—Jim Zub

"A traveling gladiatorial arena, built into a nomadic asteroid."

One short sentence and I was in.

I had wanted to work with Jim again for years, and doing a creator-owned series was such an exciting idea. I had been a massive fan of the amazing worlds Jim had been involved in creating in his previous books, so when the chance came to help craft a whole new universe . . . I jumped at it.

With Espen's gorgeous colors to help breathe life and depth into these worlds, and Marshall's dynamic lettering to ratchet up the action and emotion . . . I think you'll be just as excited as I am to discover what *Stone Star* has in store for all of us.

Thank you for reading!

—Max Dunbar

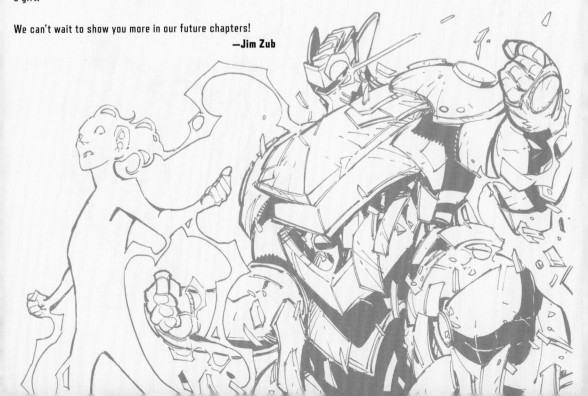

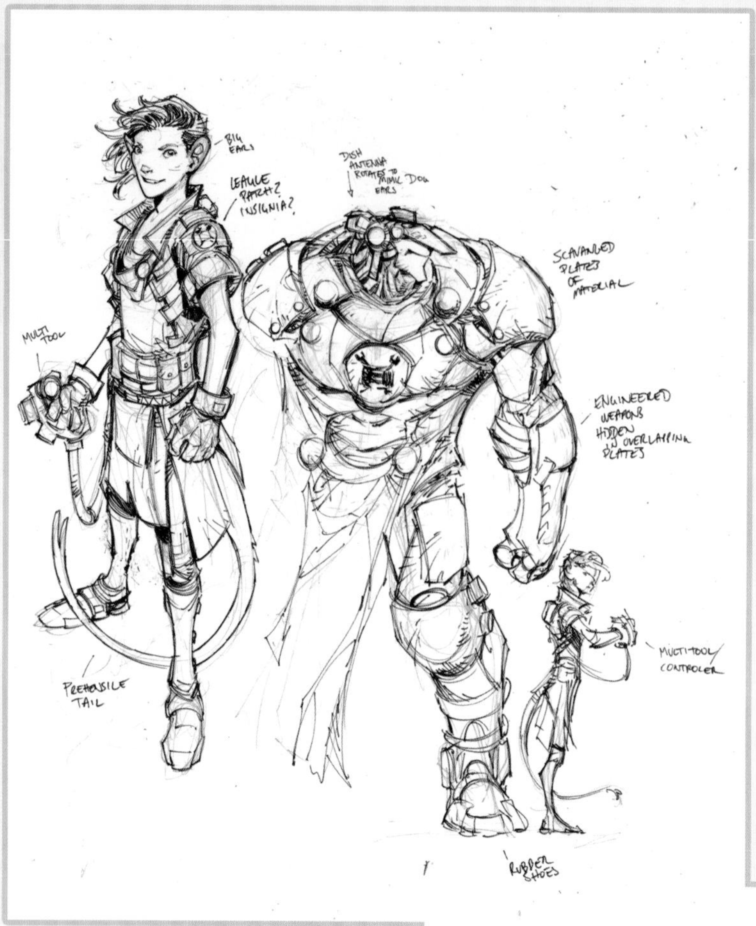
BIG EARS
LEAGUE PATCH? INSIGNIA?
DISH ANTENNA ROTATES TO MIMIC DOG EARS
SCAVANGED PLATES OF MATERIAL
MULTI TOOL
ENGINEERED WEAPONS HIDDEN IN OVERLAPPING PLATES
PREHENSILE TAIL
MULTITOOL/ CONTROLER
RUBBER SHOES

Above and Right: First concept designs for Dail and Durn.

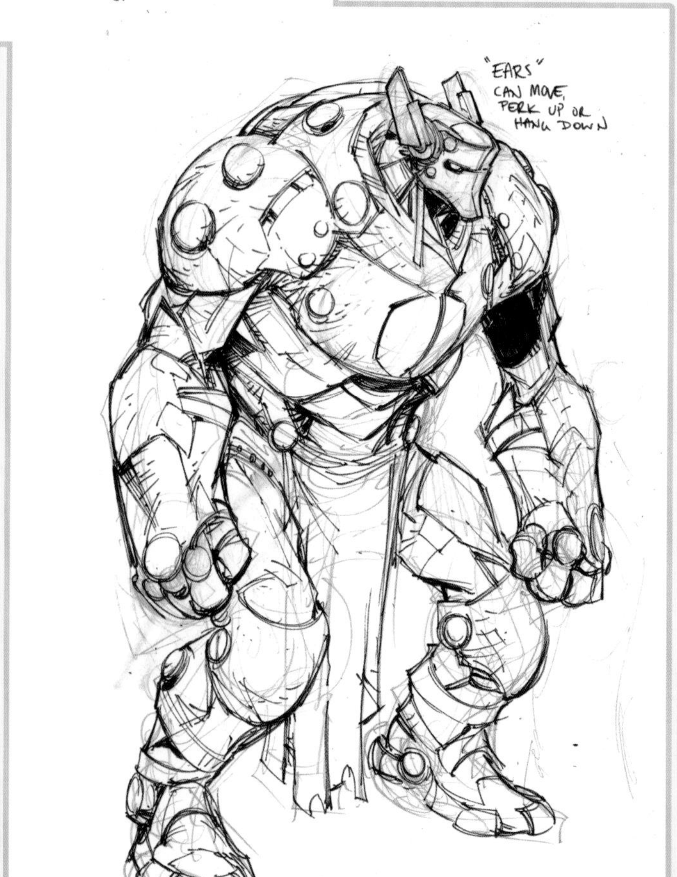
"EARS" CAN MOVE, PERK UP OR HANG DOWN

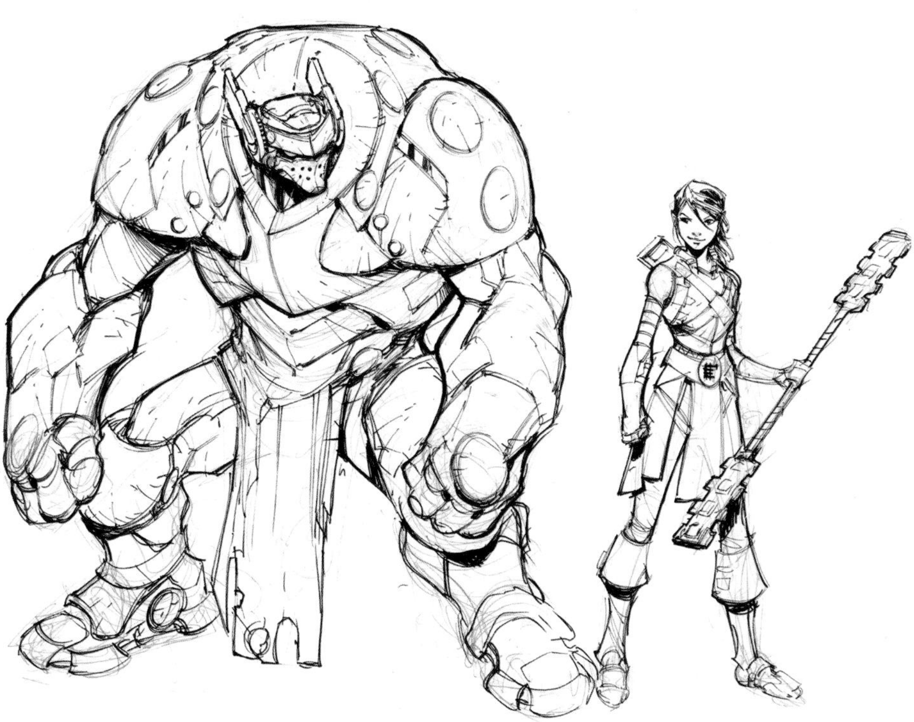

Above: Durn's development continues, and we get our first look at a potential design for Kikanni.

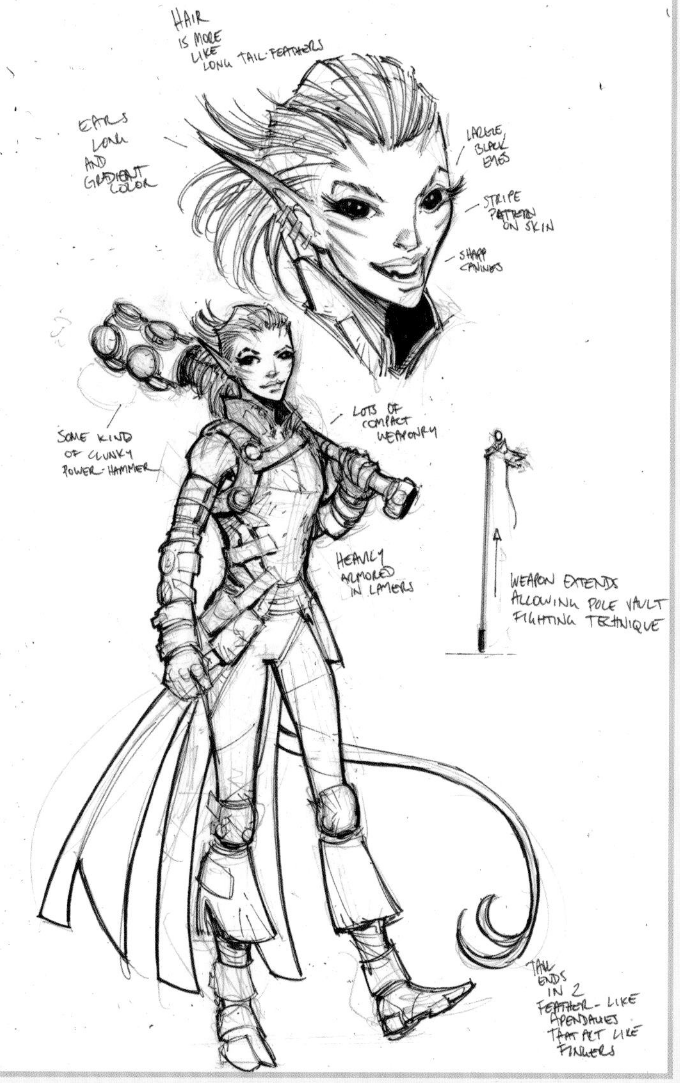
HAIR IS MORE LIKE LONG TAIL-FEATHERS
EARS LONG AND GRADIENT COLOR
LARGE, BLACK EYES
STRIPE PATTERN ON SKIN
SHARP CANINES
SOME KIND OF CLUNKY POWER-HAMMER
LOTS OF COMPACT WEAPONRY
HEAVILY ARMORED IN LAYERS
WEAPON EXTENDS ALLOWING POLE VAULT FIGHTING TECHNIQUE
TAIL ENDS IN 2 FEATHER-LIKE APENDAGES THAT ACT LIKE FINGERS

Right: Kikanni's design evolves.

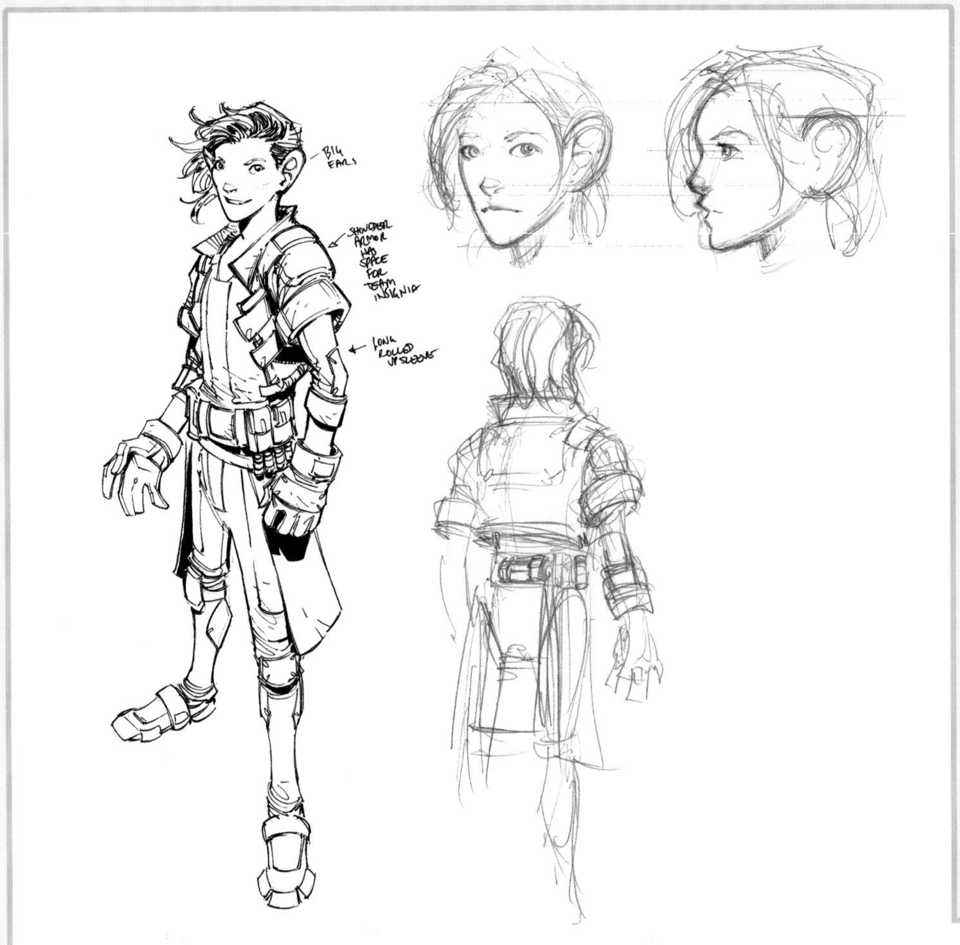
BIG EARS
SHOULDER ARMOR HAS SPACE FOR TEAM INSIGNIA
LONG ROLLED UP SLEEVE

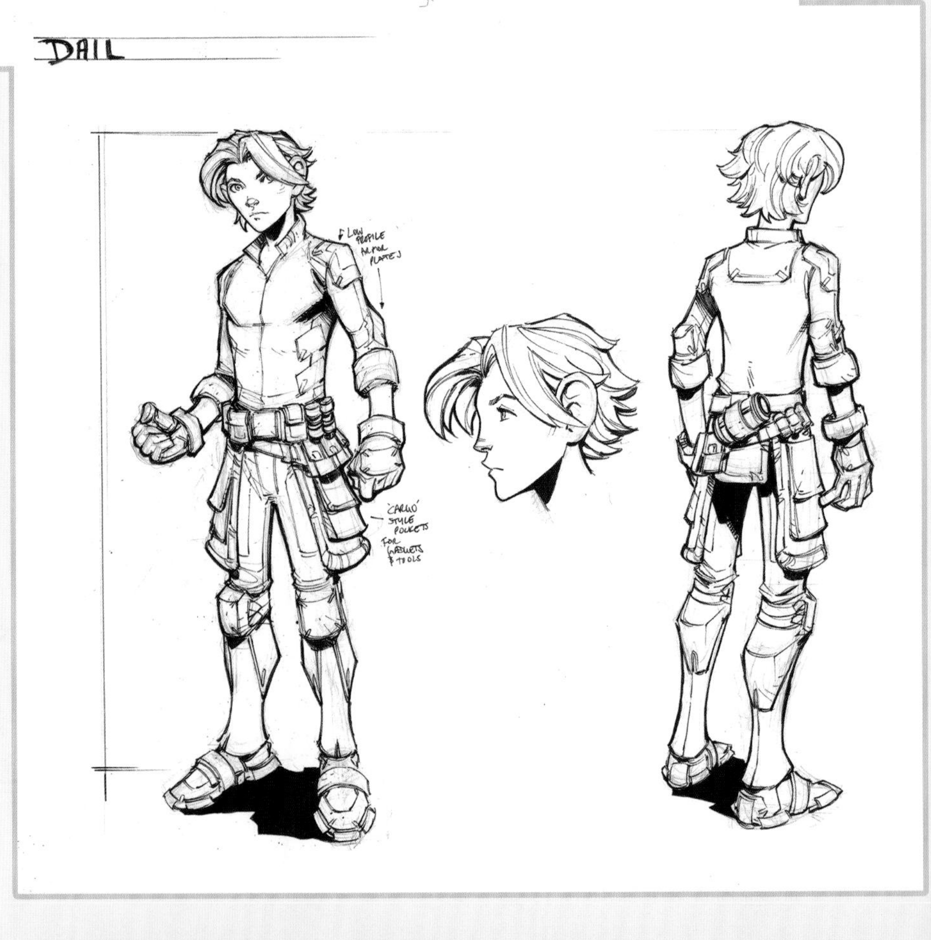
DAIL
LOW PROFILE ARMOR PLATES
'CARGO' STYLE POCKETS FOR GADGETS & TOOLS

Above and Right: More iterations of Dail's possible design.

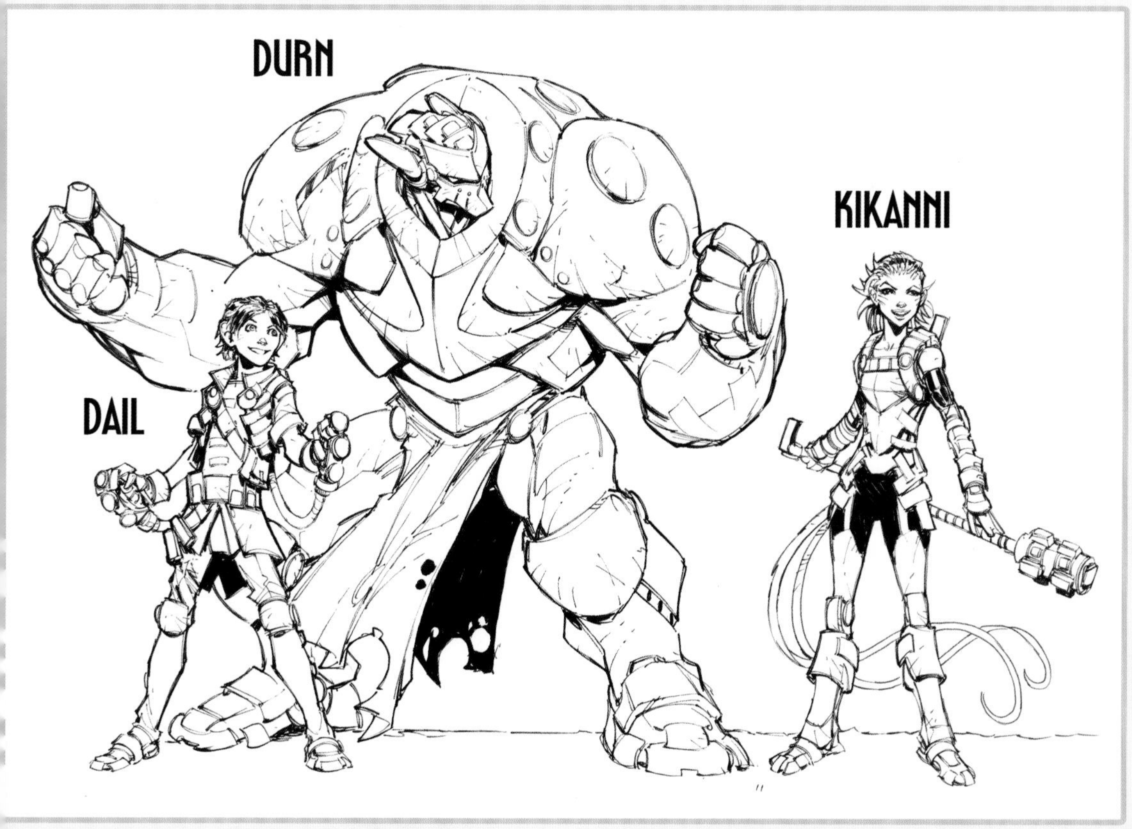
DURN
KIKANNI
DAIL

Above: The first character lineup. This image was included with the series pitch sent to ComiXology.

Below: Durn's finished design sheet.

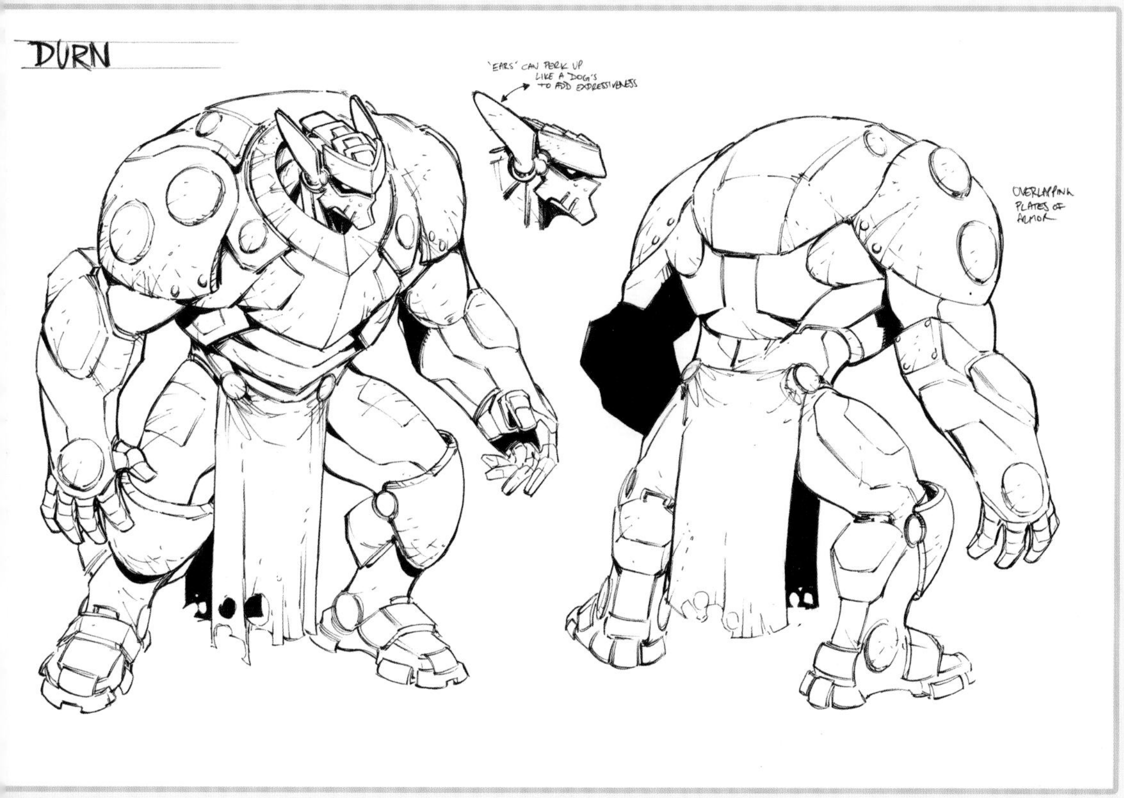
DURN
'EARS' CAN PERK UP LIKE A DOG'S TO ADD EXPRESSIVENESS
OVERLAPPING PLATES OF ARMOR

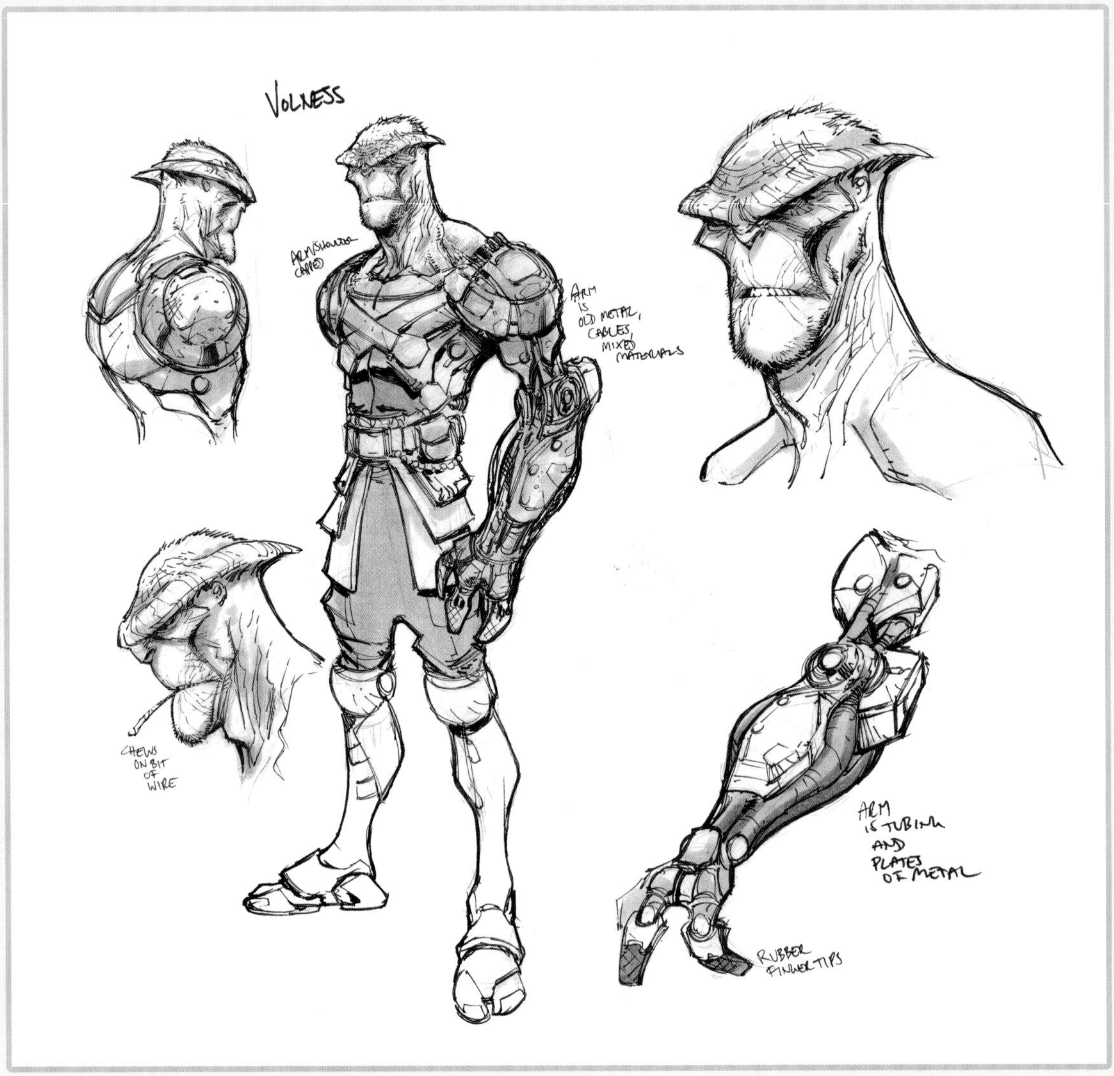
VOLNESS
ARM/SHOULDER CAPPED
ARM IS OLD METAL, CABLES, MIXED MATERIALS
CHEWS ON BIT OF WIRE
ARM IS TUBING AND PLATES OF METAL
RUBBER FINGER TIPS

Above: Design sheet for Volness Vildari.

Below: The rundown workshop where Volness lives.

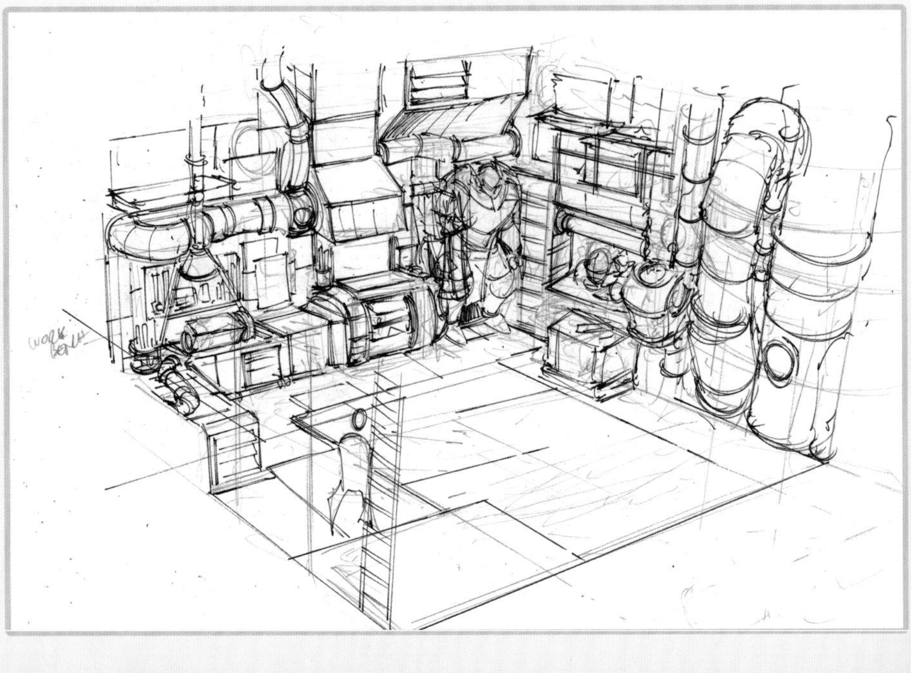

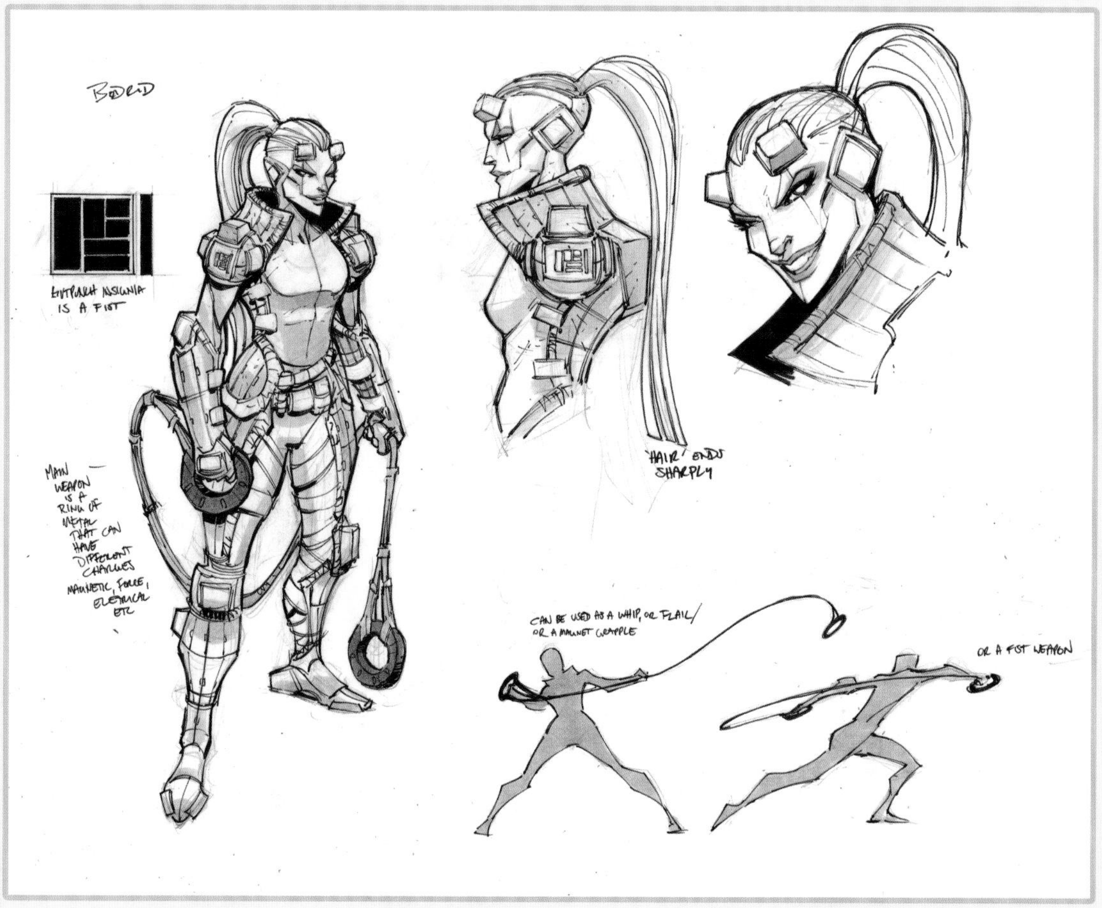
BODRID
INSIGNIA
IS A FIST
MAIN WEAPON IS A RING OF METAL THAT CAN HAVE DIFFERENT CHARGES
MAGNETIC, FORCE, ELECTRICAL ETC
'HAIR' ENDS SHARPLY
CAN BE USED AS A WHIP, OR FLAIL/ OR A MAGNET GRAPPLE
OR A FIST WEAPON

Above: Bodrid initial design sheet.

Below: Bodrid and Pierce design.

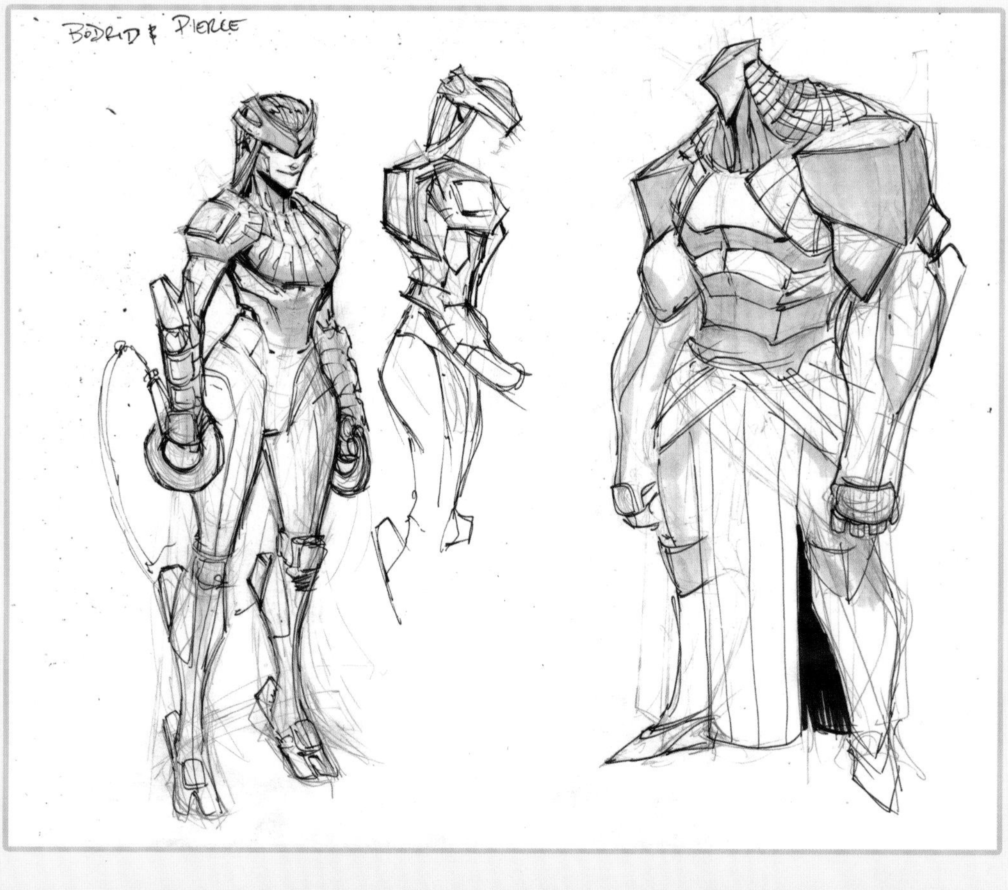
BODRID & PIERCE

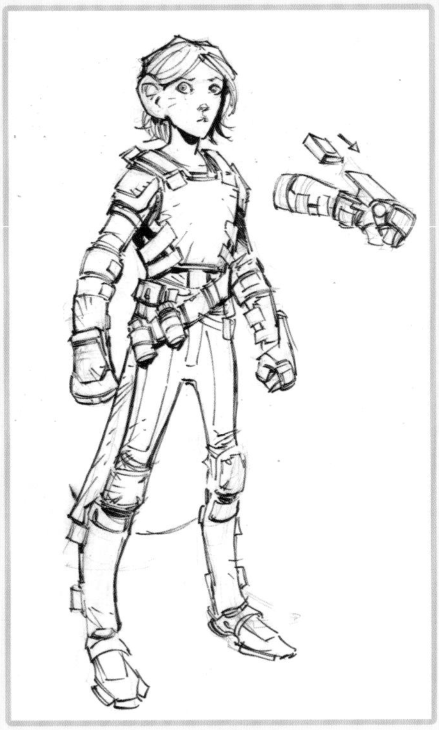

Above: Dail's gladiator gear, first pass.

Below: Dail's gladiator gear, final.

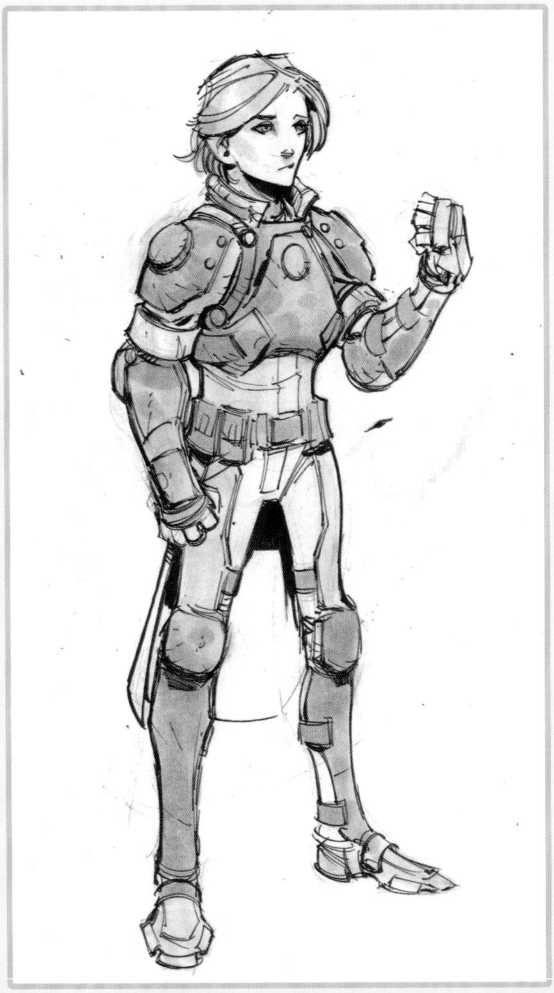

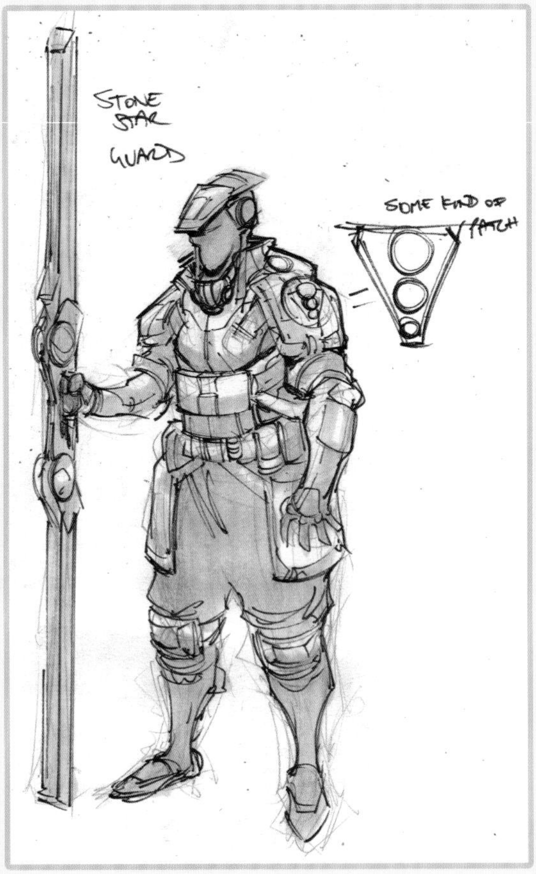
STONE STAR
GUARD
SOME KIND OF PATCH

Above: Stone Star guard design.

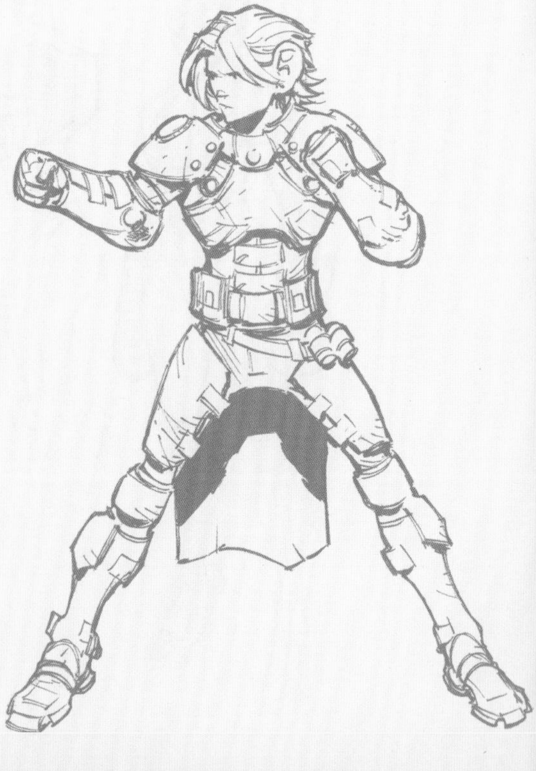

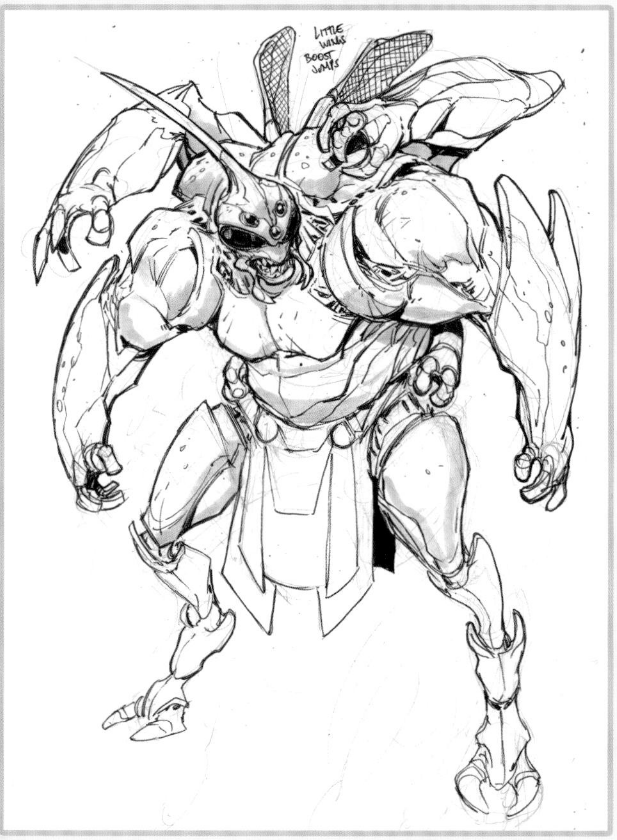
LITTLE WINGS BOOST JUMPS

Left and Below: Random gladiator designs.

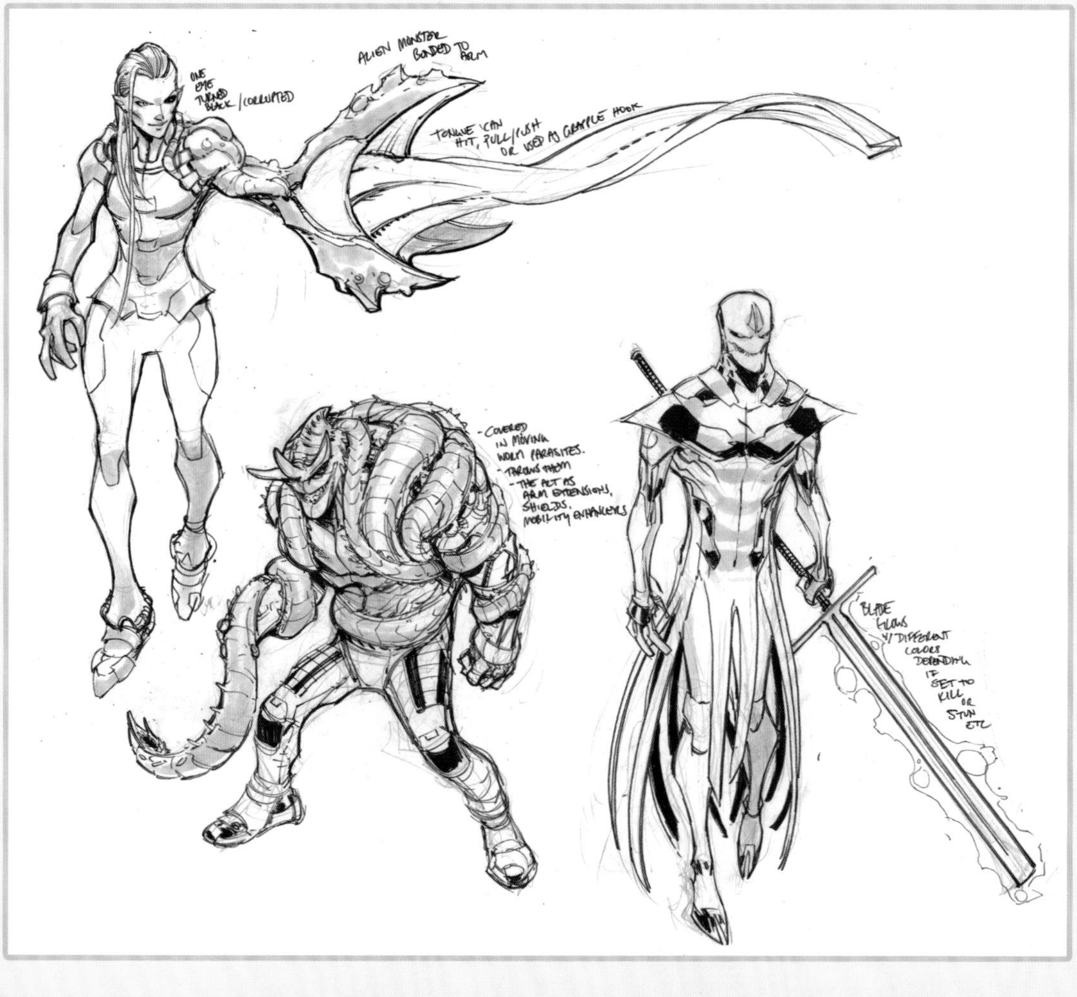
ONE EYE TURNED BLACK / CORRUPTED
ALIEN MONSTER BONDED TO ARM
TONGUE CAN HIT, PULL/PUSH OR USED AS GRAPPLE HOOK
- COVERED IN MOVING WORM PARASITES.
- THROWS THEM
- THEY ACT AS ARM EXTENSIONS, SHIELDS, MOBILITY ENHANCERS
BLADE GLOWS W/ DIFFERENT COLORS DEPENDING IF SET TO KILL OR STUN ETC

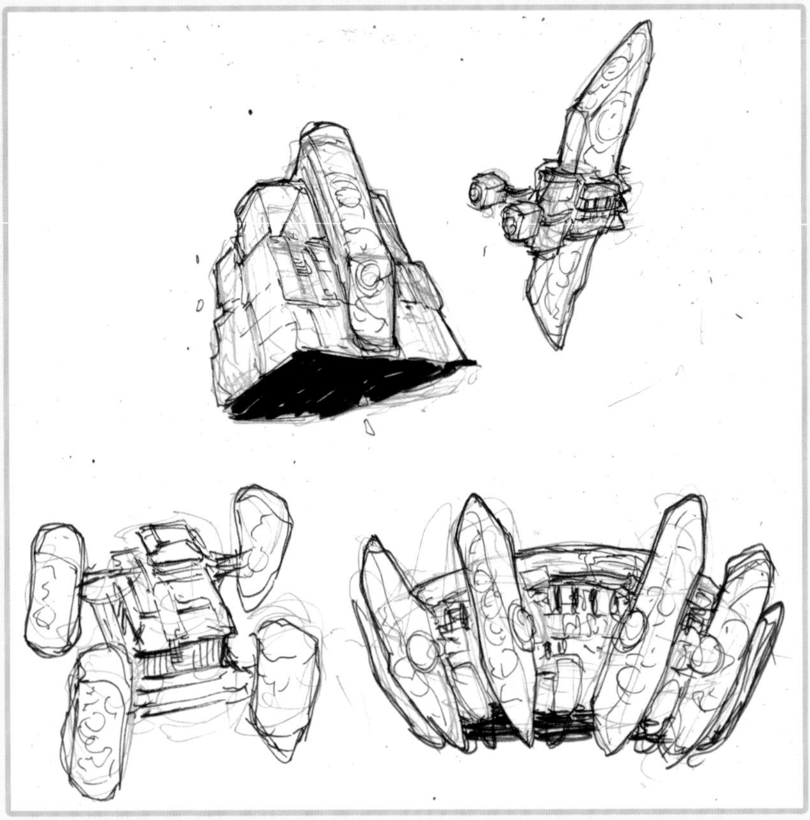

Left: Initial brainstorming for ship designs and the Stone Star station.

Below: Stone Star design development.

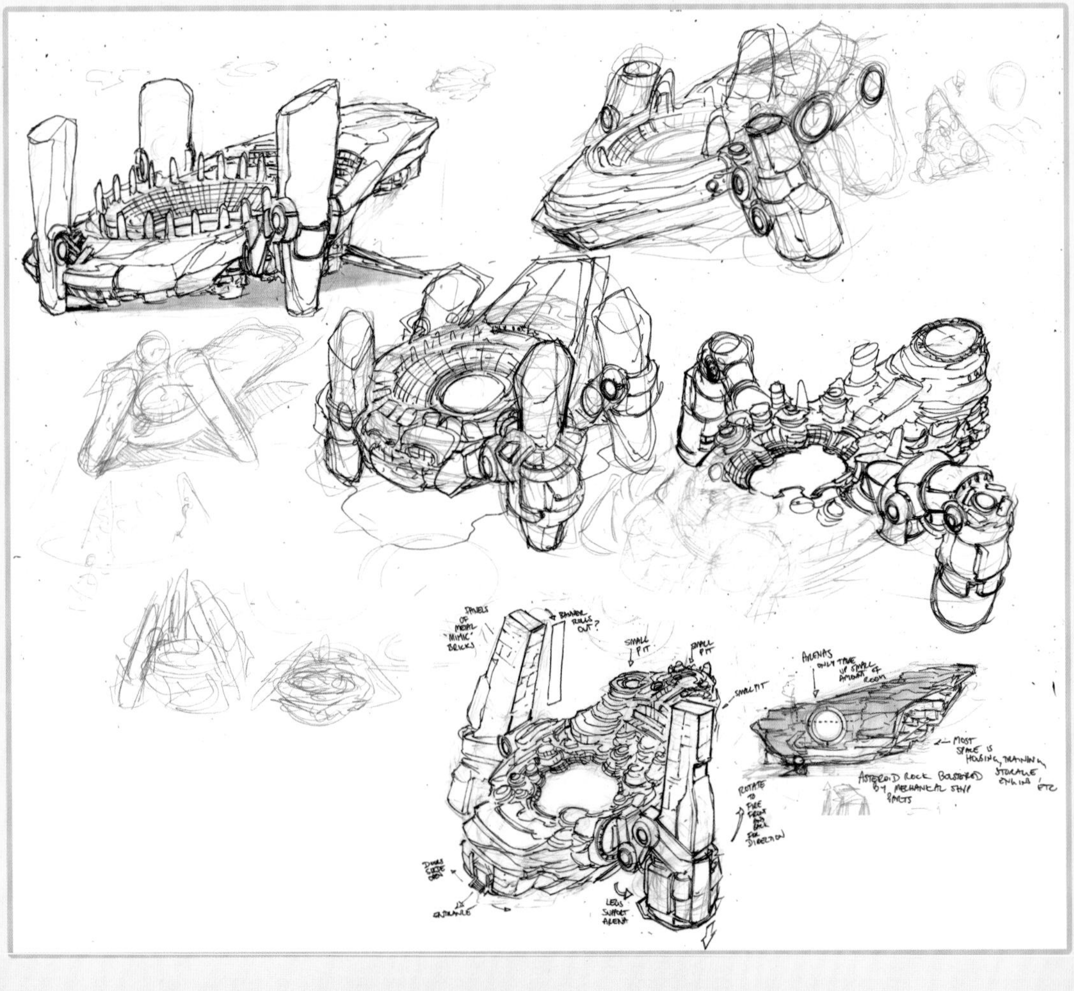

PANELS OF METAL 'MIMIC' BRICKS
BANNER ROLLS OUT?
SMALL PIT
SMALL PIT
SMALL PIT
ARENAS ONLY TAKE UP SMALL AMOUNT OF ROOM
MOST SPACE IS HOUSING, TRAINING, STORAGE, ENGINE, ETC
ASTEROID ROCK BOLSTERED BY MECHANICAL SHIP PARTS
ROTATE TO FIRE FRONT AND BACK FOR DIRECTION
LEGS SUPPORT ARENA
ENTRANCE

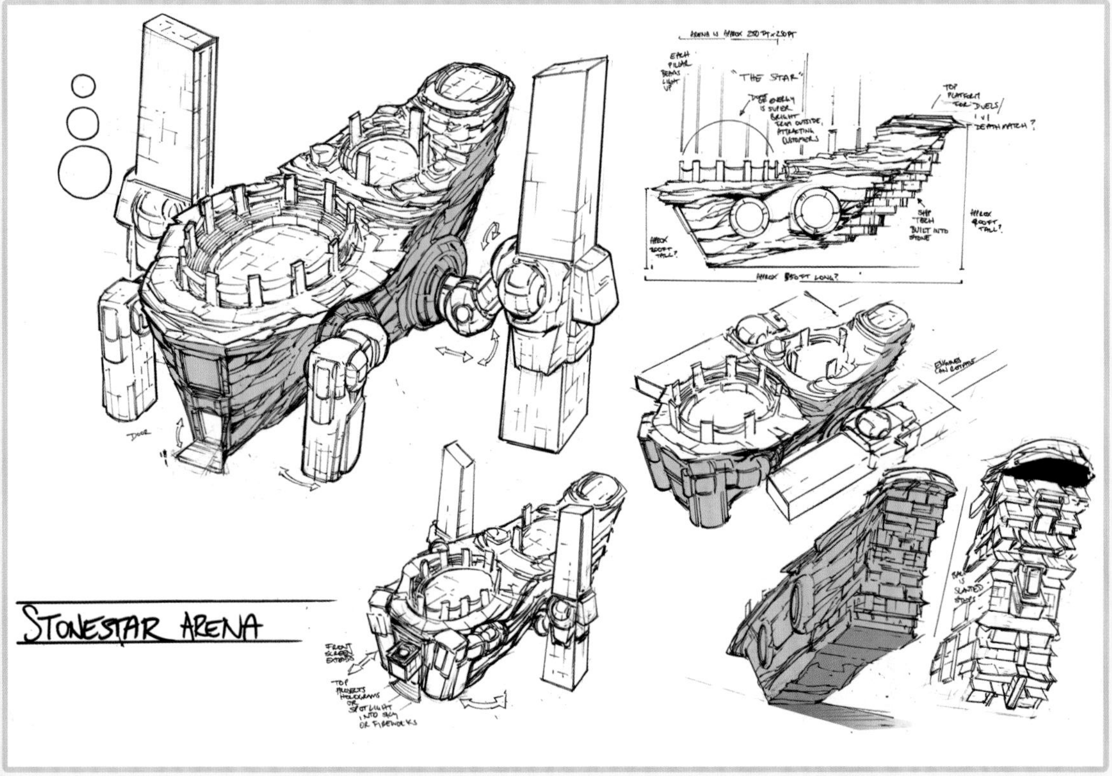

STONESTAR ARENA
"THE STAR"
EACH PILLAR BEAMS LIGHT UP
TOP PLATFORM FOR DUELS/ 1 v 1 DEATH MATCH?
SHIP TECH BUILT INTO STONE
DOOR

Above: Stone Star finished design sheet.

Below: Design development for the Pits training area.

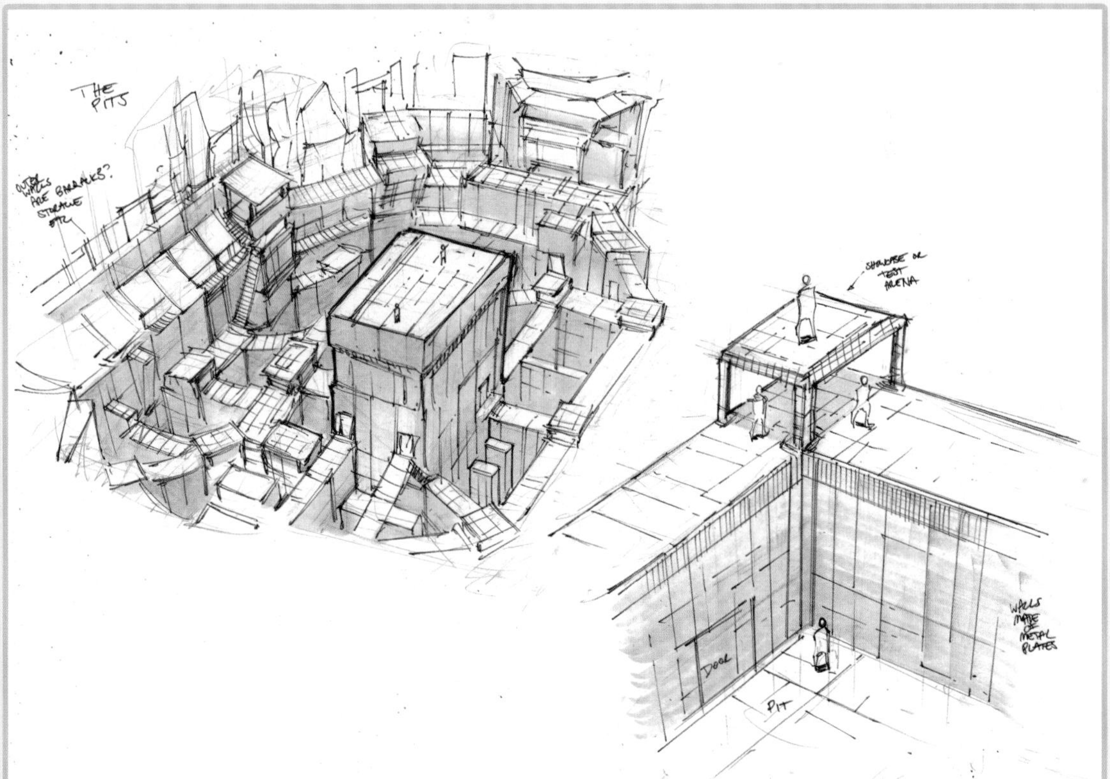

THE PITS
OUTER WALLS ARE BARRACKS? STORAGE ETC
WALLS MADE OF METAL PLATES
DOOR
PIT

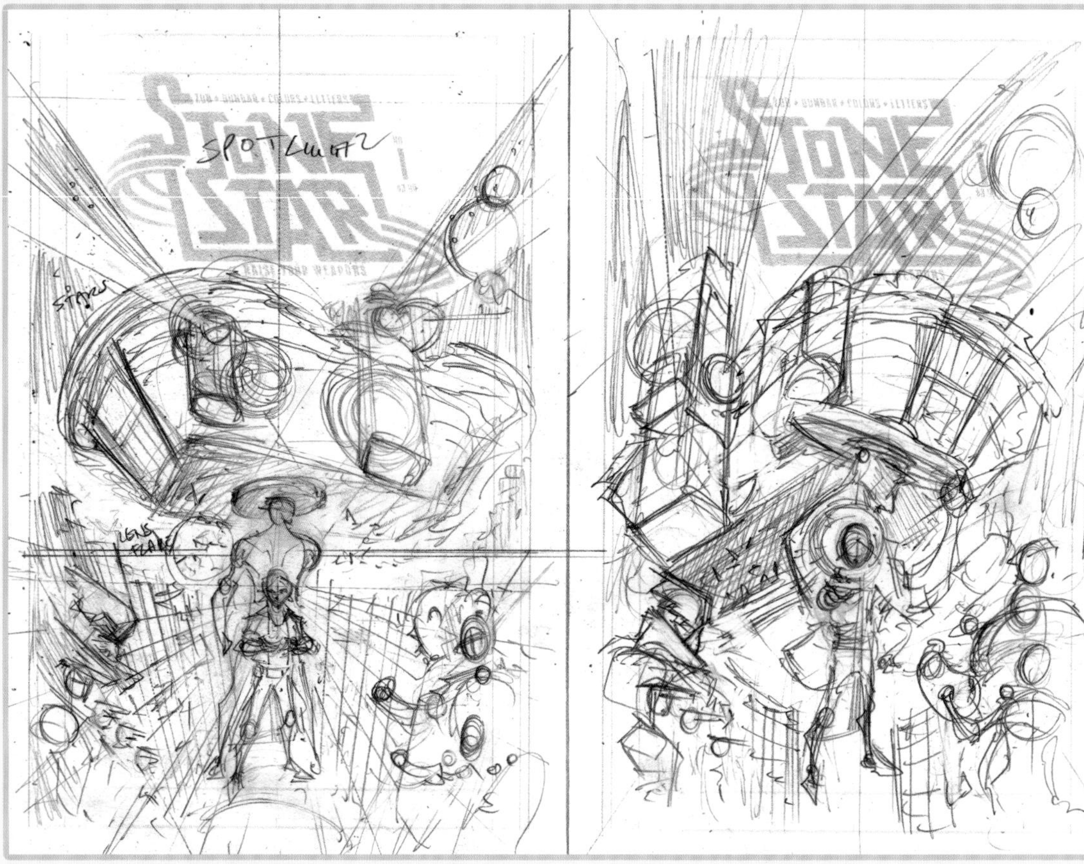
STONE STAR
SPOTLIGHT 2
STARS
LENS FLARE

Above and Below: *Stone Star* #1 cover and composition options.

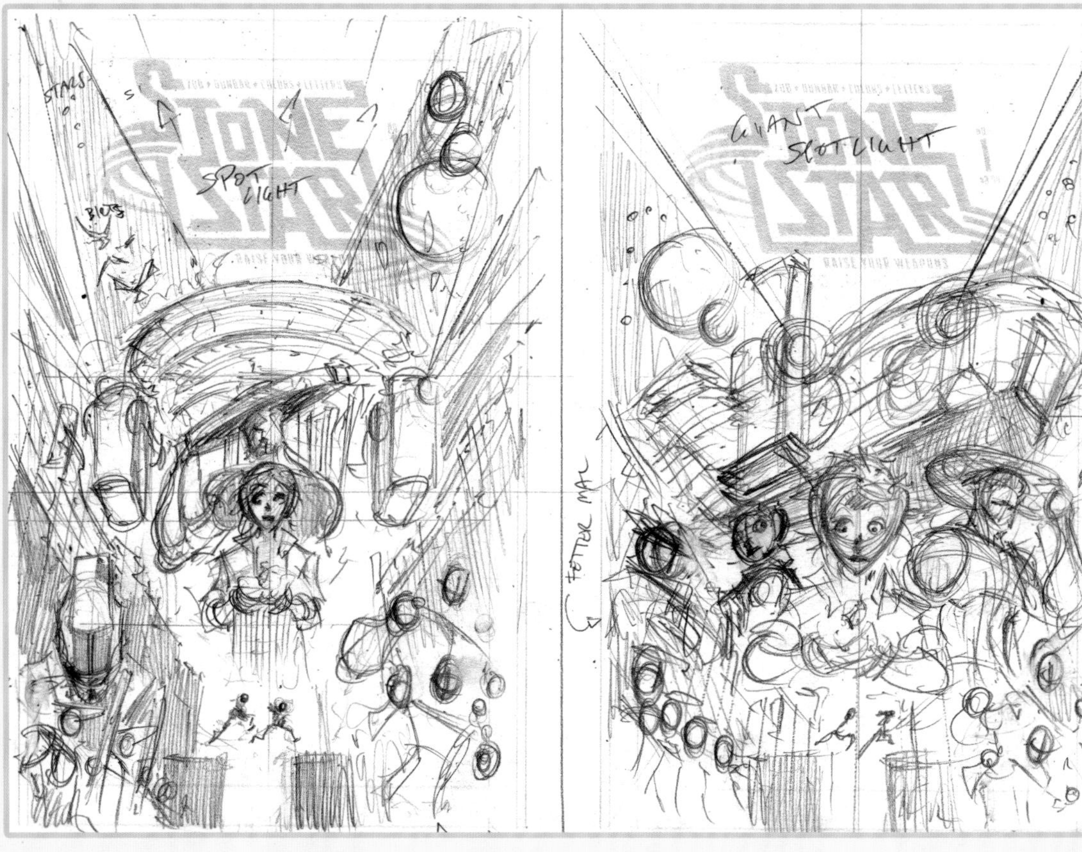
STONE STAR
STARS
SPOT LIGHT
GIANT SPOTLIGHT

Above: *Stone Star* #1 cover pencils.

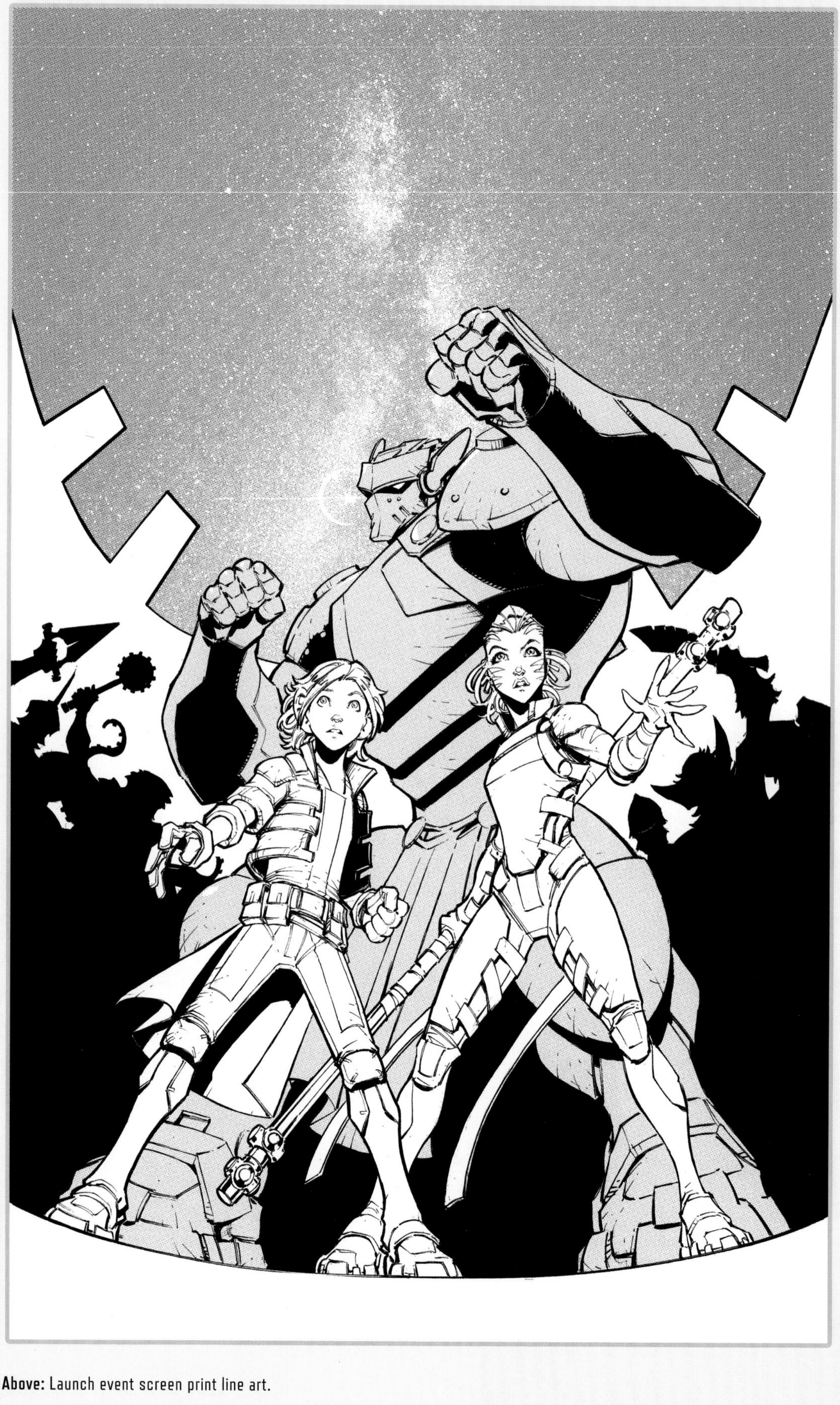

Above: Launch event screen print line art.